RUINED KINGDOM

A GOTHIC GROVE NOVEL

JA GEORGE

Bre. Because this book would not have happened without you.

And my very own mate who inspired me to add street races, because why not?

CONTENT WARNING

This is a dark romance intended for 18+. This contains heavy spice and dark material. This book was different than my other ones given the nature of the relationship between two of the characters. It is incredible abusive and one that I did not intend to go that way. However, as my characters tend to do they took matters into their own hands and decided what the story needed. As such, I caution you and encourage you to make sure to read the trigger warnings listed below. I trust you know how to take care of yourself and your mental health. Pairings within this book include fated mates that share: MF/MM/MFM/MMF.

Trigger Wanrings Include:
• Panic Attacks/Anxiety
• Depression
• PTSD
• Drug and alcohol use
• SA
• Torture
• General love of stabbings (looking at you Kallen)
• Cult-like activity
• Religious shaming/abuse

• Deprogramming religious shame of sexuality
• General feelings of self-hatred and shame
• Purity culture
• Physical and emotional abuse depicted in a relationship (on and off page)
• Dubious consent within a relationship
• Drugging partners
• Sex trafficking

The following kinks/sexual content are included:
• Cock warming
• Dom/Sub relationships
• Masochism and Sadism
• Primal kink
• Edging
• Blood Play
• Magical peens that include knots
• Degradation
• Piercings
• Voyeurism
• Exhibitionist
• Biting
• Sex magic/Use of magic during sex
• Felching/Snowballing

While I do my best to include all TW and sexual scenarios please know I'm human and I may miss some. You are always welcome to reach out and let me know: authorja george@gmail.com

WELCOME TO GOTHIC GROVE

This wouldn't be a Gothic Grove book without a few portions of a complicated timeline. This one is no different. The prologue and Part One take place historically. Part Two takes place after the events of Heavy Is The Crown and The Demon's They Forged. In fact, you'll probably recognize a few characters. With that being said, reading order is important to this series. If you're new here make sure you are caught up! Check out the list below for reading order.

Venomous Love: Little Wicked Book Box SE Halloween Novella (Please note this book is only available on author website. This book is not needed to read the rest of the series and is a prequel)
Gothic Grove
Heavy Is The Crown
The Demon's They Forged: A Gothic Grove Novella
Ruined Kingdom
Untitled Book Four (Releasing June 2025)

Ruined Kingdom was the hardest book, to date, for me to write. It was so hard fought after sitting with characters I knew like the back of my hand. This was the very first time I struggled to truly understand what my book needed or wanted. Even now, as I write this, I'm questioning the way the story arc went. About halfway through what felt like my millionth re-write I realized I wasn't actually listening to my characters, and I was attempting to shove them into a box they had no business being in. So I stopped ignoring them and started listening and wouldn't you know it went a little better.

In the back of the book you will find a guide to the 'people, places and things' within Gothic Grove. It does contain spoilers.

The desperate wail of the woman giving birth echoes through the woods that is the home of the priestesses; her cries amplified over the storm that had started to rage the moment the woman went into labor. The wind and rain pound against the small cabins the other priestesses are huddled in and thunder cracks against the sky as if hoping to open a pathway to the deepest pits of Hell for them all. Even the ground shakes, writhing against the war of the storm.

"One more push!" The elder yells at the soon to be mother.

"I cannot!" Sweat beads on her forehead; her voice unhinged with fear "You know as well as I what this child will bring. You can feel it!" She screams.

The older woman steps away from between the birthing space at the end of the bed to pull the mother's forehead to her own. "You will have this baby, Genevie, you will love her as I will. Because if you don't you will die here tonight and all will be in vain. I will not lose my daughter and granddaughter." When she pulls back, Genevie nods.

Her white hair pooling in front of her face only to be

swept back by another midwife. "One more push my dear." She says encouragingly as the High Priestess reclaims her position between Genevie's legs. "Just one more and we will meet our darling new priestess."

The babe finally pushes free, wailing as though she could beat out the sounds of the storm. Her lungs fierce and determined and face screwed up in anger. The room shook against the sound and the other women cover their ears, some crying at the pain the noise is causing. The High Priestess looks in awe at the tiny, wailing creature before quickly swaddling the furious child.

The mother cries as well, though none could tell if it was relief or fear that pulled the tears from her eyes. The High Priestess pushes the tiny baby into her mother's hands, the wails quickly turning to soft whimpers as she rooted around on her chest.

Genevie whole body began to shake, terror in her eyes as she looked at the calmer baby. "The storm. . . the cries."

The High Priestess cut her off, "She will remain here. We will never allow her to leave and therefore the prophecy will never come to pass." She said it with such authority all who heard it had no strength to protest. Genevie herself nodded and seemed at peace with the proclamation.

"What is her name?" One of the other women asked, finally stepping closer.

Genevie smiled, "Harrowlena."

THE PAST

**Part One
The Priestess and her demon**

ONE

Oisin

"There will come a time when you need to show no mercy, you will need to show them exactly what you deserve and that you can take it." My mother says as she bandages my face. The excruciating pain is now a dull ache, the slash through my eye and cheek will no doubt scar. It will forever be a reminder of the time I was unable to protect myself, a time when I was weak. "You will make them regret touching you."

I hold back the sniffle that is desperate to come out, "They said I have no place here because of my father."

She lets out a growl and her hand squeezes my face so hard I feel the slice reopen and blood pool out. "Your father may have passed the magic you were owed to someone else, but you, my son, you are the one destined to be a God." I swallow back the words on my tongue and ignore the searing pain in my face as I let her statement sink in. "You will be the one to topple Hell and any adjoining kingdoms. You will be worshiped by all, or they will pay the price. Do you understand?"

"How?" I finally manage to ask.

She releases my face and goes back to tending to the wound, her hands uncaring as they contribute to more of my pain. "Let me tell you a story, my dear, of the Gods and the witches that betrayed them. . . and the power that is destined to be yours."

TWO

Five Years Later

Harrowlena
   (Stand by Me- Florence + the Machine)
   The world feels both incredibly large and oh so small as I sit at the creek. My long white dress dangling in the water, the edges soaking in as I kick my feet back and forth. The evening sky has begun its takeover and the reds and purples painting the sky reflect down into the shallow water. It's a direct contrast to the dark woods that border the other side of the bank. I allow my eyes to travel over the vast woods beyond my home, the space that I'm not allowed to go, forbidden even.

   "Nothing good comes from that place, you must never go there." My mom and Nana echo the same statement time and time again.

   I let out a long sigh and lie backwards onto the soft grass, the cool water keeping me from truly relaxing into the ground. It's a nightly ritual now, my soul dragging me towards this spot as though I'm waiting for something to happen.

I smile as the birds fly to and fro overhead, their songs a lullaby against the soft wind through the grass. Soon the air will turn cooler, and the leaves will become crisp as we edge towards the full moon ceremony, the first ceremony I'll officially get to start helping with.

I won't be allowed to participate in it yet, no that's for adults only. But I can now officially help with supplies and escorting the men, who are brought in to help the other women. As the person destined to take over my Nana as High Priestess it's important, I understand our way of life and every aspect of the ceremony prior to being given access to the full ritual.

Part of me secretly hopes I'll see the young Prince of Hell. Rumors have swirled amongst the elder girls that he is to join his father this time to see what it means to accept the power The Well has to offer. I let out a long blissful sigh as the daydream takes shape that maybe, just maybe, we are destined to be together. That he will sweep in and rescue me from this dull life and we will fall madly in love.

"Are you an angel?" The male voice startles me upward, my feet pulling from the creek as I leap to a stand, heart pounding. Silence descends around me, no birds chirp, the wind stills and it's as though the water has pulled back to hide its sound. It goes on for so long I begin to think that I've hallucinated the voice.

"Anyone there?" I finally manage. Giving it another moment of silence I let my muscles relax a bit. "Your imagination really is getting the better of you." I mutter to myself. I turn to leave, the sun now fully descended behind the horizon leaving only the pinpricks of light from the fireflies to guide me back to my home.

"Do I at least get your name before you flee, angel?"
(Arsonists Lullaby- Hozier)
My body freezes once more as the voice washes over

me. Slowly turning back to the dark edge of those woods, movement finally catches my gaze and I see the dark figure walk slowly out into the evening air. His gait is confident, hands shoved in his pockets and dark hair swept across his left eye so only the piercing crimson of his right shows. Even from here something about him captures my attention, ensnares me and tangles me up.

I cock my head, blinking several times, "are you real?" My voice is barely above a whisper, yet it feels like a scream.

His feet bring him to the edge of the water. So close and yet so far. He chuckles, "Oh, I'm very real. What is your name?"

The wind whistles through the space between us and my body seems to come alive as it brings his scent to me, an earthy, spicy scent that sends my head spinning. "Harrowlena." I manage. "My name is Harrowlena."

His eyes travel over me as though they can strip me bare to my very essence. "I think I'll call you Lena." He says stepping one foot closer, that smile never slipping from his face. His feet practically in the very water that still soaks the bottom of my dress. "Would you like to be friends, Lena?"

Oisin

My mother's voice rings in my ears telling me the story of the girl who would be mine. Of the girl who would give me what was owed. Yet for so long I feared it had been a lie. And now. Standing just on the other side of the creek is my angel, my goddess, my avenue to gain all that should be mine. Her violet eyes blink owlishly at me as she nervously tucks strands of white hair behind her ear.

"Well?" I ask.

She drags in a breath quickly, "Sorry what?" Her voice is soft, hesitant.

I huff out a chuckle, "I asked if you want to my friend." I

push my hands into my pockets as my feet carry one step closer to the magic that keeps us separated.

She lets her gaze dart around as she too takes a tentative step towards me, her arms wrapped around her center almost protectively. She tilts her head, the movement shifting her hair to the side, and if her eye color wasn't enough to tell me exactly who she was that distinct mark on her breast would.

"I can't leave here, so it wouldn't work." She says finally, her foot stomping onto the ground in a very childlike maneuver.

I cock my head and shrug, "I don't mind staying friends like this."

"Why?" She lets her arms drop to her side finally, her body relaxing.

I fold myself into a seated position on the ground, ignoring the rough terrain that I'm using as a chair and attempt to convey the utmost relaxation. "I'll let you in on a little secret. I don't have many friends, and I think my dear Lena you are going to be the best one I've ever had."

When her cheeks flame and a small giggle spills from her lips I know I have her.

THREE

Six Years Later

Oisin

My priestess paces back and forth just on the other side of the damn water that keeps us apart. Her hair bound back in a braid slips loose in a few spots and the wind tries to carry it away. The long white dress she wears curves to her body, swaying this way and that. My mouth waters. She's grown up, the bright-eyed priestess a full woman now and in a rebellious state that I've worked hard to foster. Day after day I've whispered into her ear, been the monster in the night her mother warned her against. But to my Lena? I'm her savior. Her personal safe haven.

"She doesn't understand! I don't want to remain here!" She huffs, dropping down onto the creek bed. "I can't stay here. I want to see the world. With you." She adds the last part hesitantly. Her crush on me now a full-blown infatuation that no doubt has her convinced we are to be wed. Not that I have deterred this, no, if anything I've only helped push this narrative along.

I laugh but stop when she cuts me a hard look. "All that

is stopping you is this little creek, my Lena. And of course, your mother." She glances over at me, my posture so at ease as I lean against the tree with my arms behind my head. You would never know I just spent the morning trying to figure out a way to murder my half-brother's mother. The damn witch suspects too much of my intent with Ciaran, and I can't have her ruining it for me. "Unless of course she's given you the magic?" I lean forward in earnest.

"She won't give it to me yet," she says softly though it's not hard to miss her disappointment.

"Have you asked her again?"

She nibbles on her bottom lip. "I can't. If I keep asking, she'll eventually find out about you. She's already suspicious of the time I spend away."

I roll my eyes tamping down the urge to snap at her. Had I known the dead end this would become I would have thrown in the towel on the young priestess long ago. Her mother and grandmother holding the ceremony back from her was not something I ever predicted.

As the sun crests over and bathes us in light I decide to give the female a little more motivation to find what I seek. I drag the t-shirt I'm wearing up and over my head. Exposing the washboard abs and golden skin I've worked to perfect. Her cheeks flush as her gaze devours my body. I drop the shirt into the water before pulling it back out and allowing the drops to form rivers down my exposed flesh. I keep my eyes locked on hers the whole time as my hand caresses my body.

"What?" I say with a playful smirk.

"You shouldn't do that." She darts her eyes to the ground before pulling them back up and watching me bathe myself. "It's not right." Her cheeks now crimson all the way to the mark on her chest.

I cock my head to the side, "For a future High Priestess

you are far too innocent. You do know what the ceremony involves right?"

She flushes, this time her neck matching the color of her cheeks. "I'm not innocent," She counters.

"Oh really? Tell me, Lena. Do you think about me like this? When you're alone in bed at night?" My voice fills the space between us but the gasp of air that she pulls is louder. "Show me what you do when you're alone."

She seems tempted for a moment, her hand drifting downward but she stops and pushes to her feet, stepping backwards and shaking her head. She looks up at the sky. "I should go."

Fuck. "I'm sorry Lena. I didn't mean to push." I call to her retreating form.

"You can't say those things to me." She says, pausing in her escape.

"Why Lena? I want you. All of you." I hold my hands out to her as though she could grab them. "When a man sees his mate it's hard to control himself."

Her body freezes as she registers the term, her mouth popping into an oh as shock moves through her body. "Mate?"

I cock my head to the side, "Obviously. How else would I have found you? You called to me, and I answered. My beautiful mate. It's why I push so hard for you to be able to leave, I just want us to be together." I run my hands through my hair in mock frustration "I need to have you by my side to protect you."

"Mate. . . you are my mate." She says, the joy in her tone unmistakable. Her brilliant violet eyes snag mine, lingering only briefly on the white one that never regained color after the injury. "What's wrong? Why do you think you need to protect me? I'm safe here."

"The world is dangerous my dear. And for one like you. . . I worry what would happen should the wrong people ever touch you." I push my hand through my hair once more, purposefully exposing the scar on my face as if to emphasize the point.

"I'll get it. I'll get the ceremony. They must give it to me." She says with renewed determination. "I'll tell them about you--"

"NO!" I shout, a little too loudly forcing the birds nearby to flee the trees. Harrow stumbles backwards in shock. "I'm sorry I just. . . I just don't trust anyone who trusts the royals like your family does. They can't know about me."

She blinks rapidly, "I don't know why they are so awful to you. It's not at all how mother describes them."

"They destroyed my family! They brutalized me and left me for dead!" I point to the scar on my face, the lie falling easily from me. "I can't stand the idea of them finding me again. Finding out who you are to me. They would hurt you Lena. They would do it just to punish me for speaking out against them."

"I'm sorry," She offers softly. "I'm sorry, you're right. I shouldn't have said it. But I promise to get the ceremony. I promise."

I nod, dragging in calming breaths before painting a smile on my face. "I just want to complete our bond, Lena. Then you'll be safe. Forever."

She nods along with the words and I feel a deep well of satisfaction that she has bought my lies hook line and sinker.

(No Limit (feat A$AP Rocky & Cardi B)- G-Eazy)

I had spent another hour with the priestess, talking and placating her until the twilight began to edge into our world and she skipped off to her home with the promise to return with the ceremony as quickly as possible. Which left me to go straight for the strip club on the outskirts of Gothic Grove. A place where people are excellent at forgetting exactly who has occupied the space. Which is precisely what I need as I watch my half-brother, Ciaran, contemplate what I've just offered.

His disdain for his stepfather, Alexi, is working to my advantage as I continue to twist him into who and what I need. I may not have magic, like I was owed, but I know the power of manipulation and I'm damn fucking good at it. One might say it's my own personal brand of magic.

"So, what do you need me to do?" He asks, taking a long sip of the blood I provided him in the crystalline tumbler. The body that it came from lies discarded off to the side and out of view.

I lean against the wall of the club, the music pumping outside the VIP area I've managed to secure. "Nothing really. Just report to me the coming and goings of the city. I need eyes here that I trust and when it all goes down, you'll be there to welcome me home."

A curvy female walks by, and I watch my brothers gaze linger on her before he jerks his attention back to me. "Alexi is mine at the end?"

I hold back the pleased smile that is threatening to overtake me. "Yes," I confirm. "All yours."

He drains his cup, slamming it down onto the table and standing. Even as a teenager he's already huge. "My mother will be safe?"

"Of course she will. I would never harm her." I allow the lie to fall from my lips like sweet honey.

He pushes to a stand and nods in agreement. "You've got a deal." He says, clasping my hand hard.

He drops it after a moment and moves to exit the space, "Oh Ciaran," I call after. He pauses and turns back to me. "One more thing. . . I'm looking for a book. I need it for my plans. It would be full of magic; each family has one. Do you think you could find one for me and let me look at it?"

His gaze narrows on me and I worry I just overplayed my cards. "You want a grimoire?"

Looks like the Viking knows more than I thought. I keep my face passive as I nod. "My mother talked about some spells that could be helpful in taking over, I just want to look."

Ciaran's blue eyes burn into me for so long I begin to second guess this whole fucking thing. Finally, he opens his mouth, "Sure. I'll look around."

I let out a long breath, "thank you."

He says nothing as he continues his exit from the strip club.

The book is a contingency plan, one of two if my puppet Lena is unable to secure the ceremony from her family. The other? The other is a blonde who lives with my current lover in the royal palace of Hell.

I tilt my head back and drag in another breath with my eyes closed as I continue to visualize the end goals. The buzzing of my phone in my pocket drags me back into reality. Pulling it free I glance at the message and allow a smile to spread over my lips.

Grabbing my own drink I settle onto the couch, enjoying the liquor and music for a moment before I'm forced to head back to that god forsaken forest. Only a few more visits and she'll be yours I remind myself. After today I feel confident Harrow will be far more motivated to gain what we need. After all, her mate is waiting for her. I let out a dark chuckle at my own brilliance as the thick red curtains blocking the booth from the rest of the club push open allowing a tall female to duck into the lounge, her dark hair bound back and tight while her body is covered in linen pants and shirt. "Ah, right on time. Is everything ready?"

Lady Ornate nods her head in confirmation. "Yes, the royals have increased my time amongst the priestesses, and the women have taken me in, they are overjoyed to have a healer visit them." The female has been a helpful edition to The Order far more helpful than I would have expected truthfully.

"Excellent," I drain the rest of the contents of my drink before standing and moving past the female. "As a reward for your continued service, you are welcome to be High Priestess once the title is empty."

"My Lord," She gasps. "Thank you it would be an honor to serve you as such. Along with any other service you may need." Her voice takes on a suggestive hint at the end that makes my stomach roll.

I hold the red curtain open gesturing her outward. "I have no need for any other service from you." I say sharply.

She bows her head towards me before pushing past the half-naked female moving into the private room. My eyes already traveling over the stripper. I don't bother to see if Lady Ornate is out of the room before dropping the heavy curtain once more.

Meandering past the bouncer I can't help but give him a smug smile, my bloody hands shoved in my pockets. They'll find the stripper soon enough, whether she's alive is incon-sequential to me. I enjoy these whores for a reason. No one will miss them should they not survive a night with someone who has my tastes in pleasure.

"Have a good night." I call out as I walk through the door. He sends out a similar message completely unaware of the carnage I just left.

FOUR

One Year Later

Harrowlena
(Walking on the Moon-Ruelle)

My bare feet pad over the forest floor, the moss a springy carpet that boosts my steps. In the distance I can see my mother's white hair, the color standing out brightly against her dark skin. Everyone speculates I must look like my father given how different we look, aside from our hair, my silver is at least closer to her white. But my father has been a mystery to me my whole life, no photos, nothing. It's always been me, my mother and my Nana.

Her eyes glance over to me, offering me a soft smile as she and my Nana ready for the next ceremony. At almost 19 now they have been instructing me more and more of the magic of our people and how we help the royal family. It's also a full year later than most of the future High Priestesses learn the full ritual. Despite working tirelessly to support the others since I was eleven I have yet to be allowed what should be my right. High Priestesses before me have all been gifted the ceremony on their sixteenth birthdays. Even though we do not participate it in until we are of age, we have it within our possession. All except me.

My mind drifts to what they are denying me, not only my magical right but my mate! My mate who waits for me, who longs for me as I long for him. More and more the frustration has built up inside me. Somedays it becomes so intense it feels as though it might burst from me and destroy everything in its path. And somedays that doesn't scare me as much as it should.

My eyes glance nervously back at my mother as I ease myself closer to the meeting place of the one who holds my heart. She's been oddly watchful the last few days, making it damn near impossible to escape and see him. Since the day he appeared I've spent most of my waking time sitting near the edge of the creek, talking with him and confiding in him.

Falling in love with him. My mate.

Yet never touching him. The boundary of our homes keeping us miserably apart. Something that has begun to get under my skin like an itch you cannot scratch.

When I see that she is no longer being mindful of me I race towards the creek, quick as my bare feet will carry me until I'm panting from the effort. When I finally manage to stumble into the space I've deemed as ours I'm met with the reward of his smile. "Lena, I have good news." His voice is entrancing, something deep within unfurling towards it. No doubt the mate bond that is attempting to bloom in my chest.

"What is it?" I ask, my body still alive with tension and anxiety around being discovered. Normally no one comes this way but after this morning, after the fight I had with my Nana, and the way my mother has been? I worry that my secret will soon be discovered and destroyed.

"You can come see me. We can be together." He says with excitement in his eyes.

His words cool my body immediately. My eyes well for a moment and I close them, willing myself to swallow back the shame of my failure."I couldn't get the ceremony." I manage to choke out.

He tsks, "It's okay. I figured it out for us. All I need is for you to walk to me." My eyes fly open and his face breaks into a smile. "Come here so I can dry your tears my mate." He holds his arms out wide, welcoming me.

The violence of that frustration still too fresh within me, forces back the caution that normally exists. Drowning the voice that is meek and quiet and demands obedience. The memory of our argument from this morning still playing over and over in my head as she continued to refuse me the magic I am owed.

"Why won't you give it to me?!" My voice trembles as I ball my hands into fists at my side. "It is the right of my position!"

Nana shakes her head, sadness moving over her face. "You are not owed this magic. It is a privilege not a right to become the next High Priestess."

My body feels as though she has slapped me across the face, "You've spent my whole life telling me this is who I am to become and now it is a privilege and not my right?!" Tears of anger and frustration threaten to bubble over as she tsks in my direction.

"It is that attitude, my dear one, that makes you undeserving of the magic and position. You are not ready to ascend." Her words are final. I feel the door slam down between us, her face no longer loving but instead full of pity. I back away from her, one step at a time shaking my head. "Harrow. . ." She begins.

"No." I shout, the vase on the table vibrates with the

sound. "I will not be treated like some foolish girl. You have made it very clear what you think of me." I spin on my heels, fleeing towards the only one who truly sees me. The only one who truly understands who and what I am.

"Lena?" His voice pulls me from the memory swiftly, the sudden doubt on his face spurring me to action. Picking up my long skirts I ignore the pull in my gut that tells me to remain with my mother, ignore her voice in my head telling me to remain within our own sacred wood. *You must never travel outside our forest my dear one. This offers protection against the wild of the world that would seek to harm you.* My mother, for all that she loves me, has kept me caged here. Right alongside my Nana.

This is my mate. No harm will come to me. I argue back as I allow the wild part of my soul to guide me away from the safety of our land out into the wilderness.

I take a deep breath, focusing on Oisin as I step over the threshold.

The moment my foot touches the creek my mind screams to turn back. But I ignore it, shaking my head against the onslaught of fear.

"Just a little further my angel." Oisin coaxes. Hand outstretched. The closer I get to his side of the creek the harder it is to force my body to move, the water trying to freeze me into submission even as the current drags at my ankles.

"I'm leaving." I say stubbornly to the cosmos. As if it heard me the water rushes upward, shoving me the last few steps until my hands hit the rock covered ground on the bank. My body trembles as I push to a stand. A slight whimper being pulled from me as the bare sole of my foot slips and drags against the sharp pebbles. All around me the wind picks up, a sense of dread pooling within. The further I walk inward the more nature rages around me. Time seems to both stop and speed up all at once as my mind tries to make sense of it all, as my eyes frantically search for the mate that I could have sworn awaited me on the other side. Yet now that I'm here has vanished.

I have made a mistake. This is wrong

As I go to turn around, to seek refuge in the warm forest of my home I realize, with a jolt of fear, just how far I've come without realizing it. The creek has vanished and I'm surrounded by miles and miles of darkened wood that seem to hold an ominous presence. The heaviness of it pressing in around me. My heart beats faster, sweat prickling at my temple, and my skin feels electrified. Every part of me is screaming to run, to get away, to escape this place. Yet my limbs are frozen, locked up and unable to move.

"Lena, you came." The voice that always tempts me sounds so close now. "You're finally here." Warmth gathers at my back yet no one touches me. I'm desperate to see my mate again but fear paralyzes my body.

"Please Lena. I've waited so long to have you here. Turn around please." The pleading almost breaks me.

A warm hand finally pulls at my own, fingers twining with mine. Tension unfurls from my chest at the touch. A rightness settling within my soul shoving the doubts and fear aside.

Slowly blinking my eyes open I allow my body to be turned. The thick, corded muscles of his body bulge against the tightness of his shirt, hints of dark whirling marks peak out of his sleeves. The warmth of his body presses into mine and I feel my cheeks flame as I relish the feel of my mate holding me.

He offers a dazzling smile, "There's my Lena." I close my eyes again at the sound of my name against his lips. The beauty of it settling into my core and awakening parts of me that I didn't know existed. The wind pushes against us, cold and angry, bringing his scent into my body.

When he leans further into my space I can feel his warm breath on my cheek. Butterflies attack my stomach as I realize this beautiful boy is going to give me my first kiss. "Oh, my Lena. Always and forever, you'll be my Lena." He whispers against me before he traces his mouth over mine. The light touch edges me forward until my lips are firmly pressed against his. The kiss is all consuming making my body light up in ways I could only dream of. His hands exploring my body as he drags me closer.

I allow us, myself, to get lost in the feeling even as a small, wild part of my soul starts to push against me and him. Starts to scream that something is wrong. That this is wrong. As I start to pull back his hands grip me with renewed roughness and my head starts to swim.

Something is very very wrong.

Even those thoughts are sluggish and when I finally manage to pull backward my vision swims, and the world goes dark.

Oisin

Harrow's body goes limp against mine as I let out a breath of relief that drugs on my lips worked on her and not me. Lady Ornate swore up and down I'd be fine but trust did not come easy for me.

"So that's her?" Her voice sounds annoyed and the expression on her face mirrors it when I turn to her, hefting Harrow's limp body into my arms.

"This is her. My *mate* to you." I snap as I move past her.

Lady Ornate practically hisses. "Mate?"

"Yes, I had to get her in my good graces somehow! She may be naive but even she isn't dumb enough to trust some strange man in the woods. But the moment I said mate?

Bingo!" I can't help but shake my head and huff out a dark laugh. Lady Ornate's steps catch up to mine as we make our way back to the forest we came from.

"Did she at least bring us what we need?" She asks.

I shake my head, "No. The fucking bitch of a High Priestess kept it from her." I let out a long sigh. "But I have a backup plan."

Lady Ornate cuts me a sideways glance, "want to share?"

I huff out a dark chuckle. "You are talking to the fiancé of the princess of Hell."

Harrowlena

The scent of smoke drags me back into awareness, my eyes opening only to be met with the normally crisp blue sky of our wood darkened and the smell of smoke choking me.

"Wher—" I'm cut off by my beautiful friend dragging me upward into his arms.

He hushes me, "it's okay my sweet Lena you are safe now. Always safe with me."

Confusion emanates through me as I try to make sense of what's happening. Only a moment ago I was having my first kiss and now. . .

Looking around I finally see around me. Ash rains down from the skies that are now thick with smoke, blocking the sun that normally bathes this portion of my home. The sounds of the women, generally so loud, now are nothing. Even the birds have stopped chirping. The homes we once lived in are nothing more than ash and cinder as the flames devour the last of the structures.

A sob catches in my throat as I see the bodies of the

women I once called family. Frantically I search the masses, my eyes demanding to find the two people who I need most in my life. The two people who can't be taken from me, not yet, not now, not after all the hateful things I screamed at them. My body moves, feet carrying me around the space that once was my home. When I finally spy them my world tilts on its access, their bodies laid out and eyes unseeing as they gaze towards the sky.

Body dropping to the ground my palms dig into the blood soaked earth. "Who?" I choke out. "Who did this?" Tears fall of their own accord down my cheeks.

Strong fingers grip my chin and drag my attention back to him. "The royals."

I shake my head in confusion, "Why? Why would they do this? They need us!"

"I tried to warn you, my darling." He pulls me into his arms, and I savor the feel even as the guilt creeps in. Because he's right. He did try to warn me, and I didn't listen. "This is what they do. They destroy everything good and pure. They care for nothing but themselves."

I break apart in his arms as it all settles in, the grief and guilt. The words I flung at my Nana now the very last thing she'll have of me and I of her. And my mother? I hadn't even spoken to her today. Everything comes crashing down around me as I allow it all to drag me under, praying I don't resurface.

(Mad World (feat KJ Apa, Camila Mendes & Lili Rienhert)- Riverdale Cast)

It's been three long days of helping The Order burry my fellow priestesses. Their bodies left in broken piles by the men that ruined this sanctuary. The salty taste of my tears lays heavy on my lips as I scrub at my face. My hands smell like the earth and sweat lays thick on my back having finished the last effigies that will be burned this evening. My grandmother and mothers' bodies lay on top of the prier.

The guilt of never warning my mother or grandmother who the royals really were is a constant ghost that screams at me anytime I try to rest. *You were selfish, protecting your time with him over warning them of what could happen.* I flinch at my own voice. Of the 30 or so females who lived here I am the only survivor. The lone figure left of the Priestess order and the least deserving of the position.

Raised voices to my left drag my red-rimmed eyes over to my savior, the only person who makes me feel better for my mistakes, as he argues with one of the older men who arrived a few hours ago to help us make the journey to my new home.

After everything I'm finally getting my wish to leave this place, and it feels so gods damn hollow in my heart.

"Harrowlena," Out of the corner of my eye I see Lady Ornate walking towards me. She has been a healer amongst the priestesses sporadically for years but officially came to live amongst us not long before the royals attacked, and while my mother and grandmother have always liked her something about her aura put me off.

"Harrowlena she was sent to help us, to learn from us. It's an honor the royals want to gift us someone such as her. You shouldn't be so hard on her." My mother reminds me as she folds the bread over and over again. The rich scent of it filling the kitchen.

"But mother. . ." I attempt to counter.

"That's enough. We do not judge people." Her voice is harsh and the look she gives me leaves no room for argument.

I scrub at my face attempting to push the memory out. But it lingers. Just like everything else.

"Are you still crying?" Her voice is harsh and unforgiving. I want to yell at her that I don't know if I'll ever stop crying but instead, I suck down a shuddering breath. She raises her eyebrow and purses her lips. "If you keep crying, he'll never want to keep you, no one wants a sniffling female." Her voice is full of judgement, the complete opposite of the one she used with my mother.

Fear pulses through me at the idea of losing him, the only one I have left now. I straighten up and force myself to swallow down the grief and despair that I so desperately want to let out. I blink, clearing my eyes of the last of the tears, and paint a demure smile on my face. When my eyes glance towards where he stands again, he offers a pleased expression as his eyes rake over me and something akin to pride flows through my body.

Maybe I was wrong. . . Maybe the Lady is okay, maybe she does want to help me.

"Pack your things, we are leaving today." She says with no warmth.

And just like that my world narrows once more and the grief and despair drag me under.

"Lena?" His voice calls to me as I attempt to get my sobs under control. "Are you in here?" After the Lady had left me, I allowed my grief to drag me away, to try and drown me, before I had begun packing up my minimal belongings that had survived the fire. Nothing of true value, but it felt wrong to leave it all behind. To leave my life behind in such totality.

"Be out in a moment," I hiccup.

Warm hands circle my waist, and he pulls me into his chest. I try to stop crying, try to remember what Lady Ornate said, but from the moment she said we were leaving my grief refuses to let me go. Tears flow down my face like an avalanche and my body shakes against it.

"Oh my dear Lena, it's okay. It'll all be okay." He offers soothing sounds and words as I break apart, eventually turning me so I can bury my face into his broad chest. "I promise you my Lena I will keep you safe, I will stop at nothing to get revenge for what the royals did here."

After a few moments of allowing his body to soothe me, I manage to calm myself, stop the crying, and pull back from his embrace. He smiles widely at me, planting a kiss to my forehead. "Good girl." His praise lighting a fire under me.

I wipe the tears from my face and turn from him, closing up my bag. When I turn back around, he holds my Nana's crown, the one she wore during ceremonies. He looks at it with reverence and longing which morphs to distaste quickly. "You'll need a better one." He says, tossing it back onto the shelf he pulled it from.

My body tenses as I watch the priceless heirloom bounce against the wood. I push past him, dragging it to my chest, my eyes double checking it didn't break. When I'm assured it survived the carelessness I pause, turning slightly. "A better one?"

He offers up a huff, "I can't have my mate, and *High Priestess* in something so dull."

My heart skips a beat and I fully whirl, eyes shinning bright. "Do you mean it?"

The smile that spreads over his face lifts into his eyes. "Of course, my angel. You have always deserved the position. It's yours from now until eternity." He holds out his hand, "Come, let's leave this place. You have nothing here but ashes and death."

For a moment I look at the crown in my hands, wondering if I should bring it, just in case, as a reminder. "I told you I'd get you a new one, a better one, one you deserve." His tone takes on a level of impatience that forces my hand to drop the crown back to the shelf and place my hand in his. "There we go. Good girl."

I don't look back as he drags me away from the woods that I once called my home.

Oisin

Satisfaction when I get my way is like a drug to me. Each time I achieve it I want another hit. Watching her drop her grandmother's crown was a dose that sustained me through our travel but now I need more. I need the feeling again.

I watch as Lena wraps her arms around herself, those large violet eyes looking around the space The Order calls home. It's her first time being here, being out of those damn woods and I can't help but think she's a little disappointed in what she sees.

Stepping forward I drag her in for another comforting embrace before releasing her and grabbing her hand. "I know this is new, but it'll feel like home soon enough." I assure her. She looks at me doubtfully before schooling her face. All around us members of The Order mill about, their curious looks akin to someone watching a new animal be brought into a zoo. No doubt The Elders have already been bragging about their newfound toy to bring in.

"Come on," I say dragging her away from the crowds now starting to gather.

"Where are we going?" She asks quietly, eyes darting around us. "Shouldn't I stay here, say hello to people?"

I hold back the eye roll. "No, they'll get plenty of your time. Don't worry about it. For now, I'm taking you to my home." She sucks in a breath, and I love the way her feet seem to trip over themselves as she tries to walk a little faster.

(Wrecking Ball- Midnight String Quartet)

She stays quiet as we head further into the woods, my own home outside the general compound and tucked back from prying eyes. The scent of evergreen and soil invades the air around us and the porch cries under our joined weight as I lead her up the stairs and through the front door. The inside smells like the wood fireplace and sage. I release her hand and flip on the various lights around and begin the process of making it seem like a home.

"This is where you live?" She asks softly.

"Yes, it was my mother's before mine." I respond, grabbing drinks from the bar for us. Not that my little Lena has ever had alcohol, but tonight will be a first of many things for her. Alcohol the least of it. When I pass it to her, she frowns for a moment, as if to refuse. "It'll help with the nerves. You've been through so much." Her innocent eyes widen before softening and grabbing the glass from me. Another hit of that drug invades my veins as I watch her grimace sip after sip.

"Thank you," She mutters softly, cheeks rosy now.

I smile. "Of course my angel. My mate. You deserve nothing but the best."

FIVE

One Week Later

Oisin

"How did this happen?!" Jackson grabs at his hair as he paces back and forth. News of the destruction of the priestesses has finally sunk in and I can't help but feel pleased with his reaction. It has been slow, the trickling in of the information. The King keeping it close to his chest when he learned of the deaths. But soon? Soon *everyone* will know. Bringing even more to The Order and ripping even more of the country's loyalty away from the royal family.

"The Order needs to be hunted down; we can't let this continue any longer." Arcanna adds in. I glance towards her, annoyed at her presence. Lately she won't leave us the fuck alone and it's beginning to intrude on my influence over the soon to be King. Each time I manage to sip from his magic or slip him more of the special tincture she suddenly appears, as if the act summons her.

As if sensing my gaze, she cuts her stormy eyes towards me, narrowing them.

Thankfully, after this week, she will no longer be an

issue, the Queen agrees that her attention on her son is problematic. After all, he can't be seen with another woman when he is engaged to a princess of another country. Nor will he ever leave the city if he believes she is here for him. And we need him gone.

Pushing to a stand I grab Jackson and drag his muscular body into mine. "It'll be okay, we'll figure it out."

He relaxes into my touch and lets out a long sigh as my hands stroke over his back and arms. When I feel him grow hard under me, I can't help but glance a look back to Arcanna who looks on with pure jealousy. I smirk when I lock eyes with her before dragging Jackson's mouth to mine and claiming him for my own. The sound of the door slamming is music to my ears. I do love to win after-all.

SIX

Three Months Later

Harrowlena

My back screams as I stand as straight as I can with my head held high listening to Lady Ornate, or the High Priestess as she demands to be referred to, and The Elders preach to the community. The air is thick with heat from all the bodies packed into our tiny gathering space and the crowd feels restless. The old barn wasn't meant to house this many people, but more and more people seem to be finding solace in our cause and fleeing the tyranny of the royals.

Or at least that's what the High Priestess has told me during our lessons. Each time I think of her with the title my stomach turns and part of me twists into a violent, dark creature. One that I've worked hard to push away.

"But you promised!" I cry feebly.

Oisin scoffs, "I can't very well make you High Priestess with no training now can I?" I recoil slightly from both tone and words. When he sees the movement he softens, a bit, and gathers me in his arms despite my protest. "It's only for now,

I had to do it. The Elders demanded it given you couldn't get the ceremony from your grandmother. You have to prove yourself to them, to them you are just a weepy female. You must show them, show us all, you can do this."

My eyes glance to the clock above the exit, as the memory bounces around in my head. Try as I might standing up here this long is torture. It's been three months of this, three months and I still can't seem to be the poised and serene priestess in training they seem to want me to be. And every fidget is a reminder I'm not doing what Oisin asked of me. I'm not proving to The Elders that I can do this. But my body can only stay still for so long before I start to fidget.

"One must be poised and serene at all times. You cannot allow yourself to act like such a child. You will only confirm that you are undeserving of the position." Lady Ornate's voice rings through my head even as my heart cracks a little. My Nana never cared that I was who I was. She did not mind that I enjoyed moving, that I wasn't the person to stand and preach, I was the person to get lost in daydreams and fields of flowers.

My eyes travel to the lone window that looks out towards the woods, the dark thicket of trees that hold no flowers or warmth. Some days I long for my old home, my old life.

"The Gods will grant us reprieve when we return the power to the people. The royals have held onto it long enough. They burned the Priestesses sacred place to keep the power to themselves!" The Elder's voice booms out over the crowd startling me. Lady Ornate cuts me a glare and my cheeks flame. People nod and murmur agreement from the ground. Lady Ornate takes one last look at me before she schools herself once more. That serene smile painted on her lips that I've come to know as anything but genuine, and every time she nods the crystals attached to her sunburst crown sway, casting fractured light outward.

My mind flashes to my Nana's crown. Hers wasn't grandiose, it was simple but beautiful. No, this one is a mockery of the one my Nana wore, far too flashy. Hers was well worn, well loved, and had been passed down through generations. She had always said I would be the next one to wear it. I often wonder if it still sits on that shelf that I so carelessly left it on. Often wonder if her spirit judges me for my actions as much as I judge myself.

"They tried to take our hope but we prevailed. The Goddess allowed us to rescue our priestess here, to raise her as our own and protect her." Lady Ornate says, her voice taking on a mystical quality. "However, the Goddess is angry with those who have supported the false rulers. She will strike those down who continue to support them!"

Fear trickles through the crowd at her words and not for the first time recently I wonder if her words are truly that of the Gods. Questions about our way of life have filtered in and out of my brain more and more. Many an evening I have sat up and prayed to the Goddess to give me a sign that this is the path. And many an evening I'm met with silence. Silence that seems to fester within me.

The High Priestess' head turns towards me, as if she can hear my sinful thoughts, the chains dangling over her mask swaying and providing a delicate chime. All the other gazes follow hers, the whole congressional now looking between us. "Our little priestess will show us the way, she will be the one to usher in the changes we so desire. But only if she stays pure to us." Chills skitter down my spine at her tone at the same time I bristle at the title she uses for me. She slowly lifts her finger, pointing towards me. "The Gods know your thoughts."

Pure.

The word sends a wave of shame over me as I think about the lustful thoughts I've had recently. The lustful thoughts I've had of *him* recently. Every time I see him my body seems to come alive in new and terrifying ways, a fire I can't seem to stop from burning. The stark contrast between what my Nana and mother preached about sex and what The Elders seem to preach is confusing.

"Shame doesn't belong in conversations of pleasure." My mother says as I groan. She cuts me a sharp look ceasing the noise. She shakes her head. "I know it's uncomfortable for you, but this is our life and magic. You need to feel like you have a voice, and shame will silence that voice every time."

My mother loved to preach consent and communication during pleasure. Here though? Here they teach none of that. At first I didn't mind, after all I was considered more "prudish" in contrast to the others in our home. I hated when my mother or Nana tried to instruct me on female pleasure, always trying to tell me the importance of understanding my own body. So not being forced into those conversations around pleasure did not bother me. But now? Now my body has awoken to my mate. And sometimes I wish I could go back in time and hear her voice. Speak to her just once more about these feelings.

"We shall rise up and meet these challenges head on!" The Elder yells before turning to look at me. "And this one will remain as she should be." His smile is less comforting and holds the promise of retribution should I step out of line. Since the moment I arrived The Elders have spoken of the power in my virginity. Of the idea that I will not become High Priestess if I'm no longer pure. And since the "incident" they seem to have redoubled their efforts to keep me a virgin.

I bite the inside of my cheek wishing I had never allowed my eyes to gaze so long on his chiseled chest. Swimming in the river had seemed so innocent until it wasn't. Until my nipples pebbled and my body physically ached for him to touch me. Lady Ornate, having seen us together, had slapped me across the face so hard my cheek was marked for a week. It's not lost on me that she did it the moment Oisin had left for his mission. He would never allow this treatment.

Nor would he allow the old men to do as they have. The Elders have their own form of punishment that has been inflicted on me over the past few days. Even now my back burns from the cane, despite the marks having faded away from the magical ointment they kept applying. My jaw aches when I think about it all, a strange fire burning within it begging to be let loose. For my voice to be heard and justice to be taken. But I push it back down, push it away knowing full well I cannot lose my temper with them.

I need to please them. I need to make sure they appoint me High Priestess. I need to make my mate proud.

The applause is thunderous hurting my ears as the crowd leaps to their feet in support of whatever The Elders have continued to say.

"Pssst." The sound draws my attention to the right of the platform I'm standing on the edge of. My eyes are met with a familiar mop of black hair as the object of my lustful thoughts peeks out from behind the curtains. His devilish smile lights up his face and eyes twinkle with mischief. My own lips pull into a half smile and cheeks flush.

A curt throat clearing has me cringing as the High Priestess looks over at us disapprovingly. My savior glares over my shoulder at her, his eyes going so cold even I tremor from the power. Yet when they land back on me, they soften.

"Ah yes, our young lord is here." Lady Ornate says as she raises her hands to the sky. "Blessed our Goddess." The congregation all follow suit, murmuring the closing words as they hold their hands to the sky. My own words are quiet and movements slow as I feel that insidious doubt creep in once more.

"Lena," he calls out and beckons me forward. Lifting my ceremonial skirts to not trip, my bare feet pad lightly over the rough wooden floor, the bells on my ankles twinkling as I move. So unlike the garb I normally wear, the long skirt cuts directly below my naval allowing a thin golden chain to wrap around my belly. The long slit up the side goes to my hip allowing my pale leg to be exposed when I walk. The golden anklets that hold the bells glint each time I'm exposed. My breasts are wrapped in the simple bandeau that I wear damn near every day, but I'm allowed to adorn the gold choker that dangles long tassels down my front.

I feel pretty. And for once I'm thankful today was church because now, *he* gets to see me like this. Even if I shouldn't want his attention like that, even if I know I'll pay for it later.

Sometimes it's worth the punishment.

As soon as I'm within arms reach he drags me into his chest for a heartbeat, breathing in my scent deeply before dragging me behind the curtain out of view. His hands cup my face as he looks me over, "Fuck, you look gorgeous." He groans. My cheeks flame and my eyes dart down. His hand lifts my chin until we lock eyes again. "Never look down when in my presence, own your beauty my queen."

He plants a soft kiss to my lips and my body bristles with need to feel more. "I've missed you." I huff out. He continues to kiss down my neck and my body squirms. "We shouldn't. . ." He groans but pulls away from me.

"I'm sorry my angel, I didn't intend to be away for that long." He grips my hand, dragging me behind him quickly. "But I'm here now, let's make the most of it."

"I hate that you have to leave for so long." I mutter lamely.

He turns, offering me a mischievous smile. "But it makes my homecoming that much sweeter, doesn't it?" Our dwellings whirl past as we laugh and run through the dirt roads. But as we turn and start heading towards his private home, I start to lose the courage I had gained from that kiss, my steps starting to faulter a bit. It's one thing to remain in my shared space or even the woods but his home? The one I haven't been in since that first day here?

For some reason this feels like a big step for us. I swallow my nerves, the lump settling heavy in my stomach.

As if sensing my hesitation, he pulls me into his side, "Oh my Lena, you are a gem among these fools. Don't over-think it." He drags me up the front steps of his home. "Now close your eyes."

I nibble at my bottom lip before nodding and pressing my eyes shut. I allow him to lead me over the threshold my bare feet feeling the rough wood of his floors. "Open." He commands.

A gasp is pulled from my lips as I'm bathed in the soft twinkling lights he's hung around.

"It's beautiful." I spin around taking in everything, the lights, the soft pallet bed in front of the fire, the bottle of wine and the subtle incense smoke that lays in the air.

He presses a kiss to my neck, "Not as beautiful as you." His hands trace over my body, sending shivers through me. I bathe in his warmth and touch as he explores. "I know I've been gone far too often as of late so I wanted an uninter-rupted evening with my mate."

He pulls away, grabbing two drinks from the counter-top. I watch as he pours wine into one cup but let my eyes meander over the space as he pours the other. The beauty of the moment feels too perfect to be considered wrong, how could the Goddess frown upon this when we've loved each other so long?

He clears his throat, pulling my attention back to him. My fingers take the offered glass. He holds up his own and we clink the glasses together, "to eternity." He pledges as he sips.

"To eternity." I repeat and raise my own. The red liquid tastes sweet as it slithers down my throat, settling in my stomach. It brings a warm tingle through me that forces a flush to my cheeks. For a moment my vision sways and I shake my head to clear it.

I go to say something, but I'm met with soft lips pressed to mine and strong hands around my waist. I kiss him back while clinging to the drink in my hand. My body feels feverish and the need I feel for him feels too overwhelming.

When his body steps away I frown, "drink the rest my Lena." He says as he moves from my vision. I want to say no, to say it made me feel funny, but embarrassment makes me stop. After all, he drinks all the time, for all I know this is normal and I'm being ridiculous.

Draining the contents in one more gulp I set the empty glass down before turning around only for a deep blush to develop as I see him unbuttoning his dark shirt exposing his defined chest and abs. His gaze flickers like the lights above. He stalks forward, dragging a gasp from me as his hands cup my face once more. "I need you, Lena. I need you so badly. Promise me you'll always be mine."

"I promise," I blindly whisper because in my heart of hearts I've always known he belongs to me and I to him. And if we belong to each other how can this be so wrong?

Oisin

My hips piston into the female on all fours in front of me, her face pressed so hard into the mattress below I would wonder if she could breathe at all if not for the moans that she throws out every so often. I could care less about her pleasure, she's merely here to take the edge off from the cock-tease of a priestess currently passed out upstairs. The wine hit her hard but did little to reprogram the bullshit The Elders have placed in her brain. The old fools speak absurd lies into her ear every time I leave.

Purity is bullshit.

The culture around it nothing more than a construct for them to control the females around their old cocks. The idea that the priestess should be a virgin for her first full moon is nothing short of absurd. They only do it to keep our bond from forming any stronger than it already has, they know. . . Know she is mine and mine alone. And because of that the magic she can give us will only go to me.

Anger blooms within me at the circumstance I find myself in, not being ready to fully move against The Elders and their puritanical bullshit.

Keeping us from fucking will only delay the inevitable for so long. I will have the power that I deserve and when I do I will show them who they have denied all this time.

"Oh fuck right there!" The girl beneath me yells, her voice annoyingly loud.

My hand finds purchase against her bare ass, "shut the fuck up." I growl. "I didn't ask for your feedback. I asked you take my cock like a good little whore."

She whimpers as my nails dig into her skin hard enough that blood starts to bloom. She cries a bit and the sound is my undoing. Ripping myself free I spray my seed across her back, my hand jerking my hard shaft until the last drop is spent. She collapses onto her front before pushing to a stand. Her tits hanging from the shirt I pulled downward early.

"Clean up and get out." I growl, tucking myself back into my pants.

"I didn't get off," She whines.

Quick as lightning my fist grips her throat, fear cutting through her eyes as her hands try to pry mine loose. "It's a gift that my cock was even inside you. Now fuck off before I decide to wash my hands in your blood." When I release her she grabs at her throat, rubbing the tender skin. Not bothering to even try to cover herself, she flees from the cabin door out into the woods.

My own steps carry me back to my sleeping priestess, the steady rise and fall of her chest moving the soft blankets curled around her. Her cheeks are still flushed from the alcohol and lips slightly parted. My cock hardens at the sight of them. Leaning down I brush my lips across hers before pulling back, "Soon. Soon you'll give me everything."

SEVEN

One Year Later

Harrowlena

"Do you think we'll get our happy ending?" My voice is a whisper on the wind, my body pressed into his for warmth against the cool night air. My bare skin feels like a sin against the backdrop of such an innocent evening. Fireflies lazily meander past us, his deft fingers tracing patterns across my smooth stomach.

His lips press against my temple, "of course we will. Why wouldn't we?" His voice is so self-assured, no doubt in his mind that we will make it in this cruel world.

"It feels like they do not want us together." I tentatively say. "There are. . . rumors you're leaving, for good."

He pushes his body upward so he can lean over me. His eyes peer into mine, intense and foreboding. He doesn't even have to open his mouth for me to know the rumors are true, he's leaving me.

He presses a chaste kiss to my lips before rolling away and pulling his shirt back on. The disappointment in him so easily shown. Once again, I stopped us from having sex.

Once again, I lectured him on the importance of my purity with the Goddess. Once again, the words of The Elders fell from my lips even as the burning part of my heart disagreed with them.

"I have to leave," he says finally meeting my gaze. "But I always return. You know that." His frustration with me so very, very clear alongside the disappointed look that seems to be a permanent fixture in his eyes anytime we are together.

Tears fill my eyes. I want to scream that it's not fair, that it's The Elders who instruct me, that it's them who will take the cane to me when I return from our time spent together, that it's The Elders who inspect me and make sure the purity is intact. But instead, I crawl towards him on hands and knees, pulling his length free and taking him into my mouth. The one thing I can get away with doing.

He groans out, gripping my hair as he starts to fuck my mouth with little regard to my comfort. "Your mouth is so good my Lena. So fucking good. I can only imagine how your pussy will feel when I claim it." He thrusts hard, gagging me and causing tears to spring forward until I feel him tense, and his salty taste explodes over my tongue. "Such a good girl."

I swallow him down before sitting back on my knees, my breasts still naked to the air. Shame crawls at my throat and I shove it away. Push it down, down, down, until it's a rock in my stomach and I paint a demure smile on my face. He smiles and hands me a glass of wine again, I don't want it. I hate how it feels and tastes. But I know he'll be happy if I do it so I drink it down, desperate for his praise and love.

"Oh Lena, always so eager to please me." He presses a kiss to my forehead and leaves me half naked on the forest floor to contemplate my life choices.

EIGHT

One Year Later

Oisin

I rub my temples delicately as I listen to Lady Ornate drawl on and on about the latest gossip among The Order. I truly do not give a fuck about most of it, however, occasionally she brings news to me that piques my interest. Like The Elders telling my little priestess how important her virginity is. However, since she informed me of that nothing else has been of use to me and instead only contributes to my migraines.

It's a routine now, leaving to Hell or Gothic Grove, returning and gaining these updates and wanting to blow my brains out with how useless they are.

"Is there a point to any of this?" I finally interrupt. She stops talking, mouth pulling into a slight frown before she schools it back into the fake smile I loathe so much.

"I was merely updating you as you seem to be gone much more lately."

And there it is. "I did not realize I was supposed to be here for a certain amount of time, didn't realize there was a quota for me to meet." I lean forward so my forearms rest on my thighs.

She shakes her head quickly, "No of course sir, you can come and go as you please. It's just with the rumors of the breakup between you and the prince. . ." Pushing to a stand I relish in the fear that lights up her eyes briefly before I walk towards the bar in the kitchen.

"You can tell the Elders that the breakup was needed, after all, I am set to marry the princess."

Silence followed by a quick gasp fills the room as Lady Ornate processes the information. "Ava?"

I roll my eyes, "Is there another royal whore I was sold?"

"You found her?" She asks hesitantly before saying, "I suspect I should ready the accommodations then if you have found her, unless of course you do not actually have her. . ."

Rage moves over me as I swallow it down. Her words hitting me in a weak spot. I had found the princess but getting access to her? That was an entirely different issue. "Of course, I have, did you ever doubt me?" I snap. "We will have Ava, a *real* priestess and the magic we require." I turn back towards her, the drink I've poured in hand and savor the look on her face from my comment. She forgets her place, that she holds the title alone and none of the magic.

Lady Ornate pushes herself to a stand and smooths her long skirts out. "I will bring this news to The Elders sir, I'm sure they will be most pleased with this."

"Yes, scurry along. Tell them who is in charge and who will remain in charge."

As she bows, I see the tops of her breasts spill over the top she wears, when she stands and catches my lingering gaze her cheeks flush. "Should you need anything else I'll be available." She murmurs softly, a vein attempt at trying to portray a demure female. "*Anything at all.*" She says pointedly.

When she passes me, I grab her arm, my fingers tightening on her flesh. Her eyes light up with excitement, "Bring me a female and Lena." The words are cold water over her short-lived idea that my cock would be warmed inside her. She flashes me a disappointed gaze before she manages to wipe it away and nod her head in confirmation. I release her arm allowing her to scurry from the room before I shoot the the liquor back and prepare for my feast.

Harrowlena

When Lady Ornate had told me Oisin was back I had dressed quickly, doing my best to look as beautiful as I could manage with the meager supplies I have. She had given me a strange smile as she pointed me in the direction of where he asked for me. When I had thanked her she had let out a cold laugh before walking in the opposite direction. I hadn't understood it at the time.

Now I do.

My eyes fill with unshed tears as I watch the man I love fuck the female in front of me.

The man that left me just a few weeks ago isn't the same man who returned to me. This one is brutal, rough, and uncaring. So unlike the person who kept me safe and sane all this time. The person who was my family. *Is* my family. When I brought it up to Lady Ornate, she merely scoffed, her words making me feel small as she reminded me, I know so little of men and life.

I can't help but wonder if this is indeed punishment from the Gods for everything we've done outside of sex, for the questions and thoughts I've had. Despite belonging to him, and him alone, I damned our relationship. The High Priestess and all her teachings of The Elders weaves through my brain making my body lock up as the guilt and shame slam into me once more.

Whore.

Impure.

Dirty.

All the things I became once I started pleasuring him.

I wince as he snaps his hips forward into her, the front of her body hitting the ground. My eyes go to close. To avoid the cruel display.

"Don't shy away from me, my Lena." He growls, "this will be you some day. Someday I'll fill you so full it'll drip out of you for days."

Goddess help me my pants dampen with arousal at the hard, cruel words. My nipples peak and harden under my thin bandeau top, and he smirks at the response he gains. I hate it. And I love it. My hand finds the red wine he always brings me, and I chug it down quickly, praying for the dulling of my senses. He pulls out of the female suddenly, his release painting her bare ass before he pushes her away and stands. She cries out and it takes everything in me not to reach for her. To help her.

My body feels cold as I watch him laugh at her. She scrambles up and flees the dark room without looking back. "Stupid whore." He mutters. My eyes drag down to his cock, glistening from being deep inside her. "You want a taste?"

My eyes flare and shame curls deep within me because goddess help me I do. I know it's wrong, know that he was just inside her, but I desperately want to be a part of this. He laughs at my reaction, no doubt noting the deep flush my cheeks take on.

My heart cracks a bit as I watch him get dressed. "You're leaving again?" My voice breaks apart on the question.

He tilts his head and watches me and for a moment I see the boy I fell in love with appear. Tenderly, he cradles my face as he presses his forehead into mine. "I am. I have a job to do. The royal family must be stopped my sweet Lena. It all must be stopped if we ever have a hope to be together." He pulls back, thumb swiping away a stray tear that's fallen. "I know it's hard to watch what happened, but you are mine and I'm yours. But until you are ready, I cannot have you. Your mouth just simply isn't enough."

I nod; despite not understanding at all. Because as his mate wouldn't it still be enough?

He plants a soft kiss to my lips, "there's my good girl. I knew you'd understand." He stands back up and continues getting himself together. "I have a job for you, a top-secret job that not even the busy body Elders can know about. Something only you can do. Do you want to know?"

I perk up, the feeling that he might need me, and only me, giving me a boost of energy and I frantically nod my head. "Please, I'll do anything."

He smiles, "I knew you would."

Our goodbye had been too quick, so I had lingered until the afternoon light finally started to fade to dusk. The conversation from earlier haunting me still. Befriend the Prince of Hell and trick him into giving up the ceremony for The Well. My throat tightens even thinking about being around the family responsible for the death of my mom and Nana. Not to mention I would be leaving here, alone, and heading into the royal city of Hell. And yet, I still agreed to it. Without hesitation.

I let out a long sigh as I pull the key from my pants pocket to lock up behind me. The small move returns some pride to me, he trusted me enough to give me his key, that had to mean something in the long run. The insecurity over not having sex with him keeps creeping in, even with this new task he gave to me.

As I turn to head off the porch I come face to face with Lady Ornate. A look of disgust and judgement on her face.

"Such a whore." She mutters.

Standing up a bit taller I try to exude confidence. "We love each other." I counter. "Nothing else matters." My voice shakes but I try my best to throw strength behind it. To straighten my back and stand up to her.

She raises an eyebrow at me, "you may love him, but you are nothing to him. You were a means to an end."

My confidence falters. "What do you mean?" Fear bleeds through me at her words. The house of cards I've so carefully built up one gust away from blowing down.

A cruel smile now spreads over her face. "Didn't you hear? He's getting married. To the princess of Hell. She's finally being brought home. You'll be nothing more than a conduit to provide his wife magic that will eventually be given to him."

The room ebbs out of view and something wells up from deep within. A primal, dark, creature claws at my chest until it frees itself from the cavern and is now in my throat and burning my tongue. I hear nothing as I release the pent-up creature, the scream bellowing from my mouth as the world around me explodes. My world is reduced to ash and nothingness as it all crashes around me.

Lies.

It was all lies.

He's marrying the whore whose family killed mine!

NINE

Three Months Later

Harrowlena
(Vegas-Doja Cat)

My senses feel overwhelmed as I look around at the busy streets of Hell. It was worse when I first came here, now it's more of an uncomfortable buzz that I can generally ignore. The hot, humid air is full of the sound of coins dropping out of slot machines, beeping and jingling as lights flash overhead acting like a lure on an angler fish to drag you into the various buildings. When doors open music filters out and is added to the chorus of chaos. People of all types spill from the open doors onto the sidewalk laughing drunkenly.

Nerves pepper my body, sweat now beading under the corset that's snuggled against my ribs. The blouse under it will no doubt be stained. The dark leather pants with the matching boots and long flowing skirt that's tied to my waist also don't help to release any of the warmth. I keep the goggles firmly placed over my eyes to avoid anyone potentially recognizing me. Not that Order members come to this part of the city often, but still. It doesn't seem worth the risk.

Moving through the crowds I quickly make my way down towards the darker end of the strip, careful not to draw too much attention to myself. The further I get from the main area the fewer lights glitter. Here the shadows attempt to coax you into their deep, dark homes. Rounding the corner, I have the usual anxiety that perhaps I took a wrong turn despite having done this walk now more times than I can count.

My boots echo out as my feet pound into the ground, my thighs burning from the pace I'm now setting. I keep hurrying along until I find myself outside a small apothecary. Or at least that's what the barely illuminated flickering sign says. The windows to the shop are foggy and stained, the inside barely visible. A clever ruse, I've discovered.

Wiping my palms down the pants I step off the curb and head into the front door. The old witch at the counter doesn't bother looking up as I push past her. She knows me. Knows where I'm going and who I seek.

I keep my eyes trained to the dirty floor in the hallway, studiously ignoring the doors that line the shockingly large apothecary. I looked once, after hearing some screams echoing from behind, and learned very quickly I had no business seeing what was behind those doors.

As I approach the end of the hallway my eyes are greeted with the familiar face of the hulking bodyguard standing outside the thick, metal door. I pause for a moment as he looks me over before offering me a curt nod and opening the door wide enough for me to scoot through. I'm greeted with laughter and the smell of smoke. The music pumping through the speakers rattles the walls of the room I've entered.

I swallow down the discomfort of the amount of people in the space as I push through the dance floor. After what feels like an eternity, I finally manage to make it to the other side of the space. Pushing the goggles up top my head my eyes lock with a familiar pair of silver ones.

The Prince of Hell offers me a broad smile before gathering me into his arms for a hug.

"Good to see you Harrow, ready to go race?"

Oisin

Tucked deep within the crowd and obscured by the haze of drugs in the air, rage that I've never known claws through me as I watch my property embrace the Prince of Hell. When she left, Lady Ornate had been close to dead, my mother's home shattered around her. The fucking fool had let it slip I was bringing Ava home, igniting a fire in my priestess that unleashed a side of her none of us knew about.

A banshee.

She was a gods damn banshee.

The Elders were beside themselves, furious that such a dangerous creature had been hiding in such a demure little priestess. She had fangs and they did not appreciate that. But I did, I knew exactly how to use this newfound weapon. Because that's what she is, a weapon housed in a pretty package. She'll be my dark goddess tethered to me with a golden chain, and no one will think to stand against me once this is all finished.

I push my hands into my pockets with a smile on my face as the crowds follow Jackson towards the start of the races. My hands curl into fists, smile slipping once more, as I see him skate his hand over her lower back, guiding her, she flinches away from the contact. A flash of disgust roaring over her before she sucks it back down and becomes the wide eyed, naïve, girl she's always shown. Her gaze travels around the room, distracting herself, and for a moment I think she spots me, eyes shocked and mouth parting but just as quickly she's pushed forward by the crowd.

Relief envelops me at her reaction. At first, I had been worried she had flipped sides, but after that reaction? No. My little angel is still very much mine. An idea develops as I watch it all, a wicked, glorious idea that has me chuckling to myself as I meander out of the party and into the night.

Harrowlena

For a moment I thought I'd seen Oisin. My body freezing for a moment until the crowd pushed up against Jax and I. His friend Nyx whispering in my ear to keep moving. I'm not sure when it happened but the longer I'm away everything within me is desperate to get back to *him*. As if I very well may die if I don't find myself in his arms this very moment. And thinking he's here? Everything in me is begging to go back.

"Harrowlena, you need to keep moving." Nyx says again. Without realizing it I've stopped again while Jax has continued forward towards the sleek black machine he'll race.

I nod and smile politely at his friend. "Sorry." I mutter and quickly move towards my usual spot. But my eyes keep searching for that familiar black hair and beautiful face.

Sweat beads at my temples as I listen to the engines rev up and the excited yells of the spectators. The streets are alive with the occupants of Hell. All come to see their beloved Prince. They love him. Every one of them loves the man now folding his muscular body into his car.

Every night since I found him here, I watch him talk with those around him, laugh and drink and party with the people of the city. Even with me, he was friendly the moment he found me. His kind words and encouragement have been nothing short of supportive. He hasn't made a move to harm me or fuck me. Only protect me from those at the races that have allowed their gaze to linger a little too long, asking his longtime friend to hang out with me.

He's been a gentleman with model behavior.

And an excellent manipulator. Because how else do you convince an entire population you had nothing to do with the kill of the priestesses?

I let out a long sigh in frustration. My time spent here, thus far, amounting to nothing useful except learning how much everyone adores him.

Another failure. I think to myself. Because what else would this be if not a failure? I may have been angry with Oisin but he was still mine, my mate, and I was determined to get him the information he needed. But as time goes on, I have begun to think that Jackson has no knowledge of the ceremony and if he doesn't have it, who does?

Another sigh is dragged from me knowing it might be time I admit defeat in this mission.

"You seem distracted tonight." Nyx comments in his rough voice.

I offer up a small smile. "I just forget he is a royal sometimes. I mean what Prince of Hell street races?"

Nyx snorts. "So does everyone else. Jackson isn't like the rest of them. He is a good person, always has been, always will be. They want to mold him into something he'll never be. So, he escapes here. It's his way of letting loose and getting to know his people better." I frown. Annoyed that another person thinks Jackson is such an amazing person.

It's confusing and at odds with what I've been taught. With what I know. Nyx clears his throat, and I realize I've been silent and frowning for far too long.

"Sorry," I manage as I wave my hand in front of my face. "I think I'm just not feeling super well. I may call it a night." I push against the wall I was leaning against, Nyx moving to follow me before his eyes snag on a female. A low growl pulling from his lips as he sees her slip through the crowd and out of sight again. For a moment I think he mutters something about his stubborn mate but just as quick the words are taken by the sounds the street.

"If you need to go talk to whoever that was you can." I hedge. "I'm truly fine."

He looks torn, pushing his hand through his hair. "Are you sure?"

I offer up the most confident smile I can muster. "Yes! Seriously go."

"Gods help me for having such a stubborn mate." He mutters before he looks me over once more, "go straight back to the apothecary, okay?"

I roll my eyes, "yes yes I know. Tell Jackson I said good-bye." I don't let him say anything else before I'm quickly fleeing from him back the way we came.

Weaving through the crowds my mind wanders back to Oisin, heartache and longing filling my every bone with a loneliness that keeps threatening to pull me under. I miss him. Even if I was furious when I left, he's still my mate and I miss him.

As I near the building my mind continues to whirl, stuck on thoughts of Oisin when something flashes next to me. Cold steel and hot breath invade my senses as hands latch around me right before a sharp pain explodes over my temple and then... Nothing.

The room slowly comes into view as my eyes attempt to open. The blurred figures moving around me send fear skittering through my bones. My body attempts to push up only to find my arms locked to a cold table. I blink several times, confusion bleeding into my senses. An old man moves over me, a strange device within his hands as he looms over my face.

My awareness comes in sharply as I feel cool metal locked in place over my mouth. Firmly keeping it shut. My cries muffled through the spelled mask do nothing to stem my panic, cutting off my breathing. My nails scratch the surface of the table, desperate to break free.

"Now, now, dear let's not hurt ourselves. That mask won't be coming off." The voice comes from an elderly man wearing long cream robes. His balding head is slick with sweat and his beady eyes look at me through thick glasses. The tattoo adorning his neck gives him away as one of The Elders. But even if he didn't have that tattoo, I would know a priest like him from a mile away.

My eyes dart around, rapidly attempting to absorb my surroundings. My mind hazy and unable to figure out what happened and why I'm here. The once-white tile is now a mixture of blacks, browns, greens, and smears of red. The air smells moldy with a hint of iron under it. My body shivers against the cold medical table it's strapped to. Thick white bands go over my breasts and the apex of my thighs holding me down.

"You caused such a stir when you let loose your power and ran. But there is no need to be afraid," his tone is patronizing as he pats my bare leg with his wrinkled hand. "This mask will keep you under control. No more accidents."

My memories are slow to come back as I remember standing at the races, turning to leave, and then. . . nothing.

"When you left the High Priestess was gravely wounded from that blast of power you gave. Truly it's a miracle she survived." He prattles onward. "So, we had to make sure that mistake didn't happen again."

My eyes widen as panic pulses through me. My power flares trying to escape but as my mouth attempts to open in the mask a blinding pain rips through my jaw, and a scream attempts to break free from me as my body bows off the cold table only to be stopped by the bands.

"You'll find when you attempt to use your banshee scream, you'll be corrected." He says, unsympathetic as I lay panting, a thin layer of sweat coating my body now. "What you felt is the magic pushing iron into your jaw. I would suggest not testing the mask often. Eventually, you'll die from enough exposure."

Tears track down my face in a silent plea. Wordless prayers being offered up to the gods who have long since forsaken me.

He continues to busy himself out of my line of sight, "now that you've returned to us, and we have you under control we must get you ready to present to court. He'll be so pleased we found you! The young lord has been beside himself searching, what a lovely surprise to give him."

He prattles on as if I too will be proud of his accomplishment.

I thrash against the holds, emotions rushing through me as I realize how I failed.

He tsks. "You must calm down dear." He moves back over a syringe in his hand filled with clear liquid. "This will help you. Now you'll feel a little prick and when you wake, you'll be ready to serve."

He jams the needle into my neck and the world slowly drains away from me.

(his land- Paris Paloma)

Time has lost meaning since the mask was placed on me. It's endless pain and torment and that's all. The Elders are cruel, wicked men, and if I were a better person I would allow the Goddess to bathe me in her grace and understand what they are doing is a consequence of my own actions. A consequence of my failure to retrieve what my beloved sent me for.

Because what other reason would he have for not rescuing me?

I'm not a better person though, not anymore, and every smack of the cane, every ounce of iron piercing my jaw, has me daydreaming about their murder and questioning my devotion. A strange madness crept into my mind the moment that mask was placed on me. One that will surely condemn me to the very pits of the underworld.

Every time I look in the mirror, I see the monster they've turned me into. See the way my bones poke from my body and the unhealthy sheen my skin has. No one thought this through, how I would be fed and taken care of, until the mask was on, and I was starving. It's why I stay hidden in the shadows, and they've seemed inclined to allow it, only parading me out every so often. Their golden treasure now tarnished. A ghost now haunting their halls.

Today however is different.

I would have known he arrived even if they didn't come running in gossiping like old women that their lord had returned.

Yet as much as I want him, crave him, I don't want him

seeing me like this. Don't want his eyes to see the mask that is plastered to my face. To see the failure of being dragged back here. My shame is on display. My punishment sent from the Goddess herself screwed into my bones.

"Back straight you little whore." Lady Ornate hisses. She's dressed me in ceremonial garb once more with a crown atop my head that mocks my status here and forces me to keep my head up. I had taken to keeping my eyes on the ground, chin tucked, to keep the mask at least partially hidden, but Lady Ornate figured it out and now I wear the damn crown with hair back every time they allow me to be in the community.

She hates me. A dark, twisted, hate that she uses to torture me endlessly. I can't even explain to her that I had no idea I was a banshee, that I hadn't intended to hurt her. Though I suspect even if I could speak, she wouldn't believe me. She's enjoyed this role, enjoyed torturing me and doing all the nasty work for the men who hold church in the other room.

"Master will be so pleased, he'll reward me." She mutters to herself. I tuck my chin tighter to my chest, desperate to hide the shame that is screwed to my face. When the crown starts to tip forward again, she screeches and snatches my hair, dragging my head back upwards. My eyes watering from the feel.

"What are you doing?" His voice feels like a blessing and a curse all wrapped up into one.

Tears burn in my eyes as I squeeze them shut against the pain of my hair being pulled and my heart hammering against my chest.

"A gift, your lord! We found her!" She says as her voice pitches upward an octave.

I keep my eyes shut against the room, refusing to look at him, the one I failed.

I can almost feel his eyes roam over me as we stand in silence. When I feel his hand gripping my chin a small whimper lodges in my throat as he turns me this way and that, inspecting me. Every nerve ending raw from the mask being placed on my face and from suddenly being with him again. The silence in the room grows as he doesn't acknowledge Lady Ornate next to us, the discomfort of it causing her to shift nervously.

"Open your eyes." He commands softly.

I do. Unable to fight a command from him. My mouth goes dry and skin heats as I lock eyes with the one I failed. The months have only made him more handsome, all his harsh line and hard cut muscles. For a moment my heart skips a beat, and, in those eyes, I see that boy who loved me and saved me from my burning home. The one who made a twinkling space for us to escape to.

"My lord," Lady Ornate starts in. But he cuts her off with a single look, one that promises wrath and retribution.

My body trembles under his gaze as his fingers drop from my chin and lace through my own as he leads me from the room, leaving the "High Priestess" sputtering in the room alone.

My jaw burns and my skin feels flayed raw in the spots the mask is connected. The pain is dizzying, and my mind feels cloudy from it. Or at least that's the excuse I give myself for willingly following him and allowing my heart to skip a beat now that he's holding me again. I don't even care to notice he's dragging me into the main common room of The Order until I see all the pale robes.

(Whore- In This Moment)

"Who authorized this?" His voice is deadly quiet, but it sends a shock through me as I jerk my eyes towards him. The Elders, gathered in a small circle, all turn towards us with annoyance and confusion written across their faces.

Yet no one speaks, not a single word uttered. "I asked a question." He says with equal deadly calm.

When he's once again met with silence, he turns towards me with vengeance crackling behind his eyes that sends heat waves through my body. I cock my head to the side, the question in the movement, *did he really not have them do this to me?*

He drags me into his body, his lips ghosting over my neck, the only spot he can kiss that's close to my face and uncovered by the mask. It holds a promise, even if I cannot feel it on my lips, I know it holds a promise. I could sob with relief, he was never mad at me, he didn't do this. *They* did.

When he steps away and locks eyes with me again. "Who?"

I allow mine to shift to the group of Elders before raising my hand, a single finger points towards the one who fitted me with this contraption. And I have no sympathy for him as I do so.

"Good girl." He praises sending a flush through me that has my eyes fluttering.

A blade seems to materialize from nowhere, pressing into his palm with a punishing grip. He keeps his eyes locked on me for a moment before offering me a smile and whirling, that gleaming blade slicing clean across The Elders throat. Crimson vengeance pours from the wound, spraying him in the face and covering his hand.

Voices arise around me but all I can focus on is the blade his fingers are wrapped around. The edges are harsh in a beautifully, violent way, the blood dripping down it mesmerizing as he walks back towards me. It calls to some darker part, watching this justice be carried out. The same part that was silenced with this mask. The Elder's body drops in front of me, the life seeping out onto the dirty floor as his eyes grow cold and finally lifeless.

I don't know how long I stand there watching but when he touches me, I lean into it. "No one will ever touch you again, you are mine. My angel." The words push away any doubt that has tried to fester in me, replaced with a small amount of shame that I ever thought he could hurt me like this.

When I feel him hard and wanting against my back desire blooms fresh in my core and a small whimper escapes me. The shame taking a back seat to my arousal.

He begins to kiss my neck but pauses as his hands trail down my stomach, "You all kept her from me. Now you get to watch me take what is mine." He growls possessively. "You'll watch as I finally get what is owed to me."

His fingers dip into that untouched place beneath my skirt. "You're so wet for me." The sounds his fingers make as they slide through my mess is obscene, yet I can't seem to care, my eyes stay fixed on The Elder who he just killed. The eyes staring up at me lifelessly, yet I hope his soul is still around to see this. "I'm going to fill you with my cum and let them see who you belong to."

My eyes finally look up and connect with the faces of those around us. It causes another fresh wave of arousal to pool and my pussy to clench around his penetrating fingers. He huffs out a laugh before biting my neck.

I have to slam my lips shut behind the mask, contain the scream that I want to send to the heavens. The terrible, awful scream that I like this. I like his fingers deep inside me. I like these old men watching and most of all I like the blood pooling at my feet. The shame of it all threatens to boil over once more, springing free of where I shoved it.

As if sensing he's losing me, he uses his other hand to start working my skirt aside before backing me up. He never stops stroking me as he pulls his hard length from his pants, lowering himself down onto the seat. With my front facing forward and my back still to him the whole room can see his fingers leave and cock slowly pushing into me, can see the place of our joining.

I tense, suddenly afraid and reality crashing into me once more when I feel the head of his penis enter me. "Shhh my sweet angel. My Lena. This will hurt and then feel good." He doesn't let me adjust before he is fully sheathed deep within and the pain that seers through me forces a small scream. I feel the tell-tale sign of the warning of the iron attempting to be injected and I slam my lips shut again, eyes watering.

Oblivious to my discomfort Oisin brings his fingers to the small bundle of nerves at the apex of my thighs and begins to stroke. The soft circles send zings of pleasure through me and slowly I start to rock my hips back and forth. The pain forgotten as it all dissolves into pleasure.

He groans and sings his praises of my tight cunt and how wet I am. The words only adding to my own arousal and causing me to gush around him. My body heats, cheeks flushing and nipples pebbling. My eyes dance around the room and I feel a sense of power and justice as the men who kept this from me watch my, oh so important, purity be taken.

Movement out of the corner of my eye snags my attention and I see Lady Ornate standing at the doorway, raging. A smile appears under that mask as I push through any lingering pain. I spread my legs a little wider, push my skirt a little further, so I can be sure she sees exactly what he's doing to me. I keep my eyes locked on hers as he pistons upward into me, as my hand snakes behind his head.

"Thats it. Fuck you're even better than I imaged you would be." He groans. "I need to feel you cum, need to feel you squeeze me." My body tightens as I hurtle towards my release, his words the fuel to the fire that rages in my body.

My fingers find purchase in his hair and I pull tight as my pussy convulses, squeezing him until he too is filling me with a loud roar. The world begins and ends with the feeling and every part of my soul settles into it, a rightness pushing away the fear and shame and doubt that have been beaten into me. All the while I keep my eyes dead locked on the woman who holds *my* title.

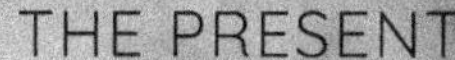

THE PRESENT

**Part Two
It all falls down**

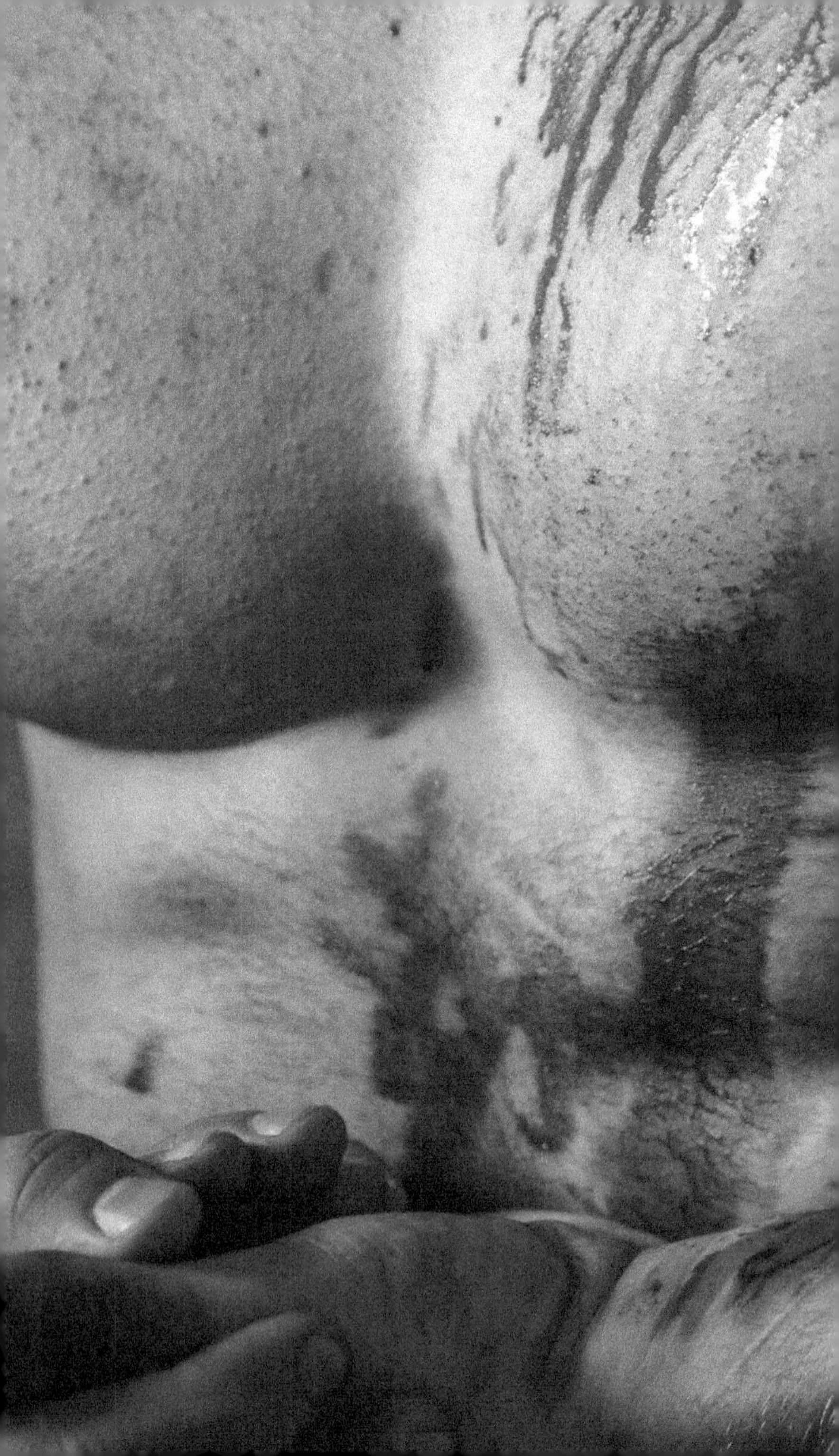

TEN

Oisin

Standing in front of Club Eufori I pick at the lint on my jacket, sneering at whomever passes by and chances a glance my way. The hour is late enough the club is closed but still too early for respectable individuals to be out and about. It's the hour of the night people like me thrive.

Gothic Grove is a city on the brink. If anything, good came from that bitch killing herself it was the removal of her dragons. Drago held this city in an iron fist after the original families were killed off. He kept most of the crime at bay, unless of course it was crime *he* was committing. Somehow everyone looked past that the fact that he was a drug dealer, and the biggest pusher of Eufori in the city.

I take a drag of the very drug that he used to create, the smoke swirling through me as I watch the employees file out one by one until I know all that is left is my query. The last to leave is a curvy shifter with headphones over her ears and dark rimmed glasses perched on her nose.

I can almost taste my victory, can almost taste the power that keeps getting snatched away from me at the last moment. I've hunted this magic for far too long and each time I have it in my grasp it seems to slip through my fingers. My anger simmers in my veins, as I stare at the curvy female, practically boiling my blood as I think of all the times, I've been so close to my end goal only to have it ruined.

As if sensing my fury she glances my way, and I hunker down for a moment, assuming the position of another junky looking for a score. She frowns but moves on, leaving the club wide open. I smile as I take one last drag and chuck the still lit Eufori cigarette to the ground. My charity of the day, providing free drugs to the streets. I would guess the moment I step off this curb someone will appear like the vermin they are to snatch it away.

As I near the back entrance I can hear sultry music pulsing through the speakers; a wide smile spreading over my face. There is nothing more satisfying than taking some-one, who thinks they are invincible, by surprise.

Lingering in the dark entryway to the main area, I watch as my query dances through the end of her shift. Her skin is radiant; the gold flecks she has painted across it stand out against her dark chocolate color. Her dark hair is made up in intricate braids, the thickness of the bun she has them looped into indicating the length is long. I stand for a moment longer, watching her work before I whistle.

The sound snaps her attention in my direction, eyes going wide as she looks at me.

"Hello Bast." I purr, inching forward. She holds her head high as she watches me, no fear in that gaze. "Shall we do this the easy way? Or the hard way?"

She regards me with her back tall, "Do you know whose club you are in?"

I let out a long laugh. "The dragon is long gone. He won't be back."

"You do not want to do this." Her voice waivers, eyes searching around for someone to step in.

I shrug, "I do. Actually." She moves to flee at the same moment I snap my fingers, using the last of my stolen magic, and Lady Ornate appears directly behind her. The movement takes her off guard and the needle the Lady drives into her neck pulls a scream from her before her body slumps forward. The High Priestess lets her drop to the bar floor, eyes glittering waiting for praise. I roll my own.

Lady Ornate looks at her with a level of annoyance that is normally reserved for the little priestess. "Why her? If my research was correct she doesn't have the type of magic you seek."

Rage renewed by her questioning I bare my teeth as I hiss out my commands. "Bring her back to my place, I can already feel how low on magic I am. I'll need her ready."

Lady Ornate pales, stepping back from me. "Yes sir."

I watch as she drags the unconscious female through the portal that had remained open.

"BAST!" The scream echoes through the bar room as I turn and find the female from earlier racing towards the still open portal. I leap forward, clearing the space as she reaches out. My hand grips the back of her t-shirt, the material ripping, and I throw her backwards. The momentum propels me forward as I hear the sound of shifting and a great howl echo outward as the portal closes behind me.

Lady Ornate stands wide eyed, the unconscious female still with her. Dusting my clothing off I let out a long sigh. "Looks like our little goddess here has a wolf shifter as a mate." I walk over to Bast, looking down at her serene face, the feeling of satisfaction rolling through me as more of my plan falls into place.

Jackson
(Fallout- UNSECRET & Neoni)

My boots crunch on the gravel thrown over the roads, barely audible over the wind currently ripping at the hood I have tugged low to hide my face. The storm came on fast and with a vengeance the moment I stepped out of the townhouse. Normally, at this time, the streets would be littered with party goers, even this deep in a residential area it would be full of laughter. Tonight, however, it's silent save for that screaming wind blowing in from the northeast.

Taking one last look at the space that used to house the home I spent so much time in. The space that felt more like a family home than my own had. I turn away towards the street, nothing was left, the memories and possessions scattered to the wind save for a few blood stains and battle marks. My friend had vanished.

I drag the leather cloak tight around my body to block the sand being kicked up as I force myself to keep walking towards the city center. I had hoped visiting would help me and assure me that he was fine. Truthfully this visit had done little to quell the deep pit in my stomach that keeps threatening to overtake me every time I think of him and the lack of knowledge I have on his whereabouts.

It's been a month since my world was shattered, a month since Ava sacrificed herself. Weeks of not knowing if my friends, my people, are alive or dead. Weeks of bureaucratic bullshit at the lake house I've been forced to remain in as my advisor's prattle on and on. Weeks of the memories of that place haunting me and trying to drown me in the gods damn past. Things I've worked hard to avoid and keep locked away.

There have been so many times now that I can't help but wonder if this is why Ava ran, if this is how she felt living in the palace. Trapped. Haunted. And gods damn miserable.

It doesn't help Dios has been gone for the past week. He had opted to help Demon and Kallen briefly, asking me to stay put until he was back, *"your magic is low, mi cielo, stay here and stay safe."* The memory of his words tastes bitter in my mouth.

The sound of scurrying draws my attention, my silver eyes dragging to the rubble of an apartment building that was unlucky enough to get the end of Drago's tail by the looks of it. The massive chunks from the structure litter the streets providing ample cover for whatever my magic is picking up. I stay still with my eyes narrowed and body alert until I see something move behind one of the large chunks of concrete. When the wind shifts again it brings with it the stench of rotting flesh.

Fuck me, please don't be an Okra.

I draw my hand under my leather cloak and pull my sword free from the sheath down my back as I keep sending the prayer outward. My magic crackles under my skin and overhead lightening splits open the sky in a violent display.

"Come out now and I will give you a quick death." I yell out into the dark night.

I'm met with the barbaric sound of hissing. "You are out rather late, aren't you little King?" As the human shaped creature slithers out from behind the structure. Its serpent-like eyes glowing yellow as its decaying head twitches.

(Sandman- izzy reign)

"Oisin must be desperate if he's using your kind." I grind out. The creature hisses again as its face splits almost in half to reveal the long fangs it keeps hidden in the decaying humanoid form. "Whatever he promised you is a lie, you know that right?"

"You are a false King who allowed the imprisonment of

our kind. Master will raise up and allow us to feast on whatever we choose." It takes an unsteady step towards me. The flesh on its body practically melting off as it drags its left leg behind it. No doubt attempting to shift to its more serpentine form. Okra are annoying in human form but dangerous as fuck when they shift. A cross between a zombie and a snake the things are poisonous and far too quick for something undead. One of the smartest things my father did was hunt them close to extinction.

It screams out as it rushes forward its massive snake body tearing through its lower half. It keeps its upper half human and I watch in slow motion as it reaches out with talonlike fingers and jaw unhinged exposing the razor-sharp teeth it plans to rip me to shreds with.

Unleashing my wings, I parry to the right slicing my sword along the scales marring the side of its body. I'm met with resistance even as I throw my whole shoulder into it and my wings push me forward, dragging the blade the best I can against the smooth scales. Too late I go to pull the blade free and the massive tail swipes back at me knocking my body across the ruined street and my sword in the opposite direction.

For a moment I can hear my father's voice chastising me as I skipped his instructions on swordsmanship. Words that I had previously countered with the idea that my magic would save me, that it would be more powerful than any sword.

"Fuck." I growl as I feel at least one rib snap when I hit the ground. My wings splay behind me briefly as I shake my head to clear the spots in front of my eyes. I go to push up and away however my movements are too slow, and the Okra wraps its lower half around me and squeezes.

"You cannot use your magic, nothing is left to replenish you." It hisses. Its human half is even more grotesque as it looms in front of me. This close I can see the patchy flesh and magots collecting in the various wounds spread over its body. "Master will reward me for bringing him the false King." It leans in until its fangs are inches from my eye. "We shall get to feast on your flesh when he is done with you."

I roll my eyes even as I feel another rib crack from the pressure as it constricts me. No doubt attempting to knock me unconscious. Or more likely eat me. Okra have never been known to be intelligent or loyal.

"You all seem to forget what I am." I say low the silver in my eyes glowing so bright I can see it reflected in the creature's lifeless eyes. My magic rolls through me, pulling the oxygen from the night air around us. The Okra's eyes dart in panic as the air thins around us, as if it never occurred to it that I would indeed use my magic. The more I pull the looser its hold on me becomes until my body slips free of the tail.

The Okra claws at its throat desperately as it writhes on the ground, the oxygen that was once plentiful now gone. Shoving my hands in my pockets I walk to my sword, grabbing the long blade from the ground, ignoring the pull of ribs, as I return to my prey. When I'm standing back over the creature, I poise my sword above its head allowing a tiny bit of air into its lungs.

"I'm the fucking King of Hell." I swing the sword and let the blade ax through the neck of the Okra. Blood sprays outward in a fountain of putrid black sludge that lands across my face and hands.

The head rolls free, the lifeless eyes landing upwards towards the sky. I kick it back with the toe of my dark boots before I wipe my blade on my pants. I drag a deep breath in as my magic falls away and I waver slightly. It doesn't escape me that I was mad at Ava for being so low on magic and yet here I am, draining my reserves because

I was so fucking determined to make my streets safe again.

Another shuffle behind me has me spinning and my stomach drops when I see three more Okra emerge from the now obvious nest they seem to have created. I take one step back as the three shift much more rapidly than their predecessor. I grip my sword tighter, mutter curses under my breath, I may be the King but even I have limits, and with my magic waning I have little hope of surviving against the three in front of me. But if I flee via the sky, I'll be leaving more of my people to be food for these beasts.

With my mind made up I drag forth a little more magic, gritting my teeth and preparing to fight. A howl pierces the air, and my eyes shift briefly to a massive black wolf stepping free of the shadows, its lips pulled back to expose gleaming teeth before shredding the Okra in seconds. I blink once and instead of the wolf my heart tugs towards the familiar man standing before me.

"Need some help, *mi cielo?*"

Dios

The taste of the creature lingers as I glance towards Jackson. His beautiful face covered in putrid black blood. Another Okra rushes forward only for a Hellbeast to intercept it. It takes Kallen's creature less than a minute to rip it apart.

"We will kill you!" One of them screams as it rushes us. I step forward letting my magic rip free and grab onto the pathetic excuse of a soul this thing has. Like a marinate obeying its master it freezes as its body goes taught, screeching for help as I taste the fear it's smart enough to finally feel. The taste sends shivers through my body, awakening that dark part of my soul that fuels the rumors people spread about me. I watch with deep satisfaction as the Okra explodes outward, its pieces decorating the street.

I let out a sharp whistle and Kallen's Hellbeast pushes off into the darkness to hunt any others that might be lingering. No doubt reporting back to Kallen and Demon as it does. The two had been arguing about going to hunt the pack of Elker Oisin had set loose on a small town, Kallen in favor of it and Demon pushing to return to Gothic Grove. I had been in favor of Demon's idea. But before I could vocalize that I felt a tug, a need to return. To him. To my mate.

I swallow a frustrated breath as I turn and look at Jax, I don't miss the wince as he slides his sword into the sheath down his back.

"What part of stay put did you not understand?" I growl as I invade his space and drag him into my body. His scent wraps around me and I try to ignore the tremor in my hand as I think about what would have happened had I not made it in time. "Your magic is low; you can't keep using it."

He pulls back, the silver in his eyes dull. "I'm the fucking King, Dios. I have an obligation to defend my city, my people, not hide in a fucking vacation house. It's been a month and my home sits in ruins still and we are no closer to catching Oisin." He frees himself from my embrace and I let out a low growl at the distance he puts between us. He shakes his head, "you confuse the fuck out of me these days."

I drag my hand over my skull, the tattoos pulsing under the touch for a moment. I had sent a message when I dragged Harrowlena from the palace, painted it in blood and made it clear that the god of death had come calling in defense of the King. It had sent a ripple into the world and alerted some *things* of my connection to Jax. So, I've kept my distance. Stayed far enough away that anyone paying attention would think we were casually fucking and that's it.

"*Mi cielo. . .*" I start. Knowing full well I can't answer the questions he has right now.

Jackson shakes his head the agitation clear in his movements. "I don't want to hear your arguments, you know what I want. You know I choose you despite any of the excuses you've presented." He steps back towards me, defiance shinning bright in his eyes.

His breath huffs against my face and when he drags his full bottom lip between his teeth, I can't help but bring my hand to his chin and pull it free. "Keep doing that and I don't care that we are standing in the street or that you're covered in blood, I'll bend you over and fuck you until you learn your place again."

Jackson's pupils expand as he holds my gaze; the air around us electric with energy. His breathing heavies and just when I think he is going to fight me he drops his gaze and steps out of my embrace once again. "Come find me when you're ready to talk." His wings flare wide, and he shoots up into the sky leaving me alone on the streets.

"Well, that was rather dramatic." The voice makes me freeze for a moment as I slowly turn to face the source.

The female offers me a smile, one that sends chills down my spine. Her white eyes are luminous against the night as she looks me over. Her arms cross over her ample breasts currently held tight with a corset that begs the question of how she can breathe. Over her shoulders is a lace shawl that blends seamlessly into the skirt she wears. One would think she was a madam at a brothel in the old west.

"Men always seem to be like that don't they?" She brings a cigarette to her red painted lips, taking a deep breath before blowing the smoke free. "I find a while in the stockade and a good cock in the ass helps put them in their place."

"Who are you?" I finally manage to ask.

She offers a soft chuckle, smiling as if I told a joke, "I'm a friend of the family." My blood runs cold at the statement but she continues as though she didn't just drop a bomb on me. "I have need of your assistance."

"I don't help my family, go to them." I snarl.

In the blink of an eye the female is in front me, dangerously close to my face before she regains composure and steps backward. "You will help me because it's your King's fault this has happened. So, unless you want me to go to him myself, I suggest you listen to what I have to say." She walks back, sitting herself on some rubble, and patting the spot next to her. "Come now dear, let's have a little talk before you race home to be with your *mate*."

The moment the word leaves her mouth I know she's got me.

ELEVEN

Jackson

The first time I had a panic attack I believed I was well and truly dying. I was ten years old and rushed to my father's office. Barging into the meeting, with tears streaming down my face, I announced to the whole room that I was, in fact, going to die. That was the first time I learned my father saw very little use in a son who cried. It was also the last time I ever admitted what was happening to me. Every day my skin would crawl, my chest would tighten, my breathing would pick up and my heart would try to beat from my chest. And every day I would swallow it down, focus on tapping my leg in a rhythmic pattern to distract myself from the impending death my panic attack was trying to convince me was coming.

As I got older, I discovered that adrenaline was a cure. It stole the panic away and filled my veins with a drug I couldn't get enough of. When I learned I could get that drug every night racing my bike or car I never looked back. The scent of exhaust and gasoline was my favorite perfume, and the sound of engines rumbling was my lullaby. At least until my father died and everything went to shit, now the anti-anxiety I crave feels out of reach.

"Are you listening?" A drawling voice pulls me back into the room as one of my many advisors cuts me a sharp look before continuing to explain. . . *fuck what was he even talking about?* Panic settles in and my fingers dance across my thigh. He lets out an exasperated sigh. "You never should have gone out last night! If you die where does that leave the kingdom?"

I almost laugh at his statement given at this precise moment I have no way to replenish my magic. At least no reliable way. My mind flits to the priestess sequestered in the room Dios dropped her in when we arrived. She's made no attempt to socialize with any of us, if anything she's avoided any social interaction. And my mate?

Pinching the bridge of my nose in a vain attempt to ward off the migraine starting to set in, I let out a long sigh "Did you not just get done lecturing me on the importance of taking care of Hell?"

Phelanais shakes his head disapprovingly. "This is not what we meant, and you know it. You have people who can dispatch the creatures, throw their lives away not your own."

"So, I'm supposed to sacrifice Kallen and Demon? Or Reaver?" I shift and wince as my still healing ribs pull. "I went looking for Nyx and Ophelia. I needed to see they were alive and well."

I hear someone let out a cough, one of the newer advisors, and I cut him a sharp look. Phelanais shakes his head with a disapproving glare. He's always hated my friendship with them. "You know a way to solve this. . ." He trails off as the room crackles with my power. Phelanais is many things but he isn't stupid, his face pales and he swallows heavily as he takes in my reaction, knowing he pushed me too far.

"And I told you I wouldn't go that route." The anger in my voice is pure venom as I glare at him.

"You cannot ignore this," he says. His voice is high-pitched and squeaky as he gets more and more agitated. "If you continue to pretend like this isn't an option you will not only doom our kingdom, but you'll potentially risk war. One we cannot hope to win. Not anymore."

"We have Kallen and Demon. . ." I start.

He cuts me off. "Who shouldn't even be involved in this. They are not of Hell nor are they royals. They are glorified thugs and no better than the creatures that ruined the city!"

"Those people fucking saved us!" I shout back. "Without them we would all be dead."

"We have no city to rule over! You'll be lucky if we ever rebuild without the help of Divinity! It's bad enough you have that. . . that wolf here! The message it sends!" The room shifts uncomfortably as Phelanais calls me out. My fingers move at rapid speed in my desperate attempt to stay calm. "Speak of him that way again and I will no longer remember how loyal you were to this family." I hold the old man's stare, my silver eyes never wavering despite the anxiety eating me alive. He clears his throat after a long moment of silence and casts his gaze downward in an act of submission. "Does anyone else want to offer up a solution?" My voice carries throughout the makeshift meeting space that has taken over the dining room. The lake house used to be a safe haven for me, but now? Now it's nothing more than a reminder of everything I've lost. Memories assault me at every turn here and I hate that I'm stuck living in this mausoleum. Every door opened is like opening a coffin and allowing the skeletons out to play.

Grabbing the drink in front of me I shoot back the dark amber liquid before slamming the empty tumbler back down. I don't have to look up to know Phelanais is judging me. "Your Grace, you cannot hope to hold your kingdom to another attack with those four people. There is a perfectly good army at your disposal should you just agree to marry R—. . ." He starts to say.

"I AM NOT FUCKING MARRYING HER!" I snap, my voice bellowing out. My wings flare out behind me as I work hard to reign in my powers. Phelanais has the decency to look nervous. "I will not continue to have this conversation repeatedly. Now get the fuck out." I bite the inside of my cheek hard in an attempt to reign in my anger and magic. I don't want to show that the idea of my mate hearing the conversation about my "fiancé" is adding to my anxiety. It hasn't escaped me that as much as I don't know about his past, he doesn't know about mine either.

The three men, in matching robes to Phelanais, men whom I have no interest in actually learning their names, file out in front of him. They seem smart enough to know what awaits them should they stay. Phelanais, however, seems as though he wants to continue arguing. That is until the man who avoided me all night makes his entrance.

My heart tugs forward as the room fills with the comforting scent of Dios, his bergamot musk a soothing balm to the anxiety that has been clawing its way up and down my spine.

The old men skirt around him, various levels of fear and distaste plastered on their faces. When he's next to Phelanais he snaps his teeth at the old man before offering up a slightly unhinged smile. Phelanais backs away from him, nostrils flaring and eyes widening before he looks to me. "This isn't over. We need to continue this conversation." He mutters before he too exits the room.

Dios chuckles, drawing his snake bites into his mouth

before releasing them back out. "The old man is scared of me."

I roll my eyes as I stand, desperate to ignore the tug of my ribs and move to the bar to fill my drink again. "Do you blame him?" Phelanais had seen the carnage left behind by Dios when he retrieved Harrow. The blood and body parts scattered; the message written within them.

He knew who Dios served and had no interest in pissing them off.

"What did he mean? What conversation did you guys need to finish?" He asks. The question is one that every anxious cell in my body is screaming that I need to avoid at all costs.

So instead, I cross my arms and shoot him a hard look, "you avoided me all night."

He raises an eyebrow, "And you left me standing in the middle of the street. I would say we are even." I shake my head in frustration before turning towards the bar.

When he comes up behind me and wraps his arms around my stomach, I let out a long sigh, the tension melting from me. "I'm sorry, *mi cielo*." He nips at my neck, the feeling going straight to my cock. He groans and it turns to a growl as his hand snakes down to my jeans, gripping my hardened length through the rough material.

"Fuckkk." I hiss as he strokes me over the denim. My fingers are quick to pull at my jeans, jerking them down around my thighs exposing my ass to him. "Please." I beg, shamelessly presenting myself to him.

"I don't know if you deserve anything after last night. Not only did you put yourself in danger, but you ran from me." He grips my hair with his hand and tugs hard. "You don't fucking run from me Jackson." His hands ghost over my bare skin, his breath warm as his teeth nip at my neck. I arch into the feeling and push into them.

"Bite me. Please." I beg. Grinding my ass backwards. His hand is a punishing grip in my hair, and I can feel the two parts of him warring against one another. "Remind me who I belong to."

I feel the graze of his teeth against my neck, the bite light and quick before he's dropping down behind me. I ignore the flare of disappointment in my stomach that he did not do as I demanded.

He groans, "need to taste you, *mi cielo*." His voice is a low growl as he sends a long lick up my tight hole before pressing inward. My cock jerks in response, precum dripping from the tip. I push back, demanding more from him which earns me a sharp smack across the ass and the loss of his tongue. The broken sob dragged from me should have been an embarrassment, but I'm too far gone to care.

He plants soft kisses on the stinging skin where his hand just imprinted on me. His tongue returns to my hole, fucking me slowly until I'm wet with his saliva. When he pulls back once more, I cry out. "Stop fucking with me, please sir. Please!" I beg, tears forming at the overwhelming need to have him deep within me.

"Is this what you want, *mi cielo*?" I feel the blunt head of his dick press against my hole as he slowly pushes inward.

"Oh yes, oh gods." He stretches me to the point of burning, yet I can't bring myself to care. I want it all. "Please, I need you. I need to feel your cum." He pauses for a moment once he is fully sheathed in me.

"Should I fuck you hard or slow?" He drags himself back out slowly before pushing back in equally as slow. "Should I force you to wait for your release until I'm sure you've learned your lesson?" His hand has a punishing grip on me as he sets an excruciatingly slow rhythm. "You are *mine* Jackson. That means you fucking listen to me. You do not run."

Incoherent words fall from my lips as his pace picks up. Glasses rattle as I'm shoved into the bar top table over and over again. My own cock painfully hard as it brushes against the rough material. When Dios's hand wraps around me finally I whimper at the relief that he is going to allow me to cum.

I pant as he starts to stroke slowly. "Yes. I'm yours. Yours."

He adds a slight twist to his hand as he continues to stroke me, up and down, up and down. "You're so hard, it must be so painful."

"Yes. It hurts, I want to cum for you so badly." I whine.

He chuckles darkly, his breath ghosting over my ear as his tongue licks up the shell. "It's too bad only good boys get to cum." He stops stroking me and squeezes the base of my dick while I feel his magic latch onto my soul. My eyes roll back in my head at the feel and even more I'm desperate to be his, for him to claim me.

"I'm going to fill you with my release, and you can spend the day with it dripping from you while you think about what you did." The feel of his cum painting my insides has my cock twitching in his grip and my soul writhing under his magic as he holds me from following him over the edge.

"Please," I beg. "Let me cum."

He pulls from me quickly and I wince from the loss before I feel the cold press of steel at my rim, and I'm filled with a plug. "Keep this in and tonight, if you're good, I'll take it and let you cum however you want. I'll even give you, my knot." Dios murmurs. He drags my jeans up my thighs, helping me tuck my still painfully hard cock into the tight pants.

He turns me around and plants a soft kiss to my forehead. The tenderness feels at odds with the savage fucking he just gave me. I let out a long, haggard sigh as I attempt to control the lust that is currently trying to override all rational thought. I want to feel his cock in me, feel his teeth dig into my neck, feel his magic hold onto me and bond. I want it all. My mouth opens to tell him this, until another familiar scent washes over me that sends my stomach plummeting.

"Don't let me interrupt boys." Her voice is a cold bucket of water on the raging inferno burning through my body.

Dios stiffens momentarily as he feels the change in my body. I pull away from him, fingers tapping on my leg. His eyes catch the movement, and his lips pull to a frown as his eyes blaze with concern before they cut over to the newcomer.

My own are already on Arcanna. She has her dark hair pulled up in a messy bun and her face clean of make-up. She's dressed comfortably in another pair of loose linen overalls and a small bandeau top that barely holds her breasts in. Tattoos of all forms swirl and curl around her body like twisting vines. While they are black right now when her magic flares, they glow gold and green.

Her eyes are a cold storm as they look us over. "Do you always fuck your toy and then make him wait?" She asks with judgement as she crosses her arms. "I certainly never make *my* pets wait like that." Irrational jealousy burns through me at her comment.

"You are far from your forest, Reaper. State your business." Dios demands, arms crossed over his chest and body slightly shifted in front of mine. As if he hopes to protect me from whatever she plans to throw our way.

Her laugh is twinkling, "Reaper huh? I guess that is a good title." She walks a little further into the room, dropping down onto one of the chairs. "You're far from your home as well." She says with a wink.

Dios cocks his head in curiosity, "And what do you know of my home?"

"I know that your being here is sending a message to all sorts of people and *things*." She smirks, proud of herself for knowing a secret. "I know that your home is far away from the little pack you were residing with in Gothic Grove."

"You know nothing of my home." Dios counters. "And as for Jax, he can attest that I take care of him quite well. His punishment tonight is deserved but don't think for one second, he doesn't enjoy it. But if you're worried you could join us, keep an eye on me."

My cheeks heat as I'm assaulted with visions of the three of us together. It feels. . . Right. Stepping out from behind Dios, I place my hand on his wrist and squeeze gently before letting go. She zeros in on the display with those unforgiving eyes, the same eyes that used to look at me with love and admiration. When she left all those years ago, I thought my heart couldn't break anymore, but now? Seeing her here? It feels as though a little more has been chipped away.

The exhaustion of the day, no month, hits me square in the face and I can feel my energy waning. "What do you need?" I ask, praying she can't hear my voice shake.

She looks between us, her eyes flashing between blue and a stormy horizon, before crossing her arms over her chest. "I want to know why the fuck The Order is running amok, why the royal city still sits in smoldering ruins and why you aren't stopping that sniveling ex of yours." She glares at me hard, judgment pouring off her. *But what else is new? Every day I'm judged by the people around me, why would she be any different?* "Oisin is all over my forest." She says, voice low and angry.

Theoretically, ruling had sounded good when it was a distant pipe dream, but now the reality of it is crashing in around me. Everyone wants their pound of flesh from me now and it's fucking exhausting.

Ava would have been better at this. She should be the one here, not me.

"You don't need me to evict him." I say softer than I intend to. It's the truth, her magic in her realm is stronger than anything Oisin could hope to have. Dios reaches for my hand and squeezes it before walking and grabbing each of us another drink.

She scoffs, opening her mouth to no doubt pour out more visceral hate she has for me when Dios intervenes "We just killed some of his creatures last night, how do you know he is still there?" He asks as he hands me the drink he just poured. "Seems more likely he has returned to the city."

She rolls her eyes, "You may have killed his beasts but he's still in my forest nosing around. That damn 'high priestess' of his is all over the place. He's even stolen souls! Parts of The Forest have already been destroyed!"

A pit grows at the knowledge that he has managed to damage The Forest of Souls. I shake my head, "I'll send someone with you." *Kallen and Demon maybe?*

Arcanna pushes up from her seat, "Pull your head out of your ass and come help me."

For a moment I'm angry at her, the feelings bubbling up until they explode outward. "It's your fucking mother helping him. Clean up your own gods damn mess!" I snap.

She sucks in a sharp breath, eyes flaring wide and her hands brace against the table. "Fuck off." She growls. "It was your bitch of a mother who sent her away, sent her straight into their arms."

My body leans toward her, the urge to wrap my hand

around her throat to shut her up overtaking the conversation as I watch her skin flush and cheeks redden. Her anger just as palpable as mine in the air. Dios finally clears his throat, the sound coming out as more of a growl than anything.

"I have it on good authority that he stole someone from Gothic Grove." He says. Effectively shutting us both up for a moment.

Arcanna is the first to react, blinking rapidly with concern. "He kidnapped someone?"

Dios drinks the remainder of his own glass before pouring another. "Her name is Bast and if Oisin has her we are facing a potential bigger issue than we originally thought." He drains his glass again, setting it down.

"I think we need to talk to the priestess." I finally mutter.

Dios grunts in agreement. "She's been sleeping most days. I'll bring her this evening when she is up, can you both behave until then?"

Arcanna rolls her eyes but nods. "Scouts honor."

I say nothing but my silence says enough. He raises an eyebrow at me before grabbing my face and planting a kiss across my lips, allowing his body heat to bleed into my own. He pulls away far too quick pulling a small whimper from me when his body heat leaves as well. He shakes his head as he offers up a soft smile before he's gone.

"Didn't take you long to find a replacement for me, did it?" Acid drips from her voice as she says it and her eyes twinkle with grief and rage before she blinks it back and grinds her teeth to keep from saying anything else.

The glass shatters as it flies from my fist and hits the wall, the years of repressed emotions bursting free from that single comment. "You fucking ran Arcanna! I won't even begin to think of going to your forest unless we talk about everything, wicked girl."

"Don't." She snaps, silencing me quickly. Rage burning bright and hot in her eyes. "Don't you fucking call me that." Her chest heaves as she drags in a ragged breath.

The room fills with awkward tension as we remain locked in a standoff, our emotions threatening to drown us both. "You need to fucking talk to me; you owe me that much."

Arcanna shakes her head as she backs away from me, "I have no interest in revisiting our past. I'm here on official capacity only." She turns and heads through the door but not before looking behind her and throwing one last barb at me. "You let him take the last remaining priestess and mask her. You let him murder Ava. Your kingdom is falling apart. You're an embarrassment to the throne, even your father would have done better."

Her comment hits me square in the chest, my anxiety enjoying the confirmation of everything it's already told me. And yet I can't seem to stop trying to defend myself.

"You have no idea what it's like being King, none. I have to make choices every day because I'm the King and no one else will do it." The response falls softly, barely convincing even to my own ears. "You'll never understand."

She rolls her eyes and scoffs. "Convenient excuse, isn't it? You get to hurt everyone around you while you hide behind that title."

She's right to be angry. The priestesses were all but wiped out by The Order. All of them died protecting the ritual to keep passing the magic to the royals. So, when I discovered what Harrowlena was, who she was, I should have done a better job at keeping her safe. I should have protected the last, true, priestess.

And Ava? Ava will haunt me for the rest of my life. Because I knew the risks of her entering the palace with him. I knew she was risking her life to help me, and I selfishly allowed her to do it. Never stopping to consider what would happen if the worst-case scenario truly did play out.

My silence is enough for Arcanna to look at me with disgust before exiting the room fully.

My head hangs and my fingers dance across my thighs as the anxiety and panic start to close the walls around me. It's moments like this that I can't help but feel as though I do not deserve to have my mate bond. That Arcanna fleeing from me was best case scenario and Dios continuing to list the negatives of us bonding is at least preventing him from being caught up in the shit storm that is my life.

TWELVE

Harrowlena

The world narrows as I feel his hands slip into my skirt. My stomach rolls with his touch, both from pleasure and shame. I both love and hate this. He doesn't seem to notice though as he strokes my clit with his callused hand and his teeth nip at the exposed parts of my neck. In the beginning he paid lip service to the mask, saying when he removed it, he would fuck me so hard I'd shatter the windows.

Now he just pretends it doesn't exist.

"Fuck I've missed your tight cunt." He groans as he spears two fingers inside me. My body responds automatically. Lighting up with his touch and dripping arousal. I groan at the feel. He chuckles at my response before dragging my skirt down with his other hand. "Spread your legs for me."

His command is obeyed without question. My legs going as far as they can with the skirt still binding my thighs. His fingers slip free of me and are replaced with the blunt head of his dick as he bends me over the desk. This is the only way he has sex with me now. He hates to look upon my face with the mask secured to it, hates to watch me cum while I'm silently screaming behind the contraption. I can understand it, even if part of me resents him for it. After all, it must be nice to get to ignore the trauma of the one you claim is yours.

"I'm going to fill you up, fill you so full it'll be dripping from you all day. So while you serve my future wife, you'll know you're full of my cum. That when I fuck her tonight it'll still be dripping from you." He thrusts into me harder with each word, the depravity of it is intoxicating. And I hate that. I hate that I'm turned on by the idea of him using me like this. And I hate that I have to ignore the statement that soon he'll be fucking Ava. Be using her as he uses me. I know what's expected of me in this role and for a long time I was okay with it. But now that she's here it feels too real. Only having met her once I can already tell she is different from the rest of them, even her brother. And it bothers a part of me that he'll be using her like this despite how aggressively against it all she is.

His hand slips forward and rubs my clit in rough circles forcing me back into my body and I feel that bond between us emanate with lust. It drugs my every movement, and I feel myself getting lost in the magic of it, suddenly forgetting why I feel the guilt and shame that I do. My pussy clenches around his thick cock.

He grunts, "that's it. I know you love this. Cum for me Lena. Cover me in it." I barely manage to withhold my cry as my orgasm rips through me just as he goes rigid, and I feel him pulse inside me. Over and over a seemingly never-ending stream of cum fills me as I ride out my wave of pleasure.

We each fall down our own rabbit hole until we hit bottom and the endless pleasure finally stops, reality crashing back in around us. When he pulls out from me the idea of his cum staying in me seems dirty now, and the feel of it on my inner thighs makes me itch. Makes me want to shower.

I press up and turn around, looking at his muscular body. I want to ask him if he does in fact still love me, if he will ever make me his queen now that he has Ava. But the mask holds me back and when he finally catches my eyes the look he gives forces me to bow my head, and not for the first time I miss the boy I fell in love with long ago.

(Enchanted- Delerium)

My eyes spring open, blinking to adjust to the dark as the dream world fades from me and reality sinks in. My hands jump to my face desperate to feel my bare skin, to remind myself the mask is gone. A small feeling of relief pulses through me, my breath leaving my body in a long exhale. The mask being removed was a silver lining to this hell I've found myself locked in.

Pushing up I keep my eyes shut as I continue to take in long, steady breaths. My chest tight and aching with every pull of air. The warm night air carries a familiar sent inward. Sandalwood. It drags me out of the sweat drenched sheets to the open patio door. Pushing the curtains aside I step my bare feet out onto the rough wooden deck.

Each night that past week has been the same, the nightmares invading, chasing me from my sleep and back into this world. As if I don't deserve the escape rest should provide. Maybe that's why it is always her form my eyes land on, under the moonlight. The Reaper who lived in the woods bordering my home long ago. For a moment my mother's voice pulls through my brain, warning me of her, of her kind.

"Do not venture towards the land of the dead, the reaper will show you no mercy when she snatches your immortal soul."

My eyes are once again drawn to the lawn, the moonlight bathing the lawn and the source of that scent. Up until now I've silently watched her from afar but something about tonight is different. Taking a deep breath, I allow myself to exit the room, feet padding down the balcony stairs and onto the lawn. Carrying me to the female currently in a contorted form. Her back end is pushed into the air while her forearms are flat on the ground in front of her. Her long curtain of dark hair covering her face.

"Hello, another night of not sleeping?" Her voice is rich and sends chills through me. A small smile pulls at my lips before I tamp it down as I watch her slowly raise her legs into a split above her head. The balance impressive. "Have you finally come to have a try at yoga?" She drops downward so she can face me.

I desperately want company to ease the loneliness that is threatening to drown me. The loneliness that chased me off the balcony and into this little patch of grass finally. I offer her a small nod that earns me a wide smile in return. "We'll start in Sukhasana." She crosses her legs in front of her, waiting for me to copy. Sitting on my own mat, the one that has been sitting next to hers since the first night she found me watching from afar, I replicate the pose. "Very good." She praises. She leads me through a breathing exercise, my body slowly letting the tension release.

"Now we'll do some sun salutations. The important part of yoga is to listen to what your body needs. Don't force yourself into a pose, let your body guide you in how deep you can go. Yoga isn't about the perfection of the pose."

About two poses in I realize she makes this look easier than it is. Sweat beads on my body and embarrassment floods me as I struggle through something called baby cobra. When I push upward into downward dog and a grunt escapes me, she lets out a soft laugh.

"Here, let me help you." Suddenly her hands are on my hips, pulling them back a bit before I feel her smooth them down my legs. My breathing turns ragged at her touch, my body so unused to anyone's hands on it. "See, there you go!" She says excitedly when my body is now somehow in the pose she wants.

I let myself fall out of the position back into the seated one we started with. She looks down at me expectantly, a smile full on her face. She looks radiant with the moon behind her, like a goddess that all should worship. I feel my cheeks burn and shame well up inside me at my admiration. If she notices she doesn't say anything.

"Thank you." I finally whisper, breaking the silence apart. "I appreciate all of this." My voice still sounds odd to me, a stranger to my own tone.

"You don't have to thank me. I'm glad you came out tonight." The words open a void in my heart and soul, a deep yawning pit. "I've seen you watching me, but I didn't want to impose and force you to come out and enjoy the night sky." She continues.

"You wouldn't have been," I whisper. The words fall from me before I can think better of it. I keep my eyes trained on the grass, not able to look at her face.

"I'll remember that for next time." She chuckles.

My eyes finally look up to her once more and note the tattoos that seem to be glowing before they blink out. Her body, so unlike mine, curvy and soft and strong all at the same time. Her smile frames the small gap between her two front teeth and her hair looks like crushed velvet. She's beautiful in her own way. She does not look like the monster Oisin described when he spoke of her.

There are many things he didn't describe accurately it would seem.

The voice is one that seems to get louder the longer the mask is off me and the longer I'm away from my old home.

"I'm Arcanna by the way, since we haven't been formally introduced."

"Harrowlena" I mutter in response.

"Yes. The last priestess finally returned home."

I dislike the way she talks about my life and the return to this place. It feels like a betrayal. Because this place isn't my home. Not now, not ever. My home is far, far from here. Another wave of that loneliness hits me in the chest, my breathing stuttering out for a moment as I try to regain my balance in this conversation.

"Harrowlena?" Her voice is deep and shakes me loose of the clutches of my mind. But the words still die on my tongue and my mouth feels just as anchored shut as it would be with that mask.

She leans down, her body at the same level as mine now. "I suspect you've had a much harder life than most. And in your world, someone being kind to you is earned. But here? Kindness is freely given. And friendship. So should you be looking for that I offer it with no strings." Her words ring with truth but they also remind me of my purpose. That every single choice I make has strings attached to it.

Strings that are going to drag me back to my home soon.

Dios

I watch the reaper lead the little priestess back into her room. My body concealed by the shadows. Harrowlena had been sleeping when I arrived, and I watched as her nightmares drove her from her bed and out to the lawn; her acidic sweat hung in the air and drenched her sheets. The yoga seemed to calm something, but not for long she reeks of fear all the time. Her eyes shifting nervously around whenever she thinks someone isn't looking. I cock my head as I watch Arcanna strip her sheets and change them,

Harrowlena wrapping her arms around her mid-section as if to hold herself together.

"There we go, all settled Harrowlena." Arcanna says as she pulls back the freshly made bed. "Why don't you go shower and get clean, that way you can snuggle back in with no memories of whatever chased you away."

She nibbles on her lip nervously before nodding and disappearing into the large bathroom. Once the door is firmly shut, I step slowly from the darkness. Any softness Arcanna had on her face drops once she sees me.

"You can stop lurking in the shadows." She growls.

I offer up a smile, "ah glad you can sense my presence so well. Reaper." Pushing my hands into my pockets I walk towards her, invading her space until the sandalwood scent that clings to her skin breaches my own senses. "You've become awfully friendly with the little priestess."

Her eyes flash an enticing deep storm blue with specks of hazel. "She is lost, scared and in need of a friend. Is it against the law to help someone like that?"

I shrug, "no but it begs the question what do you hope to gain from it?"

She shakes her head even as she huffs out a laugh, "you and Harrowlena are cut from the same cloth, aren't you? People can be kind without expecting anything in return."

"When you come from the dark places we do, you learn very early that's not true." Pity seems to cloud her eyes for a moment before she shakes it away and steps out of the space I occupy with her. A growl lodges in my throat at the idea of her moving away from me. "You should talk to Jackson."

"I have nothing to say to him unless it involves us hunting down his fucking ex-boyfriend. I made that perfectly clear earlier."

"Both of you are so fucking stubborn," I huff out a frustrated breath. "You know that's not all you two need to talk about, Arcanna."

She holds her hands up, "Don't." Her body edges away from me, towards the door she walked through with the priestess. "I have no interest in your excuses or his. I don't want an apology; I want to do my job and leave here."

"What job is that?"

She levels me with a hard look. "The reaper, as you so lovingly call me, is charged with keeping all the souls safely in the afterlife. If that doesn't happen, we have free reign to hunt down whoever is taking them." She jabs a finger towards me, "so I will hunt down Oisin. I will drag those souls he has taken back, and I will fucking end this."

"All without talking to Jackson? Your *mate*." The word drops between us like an anvil, both of us holding the other's gaze until she finally breaks it and looks down.

"You don't know what you're talking about. Just drop it." She growls.

I step closer one more time, eyes narrowing. "I know you watched us fuck for a moment before you came in. I know your pussy got wet while I filled him with my cum. And I know your jealous as fuck you weren't between us."

Her eyes go wide, mouth dropping open even as her cheeks flame red. For a moment I think she'll launch herself at me but instead she whirls and flees the room.

THIRTEEN

Harrowlena

Coming out of the shower I'm relieved when I do not see Arcanna still in the room. Her words from earlier played over and over in my mind while I washed away the sweat and nightmares that seemed to have tattooed themselves on my skin. There is a reason I've avoided everyone here; the minimal interactions I've had forcing more questions into my brain than answers.

"Can't sleep, *diosa*?" His voice is rough, rougher than when he pulled me from that blood-soaked hallway and it startles me as I clutch the towel to my chest. My eyes scan the room until they land on the dark corner where the shadows seem to be alive.

His hand is the only thing illuminated, tattooed fingers gripping a tumbler of amber liquid as he raises it to his mouth. "I asked you a question." He says, leaning out of the shadows. The fire plays across his features, it's the first time I've seen the man since he pulled me from that hallway, the one who set this all in motion without realizing it.

"You're going to let them take you, I need that fucking ceremony and if that bitch Arcanna is there she has to have

it." Oisin grips my arm hard, his fingers bruising me as I shake my head back and forth. His rage practically chokes me. *"You do not get to deny me this, you fucked this all up in the first place by not getting it from your gods damn grandmother!"*

"No," I reply quietly, refusing to let the conversation drag me under while Dios is here.

He moves towards me slowly, a predator stalking its prey. The hair on the back of my neck raises as he meanders closer. With each step forward I take one back until my legs bump the edge of the bed and I drop down. He smiles, a predatory glean as he leans down invading my space and making me acutely aware of the thin towel protecting my modesty.

"What chased you from your slumber? *Que demonio acecha tus sueños?* What demons haunt you?" His dual-colored eyes catch my own. The intensity is so brutal it feels as though it's searing my soul. "You only come out at night, never in the day light where those demons could be exorcised."

He tuts when I go to avert my eyes and grasps my chin with his calloused fingers. "Eyes on me" he says as he runs his fingers down my throat. His hand circles me, hard enough that he can feel my pounding heart but not so tightly as to cut off my ability to breathe.

He raises an eyebrow, "I'm curious about you, *pequeña diosa.* You are a mystery that demands to be solved." He muses.

I want to shake my head, deny the words but I feel frozen in his gaze.

"I see in your head," he murmurs as he leans down to my ear. His nose brushing the shell. "The guilt is eating away at you." My breath hitches. The words making my blood run cold.

"I don't know what you're talking about." I stammer in a rushed whisper.

My body feels on fire the longer he holds my throat, the longer he invades my presence.

He pulls back, inhaling deeply as he does, his head tilting to the side as if he can sense what's happening to my body. "Interesting." He murmurs. "If I didn't know better, I would guess you were a female shifter. But you are something much rarer aren't you, *pequeña diosa?*"

His voice causes my legs to quiver, a sudden aching emptiness pulsing through me. "Hasn't your King told you what I am?"

He laughs darkly, "He is not my King."

I frown, "If he's not your King, who is?"

His gaze almost burns through me. My soul comes undone as he says, "Someone darker." He pushes back away from me, his eyes trailing over my body.

My cheeks flush, a deep crimson red burning from my neck to my cheeks. He chuckles, dragging his silver piercings on either side of his bottom lip into his mouth before they pop back out. Those who are caged for so long often have the brightest awakening, and I hazard a guess you will burn so bright those of us around you will struggle to see after."

"I don't know what you mean. . ."

He raises his eyebrow at me, "you know exactly what I mean."

I shake my head, wanting to deny everything he says but the words can't seem to make it out of my mouth. They keep dying on the edge. "I'm tired." I say instead, eyes tracking to the door.

"You spend most of your day sleeping, tired is the wrong adjective." He counters.

My nostrils flare in annoyance. "Who are you to tell me what I feel?" I snap before overthinking it.

He studies me for a moment, eyes tracing over every inch of me, exposing me to whatever lies under those mismatched eyes. "Someone who sees you for what you truly are." He strolls towards the chest of drawers grabbing my clothing and throwing them to the bed. "As it doesn't seem you'll be sleeping anymore tonight, get dressed. Jackson is waiting on us. And that isn't a request."

Point taken. The King of Hell is summoning me.

I fidget as Dios drags me down the long hallway. My hair hangs in an unruly mess around my face. I tug the long linen coat around my body attempting to cover my slim frame that is on display in the cream linen pants and black bandeau wrap around my breasts. I feel too exposed in the outfit, too vulnerable. Never have I been uncomfortable in my priestess clothing until this moment.

My eyes stay glued to the ground. A ground I've come to know extremely well. Dios was right that I'm never out during the day. But at night? At night I've mapped out this space in its entirety. Like a mouse skittering around to avoid being seen, I've gone through every nook and cranny while avoiding interaction with the others. At least until this evening when I finally stepped out into the night with Arcanna. Dios comes to a stop in front of a partially cracked open door. An uncomfortable silence leaches from the inside, frowning I allow him to gesture inward. Jackson sits in a large chair by a fireplace looking incredibly uncomfortable while Arcanna sits opposite him. She looks refreshed but the tension on her face is hard to miss.

"Harrow," Jackson startles me, pulling my attention to

him. "How are you feeling?" Concern laces his voice. The question is a loaded one that comes with too many pitfalls and traps to answer truthfully so instead I shrug and offer a small smile.

Silence is best to use when you don't think you can lie. The words trace through me as a reminder of how I was trained to survive, how I was trained to get back to *him* someday.

Jackson seems to take my silence as something other than avoidance and offers me a slight smile before continuing. "We have some questions for you."

Fear peppers me, *shit.*

What do they know? Do they suspect something?

I force my breathing to remain calm, demanding my heartbeat stay at a normal pace, reminding myself Dios's wolf can hear the change. I try desperately to think of any excuse, a way to escape this conversation and avoid the pitfalls it will no doubt come with.

"We need to know what Oisin hopes to gain from all of this." Arcanna says with a soft tone. Her body language relaxing as she glances at me. She exudes calm and patience.

She would have made the perfect High Priestess. My own thought sends a spark of jealousy through me. I suck my lower lip into my teeth and bite down hard on it, the taste of blood grounding me. Giving me a moment to think without the fear and anxiety overtaking me.

Dios clears his throat, cutting me a curious look as his eyes drag to my lip.

"Harrow?" Jackson steps up as if he would guide me to a seat, and I shrink backwards, avoiding his touch. He stops, confusion and hurt flashing over his face as he sees my retreat and instead moves to sit back down. "I want to apologize to you; I allowed you to be taken that night and I'm truly sorry for my mistakes. I never should have allowed it; I should have watched you. Not Nyx. Or better yet I never should have taken you to the races. I'm sorry."

I'm taken aback by his words, eyes blinking rapidly as I hold his own silver ones. They remind me so much of Ava. My mind flashes to her time with me. Her face of disgust as she took in the mask. Her kindness. The memories continue to war within me, and my chest threatens to crack open at the memory of her last stand, at how her blood will forever paint my hands even if I was nowhere near her when she dragged that blade over her throat.

"I–," My voice cracks on the word. Guilt assaults me as I realize he truly believes he is at fault for me returning to The Order. For the mask being placed on me. And while I still cannot forgive his family for the actions against my own something within warms towards him. "How much do you know of Oisin's history?" I ask, my voice quiet as the words pour from me in an attempt to stop the intrusive thoughts.

Jackson frowns, "He just kind of appeared one day and we started dating." He looks to Arcanna for confirmation.

She nods, "We all partied and played. And when Ava was old enough she joined in. He was normal I suppose." A pang of jealousy moves through me.

He was building a life here with them while I was left behind. No. Stop it. You know it was for a reason. You were always the one he wanted.

I clear my throat once more, "But what of his history?"

Both frown, "Now that I think of it. . . I don't know anything about it him." Jackson seems disturbed as he talks and comes to the realization. "I didn't even know Ciaran was his half-brother until he and his mate told me."

"Oisin grew up in The Order. His mother was a member when he was born." The words feel heavy as they leave me as if they shouldn't be uttered to anyone. I swallow against the feeling and continue talking. "Women have two purposes in The Order, breeding and providing for the men. His mother was never supposed to hold the position she did, but she was a very clever witch and outsmarted the men at every turn until she came of age and was expected to be with child." My voice trails off, the vocal cords hurting from even a small bit of talking.

Arcanna growls low, the room vibrating with power. "Fucking pigs." She hisses.

"Calm wicked girl." Jackson says and Arcanna goes stiff, cutting him a sharp glare as her nostrils flare. I brace for an altercation but Jackson holds up his hands in surrender. "Sorry." He mutters.

"It's important to remember, for this next part, that most who are within The Order do not have strong magic, if any. They are people who seek either more power or protection from the powerful. So, when she was sent to find a husband she looked outside The Order." I hear Jackson suck in a sharp breath, as if he knows exactly where this story is headed. "She wanted someone who would give her magic, give her power. When she met her future husband, she made a demon deal with him. He would provide her an heir with magic and help her maintain her place within The Order."

"What did he get out of it?" Dios asks.

I shrug, "I'm not sure. People say at one point the pair seemed truly in love, but I only heard of the aftermath when she learned of his affair with Kara Carmine."

"What happened?" Arcanna asks softly.

I shrug, "most say it wasn't pretty. She made him suffer for his adultery. He did not uphold his part of the bargain, the heir he provided had no magic due to the child he sired with Kara. Ultimately, it's what got her killed by The Elders."

"Even if she hadn't killed him the broken bargain would have killed the demon eventually." Jackson says to the room.

"So Oisin is left mother and fatherless?" Arcanna questions looking at me.

I nod. "Yes. The Elders kept him, raised him as a potential leader. However, some did not feel he was fit to lead them, so The Elders kept the power, sending Oisin out on more jobs. Like meeting Jackson." Rage bubbles under the surface of my skin as I think about it, as I realize how different my life could have been had they let the natural way of things occur. The old fools paid him lip service when he was around, but they never intended to give him power. My hands ball into fists before I can school the motion.

"So where does that leave you?" Arcanna questions. Her voice has an edge to it, and I snap my gaze to her before I take a deep shaky breath forcing calm back into my body.

"I was brought to The Order at nineteen. Rescued from the ashes of my home. I've spent the last few years growing up within the community. As I engaged with more of their customs, I realized I did not want the life they had planned for me." More lies mixed with truth.

Dios scoffs, "Rescued from something they fucking did. Such bullshit." I don't argue with him, don't counter his statement.

Treading carefully, I continue, "When I left, I happened to find Jackson. It was lucky, honestly. But The Elders found me, dragging me back to The Order. When I awoke the mask was on me and I was a prisoner once more." The memory of that day streams past my vision, blurring the figures in front of me. My jaw radiates pain as if the iron still lingers.

"Why not escape?" Dios asks as he brushes past me and sits down next to Jackson, grasping his hand tenderly. His mismatched eyes full of lust and love as they take in the King. "If you had already met Jackson, why couldn't you run to him again?"

My tongue feels like lead as I try to think of a reason, my mind blanking to every possible scenario that would lead me to stay instead of flee.

Arcanna clears her throat. "You make it sound easy, to leave a place with so much power of manipulation" she says as she looks at the couple. They stay silent, Jackson with pink creeping up his cheeks. For a moment I want to laugh at her, laugh at them all. They are no better than I am in being manipulated given they still believe it was Oisin who burned my home. Even Jackson buys the lie that it was The Order, but I know better.

"I couldn't leave, the first time was a random accident as I was unaware I was a banshee. Without that power I had nothing." A breathy sigh leaves my chest as I work up the strength to continue the story. My throat burns. Turning to look at Jackson fully I finally allow the words to spill free. "They wanted Ava you know, but your father kept her well-guarded. You were the easier target to get close to."

Arcanna looks to Jackson who rubs his hand down his face. The two exchange a long look before he shakes his head, shame painting those silver eyes as if he accepts the weight of the consequences on his shoulders.

Dios grips the back of his neck hard, pulling his forehead to his despite the awkward angle. "You listen, this is not your fault. None of it. Oisin used you."

"He used Jackson to get to Ava. And the King just agreed to this? Agreed to let her marry her brother's partner?" Arcanna spits with disgust. "Both the King and Oisin deserve their deaths."

Swallowing against the dryness collecting in my throat as my power tries to rally against the words being thrown around, I look towards the pitcher on the table, Arcanna notices my glance and moves to stand, grabbing a glass and pouring the cool liquid before handing it off to me. I'm awed at her thoughtfulness as I sip the water; it soothes the agony my throat seems to be in constantly now and gives me a moment to pause and collect myself.

"Oisin does not have much magic himself. He had a spell from his mother to feed off the magic of others. Being with a royal was helpful." I look at Jackson. "His goal with Ava was to gain full access to The Well and use it to control Hell and The Order."

Dios finally chimes in, "so that's why he kept you so close."

"He thought you could help him with The Well." Arcanna finishes, the light bulb going on.

I nibble my cheek, shifting on my feet. "Yes and no. We didn't have the ritual so I truly wouldn't have been much help at the time. He gained the grimoires from the witches in Gothic Grove and has been working on a way to drain it himself, without me or a royal."

"That would destroy magic as we know it, from here to Gothic Grove would be fucked." Jackson replies. I don't miss the way his voice shakes. "And the magic belongs to us, to the royals, we've kept it safe all these years."

It's on the tip of my tongue to scream at him that it came at the expense of my family. That the royals burned my home and killed everyone I held dear all for that magic to stay theirs. To covet it. But I don't. I keep it in. Swallowing the venom downward. Remembering my purpose and my place.

Arcanna hisses, "He doesn't care. He's a selfish fucking prick."

"He also wanted to find a way to free me of the curse of my priestess magic as well," I say hesitantly yet still with a tone of defense. "At one time Oisin cared that I would be risking death if we didn't have the ritual once I came of age. It wasn't the magic he cared for; it was my well-being."

As soon as the words leave my mouth, I know I stepped over a line I shouldn't have.

"He's evil and you must know whatever he said is a lie Harrow. One we both fell for." Jackson says while Dios stares deep into my soul. "There is no way he'd still help you once he had The Well."

"Why do you think I finally escaped? With the chaos of it all I fled with your help." I force a choked laugh from my body and paint what I hope is a relieved smile on my face. But Dios doesn't stop staring at me, his eyes all seeing as they burn through the carefully constructed house of cards I've built.

<hr>

Arcanna

I watch Harrowlena carefully as she speaks. It's clear she's still harboring some feelings for The Order, particularly Oisin. And it's clear Jax and Dios do not understand her. And maybe it is because I have seen their way of life that I can understand just how sheltered she most likely was and how easy it would have been for Oisin to twist her into his little pawn. I can't help having some empathy for her, some sympathy for her predicament.

A young woman, orphaned and alone, placed in The Order with no real friends or family. No doubt she clung to Oisin like a lifeline. And the bullshit lie that the royals killed the priestesses is one she seems to still buy if her reactions tell me anything. The Order had worked hard to try and convince everyone that it was Jax and his family that

killed them all, but the citizens were loyal to them and ultimately their plan failed.

At least it failed on anyone outside of their cult.

"He was my friend for a long time." She goes onto say,
even as her hand ghosts over those scars left behind by the
fucking mask her so called friend allowed to be placed on
her.

"Oisin stole someone, kidnapped her. On top of everything else he has done." Dios goes on, his voice hard. "He is
not a good person or anyone's friend." She flinches backward slightly, her violet eyes wide.

"Harrowlena," I approach her slowly. Her big eyes peer
at me, partially obscured by the silver hair. "Would you
mind walking with me? As you know, I like the lake this
time of night."

"I. . ." she starts. Eyes tracking around the room. She
blinks a few times before nodding in agreement.

Looping my arm through hers I shoot a look over my
shoulder at the guys, "I'll be back!" She relaxes into my
body, the tension leaching outward and away. Her scent
washes over me like wave on the ocean, carrying the smell
of wisteria just atop it. "Enjoy each other's company! I'm
sure Jackson is still dying for that cock of yours!"

Harrowlena trips at the words but I keep dragging her
along, ignoring the daggers Jackson is currently glaring into
my back.

FOURTEEN

Harrowlena

I'm sorry. I'm so sorry.

My stomach feels hollow as I send the words out into the universe and hope they land where they should. Arcanna's link through my arm the only thing keeping me upright after the conversation.

The warm night air brushes through my hair as Arcanna pushes open the door into the large backyard. The lake is only a short distance away offering a softer ambience to the occasion.

"I loved this place when we would come here." She says, pulling us both down onto the grassy shore of the lakeside. Not far off from where we practiced yoga earlier this evening. Arcanna keeps her gaze locked on the water, a soft smile on her face. "Gods, it feels like a lifetime ago."

Envy rolls over me. I've never known what she is talking about. Never known how it feels to just fit some place. Even as a girl I didn't fit with the other priestess, and it was no different within The Order. Oisin is the only connection I've ever had.

"Over there," she points across the lake to a distant

gazebo barely visible in the moonlight. "That was where Oisin and Jax had their first kiss." I want to tell her to stop talking, that I have no interest in hearing what Oisin did while he was away, the life he built. "And right behind that is the place Ava broke her arm from falling out of a tree. Gods she was trouble. Always following us." Sadness passes over her face at the mention of the princess.

"I'm sorry that she's gone." I offer up.

She smiles at me and nods her thanks before she lets out a long sigh and drops down onto her back, hands resting across her stomach. The past playing out across her face in a spectacular display of vulnerability. She doesn't look at me, keeping her eyes trained on the night sky above. But my violet eyes stay locked on her, even in her sadness she's beautiful.

"Jackson and I haven't always been at odds, and even now, even hating him, he still means the world to me. I would still do everything in my power to protect him. And I do believe he would do the same for me. Because that's what friends do, that's what mates do, Harrowlena. We protect each other."

"Mates?" I gasp. "You are both mates? You hate one another!"

She laughs out a sad sound, "That doesn't change that we still care for one another. That when push comes to shove, we would stand up for one another. Hate is a very short distance from love. And because of that love I would not allow another to hurt him." She lets out a very long sigh for a moment. "Truthfully, I hate even being here with him because I know it causes him distress. And despite it all I do not want to hurt him." For a moment I'm stunned. Her definition of friendship and the relationship they have so unlike anything I've experienced. My memories of Oisin are nothing of what she has described.

"Tell me about yourself Harrowlena."

"You can call me Harrow." I manage while my brain still fumbles to catch up with everything. A large smile breaks over her face exposing the gap between her front teeth. "There is nothing to tell," I whisper quickly. The lie tastes bitter on my tongue.

She shakes her head, "not buying it."

I draw an unsteady breath I hadn't intended on sharing anything with anyone here, much less this woman who seems to be pulling me into her orbit faster than I can pull away. But her words have opened up the loneliness that's taken up residence in my heart, the loneliness that is begging me to let someone in.

The silence stretches on between us, her body relaxed while mine grows increasingly tense. Until I finally give in. "I grew up in The Priestess Forest. I lived with my mom and Nana but spent so much of my time alone, wandering through the forest, it feels like I was raised by the plants instead." I say quietly, deciding to give her as much of the truth as I can. "Overall, I had a good childhood, my mother was kind and my grandmother was loving. But I was different from them all. I always struggled to sit still during lessons, and the intimacy that is required by priestesses. . . I. . . I did not want to talk about that."

Arcanna nods along encouragingly with a soft expression on her face. "I wanted to be like them, so badly, but I just couldn't be. I felt dirty when my mother wanted to educate me and, on the nights when they would all perform the ceremony I would stay as far away as possible." Even speaking of it burns my cheeks. "But I truly did want to be High Priestess. I wanted to take over for my Nana. Regardless of what it would mean. All that obviously changed once our forest was burned." I leave out the bitter end to our relationship and the guilt I feel for it all.

"I can still smell the smoke in the wind every once in a while." Arcanna glances over at me, "I've always wondered how The Order managed to break the magic protecting the forest."

"If it was them." I add quickly without thought.

She tilts her head as she watches me, "Harrow it was them. It was The Order that killed your family, killed the priestesses." Her tone feels far too calm, far too quiet and the words slip through the small crack her offer of friendship made.

Oisin wouldn't have lied. . . he never would have harmed my family. Right?

I feel her gaze on me as I attempt to control the emotions bubbling up, attempt to school the out-of-control inferno that seems to always try to escape.

"Harrow," My name from her lips has me blinking my eyes several times. She looks concerned. "The full moon is coming up." My body turns cold now, the heat extinguished with her words. "You told them that Oisin did not have the ritual, do you?" She asks.

I open my mouth and close it multiple times before I manage the quiet words. "My mother never got to teach me, nor my grandmother. So, the ceremony is still a mystery to me." It feels heavy, saying it like that, not telling her my Nana outright refused. That my mother pulled away from me at the end and I was unsure if I was going to ascend to High Priestess.

"Do you know the other options?" She asks carefully.

I give a quick nod, my mouth drying up at the idea of allowing someone other than *him* to touch me. Of allowing my body to be used. Lady Ornate's words swim through my mind as the voice of The Elders join.

Impure.

Whore.

Unworthy.

They are so loud I have my doubts that Arcanna can't hear them as they scream at me. I desperately want to shout back, to tell them to stop talking, to shut up. I can feel it bubbling inside me, the innate drive to open my mouth and let it out. But I hold it in, swallow it down, until my stomach feels like lead and my throat burns.

Arcanna's voice cuts through as her gaze remains steady on me. "Part of my job is knowing at least part of the magic to help you transfer the magic to Jax. We could go to The Well together. We could figure it out so you wouldn't need to have anyone help you."

The kindness in her words along with everything else she has shared this evening ruins the admission that should have brought me relief. Instead, the words that she's spoken break me apart like a wrecking ball.

"Harrow?" She reaches for me, sensing my distress, and I flinch backwards.

I shake my head, pushing to a stand as words get caught in my throat. My mind is at war with itself as that invisible string pulls at me, wants to drag me back to my home, to the one who should be my safe haven. Yet all I feel right now is gut wrenching guilt deep within my bones.

FIFTEEN

Arcanna
(Nightshade- The Lumineers)

Harrow's rapidly retreating form holds my gaze as my eyes narrow. It was a test, an unfair one to give albeit and one she failed miserably. I almost want to laugh that she is such a bad liar, but I hold back because part of me understands the manipulation she has experienced.

I already suspected she still had loyalty to Oisin and The Order, and her reaction only gives me more confirmation. The fact that she believed The Order innocent in the destruction of her home was proof enough but her reaction to the fact that I could help her with the ceremony? It was as if two people were at war within her and neither were going to win.

The real question now is how much sway does The Order or rather Oisin have over her behaviors. Because despite having escaped physically, mentally they still hold some type of leash around her.

Shoving to my feet I brush the soft grass from my clothing as I start to head back towards the house, ignoring the pull of my magic and the ever-present heartache that seems to have taken up residence within my chest.

The clock is ticking down for me, my magic burning and writhing in my veins as it demands we return home. At this point I will have to either beg Jax to come with me or I'll have to handle it on my own. Either way I need to leave this place for my own sanity and for the sake of my magic not dragging me back against my will. As the Lady of Souls, it's my job to take care of The Forest and the souls within. Being here this long does neither of those things.

Meandering back into the dining room I see the two still occupy the space. He looks beautiful curled onto Dios's lap. I worked so hard to build up a hard layer of ice between myself and him, but it seems to be melting simply because he's in the same room and that fucking kills me.

I announce my presence by slamming the door behind me, Jackson practically jumping out of his skin and pulling himself from Dios's embrace. "She's hiding something, we cannot trust her." I say as I pinch the bridge of my nose. Jackson's face pales, "but the full moon is coming. We need her help."

My mouth remains in a grim line as Dios cocks his head, "I don't think I fully understand the way the priestess magic helps."

I let out a long breath as I settle deeper into the cushioned chair. "Priestesses naturally draw magic from The Well over the month. When the full moon hits, they are brimming with it, the intention being they perform the ritual and give the magic to the royals." I explain. The High Priestess is the one, and the only one, who passes the magic onward to whichever royal is in need of it. They alone have the ceremony." A quick glance to Jackson and I can see his fingers doing their anxious pattern across his thigh. "She admitted she did not have it." I leave the rest of our conversation out, refraining from telling him I have some knowledge of it.

Jackson takes a sharp intake of breath at the hidden meaning before muttering a curse and dropping his head in hands.

Dios crosses his arms, legs spread out in front of him. His mismatched eyes dart between us. "I'm clearly missing something."

"Every priestess absorbs the magic. But as I said only the High Priestess passes the magic on. Early on in their history, they did not realize what would happen if the magic wasn't given back by the others. It was a gruesome death. Burning from the inside out until there was nothing left but charred remains. They searched endlessly, rumor has it they even risked going to the original witch families in Gothic Grove. But no one had any solution." Jackson explains.

I watch as he drags his hands through his hair before pushing up and heading to the bar. His movements are graceful despite the powerful muscles he's built up over the years. He keeps his back to us as he pours himself a drink. "I wasn't alive at the time, but I remember my father telling me about it. It was a dark time. Priestesses went as far as to kill themselves if they weren't chosen for the ceremony. None of them wanted to endure that type of death."

Dios cocks his head to the side, "So how did they figure it out?"

"Before the fever would take them fully the priestesses would fall into an uncontrollable state of lust. It reminded one of the older females of a shifter's heat." I give him a moment, hoping he's more than just a pretty face. When his eyebrows shoot up, I know he understands.

"That's right my little death pup. The symptoms seemed to be incredibly similar to what female shifters experienced during their heat. They quickly discovered that by engaging in sexual acts, alongside some newly created spell work, the magic would be released back to The Well without harming the priestess. It would take a whole week, starting the night of the full moon, but when it was over they were good as new."

"So, if Harrowlena cannot perform the ceremony because she lacks the magic, she would need a partner or she'll die." He states grimly.

I let out a long breath, exhaustion creeping in finally. "Yes."

"So why shouldn't we trust her?" Jax frowns, finally turning towards us. "That doesn't mean she's hiding anything."

I zero in on Jackson, his fingers tapping rapidly once more, but now against the glass. His anxiety is out of control, and I'm not sure he even realizes it. "I think The Order, and Oisin, have more sway with her than we know. She spent long chunks of time being fed the lies they spread; isolated among them with no real access to the truth." I say, drawing my eyes back to his. "She truly believes Oisin rescued her, that The Order rescued her. I know some of the ceremony, enough that I think we could peace it together to help you get the magic you need from The Well and save her."

Dios shakes his head with a scoff. "Those fuckers didn't save anyone; they are the reason she had that fucking mask on her face."

Jackson nods along, "They are also the reason her family was killed." He keeps tapping his leg, the movement starting to bother me more and more. "When I first met her, she was so timid and quiet, but she also had flashes of this fire within her. Every so often she would be furious with me but would seemingly swallow it down, I never understood it at the time. Now it makes sense if she thinks I killed her family."

"I think she was sent here," I say shoving onward. "I think Oisin hopes we have the magic and is using her to get it from us."

Jackson shakes his head immediately disagreeing before Dios catches his eye. "It would make sense," He hedges. "She was unguarded and seemingly alone in that hallway."

I see the moment the anxiety starts to win and Jackson spirals. Dios moves quickly over to him gathering him in a tender embrace as if he too knows what is about to happen. "We'll figure it out." He says in a soothing tone. "We'll convince her to go to The Well. Or drag her there kicking and screaming if we have to."

Bile rises in my throat as I watch Jackson wrap his arms around the man and it propels me upward and out of my seat. "And give Oisin access to The Well and everything he wants? You guys are fucking idiots." I let my feet carry me backwards towards the door.

"Where are you going?" Jackson calls out.

At the same time Dios yells, "what is your proposed solution then?"

I roll my eyes and cast a hard look to Jackson. "I'll be in the city if you need me, doing your fucking job." Then I aim an equally as hard look at Dios. "And it's not my fucking job to think this through, it's the King's."

"Watch your tone." He growls before pulling away from Jax.

I let out a rough laugh, "oh fuck off."

Jackson holds Dios by the wrist as if worried the man will launch himself at me. I would welcome it at this point, honestly, a physical means to get out the pain and heartache this is all causing. And to help me push aside the little voice in me that seems to want the death god to comfort me as he comforts Jackson.

I flip them both the middle finger as I flee the room.

Jackson

(Fortnight (feat Post Malone)-Taylor Swift)

"Are you ever going to tell me what happened between you and her?" Dios asks, leaning against the old Dodge Charger that I currently have my head buried in. After convincing Dios, and myself if I'm being honest, not to follow Arcanna I fled here.

I don't say anything for a long moment, avoiding the conversation but knowing it needs to be said. Memories of nights spent wrapped in each other's embrace bombard me, her laughter echoing through the garage like a phantom on the wind, the smell of her skin after racing. It hits me one after another as I avoid looking at her car that is still parked off to the side of mine.

As if waiting for the next race we'll have.

"We were inseparable, from the moment we met. Regardless of anything I had with Oisin" I finally begin. "We had a possessiveness over one another that always raised questions, I think most thought we were fucking. Or at the very least would be in the future."

Dios chuckles, "you weren't?"

I let out a huff, "Not at first. No. We had a kiss right before I met Oisin. It was the kind that you have as a kid. Such a typical first kiss, clumsy and not at all hot. But still, it was our first kiss. I think things would have shifted at that point, we would have fallen in love but then suddenly Oisin was around, and I was enraptured by him. Arcanna was still in the picture, but she backed off." Regret clogs my throat as

I think about those early days, when she was so clearly hurt, and I refused to see it.

I huff out a defeated laugh. My mind replaying it all on rapid fire as Dios watches. I wince at his gaze; the sharp cut of his eyes pierces me to the soul. "I've been engaged, technically, since I was born. The Princess of Divinity was to wed the Prince of Hell. Forming an unbreakable alliance between two of the most powerful families."

The garage is silent as the statement settles in. Dios doesn't say anything only sips on his beer again. Waiting for me to continue.

"The night Ava left was the eve of the whole royal family coming to be with us. Rhea was to live in our home after her parents returned home. I didn't realize at the time it was so they could be around for my father to announce Oisin's engagement to Ava."

Dios takes another sip of his beer. He's so calm it almost makes the anxiety building in me worse. I hate the understanding he seems to have for the whole scenario because deep down I do not believe I deserve any of it. "Rhea did come to stay with us, not for long, but enough time that we formed a good friendship. We learned we had no interest in one another romantically and made the plan to eventually tell our parents the engagement was off."

Dios tilts his head, "I doubt that would have gone over well."

I shrug, "No. But Rhea is very stubborn when she wants to be and I have no doubt in my mind she would have gotten what she wanted in the end."

"None of this explains you and Arcanna though." He points out.

I drag a deep, painful breath in as I force myself to remain calm. Force the anxiety to shut the fuck up for once.

My eyes finally drag over to her red Challenger and I'm transported back to the best and worst night of my life.

(Sacrifice- kaskade, deadmau5, Sofi Tukker)

I watch Arcanna as she dances around the club. My eyes track her with a hunger that is all consuming. An obsession that I refuse to let go despite knowing how this will end. Something has changed. Deep within my very being it has changed. The sway Oisin had over me no longer powerful enough to make me ignore the addiction currently swaying her hips to the music.

Maybe it was the kiss that broke the spell. The shock of it forcing my body out of the stupor it had been in for so long. My lips still burn from the drunken fumble when she pressed herself into my body, and my cock still aches from the memory of listening to her making herself cum in the shower after.

Much like this evening, she hadn't known I was there. Hadn't know I had raced after her once I gathered myself. I was ready to demand more now that I had tasted her lips. I had remained outside the door, cock in hand, stroking myself in time to her own pleasure. When she came it was my name she groaned and that had been my undoing.

She's a drug that I want to inject directly into my veins, and I don't give a fuck if I od from her.

I groan as I see her laughing and smiling in the center of the crowded floor. Ophelia is next to her with a broad smile on her face as Nyx stands behind her with arms crossed keeping every single person away from his mate. Jealousy radiates through me. It should be me watching over Arcanna, me who is threatening to rip apart anyone who approaches the girls.

She's a vision in the short black dress that hugs her body, her long obsidian hair down in soft waves that fall to her waist. The music pounds through the speakers, lights flashing overhead to the beat. The air is thick with sexual tension from all around. Bodies grinding on one another in the dark heat of the dance floor. It's intoxicating.

I keep my arms crossed over my chest as I lean against the brick wall. A glass of amber liquid on the tall table next to me sits untouched. The condensation collecting on the sides. My resolve to remain hidden is slowly being chipped away the longer I watch.

Something has infected me, it's the only logical explanation as to why I'm thinking of giving into this strange lust that's built up for my best friend. This deep, dark desire to know what her throat feels like being squeezed by my fist. I grit my teeth against the need to drag her to a dark corner and fill her with my cock.

She's laughing, hands now above her head when I see a man prowling towards her. His hands circle around her and he drags her into his body. I tense waiting for her to push him away but instead she offers a smile and grinds into him. It's enough to spur me into action, the crowd parts for me out of pure instinct, clearing my path to her rapidly. my hand lands on the man's shoulder, yanking him back. He goes to shout but the moment his eyes lock on my silver ones he backs off, face going pale.

"I didn't know she was with you." He stammers, stumbling backwards. I don't say anything, just raise my eyebrow and let my power wash over him. He flees rapidly. Arcanna spins around, eyes flaring wide as she realizes I'm here.

"Jax. . ." She starts.

I cut her off and spin her back around before I pull her flush against my chest, grinding my hard cock into her ass as I flatten my hand against her taut stomach. Moving her thick hair to the side I lean into her ear, "Did you enjoy teasing me?"

Her body tenses under my splayed hand across her stomach. "What are you talking about? What are you doing here?"

"You know exactly what I'm talking about. It's like you want me to fuck you on this floor so everyone knows who you belong to. Like you want them to see what your little cunt looks like with my cock stuffed in it."

She lets a moan escape her before she tamps it down and digs her nails into my arm. "I don't belong to you."

"Wicked girl, I heard you the other night. It was my name on your lips as you came on your fingers. You've always belonged to me." I whisper into her ear.

(Lose You're Head- London Grammar, CamelPhat Remix)

She drives her thick ass into me harder, her head falling back onto my shoulder. I let my hand trace circles on her, the song changing to something sensual, making the room heavier with want and need. She lets out another low moan that has my restraint snapping. My eyes shoot up to be greeted by Nyx who raises an eyebrow before jerking his head towards the edge of the dance floor.

I grab her hand drawing her into the dark recesses of the club.

"This is a bad idea." She huffs out as I shove her into the brick wall, my lips landing on her neck. Sucking and kissing relentlessly. Her nipples pebble out of the dress and my hand finds her full, heavy breast. "Jax. . ." Her voice warning and wanting as I bite harder on her exposed neck. "What about Rhea?"

"I'm not marrying her, I want you. It's always been you. Fuck, how did I let you go for so long. It's always fucking been you." Her hips tilt forward as she grinds into me attempting to find friction. My fingers trace down and slip under the hem of her dress. I groan as my fingers are immediately met with wetness on her thighs. "Fuck, tell me to stop now if you really want that."

Her hand snakes up into my blonde hair and pulls me off her neck so she is looking me directly in the eyes. A moment passes and I'm worried she will indeed push me away. But her mouth slams into my own, her tongue exploring as I yield to her. I moan out low in her mouth and push my hand fully onto her cunt. The wet heat of it shoots to my painfully hard dick. I circle her clit roughly and she yanks off my mouth crying out.

"Oh fuck," she moans. I keep circling her before dipping down to her slit and pressing my fingers into her tight channel roughly.

"Fuck, my cock is barely going to fit in you." I pump in and out, watching her cheeks flush, more of her arousal flooding out. I keep up the pace, her hips now fucking my fingers hard, chasing her release. "That's it, baby, get what you need from me." I rip the top of her dress down and suck one of her nipples into my mouth. The effect is instant.

"Jax. Oh, fuck fuck fuck. Jax I'm going to cum." She screams out as the orgasm rushes through her, her pussy clenching my two digits hard. Letting her ride out the full release I only slip my fingers out once she stops quivering. I bring them to my mouth, sucking them clean; the taste hits my tongue and my cock jerks in my jeans, eyes rolling back in my head.

I don't stop to think, I rip my zipper down allowing my length to spring free. I turn her roughly, so her chest is pressed against the wall and press the thick head of my cock into her tiny cunt. I keep going, even as I feel her barely stretch around me until she's surrounding me.

Fully seated I give her a moment, just one, to adjust before I pull back out and slam back in. She cries out but I don't stop, too far gone, I keep fucking her relentlessly. My only goal is to fill her with my cum, to lay my mark on her so no one can question who the fuck she belongs to.

"You. Are. Mine." I chant over and over as I thrust into her. I barely notice my dark magic flow from my body into her. My wings flare out possessively blocking us from any eyes that may pass by. A deep knowing settling in me that I would slaughter this entire club if someone did indeed see me fucking her right now. Only my eyes are allowed to watch he come apart.

She throws her head back in a scream that the music around us gobbles up. "Oh gods. Oh fuck, right there Jax, don't stop."

My voice is something I don't recognize, feral and unhinged as I grip her hair in my fist. "Whatever nameless god you are praying to won't hear you. It's my cock inside you. Mine. Do you understand?"

"Fuck, yes, I understand. Now please please please. I need to cum. I'm so close." She whimpers. Tears track down her face illuminated only occasionally by the flash of light from the dance floor, sweat coats her body and her thighs are slick. I push my magic out further, the tendrils looping around her neck and breasts, and finally down towards her clit. I allow my darkness to caress her and tease her to an inch of her sanity. The electric side of it adds small pings of energy to each point that makes her pulse.

"Do you want me to fill you up?" I pant, pushing my magic towards her other hole. "Fuck you in both places?"

She lets out a whimper as she feels the first push into her ass, her body squirming as the feelings overwhelms her. "So full." She groans out. "I'm not going to last. I'm not going to last." She keeps repeating it over and over.

"Let go my wicked girl, let me feel that pretty pussy gush on my cock as I fill you up. Give it to me baby." She lets out a scream, her orgasm hitting her hard.

The entire club fades around us, the sounds a dull roar under the feeling of driving into her repeatedly. It isn't until I look down at my hand that is holding her hip that I see the dark runes starting to flare up and over my skin. By that point I know, in my soul, it's too late and I cum with a grunt as she squeezes me. My cock keeps jerking into her as I look horrified at my hand. As I look around us at the net of magic I've created.

I'm barely done with my release before I'm pulling out of her roughly. The feeling was painful not only in my chest but my cock.

"What the actual fuck Jax?!" She yells, whirling on me. Her fury is burning through me, a visceral feeling that sits on my lungs, compressing them. I can only look at her in horror, my eyes shifting between her and the now-white tattoos that are on my hand. Tattoos that I know will also be marked on her hip, invisible to her for now, but there nonetheless.

Her dark hair is a mess, her makeup ruined from our tris in the dark. The look on her face morphs from anger to utter devastation as I back away from her. When her eyes catch the white tattoos on my hand she stills, shock pulsing through her. I think she begs me to stay but I shake my head, turning and fleeing like a coward back into the crowd. My release still dripping down her.

SIXTEEN

Jackson

I keep my eyes locked on the ground in front of me, avoiding the judgement that no doubt resides on Dios's face. My fingers tap out patterns on my leg as I try to get my ragged breathing under control.

"What are these?" Dios's voice feels like a slap, my body flinching as he grabs hold of my hand to look at the tattoos that are barely noticeable now. I hadn't even realized I was looking at them.

"The start of our mate bond. When someone who has demon blood in them mates, we get matching tattoos." He narrows his eyes before dropping my hand and stepping out of my orbit once again. His calm nature is making it feel worse, no judgment or anger. Just a steady presence as I word vomit my shame.

I shake my head. "I regretted leaving her in that club almost immediately, I had panicked when I saw that magic. When I finally got back to the palace, I had calmed down, and knew I needed to make it right, I went to Rhea and told her we needed to move up our timeline." I snort out a laugh at the memory. "The way Rhea looked at me like I was the biggest idiot alive as I spilled everything. She told me to give Arcanna some space but to make it right sooner rather than later."

"I waited all night for her to come find me, all night to hear her sneak in. But when the sun finally crested the sky, I gave up waiting and went to find her, to tell her how sorry I was and that she was mine. But she was gone. Vanished without a trace." Anger courses through me and I throw the wrench across the room, the loud noise echoing through the garage. "All I found was Oisin waiting for me."

Dios scoffs and mutters something that sounds like he is calling me an idiot. "You ran right to the female she thought you were to wed. What did you think would happen?"

"This involved Rhea!" I snap. "If it got out it wouldn't just be me who was in trouble, but her life would have been on the line no doubt. I was trying to protect everyone." I drag in a deep breath as a shudder wracks my body. Tears of frustration fill my eyes.

"Rhea was the one to figure it out. She learned, via my mother, that Arcanna had taken up the position of Lady of Souls and fled to the forest immediately. She didn't wait for me, she just left. I went to find her and bring her home, make her my queen. But when I arrived, she told me to leave. She said that while I was a good fuck she didn't want anything else. She even laughed when I showed her my tattoo and said she planned to cover hers up. So, I left. I gave up on her and us."

I see Dios's boots come into view before I feel his fingers on my chin, tilting my head up so I can lock eyes with his. Emotion plays over them, an understanding that burns deep in my soul. Dios is rarely emotional and rarely displays vulnerability. His hand traces my jaw, playing with my facial hair that has started to grow, before dipping down and gripping my throat.

"It sounds like you both made a mistake." His voice is a deep purr. Earthy, like coming home. "And from what I see you both still want one another. You do not get the anger she has or the regret you have when there is no longer love and want. How do you feel about her now *mi cielo?*"

How do I feel now? It's a question I haven't allowed myself to think. Seeing her was like a knife to the heart. Knowing that she's been out there all this time without me, knowing what she is to me. But gone was the girl who trusted me, in her place was someone who had hardened her heart against me.

"*Mi cielo?* Answer me." Dios demands. His grip more forceful now.

"That even after all this time I want her back. I want to make this right." He doesn't say anything, but a small smile creeps over his face.

<hr>

Dios

Jax looks devastated as he leans against the car, his hair untidy atop his head and oil smeared across his cheek. "But me and you?" He trails off, the question in his voice so clear. His cheeks are flushed and his eyes hold mine with so much hope. I know what he wants me to say, what he needs me to say but for fucks sake one of us has to be rational about this.

And yet it's on the tip of my tongue to tell him I too feel a pull towards her. No. Not me. My wolf. My wolf wants her. Needs her. "If you want her, we will make it work. She is important to you, so she's important to me." I say. "If you were paying any attention when I was fucking you, you would have known she was just as turned on seeing me fill you up as I was knowing she was watching."

The little reaper had walked in as I finished, her scent filling the room and making my wolf salivate. But she wasn't ready to admit she wanted me, wanted us, so I kept quiet instead of alerting Jackson to her.

Grabbing his hand, I lead him from the garage and back towards his own room. Shutting the door with a resounding click his silver eyes barely track me as I push him into the large bathroom and turn on the shower. But I don't miss the way his pupils have blown wide, and the scent of his own arousal faintly clings to his body.

Stripping him quickly I give a gentle nudge towards the deluge of hot water. He steps under, shuddering for a moment before he tilts his head back and lets it wash down his body. The muscular plain of his stomach catching my attention as the water carves a path over it before my eyes travel back up to his face. His hair has grown out some since I first saw him in my dreams all those years ago and his eyes have collected a few wrinkles to show the passing of time.

It had been a shock when I meandered into his dreams, and an even bigger shock when he dropped into our bar not long ago and I realized he was a real person.

"*Tu alma lo buscó, él es importante. Mereces la felicidad.*" My abuela's voice echoes into my mind. She was so hopeful when I told her about him, a hope that I could never return.

"*Deja de mentirte a ti mismo, Dios. No te crié para que fueras estupido.* Stop lying to yourself, Dios. I didn't raise you to be stupid."

I roll my eyes, as if she could see me. I often wondered how she created my father, the two so vastly different. When I was young, I asked my abuela about it, it's the only time she got angry with me. Truly angry. Telling me I didn't understand what I was talking about. And maybe I didn't but as an adult I wonder why she never told me what happened to make my father so cold.

The homesickness that washes over me is a vast tidal wave. Closing my eyes I can almost smell her cooking my favorite food, hear her humming as she leans over the stove. The kitchen was her favorite place to be, her love language had always been feeding people. It's a similarity we seem to share. We spent hours in the kitchen together until my father deemed it "not manly" enough.

"Dios?" Jax's voice pulls me from the thoughts.

I offer a tight smile, "sorry, *mi cielo*. Are you all done?" He nods stepping out of the shower as I manage to grab a towel and wrap him in it. Leading him into the bedroom I push him down onto the massive bed, ignoring my hardening cock at the sight of him laid out like a meal. His own impressive length lays half hard against his thigh, the thickness of it evident even now.

"Be a good boy for me and get some sleep. I'll reward you for it when I come back." He looks disappointed but nods, accepting my command as he rolls over and allows me to cover him with the blankets.

"Are you going to check on her?" His voice is already rough with sleep.

"Si." I want her side of things. I want to understand why she ran that night, why she didn't demand an apology or answers. She doesn't seem like the type to flee; she seems like the type to fight. The fact that she flipped us off even now makes me think we are missing something.

My wolf paws at me impatiently.

"*Mierda.*" I curse, shutting the door to the bedroom. This is a complication I don't want or need. I let my shift take me, throwing my large body into a sprint and follow the rich smell of sandalwood through the woods that line the lake out onto the hill that overlooks the main city. My predator eyes scan the world as I wait to catch her scent again. When the wind finally changes directions and I'm greeted with it I throw my head back and let out a loud howl before racing after her.

Jackson

I wait just long enough to know Dios is gone, his howl that had echoed into the air no longer filling the space. Slipping on my sweats I make my way towards Harrow's room, knocking softly in case she's asleep. Though I'm doubting it given what I've observed. Arcanna wasn't wrong in what she said, nor Dios, but something tells me even if Harrow is playing both sides she is still someone who needs us. Needs friends.

When the door cracks open, I see her violet eyes peak out and flare wide when she sees me shirtless standing in her doorway. "Can I come in?" I ask finally when the silence draws out far too long.

She nods and lets me, gathering her robe around her body as she moves towards the small sitting area the room comes with. Tucking herself into one of the arm chairs she looks at me expectantly and with some confusion.

I offer up a smile as I find myself in the chair opposite hers, "Wanna talk?" I ask.

"Uh," She starts. "About what?"

Leaning towards her a bit more I brace my arms on my legs. "It seems like maybe you could use a friend. At one time we started trying to build that relationship. I guess this is my olive branch in hopes that you'll still want it." She looks taken a back, shock flashing over her face that I have no doubt in my mind she didn't mean to show.

For a while we both just look at each other, the silence building to almost a crescendo before she clears her throat. "I don't know if I know how to be a friend." She murmurs in that soft voice she seems to have adopted now.

I let out a hum of question before pushing up from the chair. "Did you know this is the room Ava used to stay in?" I ask as I start to mill around the room.

"No." She responds instantly. While my back is to her, I can feel her large, doe eyes, boring into me. Watching every move I make. I'm making her nervous searching like I am which only continues to add credibility to Arcanna's concerns.

My hand travels over the bookcase, each book being pulled forward slightly when my hand graces it. "She was a sneaky little shit. Always following us, even when she thought we didn't know. And always the life of the party." When one of the books snags, I feel a great deal of satisfaction. Pulling it forward I hear the familiar click and swoosh before a panel swings open revealing a small bar that still holds a few bottles of half drank liquor. I snag one, turning around triumphantly. "Ava didn't have many friends. Really, she didn't have any. So, I let her tag along with us. Let her have her fun secrets. But it was Arcanna who always bridged the gap between us. Making sure Ava felt seen and heard in our group. She was the one who truly made sure Ava was safe all those times she followed us."

The regret of it all wants to choke me. I take a swig to

force it away, to focus on building this relationship with Harrow. When I go to hand the bottle to her, she pushes her back against the chair and holds her hand up in protest. "Oh no thank you. I don't. . . I don't want it. I'm sorry what does this have to do with anything?"

"I watched my sister try day after day to make her own way in this world, but *I* never helped her. And I watched her die knowing I never helped her achieve those goals. In fact, I would argue most her life she thought I was against her." Harrow looks pale as I talk. "I don't want to repeat the mistakes of my past. So, should you want or need a friend I think I could make a pretty good one."

She pulls her bottom lip into her teeth, chewing on it for a moment before it pops back out. Her long silver hair hangs around her in a curtain as though she hopes to disappear into it. "Thank you, I'll. . . I'll think about it Jackson."

Shrugging and downing another shot. I place the remaining liquor on the table off to the side. "Just in case you change your mind." I say with a wink before leaving her alone.

Harrow

I stumble to lock the door as soon as Jackson is out of my room. My heart pounds in my chest so hard that I'm shocked I can't see it trying to break through my skin. My eyes lock on the liquor he pulled from the secret bookcase and I don't second guess myself as I chug the vile liquid.

It burns my throat before it manages to drop into my stomach twisting my insides.

"They are lying. Arcanna is wrong." I repeat to myself over and over. "They are liars." I say again. But no matter how much I say it my voice never sounds convincing. I take another sip, and another, the fire liquid burning me from the inside out as though it's taking aim at all the information I've been given. Searching for the ones that are the lies and the ones that are the truth.

When I go to take another sip, I come up empty, the liquor now fully consumed. Through my hand the empty bottle slips away and clatters to the floor, the glass shattering into a million pieces. It feels like an accurate representation of how my mind feels. A thousand glittering pieces sprawled out and no way to make sense of them all.

Just send the message, send it and you'll be done soon. You'll be able to go home soon, it can all go back to how it was before this started.

The voice speaks partial truths in my head, yet I can't seem to bring myself to fully believe that inner monologue. Watching the three of them interact, despite the hurt they've caused each other, has made me question everything. Arcanna's words on friendship joining the others as they roll around my brain. And Jackson coming here, coming to see me, it only makes it more confusing.

"Why did you have to come here?" I cry quietly as I grip my curls hard and tug. I hiss, and tears form in the corner of my eyes. This was supposed to be easy. It was supposed to give me freedom. Now all I feel is more trapped.

Looking down at my palm I tilt it to and fro to see the small, silver scar, barely visible to the naked eye yet to me it appears like a beacon. I trace it with my thumb lightly, back and forth, back and forth, the motion almost hypnotizing me as the liquor starts to provide that tingle in my body that washes everything else away.

Sweat starts to bead on my forehead and shame threatens to dump the contents of my stomach back out on the ground.

"You have to do this." I say out loud. "Everything will

be different, he promised." The words sound lame to my own ears and feel less like a reason and more like an excuse. I whimper as my body tenses and my vision swims.

"You failed me before my Lena. You don't want to do it again do you?" Oisin's voice seems to come from all around me yet I know it's nothing more than a hallucination from the booze and my subconscious pushing me.

"I'm sorry. I'm so sorry." I say out loud regardless.

"Come home to me and I'll give you everything you want. Everything you need. My mate."

The words draw out a new reaction deep within my body. I can feel the dampness of my panties now, feel my nipples tighten and my breath heave as my vision swims with images of his cock deep within me. My pussy convulses and I stifle my cry as arousal hits me square in the chest. My thighs press together tightly, desperate for friction on that sensitive area.

No.

Not friction.

I want to be filled.

I want to come apart while riding him and feel him unleash himself on me.

I stop stroking the scar and my hand dives down into my soaked underwear to my swollen, hot, pussy. My small fingers feel like a tease compared to his but I plunge them in anyway as I rotate fucking myself and stroking my clit. It doesn't take long for me to cum, for my body to release the tension and I scream out with my head thrown back. His name a prayer on my lips as I do.

When I finally pull my fingers free, I go back to stroking that scar, now with arousal painting it. And when let myself press into it, my chewed nail digging into the flesh, the relief I expect it to provide does not appear, instead, I feel more shame and regret than I did when I started.

Arcanna

The first rays of sun crest over the horizon as I rip my glaive free from the chest cavity of whatever fucking creature I just slaughtered. Its putrid insides oozing out as it starts to melt, spearing its heart had caused a chain reaction deep within it.

"Fucking gross." I grumble. My eyes scan the streets and snag on the other things I've managed to kill while unleashing my emotions. It seems like since coming here I've done nothing but either shove the emotions into a box labeled 'avoid at all costs' or felt as though I was drowning in them. All in all, it has worked to my advantage that Jackson is low on magic and avoiding the streets of Hell. Swinging my blade, I move to wipe it across my pants when the back of my neck tingles, the feeling of being watched pressing into me. All around the world goes quiet, as if the night itself knows a predator is among us.

A low, deep growl has me cautiously turning, my glaive held so tightly my knuckles are white. Slowly, ever so slowly, I come face to face with a massive black wolf. For a moment my stomach bottoms out but instead of fear a strange familiarity rises up allowing my muscles to relax and the grip on my glaive to loosen.

"I don't need your help, Dios." I bite out, annoyed he did indeed follow me. He huffs out through his nose, the feel hitting me even at this distance. "Jax needs you more, his magic is stupid low. Run along and help your little mate." I spat the last word, and the wolf flattens his ears letting out another low growl. His massive paw scratching the ground in front of him. I smirk, satisfied I hit a nerve.

The wolf pulls his lips back exposing his bright, white teeth. The action lighting a flame within my body, a desperate and hungry flame. Any other moment I would be worried that I was about to be eaten but something tells me the only way I'd be eaten by this beast was if he was kneeling between my legs with his tongue pressed into my pussy. The arousal that pulses through me is swift and powerful, my knees squeezing together.

(Eyes on Fire- Hahlweg & wayfie)

"I can smell you." The words start animalistic as the wolf in front of me shifts into his human form. Dios stands naked, his cock hanging heavy between his legs. "I wonder if you would taste as good as you smell." He muses as he takes a step closer to me with a swagger no one should have after just shifting from the massive form.

"Why don't you ask your boyfriend? He's had me all over his body." I breathe out. Something deep within me flares to life like an ember finally given oxygen as I continue to take in his naked form.

Dios smiles, eyes alight with mischief as he steps into my space. "Why ask when I could taste you myself. Tell me, would you enjoy knowing my face was covered in your cum when I go home to him? Do you think when I kiss him, he'd taste you?" He leans in so our breath shares the air between us. "I'd make him lick it clean." An involuntary shiver rolls over me at the words and my pussy clenches.

"Fuck off I have no interest in whatever game you want to play," My voice shakes, the arousal barely contained as that stupid ember turns to an inferno.

"So, you didn't fuck your own hand after watching us?" He purrs.

I grind my teeth hard, jaw clenched. "Fuck. Off." I growl despite more wetness pooling from me.

Dios's eyes reflect that inferno as they look me over, his nostrils flaring slightly as though he is catching my scent on the wind. "I know what those marks on him mean. You ran from a bond..." his gaze seems to cut through me to my soul, flaying me open to an uncomfortable degree.

The statement only cools my body slightly. "I could never be what he needed, bond or no. He can't pull magic from me." I counter, knowing exactly where he is going with this. He walks around me, the heat of his gaze burning a path along my skin.

"You are fighting fate." He says stopping in front of me once more.

My glaive pushes upward, the blade pressed just hard enough into the dark skin on his neck that blood bubbles upward. He smiles widely his mismatched eyes flashing with magic. "Jackson didn't want me. He wanted the Queen, the one he was engaged to." I bark out with rage and hurt. He frowns, taken back slightly. "You ran."

I huff out a dark laugh, "Is that a question or a statement? I left because he demanded I leave. He doesn't get to put this on me."

Dios crosses his arms over his naked chest, eyes narrowing on me. "I think you need to talk to him."

"No." I bite out. "He can kindly go fuck himself." Dios growls, the sound vibrating every part of my body making me want to tilt my head and submit to him. I grind my teeth together to stop myself. "Stop using your wolf against me." The feeling washes over me again and again leaving me no doubt in mind that if he wanted to fuck me right now his cock would have no resistance sliding right in.

He smirks, a lazy satisfaction moving over his face but doesn't stop. My body shakes and I ball my fists up forcing myself to stay put, refusing to bend over and let him have me. "You need something, *segradora*?" He presses into the blade a little more forcing me to step backwards.

"I don't need anything." I snap. "I don't need you or Jackson. Now let me finish hunting."

"I don't think I will". Slowly his hand comes to rest on mine, forcing me to release the weapon that's held him at bay. He steps closer, so close I can smell the rich leather and bergamot scent he carries.

"I don't want you." The words tumble lamely from my mouth my voice a breathy tone.

He raises an eyebrow, biting his bottom lip before he closes in and presses his mouth to mine. My hands press against his chest firmly and my nails bite into him as he claims my mouth. The world narrows for me, the kiss consuming, turning into an inferno that burns all clarity away. Until he lets out a groan and the sound reminds me of reality.

I bite down on his lip hard, the taste of his blood filling my mouth. He offers a chuckle, even as he pulls back and I can see the blood shinning on his lip, he still chuckles. "Oh, we are going to have fun."

In a quick movement he's behind me, pulling my body into his so my back is pressed against his naked front. My mouth goes to open but the soft stroke of his hands on my body forces it closed again. My eyes flutter shut despite my best efforts to avoid falling into this trap. When they get to my collar bone, I can feel his lips follow the path his fingers have created. His nose nudges at my neck, a silent ask to tilt and submit.

"You're fucking high if you think I'm tilting my neck for you." I have to grit my teeth as I say it, my body, a traitor to the lust this man is building inside me, demanding I submit. Demanding I let this wolf bite and claim me.

That growl rises up again, this time louder and more powerful, one that makes me think if I were to turn around, I might see more wolf than man. The growl continues as he grips my breast, his fingers tweaking my nipple through the shirt. A low moan comes from my throat and more arousal floods from me. My head lulls to the side before sanity and control can return to me.

He pauses for a moment and utters a curse before he kisses into my skin, his teeth grazing but never biting. When his hand dips down to the band of my pants a low whimper escapes me.

His fingers graze my bare sex, and he groans loudly. "So wet for me, fuck." He strokes my slit before resting on my clit and gently circling the tight bundle of nerves. My legs spread wider to give him more access, a silent plea to give me everything. That deep growl still pulling at my chest as his wolf demands it all from me.

Two thick fingers press into me, filling me to a delicious point. "Yes," I hiss out as he starts to stroke my inner walls. My nipples pebble and press painfully at the tight top I have on. His left hand now grasping my breast and stroking them through the fabric.

"You have some modifications, reaper?" He says as he feels the metal barbell pressed through the bud. I pant as I struggle to find words as the lust clouds my mind and drags away all thoughts. "Someday I'll find out what they feel like with my mouth around them. But for now, I want you to cover my fingers." His lips find my neck again and when I feel sharp teeth graze the skin once more, I cry and cum on his fingers. "Fuckkk that's a good girl, I can't wait to feel that around my cock."

He keeps praising me as I ride out the orgasm on his fingers, my hips rutting into his hand while my one hand holds his mouth to my neck and the other grips his wrist.

When he finally removes his fingers, my body feels limps against him and my head swims. A strange buzzing sensation moving through my bones. He stands holding me against his body before bringing the fingers I came on to his mouth and presumably licking them clean based on the sounds behind me.

"You taste like mine." He growls.

I spin abruptly, nostrils flaring but as I go to argue the world is rocked by a massive explosion, a massive hole opens beneath our feet sending the two of us plummeting. A scream lodged in my throat.

EIGHTEEN

Arcanna

Confusion meets me as I slowly blink open my eyes. My vision spinning. The scent of smoke and earth invading my nostrils. Trying to drag in a deep breath I cough as it burns through my lungs and chest. My head swims as I try to push up, but searing pain scorches through my body and reality slams into me.

"Motherfucker." I curse looking down. My stomach rolls at the sight of the metal sphere piercing through my thigh, effectively keeping me locked to the ground.

"Arcanna?" Dios's voice echoes through the cavern making it difficult to establish where exactly he is coming from.

"I'm here!" I manage to cough out. I try to wiggle my body, but it drives more seething pain through me wrenching a cry from my lips as I grit my teeth against the wave of nausea that follows.

Warm hands grip my face alerting me to the fact that I closed my eyes again. Dios's face swims in front of me as soon as I open them. Blood drips from his right eyebrow down through his eye and small scrapes cover his bare chest.

"Where are you hurt?" He says quickly.

"My leg." I pant out. He curses when he sees the metal stuck through the flesh. "What the fuck happened?" I ask through gritted teeth.

He doesn't answer, his gaze locked on my wound. My blood pools around me from the wound and I know from the look on his face I'm fucked.

He doesn't look at me right away and his voice shakes as he whispers, "We need to pull it out."

I roll my eyes, "no shit."

His fingers press around my thigh and I wince at the pain that shoots up through my body. He continues his exploration, slowly moving his fingers around the wound. "It's clean through into the ground. I think our best bet is to snap it free and leave most of it intact in your leg. Otherwise, you might bleed out before we can get you back to the house."

I lean back on my forearms, "just hurry it up." I groan before pressing back into a seated position. "I don't like being down here."

He nods and his mouth forms into a hard line. "This is going to hurt."

I give him a blank stare trying my best not to show any fear as his hands grip the metal. Even that movement pulls a whimper from me.

"Sorry *segadora*. Take a deep breath for me."

I start to drag a deep breath in but pause. Something tickles at the edge of my awareness and my eyes shoot up and over Dios who continues to look contemplatively at my wound. "Dios." I hiss. "You need to move, now."

He looks up at me with a frown. "What?"

My eyes dart to him and back over his shoulder. The

darkness may be hiding the bodies of the creatures, but their eyes are not hidden and even from here I can tell there are too many.

"You need to leave me." I say again. His pupils dilate and I know he senses the things that have gathered around us.

"I'm not leaving you." He says firmly before standing and looking around the cavern to face off against whatever the fuck is down here.

<hr>

Jackson

My stomach bottoms out as I jolt awake. Sweat clings to my bare chest as I fling myself from the bed wings bursting free. Panic is lodged in my throat alongside agonizing pain. It's disorienting until I realize it's coming from the bond, the one that while not fully completed still links me to Arcanna. The one she *always* keeps shut.

The sweats I had pulled on earlier still cling to my legs as I head to the bedroom door. Ripping it open my heart hammers as I race into the hallway of the house, the eerie silence that greets me only drives me faster through the empty home. When I burst out the front door my eyes scan the yard as my chest constricts and panic floods my veins.

"Sir!" Phenalais voice has me spinning towards him as the old man runs up the sidewalk toward me. "There has been an attack!"

It's all I need to hear before I'm leaping into the air, "Make sure the priestess stays here!" I yell before my wings lift me out of range

When my gaze lands on the rising column of smoke in the distance my chest constricts as I force them to carry me towards it. My muscles strain as I push my wings and body as hard as I can. Desperation crawling through me to get to my mates.

The outskirts of the city appear quickly and it's easy to see the culprit of the smoke. The ground below has been blown open exposing the older, abandoned city beneath the kingdom. A city that had been covered up decades ago so Hell could grow into what it is now. My eyes scan the rubble even as I'm already following the pain radiating from the bond.

The world tunnels as I spy Arcanna's bloody body pinned to the ground, her face ghost white, while Dios stands in front of her in wolf form. Blood matted against his dark fur and teeth bared as he protects her from the wave of creatures attacking them.

Rage blacks out my vision as I tuck my wings in tight free falling into the fight.

Dios
(Don't Fear The Reaper- Tom Rhodes)

Wave after wave of creatures swarm us, my wolf struggling to keep them at bay as Arcanna does her best to send her own magic out when she can. The scent of her blood is the only thing that keeps me standing and fighting, the amount she is losing is alarming. Even for one like her, she cannot keep up with the flow of it.

My dark magic swirls deep within, the desire and temptation to dip into it the main reason I shifted. It whispers to me, a lullaby, a soft voice that sounds so reasonable to just give into it and destroy everything around us. Even the pathetic souls of the creatures around me call out, almost beg for me to touch them and take them.

My wolf paws at the ground as I force myself to stay shifted, to stay focused.

"Dios. . ." she says from behind. I don't turn but my ear twitches to indicate I'm listening. "You need to go." I let out a bark in protest as I rip apart another creature, its foul blood clogging my mouth as pieces of it fling apart.

"He can't lose us both." She says it weakly. And she's not wrong. But I know that if only one of us walks out of here he'll never forgive himself and the survivor will never get the same Jackson again. "Don't be stubborn you idiot wolf, fucking go." She hisses.

I press backward until I can feel her against my hind leg. Her hand grips my side and she squeezes the fur, glancing back at her I see the resolution in her eyes. I shake my massive head. She grips her glaive in her hand, having manifested it at some point, the massive end of the blade spearing a creature making its way for us. The movement pulls at her strength, and I can see the way her lips have paled, the once golden colored skin now waxy. Even her tattoos are barely glowing.

I shake my massive head again. My wolf whimpers, even my beast is now on the side of that dark magic. The reality of it all crashes into me. If I don't allow the darkness out, if I don't use it, she'll most likely die.

Her eyes look at me sadly, not understanding my hesitation but seeing it none the less, before they track upward and widen with awe. "Oh fuck." She whispers.

I whip my head around and watch as Jackson drops into the cavern. His feet land hard sending cracks through the ground as his wings splay wide, all the grander given he wears no shirt to cover his sculpted torso.

Everything pauses, the creatures suddenly unsure and nervous as they take in the newcomer. His magic fills the space in a crackling energy and overhead thunder booms.

The energy manifests over his body in waves, my own hackles raising at the feel.

"This isn't good." Arcanna whispers. Her voice drags his attention to us and instead of being met with silver I'm met with full blacked out eyes. His pupils having taken over completely. His nostrils flare as he takes in each cut and abrasion left on us. The grip on his sword tightens just as a creature finally gets brave enough to attack. The blade slices clean through the body of whatever the fuck it was. His eyes never leaving us.

"Tell your master I am coming for him." He says in a deep growl before he unleashes his power. I shift rapidly and throw myself over Arcanna's body only seconds before the magic hits the space we are in. We cling to each other as it flows over us before an ominous silence fills the space around us once more.

Slowly peeling myself up and off Arcanna my eyes glance around the cavern. Nothing is left. Not a single creature still lives, their bodies dissolving slowly as the life leaves them. Their souls drifting about in the cavern before they too dissolve.

This is the King of Hell.

The one they all fear.

And my mate who I can never have. Because linking magic like ours? We would never be allowed to live.

"You need to get him to calm down" Arcanna says quietly gripping my hand hard. "He's using too much magic he needs to stop or he'll die." Her voice edges towards panic and those storm cloud eyes hold nothing but fear in them.

I reluctantly let her go and stand, turning to my mate. Jackson watches me with those dark eyes, his movements so unlike the person I've come to know. As if he's locked himself away and given into the killer deep within.

"*Mi cielo,*" I say as I approach. "It's time to let it go, you rescued us." His magic crackles around us and he blinks slowly. "She needs you." I jerk my head behind me at Arcanna's bleeding form. He blinks again, slowly. When I'm within arm's reach I take a chance and grab him by the throat. His magic claws at my arms as it bites into me. "Fight me all you want Jackson. You. Are. Mine. And no amount of this magic will change that. Now let it go so we can make sure *our* girl survives."

I squeeze his throat with just enough pressure to make breathing more labored. He closes his eyes and I feel his pulse steady under my thumb. When he finally lets out a shuddering breath, I'm greeted once more with his silver gaze.

"There's my good boy." I plant a soft kiss to his mouth as he continues to come back to me. When I'm sure he's fully present in his body I release him and step back.

"Thank you," he says. "For bringing me back."

I nod and smile. His gaze tracks around me and horror blanches over his face as he takes off. "ARCANNA!"

Turning I see our reaper laying in a pool of her own blood now solidly unconscious.

NINETEEN

Arcanna

My eyes blink open in a fluttering fashion before I gasp, and my forest comes into view. I drag in a breath, the cool tones of evergreen, rain and moss filling my lungs and removing the smell of blood and carnage.

"Well, this is unexpected." The voice draws my gaze. The cool wind blows the long blonde hair around her face, the dark raven on her shoulder nuzzling into the strands every now and again. And just behind her the massive bone dragon watches me with those black eyes.

"Fucking hell." I grumble as I push to a stand and eye my friend. The jagged scar across her neck, painted an angry red against her pale skin, draws my gaze for longer than I wish. When I asked if she wanted me to remove it, she refused saying she wasn't ashamed of what she did to save those she loved.

"Arcanna?" She tilts her head in curiosity.

I rub at the spot on my body I should have a gaping wound and can only hope that Dios and Jackson are okay wherever they still are. "Sorry, I'm a little lost. The last thing

I saw was Dios trying to help bring your brother back down. Fucking Oisin sent his pack of creatures after us."

"Is everyone okay?!" Panic laces her tone as her silver eyes widen. A huff of hot air puffs out against my body as a massive dragon lumbers past me to join the skeletal one currently keeping watch just beyond my dear friend. She smiles softly at the black and gold creature as it affectionately bumps her with its snout as he walks by.

"The fucking hunk of metal through my leg wasn't great." I grumble and then wince, "I passed out just as Dios reached him. He killed every single enemy though; nothing was left alive."

She visibly relaxes and nods. "Good."

I push to a stand and stretch my astral body out. "How is it going here?"

"About as good as you can expect. We took out two Elker packs that crept over the border before they managed to infect any more of the land." Her voice sounds distant, despite my astral projection being right in front of her. "The portions that were previously infected have remained the same."

I let out a sigh of relief and offer a thankful smile to her.

"How are you holding up?" She asks with an arched eyebrow

"Aside from being injured?" I let out a long sigh, "It's complicated. I left for a reason and being back is harder than I thought it would be."

She reaches out before dropping her hand, remembering she can't touch me. "You are meant to be in his life, Arcanna. Do you not know that?" Her eyes trace downward to the matching white tattoo peeking out on my hip. Faded but always there.

I huff out a laugh even as I squirm under the scrutiny, "have you seen the god he spends most his nights and days with?" The words feel wrong given I just had that same god's fingers deep within me.

She cocks her head, curiosity moving through her gaze before a smirk spreads over her lips. "Two cocks are better than one you know."

The dragon nearest lets out a sound that resembles a cough and Ava cuts it a sharp look before shrugging and turning back to me.

I close my eyes for a moment and drag in a deep breath before letting it expel out. "We'll figure it out after this is all over." It's a cop out, she knows it too judging by the look on her face. "We need to figure out what to do with Harrowlena before we can even think about figuring out what the fuck is happening between us all."

"Harrow is there?" Her frown deepens.

"How do you know her?" I ask.

As she goes to open her mouth again, I feel a tug on my physical body. Desperate to stay in I re-focus on her face, grounding myself to The Forest around me.

"Wait!" My friend yells. "I need to tell you—" But it's too late, I'm yanked back into reality unceremoniously. My friend left behind in my home.

(Numb- Tommee Profitt & Skylar Grey)

I'm ripped from my forest hard and slam back into my body with a desperate groan as the pain overwhelms me, nausea swelling in my gut.

"Arcanna?!" Jackson's fearful voice rings through my ears. My eyes feel heavy as they try to open, my body refusing to comply.

Dios's scent washes over me next as I feel his calloused hand caress my own. "Come on *pequeña segradora*, open those eyes."

My leg burns at the spot of the injury and my head swims as I finally mange to pry open my eyes at the command of the death god hovering over me. "Fuck off you don't get to take me yet." I mumble with a heavy tongue. I think I hear a dark chuckle before Jackson's scent sweeps by with a warm brush of wind and the bed dips by my leg. A scream lodges in my throat as he shifts the injured appendage.

"Fuck this is bad." He growls.

Dios moves away from me just as my vision becomes clear. He settles next to Jackson with his mouth painted in a firm line. The once pristine sheets are covered in blood. My blood. Even with the tourniquet around my leg it still seeps free of my body.

"Can you heal her?" Jackson asks quietly as though he hopes to avoid bringing it to my attention just how bad off I am.

A desperate chuckle falls from me before I start coughing. "He's a death god, not one of life." A strange feeling of acceptance washes over me as I realize soon, I will be a soul within my forest. It doesn't feel as scary as I thought it would. It feels like a welcome reprieve to the torture of being around Jackson and Dios.

"Don't you dare!" Jackson growls as he appears in my face. His warm hands cup me on either side, forcing me to hold his gaze. "You are not fucking dying Arcanna."

Another laugh tries to bubble up from my mouth, "Not your choice."

A fresh wave of wisteria and ocean flows into the room accompanied by a soft gasp. "No!" Harrow's voice battles within me to stay conscious. "What happened?!" Her soft hands land on my body but my eyes refuse to work, refuse to open now. Distantly I think I hear the two explain to her what's going on, but I'm pulled away once more, this time, though, I stay firmly trapped in my body.

Dios

(Burn the Witch (acoustic)-Shawn James)

The coffin I have nailed shut in the corner of my mind is moving, the skeletons screaming to be released. I've kept them at bay next to my dark power for so long I doubt I'll be able to control them once they are out. Already I can feel the dark magic tingle at my fingertips and I know if I look down they'll be hazy as this form tries to dissolve. My wolf growls low, digging his claws in, refusing to let me drift away.

I've left a long trail of bodies from here to my home, created a name for myself that's been whispered in only nightmares. I'm the one they all fear.

Harrowlena asked me, long ago, who I serve.

I wasn't lying when I said someone darker. . .

My mind whirls a mile a minute as I watch Arcanna fade from us. I dig my nails into my palm as I send a prayer outward. I know exactly what I'm about to do is going to open that coffin I have no interest in opening again but for her, for *them*, I'll fucking do it.

Slowly I allow my magic to build within letting part of it latch onto Arcanna's soul forcing a wheeze from her pale lips.

"Dios?" Jackson's voice echoes through the room like a damn scream.

"I'll fix it *mi cielo*." I vow as I latch onto the other half of my magic and pull towards me, despite it violently fighting against me.

Bright white light bursts into the room and Jackson throws himself onto Harrowlena and Arcanna, wings wide, as he blocks them from what I've summoned.

"*Hijo de puta!*" The familiar voice pulls the white light back until once more it's dimly light in the bedroom. "I should have known it was you brother."

I close my eyes briefly before allowing them to re-open and land on my younger brother. "Hello Luz."

He narrows his eyes as he dusts his dark shirt off and crosses his arms over his chest. His double nose piercing glitters silver in the light of the room. His body is still slimmer than mine, but he's bulked up with muscle now and freshly inked tattoos crawl over any exposed piece of flesh I can see.

He pushes his hand through his already perfectly slicked back dark hair before smiling wickedly. "To what do I owe this summoning?" Silver flashes on his tongue as he asks.

"I need your help." I say through clenched teeth.

He lets out a barking laugh, dramatically doubling over. "Oh that's rich coming from you. You've got to be fucking kidding me."

Jackson steps forward so he's in view of my brother now, his back rigid as he looks between the two of us. "What is going on?"

Luz looks at me with smug satisfaction, "Who is the delectable creature you have to play with." His eyes travel over Jackson, his bare chest still on display, before they widen. "He smells of you." When his eyes cast around the room landing on Arcanna he makes a noise of understanding. "Ah, god of death cannot keep one from dying. You need a god of life to pull her blood back."

"Yes." I grind out. "I need you to save her."

"Why would I?" He asks with his typical cocky arrogance. "What do you have to offer me?"

"Please." The broken sound of Harrowlena's voice makes my brother whip around, his eyes going wide as they roam over her, head to toe. "You must save her." she begs, hands in prayer like fashion.

"Ah such a beautiful ángel caído" He purrs. She doesn't

move as he walks towards her, like a cat stalking his prey he moves slow and with purpose until he's invaded her personal space. "What will you give if I save her?"

"Anything!" Jackson says before Harrowlena can utter a word, or I can stop him.

Luz lights up with a smile as he turns and looks at Jax. "Alright King, you have a deal."

"No," I growl. "No deals with them, this isn't up for debate."

He smirks and shrugs, "then she dies. Already she has so little life left in her. Tick tock big brother, times wasting for her." He looks back to Harrowlena whose eyes are wide as they flit between all of us. "I won't ask for much, just a little visit home. Come see mami and papi."

"Done." Jackson says earning a hiss from me.

"Not done," I say. "I'm not bargaining with you Luz; you'll do this for me because I command it."

His laugh bounces off the walls as he throws his head back. "I don't take commands from you; you lost that right long ago." He slips past Harrowlena and plants himself in a seat as he kicks his legs up on the bed Arcanna's uncon-scious form is currently on. I shake my head, defeat settling in my bones as my grip slips on Arcanna's soul. For them it is a small sacrifice, it's easy to think of going home. For me it is the end of life as I know it currently. Luz's grin shows he knows exactly what he's doing in asking this of me. He raises an eyebrow, waiting for me to confirm what he already knows.

"Fine. But these three will leave unharmed when it's said and done. Do you understand?" I spit out.

Luz holds his hand to his heart, "on my honor."

"You have no fucking honor," I scoff. "Now heal her."

A brief flash of hurt moves over his face like a wave cresting against the shore before it pulls away and I see nothing but the cocky asshole my parents have created. For just a moment I feel guilt for my part in everything but I shove it aside.

"You wound me to insinuate I have no honor." He pushes to a stand with a clap of his hands. "But no matter, I'm a man of my word and the deal is done. Let's rescue your little plaything."

I nod and release the soul I was gripping allowing it to drift, barely tethered to her body now. Luz looks at Arcanna with the same interest he had in Jackson before looking at me and giving me a wink. It's enough of a gesture to have me leaving the room before I try to smash his head into the wall.

"Dios! Wait!" Jackson yells after me. I don't stop at his calls, my legs pushing harder to get away from him. When he grips my shoulder to spin me, I launch myself out of his hold and shove him back forcefully. His eyes widen and his mouth parts in surprise.

"Fuck," I groan. "FUCK!" My fist lashes out and punches through the wall nearest to us, the drywall piercing the skin of my knuckles. I rage against the well of dark magic moving through my veins like black tar, gobbling up every ounce of light I managed to put into myself. My world starts to shrink and all I can think of is the leash that'll be tethered to me if I step foot back home.

"Sir?" Jackson's voice has me blinking rapidly to clear the rage filled haze that had settled over my vision. His face swims into view as he slowly turns me towards him, taking my injured knuckles into his hand with a gentle touch. "It's okay." He whispers.

I let my forehead drift to his and breathe in his scent to ground myself again. After a few, long and deep breaths that fill my lungs to capacity I step back from him once more. "You never should have agreed to us going back."

He crosses his arms and frowns. "And you should have told me you have a brother."

"I had no intention of you ever touching that part of my life." I sigh out. Jackson stumbles back dropping my hand in the process, the hurt in his eyes shining in the pool of silver. "You have no idea what you have agreed to, no fucking idea" I say.

He shakes his head as his shoulders drop. "I thought. . . ." he starts and stops. Shaking his head once more before turning his back to me. "I'll be with Arcanna." He mutters.

I desperately want to reach out to him, drag him back to my body but I stay put. Still angry at him but now angrier at myself for all the secrets I've kept from him.

TWENTY

Harrowlena

The man in front of me holds my attention in a terri-fying way. His dark hair slicked back shines under the light that plays over the various piercings he has in his face. His eyes are the color of the sky at sunset, a deep reddish purple. And when they land on me it feels as though they suck the oxygen directly from my lungs. He is not of this world, every fiber in my body screams it at me. My heart stutters at the reality that I am surrounded by gods.

He cocks his head, assessing me, dragging in a deep breath before a sneer moves over his face. "You have someone tethered to you."

I frown, "what are you talking about?"

His gaze sends chills down my spine, "you should get better at lying little goddess. Not everyone is as dense as my brother and his. . . people."

I force myself to stand tall against his continued watchful eye. But inside? My stomach drops out towards my feet and my throat constricts, as though every lie I've told is threatening to choke me now. He smirks at my struggle that is so clearly played out on my face as sweat starts to bead against my temple.

He invades my space, nose pressing into my neck before I feel the tiniest swipe of his tongue. "You could be your own master you know," he whispers against my skin forcing shivers to erupt over me. "The one who holds your leash would have no sway over you. You could be a gods damn empress if you chose to."

"I. . . I don't know what you mean." The words stumble from me, tripping over themselves as I try to keep my heart rate calm and my body still. He pulls back and shakes his head with a look akin to disgust as he steps back and moves towards Arcanna. "What are you doing?" I ask in a soft voice.

Luz turns and looks at me, "I'm a god of life. I'm doing what I do best. Healing." He says it sarcastically, as though he resent his powers. "Someday maybe you'll let me heal you. . . Should you ever get tired of your master that is."

"I have no master." Even to my ears it sounds like a lie as the words stumble from me.

He smiles at me as if he sees it, "run along," he coos. My body stays frozen, not wanting to leave him. The feeling confusing and foreign given the threats he's laid out and the fact that he's a stranger. As if sensing my hesitation, he moves towards me, invading my space and dragging his nose up my neck. "Have no fear. I'll be seeing you again soon."

Arousal blooms in me and I stumble backwards. Fleeing from the room, my own guilt running right alongside me. My body meets resistance as I shoulder check Jackson, wobbling slightly as I catch myself on the wall. I don't stop, don't apologize, I focus on getting to my room and locking myself in.

Arcanna

(Recover- Ruelle)

My breathing feels constricted and ragged as I struggle to regain consciousness once more, my blood moves through my body like molasses and my skin feels warm against the cool air. My eyes fight hard against opening, preferring the calming nature of the dark but something deep within pulls me forward against my will and my eyes manage to crack open.

The room is dimly lit now, the sheets clean of my blood, and my body is wrapped in a cool blanket. My previously injured leg is propped up on pillows with a bandage tight around my thigh. I lift my upper body onto my forearms and brace for pain, but my leg feels. . . fine. Maybe a little tender but nothing compared to the agony that I had experienced before.

"My brother paid a large price to save you." The dark voice startles me and my eyes swing towards its owner.

"Who the fuck are you?" I ask. My teeth grind down as I reach for my magic, for anything, to protect me against this unknown person.

He smiles, the gesture doing little to put me at ease. "Someone who saved your life."

"You'll excuse me if that provides little comfort at this point."

The man laughs and shakes his head, "leave it to my brother to have a mate like you." He looks at me once his laughter has subsided, cocking his head to the side. "He needs someone like you."

I blink rapidly at his words, opening my mouth to question him when the door swings wide and Jackson's scent invades the room. "Arcanna, you're awake!" He rushes to me, hair disheveled and wet and dark circles under his eyes.

He leans in, gathering me into his arms and his warmth leeches into my body.

He pulls back, no doubt feeling me tense the longer he holds me and glances to the stranger. "Thank you," he says quietly. "I'm in your debt."

The stranger shoves his hands in his pockets as he heads towards the open door that Jackson just walked through, whistling a haunting tune as he does. When he gets to the door he turns and offers up a smile that sends chills down my spine before nodding and vanishing from the room in a blink.

"Who the fuck was that?" I finally manage to ask.

Jax looks back to me with those silver eyes that made me fall in love so long ago, "that was Dios's brother, apparently." He shoves his hands through his hair in frustration.

I cock my eyebrow, "trouble in paradise?" Even as the words leave my mouth, I feel bad for saying them. My tone is sarcastic at best and venomous at worse. But truth be told I'm exhausted. Exhausted from the anger and lust and loneliness.

He shakes his head, not rising to the bait of the argument I'm clearly trying to cause and moves towards the side of the bed. The calming nature of his scent invades my space and sends shivers cascading down my spine as he allows his hands to trace over my body.

"Fuck I was so scared. . ." He mumbles, more to himself than to me. When he gets to my leg his finger tips graze the top of my bare thigh and I feel the first tingle of arousal seep into my core. "I felt it you know, the bond? You let it drift open when you were hurt. It's how I found you."

My mouth opens and closes multiple times, no words coming to defend myself or deny the statement. Said bond reaches for him, lazily and filled with need. His nostrils flare and eyes shoot up to my own. Every word that needs to be said trapped between us in that hard gaze, every emotion, every memory. All of it sitting in that small space and on top of it the scent of my need.

He goes to open his mouth, and I hold my hand up, "don't Jackson." I say quietly. "Just please don't." The well within me threatens to spill over and every emotion I've kept contained tries to invade my heart.

His face softens with understanding but still he speaks. "I made so many mistakes in my life but my biggest was not hunting you to the ends of the earth when you left. Not ripping that forest apart and dragging you back home. I never should have allowed you to drive me away. So now? Now you aren't getting rid of me wicked girl, I'll hunt you from here to the forest and should those fucking trees deny me I'll burn them root to leaf until they give you back."

My nostrils flare as my body wages war against itself. Half of me wanting to rip him apart and the other wanting to fuck him. The close proximity has my head spinning from his scent forcing all rational thoughts to flee. "Fuck you, Jackson." I say quietly. "Fuck you for all of it and fuck my own gods damn heart for still fucking wanting you."

Despite my injuries I launch myself forward and claim his mouth. I pour my rage into the touch as my fingers find his hair and my nails dig into his scalp and I bite down on his lower lip until I taste his blood. His tongue sweeps into my mouth claiming me while his hands find my face to hold me to him. We get lost in the taste of each other, the feel of it all, and he takes every punishment I throw at him in that kiss.

He manages to untangle himself and begins kissing down my neck. "Fuck Arcanna." He moans out between them. "Take everything you want. I'm yours. Always yours."

The words are a cold bucket of water on my overheated

body and for a moment I want to scream at him and ask why he needed to open his fucking mouth. I pull back and lock eyes with him, "You've never fucking been mine."

Jackson

I see the moment I've lost Arcanna. Her eyes going distant and cold as she pushes herself as far back as she can on the fluffy pillows, I don't miss the wince she makes. The bottom of her lip is painted with blood, when I sweep my tongue out I'm greeted with the metallic taste. I want to go back to kissing so hard that we don't realize we are bleeding, I want to slide my cock home inside her and feel the rightness of that belonging but she has no interest in that now.

"You've never belonged to me, Jackson. That's why this was never going to work. Does your fiancé know I'm here? Does she know you are warming your bed with Dios?" She lets out an unhinged laugh, hands pushing through her messy hair. "Fuck you are in bed with an *actual* god, engaged to a *queen* and here I am lusting after the taste of your blood and the feel of your hands." She shakes her head.

I shake my head, gripping her chin to force her gaze up on me, "Rhea and I aren't engaged. I waited, I waited for you to come home so I could tell you everything, apologize, beg for forgiveness but you never came. Why?"

"I TRIED!" Her voice elevates in the room, heat starting to prickle my skin as if her rage is warming the air. "I tried to come find you despite you leaving me alone in that club! Fucking Nyx took pity on me and gave me his jacket so I could wipe off the cum you left dripping down me. And still I fucking tried to find you. YOU DIDN'T WANT ME!" I watch as she pushes herself further from me and backwards off the bed until she's limping to the wall and leaning against it.

"You never came to me." I say again. "It's not like you didn't know where I slept. Christ you've been sneaking into my room our whole lives!"

She laughs, shoving her hands through her hair. "You've got to be fucking kidding me! This is bullshit Jackson."

I push to a stand now, taking a step towards her, confused. "I have no idea what you are talking about."She looks at me, truly looks at me as if it never occurred to her that maybe I was missing part of the story. But her mouth stays shut, stubbornly so.

"I fucked up, I should never have left you in that club." I state bluntly trying to break the silence. "I panicked when I realized. . ." I pause knowing that once I go down this path I can't backtrack. Once I admit to knowing exactly what I started, what she is to me.

Tears start to pepper her eyes. "I looked it up, you know. That type of bond. It hadn't been recorded in centuries. Took me forever to find the information, I had to hunt through so much shit." She lets out another bitter laugh. "In the end I was nothing more than a place to warm your dick." The way her voice cracks and the tears start to spill over breaks me apart.

(Arcade feat. FLETCHER- Duncan Laurence)

Words stall in my throat, my tongue heavy and mouth locked so tight it feels like I have Harrow's mask on. A thousand things are trapped within begging to be brought out but still, I'm frozen. Caught in between freeze and fight. Desperate to be understood but terrified of what that could open. Terrified of the vulnerability and the potential for it to go sideways so very quickly. My pulse picks up, every muscle needing to flee while simultaneously unable to bear the thought of being alone.

Touch me. Hold me. I need to know you still want me. I love you, I always have and always will.

The words are there. On the edge of my tongue, right behind my teeth. Desperation has me trying to communicate through my eyes, praying that she notices I'm drowning right now. Because that's what this feels like, being pulled under by the crushing weight of the ocean. The closer I get to the bottom the harder it is to open my mouth.

Say something. You can do this. It's not hard, all you have to do is start. Start anywhere.

I'm begging whatever gods are willing to listen, or maybe I'm begging myself. Either way, I make promises that I have no business making to deities just so I can open my mouth and let it all out. My head is so fucking loud.

It's moments like this where I see the appeal of what Shadow used to do. I can understand why he would escape to the blade or the joint. If it makes this feeling better, why wouldn't you? If it allows the pressure to release. . .

Desperation claws at me. A living force that is about to rip through my chest. And gods do I want it, I want to look down and see the gaping hole, so I know that this torture is over. This silent battle that isn't silent at all. It's a maelstrom of emotions and words that would make my life so much easier if I could just get them out.

Something tells me I'm alone, that she's somehow managed to flee the room despite her injury. Left me. Just like I deserved after everything that I did to her. I didn't deserve her forgiveness then and I certainly don't now.

Sadness creeps in around the edges as I allow myself to get dragged under, to get lost in the poisonous thoughts that now go along with my imaginary gag order. Those oh-so-horrific thoughts tell me I'm not worth the trouble, that love is a fictional aspiration that never actually existed. And even if it did exist, it wouldn't be something I deserved. With everything that's happened maybe this is a fitting punishment. To suffocate under the weight of it all.

My fingers dig into my palms, the nails cutting half-moon shapes. Not even tapping is working to calm my mind down.

Nothing is working. I'm going to die like this.

The familiar constriction of my chest pulls the air from my lungs and sends shooting pain down my arms. My rational mind knows what this is, but it can't save me from this spiral I've already been thrown down against my will. Because now I'm certain I'm going to die. The words that are lodged in me have cut my air supply off and my heart is about to burst from my chest. All around me, the world starts to fade to black. Spots dancing in front of my eyes as my vision goes fuzzy. I stumble, dropping to my knees hard enough that I'm sure I'd be concerned if I wasn't already certain this is the end.

My fingers move on their own volition, clawing at my t-shirt that now has turned into a noose around my neck. Desperate to rip it away, to ease the breathlessness I'm experiencing. A landslide of exhaustion bowls me over until I'm flat on my stomach, face pressed into the carpet, the feeling not helping my ability to breathe. In the distance, I think I hear someone saying my name but I convince myself it's an illusion. After all, no one is going to come help me.

I let my mind start saying goodbye. My thoughts turning to my mates and my hope for what will transpire after I die here.

I hope Dios and Arcanna take care of each other. Fuck, I hope Harrow finds some peace and happiness in this life now that she's free. At least I'll see Ava now, I don't have to be alone in the afterlife.

There is some peace in the surrender. In knowing at least I'll see my sister again, and in death, I can't suffer from this right? No one has ever had a panic attack or crippling anxiety in The Forest.

Surely that would be written somewhere, or someone would have told me, being the King and all that feels like important knowledge.

A cool touch drags me into some awareness, the room starts to come into focus as I'm rolled onto my back. Blurred faces move into my line of sight. The scent of sandalwood floating over me followed by leather. Scents that pull me back from the edge, that cradle me, force my breathing to even out so I can enjoy them.

"That's it, *mi cielo.* Just breathe for us. Focus on that." The voice moves over me like silk, wrapping me up in comfort that I worry I don't deserve.

The familiar pull of a headache sharpens my reality. Bringing me back down and reminding me what just happened.

A panic attack.

I had a panic attack while talking to Arcanna. While trying to plead my case for forgiveness.

TWENTY-ONE

Arcanna

Nothing could prepare me for seeing Jackson spiral that quick, even knowing him for years this was a different level. One minute we were fighting, the next a switch flipped, and he was gone, not seeing me or the room, only his demons. It had been so gods damn long since he had a panic attack in my presence, and even then, it had never been this bad.

My leg screams as I limp from the room as quickly as I can to find Dios, desperate for help. My body waivers and sweat beads across my forehead, "Dios!" I scream. "Dios! Please!" My words break apart. Tears well as I grit my teeth against the agony ripping through my leg. My body shakes with the exertion and there is a small voice telling me to stop, to take a break.

I used to be the one who helped him, and now he is like this because of me. I can't leave him alone this long. Fuck fuck fuck, he's going to think I abandoned him, again, just like that night.

I allow myself to take one quick moment against the wall, my weight settled against it and eyes closed before I shove off and drag my uselessly healing appendage behind me. I make it around a corner as my vision waivers and my body starts to fall.

Warm hands grab me before I hit the carpet, propping me up against the wall. The smell of bergamot floating through the air.

Dios.

"*Segadora?*" He asks with concern as one warm hand frames my face.

My own panic grips me as I lean into his body, "It's Jax." I pant. Words faltering as I try to indicate to follow me.

Grabbing my neck Dios drags my gaze to his own, "breathe, *mi segadora*. Breathe." His touch and voice pull me inward focusing on my rapidly beating heart until I can slow it all down. "You're going to hurt yourself again. What's wrong?"

Dios rubs soothing circles along my back until I can choke out the words. "He's having a panic attack, I think."

Dios doesn't respond, instead sweeping me into his arms and carrying me bridal style back towards the room I had been in. I keep focusing on steadying my breathing, trying to absorb how calm Dios is. Dragging his rich scent into my nostrils as I tuck my head against his shoulder.

I see why Jax loves him. And I can see how easy it would be for me to love them all.

The thought rattles around in my brain as we push through the door once more and my body is being placed on the bed. Dios drops down to the floor pulling Jax into him and whispering. Those silver eyes are unseeing as Dios continues to speak calming words. I nibble at my thumb, "it's never taken him this long to come out of one before."

Dios continues to stroke Jax's hair, "He's not in a good place, between the fight and almost losing you I would imagine things were brought to the surface that are hard for him to swallow back down." I wince as I look up at them, but the judgment I expect to see reflected back at me isn't there. Only a level of understanding that I did not think he was capable of. "He needs you, *segadora,* and having you walk away broke him maybe as much as it broke you."

My arms wrap around my midsection, "that's not fair." I whisper. "He was the one who left me in that club."

"And you left him." Dios shakes his head. "You two are so similar."

A small gasp from Jax cuts the conversation off.

"There you are, *mi cielo.*" Dios purrs while offering a soft smile. He helps Jax sit up slowly, "keep breathing. Focus on that." Jax falls into the command easily.

Closing my eyes I do something I've been consciously avoiding. I let the bond open up between Jax and I. The one that almost killed me when I fled from the palace and made my home in those woods. Agony so intense and blinding rips through me, dwarfing my physical pain as it pulls a whimper from me.

He's felt this. The whole time.

Jax's eyes shoot to mine as he feels me against the bond, and they widen when they realize I'm letting myself feel *everything.* The question of what happened between us floating in those silver eyes.

I grip my side, nails digging into my flesh as I think of that night. The way I stumbled into his house, angry but also content knowing that once we had this fight, we would be together. Neither of us would run. It would be okay. "You're telling me that you didn't send your mother to talk to me that night? Didn't send Oisin?"

"What the fuck?" He growls. "You know me better than that, you know I'd never do that."

"I also thought you'd never leave me in a night club

after fucking me," I say, sinking to my knees. "So, I was second guessing everything that night."

"What did she say," Dios asks with a deadly quiet voice. "His mother, what did she say?"

I glance between them, Jackson's eyes still hazy from the panic and Dios looking furious. I let out a sigh the night's memories hitting me as I tell them what happened.

Rage like I've never known before is the only thing keeping me upright. Otherwise, I would have crumpled into a sobbing mess after Jackson left me. I shake my head at the audacity he had to fuck me against that wall and then flee.

And yet you are still running to him.

"Shut up." I growl at myself.

My bare feet carry me up the pathway to the palace. The same pathway I've used most my life to invade Jax's space. My body knows it well and I could traverse it with my eyes shut at this point. It's why I'm not paying attention and find myself slamming into another body, stumbling backwards, and hitting the ground hard.

"See, just like Jackson said." Oisin's voice has a nasty tone to it, degrading and condescending. As I look up I spy the queen next to him, the two regarding me like a piece of trash. "Bringing herself in through the backdoor like the common street whore she is."

I push to a stand, brushing myself off. "What can I do for you your majesty?" I ask the queen. Ignoring Oisin's horrid words and the unease starting to take up residence in my gut.

She says nothing, eyes glancing at the runes that showed up the moment Jackson fucked me. "I pity you my dear. I understand what it's like to fall for a man who will never love you in return. But forcing a bond. . . that's just abhorrent."

I rear back as though I've been slapped. "I didn't force anything what are you talking about?!"

"Lies." Oisin hisses. "Jackson told us everything!"

My mind whirls and struggles to catch up with itself. The words not making sense.

The queen tuts, "Jackson has asked we give you the position of Lady of Souls. Effective immediately."

"What?" I manage to whisper out. "Let me talk to Jackson, this has been a misunderstand." I plea as my heart starts to splinter. Everything in me breaking apart.

"No," Oisin growls. "You will not be speaking with him. Take the handout and fucking leave."

My knees buckle as I drop to the ground in front of the queen, "just let me speak with him. Let me hear it from him and if it's all a mistake, I'll leave." My body screams, the bond we had started refusing to allow the idea of leaving him become reality.

"You have two options here Arcanna." The queen says, stepping into my line of sight. "One, you can give yourself over to the position of Lady of Souls. Leave this place and never speak to my son again. You'll be allowed to live happily and in peace until The Forest is done with you."

I almost scoff at her description of living in peace. Because without my bonded? There would be no peace. I look between her and Oisin, confusion painting my face. "What are you doing here?"

He tilts his head, "Out for a walk with my future mother-in-law."

Laughter bubbles up in my throat for a moment before the reality crashes into me. Jackson isn't engaged to him but he is engaged. . .

"Judging by the look on your face you remembered Jackson is indeed engaged and not to you." The queen drawls cruelly. "Simply put my dear, you tried to trap him into a marriage and that simply will not do."

My cheeks heat at the statement. "I'm not leaving here." I say despite it all. "Not without him talking to me."

The queen tsks. "I think you will when you hear the only other option." My face pales as she leans in closer to me. "Jackson isn't the only royal here; I don't need him. It would be all too easy for him to have an unfortunate accident, what with all the street racing he does it's only a matter of time before something catastrophic happens."

I rear backwards. "You're threatening to kill your own son?"

Her red painted lips lift into a wicked smile, "I have two children. Ava's future husband is more agreeable than my son anyway." My world tilts on its axis listening.

"I'll tell everyone." I whisper.

Her laugh fills my head, "It's your word against mine. Who will they believe? A used-up whore or the queen and her son in law?"

Nausea pools in my gut and bile rises as I look at the two in front of me. Those words turning to lead. "What do you get out of this?"

Oisin chuckles, "everything. I get everything."

Jackson

For a moment no one says anything at Arcanna's admission. The room allowing it to sit with us, heavy and oppressive.

"You thought. . ." I start. "You thought I didn't want this?" I gesture between us. "That you forced me into this?"

She flushes and her eyes track downward to the carpet beneath us. "Is it so hard to believe? You left me there and then suddenly Oisin and your mother appear."

I shake my head as Dios mutters a curse. I push against the hold Dios has on me and launch forward, gripping her face between my hands. "I wanted you more than life itself. You are all I wanted. I went and called things off with Rhea immediately. I wanted a life with you."

She lets out a soft whimper and I slam my mouth into hers. All the words that I want or need to say lay jumbled on my tongue and are poured into that kiss. A labyrinth of apologies and condemnation alike twist and weave through me. The very idea that she fled thinking that I didn't want her, that she believed my mother, sends rage through me that has me moving a hand to her hair and tugging it hard.

When I rip my mouth free of hers, we are both panting and her pupils are blown wide. My forehead braces to hers, "I'm so mad that you even believed them."

"She threatened to kill you!" Arcanna counters. "Even if I didn't believe her, I would never have risked your life."

I pull back slightly, our breath still heaving before she dives back into the kiss cutting off our verbal communication and allowing our bodies to do it for us.

Arcanna

(Madness- Ruelle)

Our hands collide as I move to rip his shirt free of his body and he moves to rip my own clothes off. We somehow manage to free each other, despite our frantic movements, and for a moment we both pause, drinking in each other's naked forms. Jax has grown up, filled out, his golden skin covering harden muscle. My mouth waters at the sight of him, his own eyes mirroring my hunger.

I suck my bottom lip in to my teeth biting hard and the movement breaks the standoff.

Jackson launches himself at me, caging my body with his own as his mouth devours the moans now falling from me. His hands grip me hard enough I know I'll bruise. The intensity of it has me squirming under him and pressing myself up into his hard cock now trapped between our bodies.

He pulls from my mouth and bites down on my neck, hard and punishing. As if he understood at that moment, I needed to feel that small measure of pain.

"Tell me I can take you, wicked girl. Let me fucking worship you like the goddess you are." He begs as he keeps kissing down until he's at my ample chest. My nipples tighten against the gold barbells. His eyes go feral as he eyes the glittering piercings. "Tell me I can suck on these perfect tits."

My head falls back, and I moan out, yes, my core dripping.

"Fuckkk, my wicked, wicked girl." He moans before dropping his mouth to my breast and sucking that barbell in hard. I let out a scream, the feeling so overwhelming that my hand comes up and digs into his thick hair pulling hard. He doesn't stop; his body just pushes me into the soft bedding beneath me.

We are in a battle of wills right now, each letting out all our feelings that we have kept pent up for too long. My magic flares out threatening to burn the gods damn house down around us. Flames flicker in my vision, the ground below us rumbling with the pressure it's taking to hold back. It surprises even me, that my magic can flare this much given what I just went through, but Jackson only groans and urges me on as he presses two fingers to the entrance of my dripping cunt.

I spread my good leg wider to give him access. My back arches up off the bed as he penetrates me, slowly pumping in and out. I'm too lost in the ecstasy of it all to notice he's unlatched from my breast until I feel the first swipe of his tongue against my clit. I cry out and stars explode around us as I arch my hips up to meet his thrusts.

"Oh fuck, yes oh gods. You feel so fucking good." I cry out. "Don't stop, please don't stop." I beg as my fingers grip his hair hard. He groans and continues to eat my pussy like it's his last meal.

"You both are making me hungry." Dios's voice is the last thing I hear as I topple over the edge and my orgasm rushes through me. My eyes lock with his as I cum on Jax's fingers and face. The scenario strangely erotic.

He drags those two silver piercings into his mouth one by one as he holds my gaze. Only releasing them when I finally push Jackson's head away from the oversensitive feel.

"*Mi cielo.*" Dios leans forward as Jax turns to look at him. He beckons the King forward with two fingers and Jackson obeys. Dropping to the ground, crawling over to him. Dios leans in and licks the arousal I left on Jax clean from his lips before grabbing the two fingers that had been inside me to his mouth and sucking. From behind I can see the tension in Jax's shoulders as he holds perfectly still and allows Dios to clean him.

Dios rases his eyes back to me as Jackson's fingers finally pop free of his mouth. "You taste divine on him." He practically purrs. Shivers erupt down my spine and the half-completed bond between Jax and I drips with arousal.

Jax turns to look at me slowly, his silver eyes on fire with hunger as he makes his way back to the bed I'm still reclined on. His hard cock stands out from his body, the tip has a bead of precum on it that he swipes with his thumb and drags down his shaft as he strokes himself in front of me.

"Tell me you want this." He begs. "Tell me you want me inside you." I spread my legs wider and nod, unable to form the proper words as I'm hit with all the feelings his end of the bond holds. He grins, the kind that I haven't seen since we were kids and raises his eyebrow in challenge. "I need your words wicked girl."

Dios moves up behind Jackson and I watch his tattooed hands trace his abdominal muscles before he plants a soft kiss to his neck. "Yes." I finally manage to say. My voice feels quiet in the large room as my eyes stay glued to the two of them.

Jackson moves so his body is positioned over mine. His thick cock notched at my entrance.

Dios, however, steps back from us and settles into the adjacent to the bed. His eyes watching where our bodies are about to join. "Go slow *mi cielo*." He commands. "Make her feel every single inch of that beautiful cock."

Jackson's cock stretches me out slowly as he pushes in. I arch my back upward at the feel, the pleasure over taking me as I'm overwhelmed by the bond that flares to life. The magic desperate to complete. When he's fully inside he pauses and glances to Dios for further instruction. Words still fail me, but I arch my hips up in a silent plea to get him to move. He groans at the feeling and a large smile spreads across my face as I do it again.

"How does she feel?" Dios asks.

"Like she was sent from the gods themselves" He moans as his own hips start to move.

I feel drunk on his cock as I meet each of his thrusts with my own and race towards my goal to feel him cum inside me. An animalistic part of my brain demanding he fill me up. Mark me. Make me his.

I grip his shoulders hard enough that my nails dig into his skin as I press my ankle against his ass to keep him deep within me. "Need to feel you." I pant out. "Need you to fill me."

"Patience. I've spent too long without your pussy. I'm not rushing this." He chuckles darkly.

My nostrils flare in frustration and the sound that comes from my lips is an embarrassing mewl. He moves slow, allowing himself to drag fully out and push back in with long, measured thrusts until tears are pouring down my face and everything in me is screaming and begging.

"Harder!" I cry in a pathetic demand.

Dios huffs out a chuckle. "Make her remember your cock for the rest of the day, *mi cielo*." His restraint seems to snap at the command of Dios. His hips piston into me harder as he holds my legs in a punishing grip spreading me wide so he can see the mess he is making of me.

"I can't hold on." I cry two seconds before my pussy starts to milk his cock. The orgasm sends me reeling through space, magic exploding from me as my body releases. Jackson stiffens above me, and I feel his cock start to pulse and the warm feeling of his cum splashes deep within. His cries echo my own and his breathing fills the air around me. I can feel that bond reaching for him, yearning to complete.

Jackson's eyes glow above me, the question in his eyes clear.

And for a moment I want to say yes, want to allow the bond to form completely. But I can't. Not yet.

I give a subtle shake of my head, tamping the bond down.

Dios

My cock rages against my pants as I watch the two. The magic of the bond fills the room as the two come apart before it's abruptly cut off. Arcanna glances away, cheeks still red, as Jackson shakes his head and pulls free of her. He drags her back into his embrace, their bodies pressed close but Arcanna keeps her back to him as she curls inward, sleep claiming her.

I can see the distress in his face. The hurt flaring up

from her refusal to complete the bond. "Give her time," I say softly to Jackson. "She'll come around."

He doesn't look like he believes me but curls around her and lets his eyes close. I allow myself to back away from them, edging towards the door to the hallway.

My abuela had a name for bonds like theirs, *guardián da alma*. The rarest of bonds. A *guardián de alma* exchanges fragments of the other's soul. During the time of the gods, it was how they bonded to one another when they found mates.

My wolf paces restlessly deep within, wanting to claim Arcanna for our own while my magic demands we claim Jackson. My two mates. Naked in bed and oh so tempting. The feeling is momentarily overpowering and my muscles strain as I hold myself back instead forcing myself to leave the room.

A growl vibrates through my chest in frustration, my dark powers pulsing out enough that cracks form in the walls around me before I'm able to regain control. Plaster sprinkles down from above. A small squeak pulls my gaze away from the destruction. Violet eyes look at me, wide as saucers and the long silver hair that frames them hangs messy around her shoulders.

"*Lo siento pequeña diosa.*" I take a small step towards her expecting her to flee, but she remains rooted to the spot. Her hands tuck her wild hair behind her ears. The movement flashes the healing wounds from the mask, drawing my eyes to them before I look back into her gaze.

She opens her mouth, shutting it again and closing her eyes tightly. A deep shuddering breath moves through her whole body before she goes to open to try again.

"I was looking for the kitchen." She finally manages. Her voice is a whisper on the wind, but she may as well have yelled it in the deathly quiet hallway. She takes a small step towards me. The explanation feels plausible but Arcanna's suspicions drift through me and I can't help but narrow my eyes for a brief moment before I decide to get to know our priestess a little better.

"Well let's go find you something to eat, *pequeña diosa*."

TWENTY-TWO

Harrowlena

For a moment I worry that Dios knows my secret, that his brother told him whatever he seemed to know. The way his mismatched eyes narrowed for a moment as though he did not believe my lie make my stomach drop out.

"Well let's go find you something to eat, *pequeña diosa.*" My breath leaves me in a giant sigh of relief and I offer up a small nod.

It had been risky coming out tonight, searching for answers. So fucking risky. Yet I still did it because the scent of Dios's brother seemed to haunt me, his voice a ghost that wouldn't let me rest.

Luz. . . just the thought of him sends shivers down my spine and awakens a strange space, deep inside, that has seemed dormant most my life. A pull that is battling against the leash that currently holds me. My skin feels too tight, my body almost on fire, and the paper he slipped me feels like lead in my pocket.

Look up the true history of the gods. Look up mate bonds. Educate yourself and should you have questions come find me. Do not trust the one who holds your leash.

"Just through here" Dios's voice pulls me from my thoughts as he steps in front of me pushing the door open. Light floods the space around us causing me to blink rapidly. The smell of bacon sits in the air, and I let out a low moan involuntarily, my mouth salivating. I used to love to eat and cook, before the mask. After it I tried to still love cooking but not being able to taste the food I made killed the joy in it.

Dios lets out a soft, dangerous, chuckle. "Come on. Sit. I'll make you food."

He points me to the other side of the granite countertop where three wooden barstools sit. The kitchen feels homey, with a small table that encourages an intimate setting next to a large window overlooking the beautiful lake. For a moment I can imagine them growing up here, I can imagine what a life that would be. A peaceful life, no more lies or hiding. No more pain. Just being with people who love each other. For another moment I picture Oisin and I here, happy and away from The Elders and The Order.

We could have been normal.

"Penny for your thoughts?" Dios asks. My eyes snap to his and I can't help but panic, just a bit, that he can see my failures. Can see all my faults I've tried to hide, and all the secrets that are currently shoved deep into the closet of my mind. He continues to watch me out of the corner of his eye as he cuts up various vegetables next to the stove.

Come on Harrow, say something. I urge myself as silence deepens in the kitchen.

Words fail to remove themselves from my tongue and instead when I open my mouth my body locks up, the muscle memory of what that mask did to me still so prominent. Whether my magic was infused with it or not, that mask punished me. The burning, acidic feeling of the iron being injected into my jaw still radiates through me like a ghost unwilling to rest in peace. The silence gets thicker, my heart pounding, my breathing feeling so loud I worry that Dios will notice.

You can do this. Just say something. Anything.

"What are you making?" I let out a whisper finally. My body is bracing for the pain on instinct. When it doesn't come, I relax.

"My *abuela* was convinced that there isn't anything that couldn't be solved by good food," he lets out a laugh but his tone is one of sadness and loss. "If she had it her way she would have marched into the middle of a war and demand both sides sit down to eat."

I cock my head. "You are sad."

He looks towards me, surprise on his face as if no one takes note of his emotions.

"I miss her." My stomach bottoms out at the implication. Death makes me squirm, having spent so much of my life near it.I hate to think of it. He goes back to adding spices to the pot he is currently browning veggies and meat within.

"That's nice you had someone you were that close to." I respond. He shrugs and nods as he continues to cook. My curiosity rages with my common sense as I think about the rest of his family.

He turns, as if sensing it, "my mother and father tried their best. But they had goals and ambitions of their own, so in the end we were nothing more than tools for them." His voice doesn't sound sad, per say, but resolute instead.

"And your brother?" I ask, my curiosity finally pushing through.

Anger seems to radiate from him causing me to shrink back. His whole body bracing as though he's holding back a tidal wave. "Luz is. . ." He growls before taking a deep breath and calming his emotions. "Luz is a product of our environment." I wait to see if he'll explain more but he only frowns as he looks at my stiff body before dropping his eyes to my curled fists and tense body.

I release my fists and let out a shuddering breath. "Sorry," I mutter. "I didn't mean to ask such a personal question."

He shakes his head, "It's okay, you have done nothing wrong. I just haven't talked about home in a very long time. It's a topic I generally avoid. And after having seen my brother today I'm feeling a little raw."

My cheeks burn with regret, leave it to me to bring up the depressing topics. When a plate appears in front me, I'm grateful for the distraction. The smell of onions and peppers drifting up towards my face. My eyes are greeted by a tortilla oozing with cheese, meat, and veggies.

"This was my favorite as a kid and the first thing I learned to cook. I still remember the first time me and my brother tried to make it without her, she was so pissed when she saw her beloved pan with the dinner burned to the bottom." The pride in his voice is unmistakable.

I tentatively bring the hot food to my mouth. Taking a small bite, I let out a loud moan as the flavors assault my tongue.

"Oh, goddess. This is the most amazing thing I've ever tasted." I say between bites, not caring that the cheese is burning my mouth. Dios watches intently as I devour every piece.

A small part of me knows this is a poor choice, eating this rich food after having been on a liquid diet for so long. But I can't seem to stop. I've nibbled on the bland bread and oatmeal that show up in my room daily, but the taste is so boring I can't bring myself to eat all of it. This however is the opposite of boring.

"Did you know that some witches use food as a way to

channel magic?" I'm not sure why I say it, but I want to share something with him while he watches me eat.

He shakes his head no, eyes still following my hand as I feed myself.

"It's an old magic, one long forgotten because most covens saw no use for it. My Nana, however, always told me about it. She warned me to never cook food for someone when you were in a bad place, that the energy you give to the food would transfer to someone else. It's why she always said love was the most important ingredient." My cheeks flame at how lame it sounds coming from me. Oisin always made fun of me when I said things like that so part of me braces for the same reaction.

Dios, however, looks at me intently. "She sounds like a very smart woman."

My eyes widen slightly at how genuine he sounds. "She... she was." I manage to get out.

He crosses his arms over his chest. "You must miss her a lot. It sounds like you both were very close before she was killed." He says casually.

My cheeks heat to the point of being uncomfortable and the food in my stomach turns sour at the words. Guilt weighs heavy on me alongside the fiery anger that I still have towards her, and my mother, for never giving me the ceremony. A sick, twisted part, blames them for being where I'm at today and yet anytime those thoughts come up I'm immediately sent into a shame spiral.

"Tell me Harrowlena, how exactly did you survive the massacre?"

The priestess freezes, face going white in response to my question. She bites down hard on her lower lip as her violet eyes dart around the room. As if she can find an escape from the question, from the conversation as a whole. When she comes up with no way out her eyes return to mine and I slowly lift my eyebrow. "How did you survive?" I ask again. "You were there, right?"

The quiet in the room is heavy. Almost to the point of discomfort as I stand and watch her struggle to find the words. Each passing minute of silence only confirms my suspicion of her.

"I had. . . left the forest for the first time." She finally says. "When I came back, I returned to the carnage."

"And The Order?" I push. Her nostrils flare and I sense the frustration building within in her. *Good. Get frustrated. Make a mistake and give me your secrets.*

"They rescued me. Brought me to their home. Without them I would be dead." She says it with the utmost conviction and with her head held high.

I would laugh if I didn't know how dangerous the cult mentality was. Instead, I shake my head sadly. "You never wondered why they were there that day? What they were doing?"

She shakes her head, the silver hair shifting so the scars show on her jaw. "They didn't do it." She practically growls. "He didn't do it."

"The Order killed your family. At the order of Oisin."

Raw flame seems to crawl up her body as the violet in her iris's practically glow. "You're lying. It was the royals who murdered everyone." She bites back.

This time I do laugh. "The royals would be dumb to kill their only source of magic. It makes no sense for them to have done it." Moving closer to her I crowd into her space. "I've been curious lately. About you and Oisin. And I wonder if you've ever asked yourself what *he* gained from all this."

TWENTY-THREE

Harrowlena

Try as I might the words Dios spills into reality make their way into my subconscious. They twist and turn and seem to seep into every memory and interaction I have with Oisin and The Order. And I hate it. Hate it because a portion of me, a very small, confused portion, knows that Dios speaks some truth. And even if it is only partially true, it's enough to make me want to throw up. I want to argue with him, tell him he's wrong but my mouth won't open. The words won't come.

"If they truly saved you, why did they cage you in the end?" He asks.

His voice is a bomb that's dropped into my body and for a moment all I can do is focus on breathing and not screaming. My throat tight and jaw tingling as that other side of me rises up in response to the chaos happening in my mind.

"Are we eating? I'm starving." Arcanna's voice has my body suddenly shooting upward as I startle, shutting off the magic I was about to lose control of. "It smells divine in here." She groans as she takes a deep breath. Standing in the doorway my eyes take in Jackson and Arcanna, her raven black hair lays in a rumpled mess atop her head.

"Oh my god did you make your abuela's quesadillas?" Jackson rushes forward and Arcanna follows quickly after, the two playfully shoving at each other to get to the stove. And oblivious to the tension they just walked into. Oblivious to the fact that I want to vomit all over the floor because my whole life feels like a giant fucking lie.

(Various Storms & Saints- Florence + the Machine)

Dios moves past Arcanna, who is currently eating shredded cheese from the bowl, towards Jax who leans against the countertop. I watch Dios applying a kiss on Jax's cheek before nuzzling into his neck in a tender gesture. My eyes dart to Arcanna, but she looks on lovingly, as if the sight of them fills her with joy. So much joy and love. The longer I'm in the kitchen with them the worse my skin crawls—the poisonous feelings threatening to choke the very life from me.

This. This is what love looks like between friends. Between mates.

And I realize I don't think I've ever seen it.

"You could have that you know?" Arcanna asks, her eyes sliding towards me and voice soft.

I blanch for a moment, "what?" Confused by her comment and worried I missed something crucial.

"Friendship." She smiles warmly, "You don't have to be alone anymore Harrow, you're free."

My mouth forms an O and a quiet puff of air comes out of my chest. She winks at me before directing her attention back to Jackson and Dios. "Someone better feed me soon." She yells playfully.

I watch their interactions for a moment longer before I quietly ease out of the kitchen. No one says anything but I can feel eyes on my back as I exit. The walk to my room feels like it takes a century and when I finally flip the lock on the door with my back pressed to the wood I break apart, my body sliding down as the world cracks apart. As my world cracks apart.

"I can't do this." I whisper into the empty room. "I can't fucking do this." I press my fist into my mouth to stifle the sobs that are now breaking through my heart. Burrowing my face into my arms.

"You are my everything, Lena. Forever and always."

"I love you. Promise me we'll always find our way back to each other." I beg.

He holds my face with his calloused hands. "I promise, Lena."

The sound of his voice meandering through my head forces my tears out faster until my body shakes with the exertion of holding myself together.

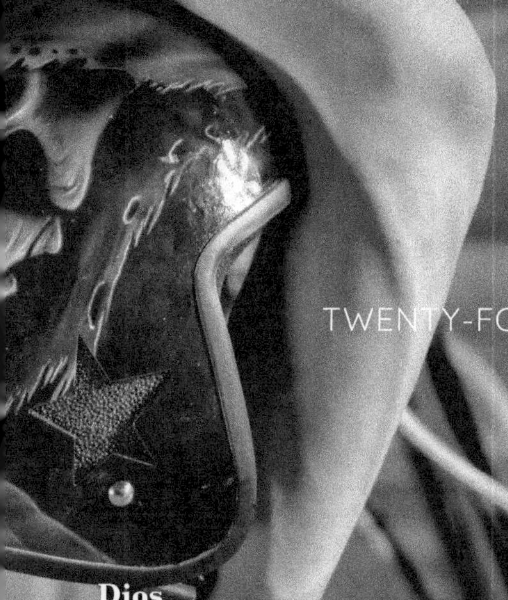

TWENTY-FOUR

Dios

We all watch Harrowlena flee. None of us making a move to follow.

"She's very confused." I say once I'm sure she's out of earshot. "In her eyes the royals killed her family and fellow priestesses."

"And she never questioned it? Even after spending time with me on the outside? They fucking kidnapped her! Put a mask on her! How could she still be loyal to them at all!" Jackson says with frustration.

"If she even escaped that time." I counter.

Jax frowns, "are you saying they let her go?"

I shrug. The thought had crossed my mind. Harrowlena would have been an excellent way to gain information. "If Oisin's goal was The Well the whole time, it would make sense to send her in. Because you would have given her the ceremony. Of course you would have."

"That would have been dumb, all it would have taken was me telling her the truth of it all and she'd have never gone back to them." He counters.

But Arcanna shakes her head, "The Order is good, and

Oisin even better, at manipulating. I don't think she would have believed anything coming from you, not at that time."

"And now?" He asks, mouth pulled down in a frown still. A hurricane of emotion swirling in his eyes.

"I think she's confused. I think we've given her information and showed her things that are a direct contradiction to everything she's been taught." I respond.

"How can she still think that given everything we've been through? We rescued her." Jackson counters.

"It's going to take a lot to get her to understand she's safe here," Arcanna says popping some cheese into her mouth. When she goes to grab another handful I snatch her wrist, my fingers closing around it. She glances at where we are connected and back up to me with a raised eyebrow.

"If you're hungry I'll feed you."

I watch her shudder and my cock responds instantly.

Jackson comes up behind her, hands starting to explore, dipping down across her chest close to the tops of her breasts. She lets out a sigh, her legs spreading a bit allowing her scent to wash over me. "What are you going to feed me?"

I chuckle, my lips finding her arm and tracing her veins. "Our cum."

Jackson lets out a groan, "come on. We aren't doing this in the kitchen." I let him lead us back out and into the sitting room. I release Arcanna's wrist and push her onto the couch before taking up residence on the deep red one opposite her.

Jackson stands behind the Reaper, and I watch as he dips down and starts to kiss against her bare skin under her ear. She bites down hard on her lip as his hands travel down her arms and back up, slow strokes up and down with his fingertips.

She reaches up behind and I watch her fingers thread

through his hair before she drags his mouth to hers. I lean forward as I watch the exchange, my body responding to the two of them. When she finally pulls away, she catches my eye first and raises her eyebrow.

An invitation.

My eyes snag on the outside, the gentle waves of the lake pushing against the shore line. Stripping my shirt off I move over to the large back door. Pushing it open, the warm air breezes inward carrying the fresh scent of the forest and lake with it. "Come on you two, let's go for a swim."

Jackson

Arcanna pushes to a stand and away from my embrace, following Dios outside. My own body close behind the two. My eyes snag on Dios's caramel skin in the sunshine as he pulls his pants off. His cock hangs between his legs, long and heavy despite not being hard. He raises an eyebrow at me before beckoning us towards him.

"If you need time alone with him it's okay." Arcanna whispers, her sandalwood scent mixing with the air around us. She grabs my hand giving it three quick squeezes.

"You haven't done that since we were kids." I respond, giving the same back. It was a thing we did when we wanted to give one another comfort but couldn't talk. "And I want you with us. Whatever is happening, it involves the three of us. You me and Dios. We belong together."

Her head drops to my shoulder for a moment. The two of us basking in the warm sun. Before she walks forward, stripping her clothes off, leaving a trail on the grass. My mouth dries up at the sight of her full body. Her thick thighs and ass making my dick jump to attention. When she turns, I catch a glimpse of her stomach, still toned but softer, no longer a six pack. Small stretch marks dance in the sunshine and I'm hit with a wave of sadness that I didn't get to see her grow into this woman.

I watch in rapture as she cautiously makes her way towards Dios, careful of her still healing leg. It reminds me how fast things have gone lately. He wraps his arms around her waist before dragging her towards the water.

Home. These two are my home. And I will destroy anyone who threatens that.

Following their lead, I strip down quickly and meander to the water's edge. The two still cling to each other as they lounge in the cool water. My cock gets hard as Arcanna pops her chest up and I can see her hardened nipples. Dios catches one of them in his mouth, sucking the barbell that adorns it into his mouth. She throws her head back, a low moan pulling from her.

(Do I wanna Know?- Hahlwg & Nicky MacKenzie)

I wade into the water until I'm able to catch Arcanna's mouth with my own, kissing her deep as Dios still worships her full breasts. Arcanna's hips thrust and when my hand pushes downward I feel Dios's fingers pumping in and out of her pussy.

"Do you think she can fit both our fingers?" Dios asks.

I hold back a laugh when I hear the desperate moan fill the air and I allow my own two thick digits to join Dios's one.

"Oh gods," she cries out. "Fuck this feels so damn good."

We play with her, bringing her to the edge and back over and over.

"I need someone inside me." She begs.

Dios catches my eye, and we meander back towards shore, my fingers pulling free of her tight heat along with Dios. "Sit down." He commands me.

I obey without question, my cock jutting out in front of me. He pushes Arcanna towards me, her thighs coming over on either side of me, lining up her entrance to the head of my dick. Without waiting for Dios, she slowly lowers herself, inch by inch onto me until I'm fully sheathed within.

"You two look beautiful together." Dios murmurs. I watch his eyes as he strokes himself up and down. I open my mouth in offering, tongue out waiting for a taste. "Such a good boy." He grins as he slides himself into my warm mouth.

Arcanna starts to tilt her hips in slow motion, her moans of pleasure echoing over the lake. "Touch my clit." She demands. I obey quickly, even as I gag on the thick length being pressed down my throat. The rightness of it all, the feel of her pussy gripping me, the taste of Dios on my tongue, settles into my chest.

The bond flares between us, desperate to complete, as though it knows the three of us should be together. It pulses forward, inching its way towards Arcanna and Dios, ready to join with them. Arcanna shoots me a look, her eyes glazed over with arousal but still the message is clear, she isn't ready.

Dios lets out a long groan, "Oh fuck, I'm going to cum." He grips my head and fucks himself down my throat. The salty explosion of his release pushes me over and my own orgasm starts to fill Arcanna, her walls fluttering around me as she screams out. I tamp down the disappointment and focus on the feeling of it all, enjoying what we have, but worried this might be all it ever is.

Harrow

The sounds of pleasure drift through my window, pulling me towards it like a lure. Looking out my eyes stumble on the three naked forms. I watch as they lose themselves in one another, fascinated almost. The way they seem to know what each other need. They can read the others body in a way no one has ever read mind. I stumble backwards from the window ashamed of myself for invading their privacy.

Anxiety claws at my throat as I practically choke on the all the lies I've told to get to where I am now, and all the lies I've seemingly been told. My breathing becomes ragged. My fists ball up, my dull nails digging so hard into my palms I know they'll leave marks.

Why? Why is this my life? Why did I have to be born into this role? I hate it, I hate what I'm harboring, I hate the questions they've put into my head and the loyalty I still feel. I'm swept up in a tornado of it all. The roaring in my ears deafening as I'm pummeled with the thoughts over and over again. I grip the sides of my head, pulling at my hair as if that will rip the noise away.

Dios's face swims in front of my own, like the beam of a lighthouse piercing the storm. My eyes lock on him as he grabs hold of my face. He's yelling something but I can't hear him over the roaring. I frown, shaking my head as if to tell him to speak up and that's when I realize the reason I can't hear him is my screams are echoing through the room.

Pushing free of him I slap my hands over my mouth, desperate to stop my magic. All around me, I can see cracks in the walls, floors, and ceiling. Glasses have shattered, and the patio doors are blown wide.

"Breathe." Dios repeats, holding his hands out to me, despite me attempting to scurry away from him. "Just breathe." From his ears I can see small amounts of blood trickling out, his fast-healing working wonders so he can hear me.

He creeps towards me, slowly, as if he doesn't want to startle me. When he is finally back in my space, and I'm not attempting to flee, he brings my hands away from my mouth gently, taking them into his calloused ones.

"There you are, *pequeña diosa*." He traces circles with his thumb on the back of my hand. The feeling comforting and caring.

"Dios?" Arcanna's voice echoes into the room. My gaze snaps away from Dios to Jackson and Arcanna standing just inside the door to my room. Jax has no shirt on, and his flannel pants hang low on his hips showing off the deep-v that's chiseled into his body. Arcanna is dressed in a long t-shirt that hangs off her shoulder and brushes the tops of her thighs.

When did they come inside? How long was I screaming for?

"It's fine, I'm fine," I try to say to them. But my voice comes out horse and weak.

"I don't think it's fine she just about blew half the house apart," Arcanna argues, I wince at her tone. "We need a fucking plan." Warm air blows into the room from the now shattered window, and the sounds of the lake water kissing the shore follow close behind.

Jackson must say something to her, a warning of sorts, but she growls at him. "No Jackson. I'm not backing down on this."

In a matter of moments, she drops down onto the bed next to Dios, Jackson remaining further back with his silver eyes watching us. "Harrow, we have to go to The Well, you need to let us do the ceremony. We can figure it out, I know we can. But you have to do this, we need Jackson to have his magic full."

My body tenses as the reality crashes in around me. Time is a luxury I do not have right now.

Arcanna scoops her hair up into a bun, the humidity from outside now flooding it making the air sticky. Her eyes stay on me, and I squirm under the attention. I hate how observant she is.

"The full moon is coming up." Jackson offers as he now joins the other two on the bed. Dios leans back, eyes still on me, dragging Jackson against him in a lover's embrace. His dark, tattooed hand splays across Jackson tan stomach, his fingers rubbing the smooth skin absently. A small smile plays across the King's face, every muscle in his body relaxed.

"Aren't you two mated?" I ask her, gesturing towards Jackson. "You two could do it alone couldn't you?" My throat burns as I speak. Not just from the screaming but from the betrayal it signals deep within my belly.

Arcanna wraps her arms around her mid-section before pushing up off the bed. Jackson follows her with his eyes before refocusing on me. "We haven't completed the bond yet. And even if we had that's not an option, with the magic flowing through her of The Forest she cannot help me."

"Why are you so resistant to this?" Dios asks, not unkindly but his voice is firm, and his eyes? His eyes say it all. He does not trust me. It makes me want to shrink back against the headboard even further.

"Shit."Arcanna mutters. It's the only warning we get before her body drops to the ground unconscious and I'm saved from answering the question.

TWENTY-FIVE

Jackson

"Fuck." I vault free of Dios and scoop Arcanna up from the floor. "Gods damn it wicked girl," I grumble as I place her on the bed. Dios moves to inspect her for injury right behind me.

"Oh my god what happened?!" In a panic Harrow moves towards Arcanna, worry etched over her face. Her hair is stuck to her neck in spots from sweat, and her cheeks are flushed red.

I shake my head, propping Arcanna up as comfortably as I can against the headboard. "She astral projected some-place, and if I had to guess it wasn't her choice." Harrow looks pale as she takes in Arcanna's form.

Astral projection is the second-rarest form of magic, realm walking being the rarest. She didn't acquire this until she became Lady of Souls, until she became the Reaper that she is now. She's changed so much since she left, and a part of me misses who she once was. For a moment I wish I could kill my mother; wish I could bring her back from the death the Harbinger gave her and destroy her all over again for putting the wedge between us.

"She'll be fine." Dios says. "Her soul is safe." His voice pulls me back into the moment. I glance over to my death god and offer a smile of thanks to him for the reassurance before I refocus on Harrow.

"Harrow, why are you so resistant to helping with this?" I ask with a tone of understanding. "You can tell us. Like I said, we could be your friends if you let us."

Her anxiety about the topic is off the charts and her face has turned pale as she glances between us all. "I just thought it would be better for all if Jackson got his magic from his mates, I mean you both are mates as well. . . why can't *you* help him?" She directs the last part at Dios. Her tone almost sharp and accusatory.

Dios scrubs his face with his hands. Exhaustion in the movement. I let out a long sigh. "We cannot decide on bonding." I finally say. "Dios does not think we should. I say fuck it we most definitely should."

"*Mi cielo.*" He huffs out in frustration with a hard glare at me. I only shrug.

Harrow frowns. "I don't understand." She glances between us with a furrowed brow.

Dios shakes his head, "we aren't talking about this. We are talking about why *you* won't help us."

While I know we need the answers from Harrow it still makes me recoil, the rejection and implication that he does not want me. Dios mutters a curse but I don't look at him, I keep myself trained on Harrow.

"I'm sorry I overstepped." She says softly, almost sadly. "I'll help. We can go to The Well. I misunderstood the situation."

I let out a relieved sigh anyway, "thank you Harrow."

I hear Dios push free of the room, muttering his own thanks as he escapes. I stare at the empty spot on the bed he occupied, my heart pulling me to follow him and confront him, put an end to this argument once and for all.

"You can go. I can sit with her." She says as she moves closer to the bed. "Really, I don't mind. I mean it is my fault we are in this mess." Watching Harrow I hesitate for a moment, something in me flashing with an ounce of distrust towards the priestess. I frown at the sensation, part of me trying to pushing it aside, while the other part refuses to leave my unconscious mate with someone I don't fully trust. With someone I know she doesn't even fully trust.

"It's okay," I respond. Settling in next to Arcanna. "I'll wait with her and find him after. You can go find a different room and get some sleep."

She hesitates for a moment before nodding and slinking off.

***

Dios

Standing outside I watch as the sky bleeds from purples to deep blue as night begins to take form. My arms brace on the wooden porch frame as I try and force myself to breathe through the onslaught of emotions today has brought up.

Two people.

One mated to my wolf one mated to my darkness.

It was already complicated being mates with Jax, our power, should it combine, would be unstoppable. But adding Arcanna as well? We would be targets for the rest of our lives, our children would be targets for their lives. It would be a never-ending battle with my own gods damn family to regain control of what I took from them.

I drag in a deep breath, the air filling my lungs to capacity before I blow it back out.

"Trouble in paradise big brother?" Luz's voice floats in just before I see his form appear out of the corner of my eye.

I groan, "go away Luz. I don't need you here."

He laughs, "too bad for you, you opened the door and now I'm here. Fuck I've missed that." I glance over to him as he leans against the balcony. His body holds tension despite the smile on his lips and relaxed expression on his face. At one time we looked so similar that people confused us for twins, but now? Now we are nothing alike. "You should mate them." He finally says.

"You know why I can't." I growl.

He shakes his head, "you always were stubborn as fuck but I didn't think you were dumb."

My body vibrates as I hold myself back from landing my fist into his face. "You know what will happen if I mate them." Resentment bubbles up from deep within. Luz is very well aware of what my father would do should I take a mate, particularly two as powerful as Arcanna and Jackson. And yet here he is telling me I should do it anyway.

When he turns to look at me his eyes are almost swimming with pity before they are wiped clean and return to that bleeding sunset. "I know what *you* think will happen, hermano. And that is very different from what I know."

I push away from the railing we both lean against, "stop being so fucking cryptic Luz." I snap. At one time Luz and I were best friends, the one person in the world I trusted most with my life. But after my father got done with him our relationship was nothing more than a smoldering pile of broken promises and lies. His annoyed sigh only makes me more furious that I've allowed him back into my life and the life of the people I care for.

"Before your temper forces your little wolfy to come out and play I did have another reason for meandering through the door." He grabs a joint from his pocket, lighting it and dragging out the suspense. Another thing he has always done, made you be on his timeline and his terms. And again, at one time I fucking loved that about my brother.

When the red smoke from the joint finally clears it feels like it's been an eternity. "Luz, for fucks sake, why are you here? You hate me just as much as I hate you."

He flinches, the movement small, but clear. "I don't hate you." He offers up his voice soft and hesitant. "I would even go so far as to say I miss you."

I scoff. "Feed your lies to someone else Luz."

He straightens up, back ridged and eyes tight. "I came here to offer up some help, but it seems maybe I should keep the information to myself." His magic gathers around him, opening the door to take him home. "But being as I have my own agenda, I'll offer it up anyway. Do you trust the little priestess?"

I narrow my eyes at him before shaking my head no.

"Good."

I narrow my eyes at him, "What the fuck do you mean good?"

He smiles lazily. "Exactly as I said." He offers no other explanation before walking back through that door between us and disappearing, leaving me racing from the room and back to my mates.

Arcanna

Unceremoniously I'm dropped into my Forest. My projection barely remains standing as the magic rips me into this space. Vision swimming, I tamp down the nausea that is building as I brace myself on my knees. Despite knowing I can't throw up in this form I have no interest in it happening once I'm back in my body. While rare now, the memories are still fresh from when I first began projecting. Every time I projected; I would vomit as soon as I returned to my physical form.

Finally standing upright with clear vision I'm startled by the massive bone dragon glowering at me. I involuntarily take a step backward. Despite having seen it before, seen him before, it feels unsettling to have those bottomless black eyes boring into my soul.

"He won't do anything." A dark-haired man walks from behind the massive creature. His body is covered in tattoos, his thick dark hair short on the sides longer on top. His tight black t-shirt conforms to his muscular frame. "My mate sent us."

"The last time I saw you, you were also in dragon form. Nice to meet you in person, Shadow."

This earns me a bigger smile, "glad you know who I am." Placing a hand on the beast next to him he moves towards me. The dragon follows closely and despite its massive size, and the fact that it is made from pure bone, he is silent as the death that follows him. The death that he is making his own.

"It's hard not to, even if I didn't know Ava. Everyone knows who that dragon is behind you, and everyone knows who he belongs to." I ramble. It unnerves me having two very alive dragons in my home. Despite allowing them in, and knowing they mean my forest no harm, it still makes me nervous. This place has been both my prison and my sanctuary. Despite my feelings around my lack of freedom I don't want it harmed anymore.

The death dragon drops his head and nuzzles Shadow. It feels intrusive, standing here as the dragon offers comfort to him.

"Has he shifted back?" I ask to cut the silence and remind them I'm still here.

Shadow's whiskey eyes look sad as he shakes his head no. "Ava and I both have tried to convince him to do it but he just. . . won't." The dragon offers a low rumble and steps away from Shadow. A snort of hot air blowing over me as he shakes his head.

I frown but refocus on Shadow. "Why isn't Ava with you?" Discomfort pierces my heart as I look for my friend.

"If she was harmed, do you think either one of us would be here? We followed her into death, I doubt we'd leave her if we thought she was unsafe." He responds. Despite his assurances, the dragon behind him is restless, his energy agitated as if he dislikes being separated from her. Understandable given the last time he was she died.

Shadow shoots an exasperated look behind him at the

dragon. "She wanted us to check on you, after last time, but also we wanted you to know there are more souls missing."

Chills go down my spine. "Fuck."

"Ava noticed first. Oisin had been noticeably quiet for a while until he suddenly wasn't. We traced his path to the City of Dead, but it veered towards an area we could not follow." My throat closes at the mention of the Land of the Damned, the only place in my realm I truly hate. "When he finally fled this realm, he did so with great haste and the destruction. . . ." He trails off leaving me to believe the damage is worse than I can imagine.

"If he took souls from that place, it makes sense, the more powerful the souls the more damage will be done should they manage to leave here." Trepidation washes over me. Closing my eyes I ask the question I'm dreading the answer to. "Do I want to know what souls he took with him?"

Silence follows the question. A deep, horrible silence before a low rumbling growl comes from the bone dragon, from Dargo. "The original families." He spats out, his dragon form speaking for him.

Everything drops away. "All the original families?" My voice is a shaky whisper as the truth settles in my gut.

Shadow shakes his head, "we think just the heads of the families, but we can't be sure."

Fear runs through me. The original families were evil in life, they were no different in death. I had spent days weaving the magic to keep their souls locked into the Land of the Damned. Arthur Mori was particularly difficult to keep contained.

A light flares in the distance, distracting me from Shadow and his guardian. A signal that new souls are entering The Forest. My Reaper form takes over. I move the three of us rapidly to where the souls enter, earning me a low growl from both dragons.

"Warn a guy, will you?" Shadow grumbles, bracing his hands on his knees. "Fucking hell."

"Sorry," I mutter. "I forget what it's like to do that when you aren't you used to it." My eyes scan the area until they find the new souls waiting entry and judgement. A wicked, feral grin spreading over my lips. "Well, isn't this fortunate." My glaive appears in my hand and Shadow shifts to his dragon form, the two massive beasts framing me as we spy The Elders of The Order cowering before us all.

"Please. . ." One begs. "Have mercy on us!"

Dragos answering roar brings the souls to their knees in terror.

Feigning boredom I glance at the shining blade of my weapon. "I don't think my friend here knows the word, mercy. And come to think of it? Neither do I."

Oisin

Pushing my hands in my pockets I step over the warded threshold of the prison cell. The lights flicker throwing off a slight buzzing noise as the electricity struggles to remain steady this far underground. My eyes land on the filthy female in front of me, her body a crumpled mess on the dirty floor. My polished boot reaches forward and nudges her side, she lets out a small whimper as I see her two golden eyes peer out from under her hair.

Bending down I brace my arms on my knees as I lean in a little closer. "Lilith would be so disappointed that one of her chosen has given up so easily." I say.

She has no response for me, the fire in her eyes no longer flickering but instead a dull ember. The first few days were fun, the fight she put up, but now it's almost boring. "Nothing to say?" After a moment of silence, I let out a long sigh and stand up. "You know, when I brought you here, I thought I would be able to drag that magic from you with no effort."

The statement earns a snort from her, the first real sign of life. It has my smile pulling wide across my face. With life you can still have the ability to break. And I love breaking pretty things.

Behind me I can hear the shuffling footsteps of someone being dragged down the hallway and I smile wider. "So, you can imagine my frustration when it hasn't worked out that way. Then it occurred to me, we were just missing the proper motivation."

"You will *never* have my magic." Her voice is rough, barely above a whisper but it fills the room.

"Ah, that is where you are wrong."

Lady Ornate turns the corner dragging behind her the wolf that had been outside Club Eufori prior to me snatching the female.

Bast's eyes go wide with alarm, her broken body struggling to reach the other female. "So, here is what we can do. Either you can freely help me, give me that magic of yours and I let this little lamb go free or you get to spend your immortal life watching me torture your mate."

As if the point needed to be proven I pull back and drive my fist into the girl's face, my knuckles cracking across her cheek bone. She cries out as her body drops to the floor.

"No! Please!" Bast cries as I lay another kick into the girl's stomach.

Pausing I glance back at Bast, "well?"

She glares at me, fire returning to her, so much fire that my cock hardens at the idea of breaking her apart all over, of extinguishing that fire as I drain her.

"I'll do it."

"Excellent!" I say, clapping my hands. Lady Ornate

drags the other girl free from the room by her hair. Bast screaming for her as she does.

"You fucking bastard!" She seethes. "We had a deal!"

I smile "I take my deals very seriously. I will release her when you tell me something I don't already know. Like exactly how to drain that magic from you."

Bast locks eyes with me, the whirls of color like an inferno. "You are starting a war you won't win." Her voice is low but the strength in it gives me pause. "Do you know what you're waking? Do you know what will happen when you open that door?"

I lean closer to her and to give her credit she does flinch back; she holds steady even as I'm barely a breath from her. "I'm counting on it."

<hr>

My nose crinkles at the stench of the city. It might be the dead of winter, but nothing has helped the smell of this festering shit hole. My veins thrum with the magic freshly "donated" by Bast and I allow it to wrap me in a warm cocoon. The look on her face when I told her I wanted the war she promised was priceless. I've been politely knocking on the door for years, now I'm ready to blow it wide open.

Looking out at the city I can imagine the mayhem I will unleash here. I imagine what it will feel like to destroy everything Ciaran has built with his mate. His betrayal has cut deeper than I care to admit. But in the end destroying this city will serve as a way to keep the idealistic ones busy while I go after my end goal.

My mood sours thinking about how much easier this all would have been if Ava hadn't run on our wedding night. Her fucking father got cocky thinking he had complete control over her. I had even sent the queen to try and keep Ava locked up tight, she scoffed though eventually relented to check on her "distraught daughter". No one believed me that the little slut could run. The King laughed in my face when I mentioned it.

The bastard never did allow himself to be humbled, even as I slit his throat, he had a look of disbelief that anyone would dare end his life. Particularly someone like me. Just picturing it again makes my cock harden. I had fucked his son right after, enjoying the fact that his father's body wasn't even cold yet. When I was finished with him, I went back to her, my precious priestess.

My chest pulls at the thought of her. Once such an innocent creature, now twisted and tainted into my creature of darkness. A pretty package sent to destroy my enemies.

Shoving my hands in my pockets I stand in the middle of the old coven grounds. The area around me burned away, the Harbinger magic laid waste to this place, nothing lives nor grows here anymore. Animals won't even fly over; it's like the touch of that deadly magic made a vortex that everyone avoids. This is a place touched by the magic of the gods.

The wind picks up blowing small flakes of snow into my face, and the sky above darkens rapidly with the approaching storm. Pulling the hood of the jacket up and over my head the scent of wisteria blooms with just a hint of ocean water under it. I grit my teeth against the feelings it drags up. Both hating and loving the lingering scent.

"Here. You look freezing." I shove the jacket towards her.

Her eyes glisten, warring between the same feelings I'm struggling with no doubt. The push-pull of who we are and who we could be.

"You look beautiful." The words are out before I can pull them back in. Her cheeks flush with a beautiful pink...

"My Lord," Lady Ornate's voice drags me from my

memory unceremoniously. Her long winter coat pulled tightly around her frame. "We are ready to begin." She places her hand on my arm, her perfectly manicured fingers delicately stroking the rough fabric of my jacket. Visions of crushing the life from her flood my brain.

Lady Ornate has always been a means to an end. And she's grown far too bold through the years we've worked together. She is delusional enough to think she's indispensable now. It's laughable really. But the idea has made her behaviors around me, and with me, reckless. Including the part she played in Harrow's life at The Order. Jealousy made the High Priestess into a cruel tutor for Harrow.

Though, in the end, it worked to my advantage. Afterall, she was so damn proud of the mask she helped place on Lena. No one would have guessed it was me, whispering in her ear, of a magical device to control a banshee. Certainly not my little angel who still believes I had nothing to do with the cruel device.

I push away from the High Priestess, forcing her hand to drop as Feather Hoar walks over, the stack of grimoires held tightly in her slim arms. She was a surprise. A member of an original family hiding amongst us in Hell, and an even bigger surprise that she aligned with my wants and needs.

"Well?" I ask impatiently.

"It can be done, sir." She says with a pleased, albeit bored, tone. "Already they await."

My face splits into a grin, relief, and satisfaction pulsing through my body. "Now that's what I like to hear, Feather. It's that type of positivity that will get you far in life."

She doesn't react, only shrugging as her dark hair shifts in the wind. Her eyes glance behind me and I don't need the verbal acknowledgement that my prey is here.

My face peels into a satisfied grin, "Ready the magic." I command her.

The Order Elders come walking towards us, their cream robes dirty on the ends from dragging on the wet ground. Their bald heads gleam even in the darkness and the look of insult at being summoned is painted across their faces.

"What is the meaning of this?!" The four stop directly in front of me, not noticing the circle of salt they stepped over. "You have no right to summon us!"

"Am I not the head of this organization?" The old men huff, a few shuffling on their feet with obvious discomfort at being called out. For too long I have allowed them to believe I had no idea of the little coo they were planning behind my back. "I'm curious, how long have you all been plotting to take my rightful position as head of The Order?"

Josiah, the man who has fashioned himself as head Elder, is the first to sputter to life as the initial shock of my statement wears off. "You have strayed from the path, strayed from our ways and you have been punished."

I nod as if I'm genuinely listening to them while I force myself to keep the laugh that is bubbling upward down. *The old fools.* "I'm curious, how long have you thought I strayed from your path? Because if my sources are correct, you all were keeping something that was rightfully mine from me." More silence enters the space as the old men look between one another. No one willing to fess up to anything now. "I'll refresh your memories. My priestess. . . the one I brought, the one I managed to gain after killing the rest of them. You all filled her head with nonsense about purity to keep her from me."

"We only told her the truth!" Josiah countered. "You would have defiled her and tainted her. We were keeping her pure for the ceremony."

This time I do laugh, long and loud, as I listen to the bullshit he spews.

"You ruined her and she is now gone!" Josiah yells over

the laughing. "The gods are punishing you, punishing us!" Another Elder chimes in now, emboldened by his leader. "That's right! The loss of the princess first and now the loss of the priestess. The gods no longer see fit to have you lead."

My newly acquired magic surges forward and grips the man from within, his heart clenched between the invisible fist I have shoved through his chest. He gasps, face turning purple, as I casually walk towards him. "The gods don't give a shit about us."

"Blasphemy!"

I squeeze the last bit of life from the old man's body and let him drop dead in front of me. "I've always found it ironic that you all think you're so above the rest of us, that your sins aren't sinful."

"What have you done?" Josiah shakes his head, face flushed with anger, his eyes dropping to the dead man at my feet. "There is no coming back from this."

I scoff, "Oh and you all thought my soul was somehow fit for redemption before this? Please. You all were fine with me killing as long as it suited your purpose. You were fine with me fucking whomever I wanted as long it, again, suited your purpose."

From behind, Feather's voice can be heard as she activates the magic within the salt circle, the trap springing to life. One by one all the coven heads of the original families appear within the salt circle. A representative from each of the families save one.

The Carmines. Kara had refused the call, somehow, and the only other who could be reached was too dangerous according to Feather. The one who had created The Harbinger magic in the first place, Lucy Carmine. I had gone to argue with her but she had assured me that there would be enough with the ones that did answer.

Feather moves about, handing each their family grimoire. The Mori witch, Arthur, allows his face to spread into a cheshire like grin. His beady eyes lighting up with sheer delight as his greedy hands cradle the family book.

My boots carry me directly in front of Josiah, his face now pale and slick with sweat as he looks around. "You've spent my entire life acting like I wasn't dangerous, wasn't worth your time. Even after I killed the last King you couldn't admit that I was the rightful heir of The Order. I used to think it was because you thought I was powerless, unworthy. But I finally figured it out."

Josiah's face goes red, "We should have killed you right along with your whore of a mother."

A low, dark chuckle emanates from me. "You were all too cowardly to do what needed to be done. To grab the power, we've always had at our fingertips." I hold up my hand as the magic crackles forth through my fingertips and dances over my knuckles.

"Where did you get that?" This question comes from Toby, a rather mousy Elder. And the one who often preached to my little angel the most about what would happen to her, and us, should she give into her lust.

I chuckle darkly, the sound vibrating my bones. "I'm so glad you asked Toby." My feet carry me around the group, casually looking them over.

Pulling a blade from my thigh I slowly inspect the spelled etched into it, "I found a rather handy piece of magic, with the help of the witches here. It has allowed me to take donations from a lovely creature. Her magic has given me the ability to do what needs to be done until I can get to The Well, until I can take that magic for my own."

Toby's face is laced in horror, his face going pale and eyes wide. "You will be an abomination."

"I will be a fucking God." I say with finality. Snapping

my fingers the resurrected witches begin to chant. The magic coming alive around us. "To get The Well and finish my goal, however, I need to not only create a distraction but also finally retrieve something that is mine. What better way to kill two birds with one stone than by creating a new gate, right here."

When I drive the spelled blade into Josiah, he barely registers it before I pull it back out and slash the throat of Toby followed by the other two. Their bodies plummet to the ground.

Magic surges up around us as each of the shades become corporeal, their bodies returned. More magic flows out, shattering the air and pulling open a gate. A smile spreads over my face as I look over the waiting demons and creatures that have collected for me. And as they step through, racing down towards the city, I can't help but feel satisfaction at the ruin they are about to cause in Gothic Grove.

TWENTY-SEVEN

Jackson

Something is wrong.

Horribly wrong.

I frown, rubbing at my chest as I try to figure out why my skin is crawling and why my body feels as though I should be prepping for a fight. I scan the room, Arcanna still resting peacefully next to me.

The bedroom door swinging open violently has me springing to my feet as Dios falls inward. "*Mi cielo!*" His chest heaves as he catches his breath and glances between Arcanna and I. "Are you okay?"

I frown again, confusion moving over me. "No, I don't think I am." I push my hands through my hair in frustration as my magic continues to urge me, to warn me.

Dios moves towards us as another shiver flows over me, my body moving on its own accord towards the window that's still shattered. The hot air pushes in with the wind, my eyes survey the outside, looking for whatever has caused this feeling. But it all looks peaceful. The lake calm, trees still, nothing amiss in our small oasis.

"Something is wrong." I think I say.

From behind I can hear Dios saying my name. But my gaze is still held on the outside world. My eyes narrow as I search the inky darkness of the forest and lake until I'm sure the feeling is wrong and I'm going crazy. As I go to turn back to Dios, that's when I feel it, the faint shift of tectonic plates. The earth beneath my feet starts to rumble, low at first, until it sounds like the growl of a great beast slowly getting louder as the movement picks up until it feels like a deafening scream.

Dios tumbles towards Arcanna. Bracing her against his body as he shields her while I brace myself against the wall. The earthquake trying to throw me to the ground. My eyes catch the lake outside, the water rippling with massive waves that crest and fall against the shoreline in a battle against the sand.

"What's happening?" Dios yells over the noise. Dust, now starting to fall from the ceiling, rains down on him as he covers Arcanna even further. Glasses topple off the table, shattering into thousands of glittering pieces. Lightning cracks overhead, the noise of the thunder lost within the sounds of the earthquake.

My mouth feels like I swallowed ash. Horror washing through me with understanding right behind it. My mouth can't seem to form the words to explain, the utter insanity of it clogging up in my throat. Even as the world settles and calms, I remain frozen with the words stuck in my throat.

"He opened a new gods damn gate." Arcanna says with fury as her voice finds its way back into her body, her soul now returned. "Oisin opened a fucking gate."

Even if I know it's true the words of denial still flow from me. "Creating a new gate takes large amounts of magic and a blood sacrifice." I say, like an idiot.

I watch as she untangles herself from Dios. "I saw The Order Elders when they tried to enter my forest. As if they thought they were deserving of such peace." Arcanna spats with disgust. She begins to pace back and forth.

Dios cocks his head towards her, "tried?"

A feral smile spreads over her face, pure delight lighting up those hazel eyes as her glaive appears in hand, fresh blood dripping down the blade. "They didn't make it." Her eyes look at the blood with longing.

"They'll reanimate." I remind her.

"No. They won't." She says, leaving zero room for argument.

I tilt my head taking a small step towards her, "how Arcanna?" I ask unsure if I'm asking about the souls or how he managed the magic.

She doesn't answer, only shaking her head before she spears onward. "He's taken the original family heads, their souls. They no longer reside within The Forest or any of the lands outside. And he used The Elders as his sacrifice."

"He cannot bring people back from the dead." Dios growls. Arcanna snorts. "He has the grimoires, the witches had endless magic in those. The Mori one holds many spells that could fall under necromancy."

Dios curses, the feel of his magic tingling across my skin before it's pulled back in. "We need to tell everyone. Warn them."

Arcanna shakes her head sadly, "It's too late to warn anyone. The gates are open. Hell is unleashed. All we can do is try and stop Oisin and close the gate now."

I look to Dios, "text Demon. Get him and Kallen and Reaver here. Now." I grab my shirt, throwing it on over my bare chest as I head towards the door. "And get packed. We are leaving."

Neither Arcanna nor Dios argued when I left, heading straight for the makeshift throne room. Having no doubt the council is already there, or on their way. They aren't stupid, they would understand what just happened.

Fuck. A fucking gate opened. It feels like a failure of monumental proportions that this happened under my reign as King. Everything that has happened feels like a failure. And no doubt my council will want my head on a spike for this, which truthfully feels like no less than what I deserve at this point. If a King cannot protect his people he does not deserve to rule.

Pushing open the door, I see the old men sitting around the large table. Not bothering to greet them I pour myself a hearty drink before sitting down. "I assume you all know what just happened?"

"Took you long enough to get here, of course we know." Phelanais mumbles sternly before he goes back to talking to the other members. Their raised voices are a symphony of arguments against providing aid, every one of them attempting to talk at once.

"I will be heading into the city to assist them." I say over the chaos.

More yelling explodes outward but it's Phelanais who looks at me and shakes his head, "So you can die by draining your magic? You are needed here, not there. You are our King and our people need the protection "

I say nothing in response, just continue to sip my drink as another member starts in, "We have heard that many number of beasts are roaming Gothic Grove. The Harbinger and her mate, the Helvig Vampire, have been seen engaging in battle with them. You will not be needed."

"This is our mess to clean up," I respond with a calm voice. Even though calm is the last thing I feel right now.

"However, you do make a good point about my magic. I'll be leaving immediately, we will head to The Well after which I'm taking Arcanna, Dios and Harrow to the city. We are going to hunt down whatever The Harbinger and Ciaran don't find." I say with an authority and confidence I do not feel.

The room seems to explode. "You cannot go to the city! That is not our place! What about us?! We live in hovels while you plan to lend aid to the city beyond?" Downing the contents of the glass in front of me I savor the feel of the liquor burning down my throat. I rub my temples with my other hand, the headache forming is already rapidly turning to a migraine and my anxiety is trying to crawl its way out of the dark hole I've shoved it in. My body needs to replenish, whether by Harrow or Dios, I need to get my magic up.

I snap, my patience finally evaporating. "First, you do not live in fucking hovels. All of you have nice cottages provided to you by me on this lake. If you truly wish to live in a hovel, I'll happily have Dios set something up." They all pale at my mate's name. *Fuck, we need to talk about it. Complete the bond.* "Second, we owe the city help, Oisin unleashed *our* creatures on them. Therefore, we need to close the gate and track down the asshole."

"They do not need us! They have The Harbinger!" One of them yells as if to make the point once more.

More arguments erupt as everyone starts to yell over one another again. Despite only being a handful of us it sounds like a full room. My face remains passive as I watch them bicker but inside my anger is bubbling up and threatening to boil over. None of these men care about Hell, or Gothic Grove, they don't care about the citizens. They care that their normally cushy lives have been displaced. My magic rolls through my veins, my hands clenching as I try to keep control of it all. My eyes squeeze shut, blocking the room out.

Do not kill them. Do not kill them.

"Well, looks like we came at the right time." My eyes snap open.

Reaver's massive body stands in the doorway, arms banded across his chest. Kallen and Demon flanking him. Demon is dressed in his typical jeans and vest showing his pres patch while Kallen is wearing ripped-up jeans and a baggy t-shirt. Her golden whip curls around her arm like a snake before it tucks up under the sleeve of her shirt. Her eyes glimmer with the promise of violence and chaos as she takes in the council.

"That was quick." I say with a smile at the sight of them all.

Demon shrugs, "it pays to know someone who is a Realm Walker."

Kallen lets out a long sigh. "I am truly amazing, aren't I?"

Reaver rolls his eyes, "you couldn't have put me with a cockier bunch, could you?"

A smile breaks over my face at the sight of my best friend, at least until from behind the curvy, lavender-haired woman steps out.

"Honey I'm home!" Rhea jokes. The sound of her voice sending a deep pit into my stomach. Her smile falters as she watches me. "I'm not here to cause issues." Her voice is light and airy, as if she knows how anxious her presence is making me. "I came because we have a mutual enemy."

My mouth goes dry, anxiety ratcheting up immediately, and my fingers dancing across my thigh. Worst-case scenarios begin to play through my mind as I picture Arcanna seeing this spitfire of a woman. My stomach twists and saliva pools in the back of my mouth as bile rises. We may have figured out what drove us apart but that doesn't mean we've healed and seeing Rhea won't help.

My gaze cuts to Reaver who looks apologetic, his hand scratching the back of his head in an awkward gesture. Kallen and Demon don't say anything, either unaware or uncaring as to what they just stepped into. My bet is on the latter.

I feel frozen in time, unable to speak or move as my anxiety continues to whisper sweet nothings to me about how this will end, about all the worst-case scenarios that are bound to happen.

After a long moment of silence, Phelanais has the audacity to step forward. Clearing his throat as he does and cutting me an angry look. "Princess Rhea, welcome to our humble home." He bows low. "The King will, of course, welcome you with open arms. I was just talking to him about the wedding between our two great cities. Such an event would bring so much joy to those who need it most right now."

"You think a royal wedding is what would bring people happiness right now?" Reaver scoffs.

Rhea looks at Phelanais with a sneer only she could pull off, her hip pops out as she braces a hand on it. "It's *Queen* actually, and my fiancé will be glad to hear another King believes he is also engaged to me."

Sadness pierces her eyes as she turns towards me, "We have a lot to talk about." Her voice suddenly lacking the normal bravado. Reaver steps closer to her, his hand a ghost above her shoulder, as if to provide comfort, but she cuts him a look and his hand freezes before it drops down once more. His body inches closer to her, however, as though he can't help but be drawn into her orbit.

"Oisin killed her family." He reports. "She's all that's left of the royal family of Divinity."

There is a collective gasp from the old men and that sound spurns me into action. Cutting them a glare that promises violence should they interrupt before glancing to Rhea. "What happened?"

She shakes her head, "Oisin is very cunning. He knows how to make people feel important. He did a great job at that with my parents, despite my arguments against him. You know I never trusted him." I nod, remembering vividly her arguments against the man I was dating.

"What about you're brothers?" I ask hesitantly, knowing fulling well how Reaver feels about the twins. And knowing how complicated Rhea's relationship is with them.

"I tried getting Aelius and Kalani to help me but. . ." She trails off. Eyes misting over. "They haven't been the same since they lost *her*." I flashback briefly to the day the twin's mate died, Kalani had been a quiet storm but Aelius? Aelius had raged and raged until he was little more than the beast that occupies his body.

"They are going to burn that city to the ground!" Rhea yells, fear controlling the tremor of her voice. "She's gone Jackson, they lost her. And I don't think they will survive this."

The memory plays through rapidly as I think back to my standoff with the two. It was the one time I have ever been truly worried I would have to drain my magic to stop them from killing everyone in their path. But just as suddenly as their rage had started it had stopped. The two cocooned themselves in the underworld, allowing a darkness to penetrate their souls that only the loss of a mate can do. A loss I hope to never endure as they have.

The mention of her twin brothers manages to force my threat from my advisor's brains and the silence that we had is suddenly filled with their whispers as they gossip to one another about them. I cut them all a hard glare.

But it's Kallen who sneers with venom, "Get the fuck out old men. We have things to do."

None of them argue with her, scurrying to escape the room. Phelanais, however, takes his time getting up making sure he is the last one to leave. His withered hands grab onto Rhea's and offer a kiss to her. "My dear please come to me with anything you may need, I will be happy to help in all that I can." Reaver growls low and Phelanais startles backward from my friend.

"Touch my future wife again and I will pull your intestines out through your nose." The room drops in temperature. His fangs descending.

Phelanais goes white, eyes wide. "Your. . . your future wife?" He manages to stumble out.

"Yes," Rhea says, stepping between them glaring at Reaver. "Like I said, I have no interest in marrying Jax."

Phelanais' face goes pale as he bows again, before quickly exiting the room. Reavers' dark eyes follow the movement. When he turns back to me the black pupils withdraw and his fangs shrink back down. Rhea rolls her eyes before sitting down as far from Reaver as she can get, my friend does not take the hint and manages to place himself directly behind her, arms crossed over his chest as though he is standing guard over her.

"Honestly what do you think is going to happen in here?" Rhea grumbles. "This is why I had no interest in marriage."

Kallen chuckles, shaking her head, muttering something about alpha men, as she grabs a bottle from the bar. When she sits down, she takes a long pull of the drink before offering the liquor to her mate. He grabs hold and takes a healthy swig, wiping his mouth with the back of his hand when done. "I was having a delightful time hunting and killing." Kallen says with a long sigh. "Please tell me you have someone else for me to hunt."

"You shouldn't sound so gleeful about killing." Rhea counters with a chastising glare.

Kallen rolls her eyes, "I've been around a lot longer than you have little queen, seen far more than you ever will. I can promise you it's far better for me to be hunting something with a purpose."

"A bored Kallen is never good," her mate rumbles from behind. She laughs, the sound light and airy.

Shaking my head I grab the whiskey from Demon and chug it down before letting the words flow from me, "Oisin opened a gate in Gothic Grove. He's flooded the city with creatures."

Rhea gasps, "He'll kill everyone in the city."

Reaver cocks his head, "What's his end goal here?"

"Chaos. No doubt. He wants the city, and us, in chaos." Kallen's gaze cuts around the room, "we cannot bring Astrea into this."

"It's too late, they are already involved and hunting the creatures." I say, pointedly ignoring her face as I go on. "And it would benefit us to have them help, I would go so far to say as we need them."

"You are powerful enough to stop them." Rhea counters even as Kallen lets out an angry hiss towards me.

I shake my head, "My magic is too low." Her eyes widen but Reaver places a hand on her shoulder, squeezing once. A warning for her not to ask questions. I offer him a thankful smile.

Kallen lets out a long sigh, a weariness passing over her. "Grief does things to people. Particularly with that magic. Astrea broke when your sister died. She isn't the same person, and she does not have a handle on that magic any longer." The mention of Ava pulls at my heart. Regardless of my relationship with death I still miss my sister, and I still have guilt that I haven't allowed myself to honor her the way I should.

"We can bring the pack in," Demon cuts in. "The Primal Knights can help."

"Speaking of, where is my second favorite play thing?" Kallen asks. Demon growls low and possessive. "What? I said second! Your cock will always be the first." Kallen counters with a giggle.

TWENTY-EIGHT

Arcanna

My hands tremble as they pull my hair up and off my neck into a quick ponytail. The events of the day seemingly crashing into me all at once now that I have a second to try and breathe. It was on the tip of my tongue to tell Jax who helped me with those souls, *why* they would never regenerate. But I held back, unclear on if the hesitation was because of exactly who helped me or because of the rules that bind me to that place. Either way he ran out before I could figure out my own mind, leaving me with far too much time to hyper fixate over it all.

A long sigh drags my gaze over to the window. Dios lays back on the chaise lounge in my room. His long body is draped across the plush fabric, his head tilted back towards the window I have thrown open, beckoning the warm summer air into the room. The wolf had followed me as soon as Jackson left. Meandering behind me and pushing in close once we got to my door. His scent washed over me when he squeezed past, and despite his back to me I have no doubt he smelled the slick arousal that it inspired.

My eyes rake over his body now, shirtless and covered in

tattoos. His dark skin is gorgeous in the early pre morning light and his abs ripple forward. A hunger pools in my belly. A feral need to feel his hands on me as I drag my teeth over that skin.

"*Tu mirádome.* You're staring at me." He doesn't lift his head, eyes still closed, as he calls out to me. My skin flushes hot at the sound of his voice. "You want to talk about why you haven't bonded with Jackson?"

I cross my arms over my chest, leaning up against my four-post bed. "Do you?" I snap.

Dios finally raises his head. Like a cat stretching from a nap, he lets his arms reach up, the muscles of his abdomen becoming more prominent as his tattoos follow the movement of his skin. He allows his arms to fall back down after the long stretch, one hanging over the back of the lounge. The silence between us goes on forever as his green and blue eyes bore into my soul.

"Well?" I finally ask, annoyed that he isn't saying anything and just staring.

"Let's make it into a game, shall we?" He pushes to a stand, his body unraveling to its full height.

My mouth goes dry. "What type of game?"

His hand pushes across his tattooed skull, the designs are delicate, and yet underneath is brutality. For a moment I picture those fingers fucking me to release and remember the feeling of his lips on me, the graze of his teeth. I press my thighs together to relieve the ache suddenly building. His eyes miss nothing, the movement caught. "I catch you and you talk, tell me why you haven't bonded."

I cross my arms and force my face into neutrality, refusing to show how much I want to let him catch me. "What would I win?"

"If you evade me, I'll tell you everything." He surveys me, his eyes cutting straight to my core.

"For how long? How long would I evade you?"

Shrugging, he stands slowly, his feet bringing him directly in my bubble. My breathing picks up, his scent flooding me. "Five minutes. Five minutes of running from me, of letting that sweet little cunt get wetter, and wetter, until you finally let me catch you and fuck you." His words send a ripple effect down my spine and deep into my core. "Because make no mistake, I may be pulling secrets from you but I also want your cum painted on my tongue and cock."

His nostrils flare, scenting my change. His pupils slowly expand. "Do we have a deal?"

I swallow, "You catch me before the five minutes, and I have to talk to you? But if I escape you, you have to spill your own secrets?" I whisper, my voice barely audible.

His eyes trace over my body, noticing the tension building. "Don't forget, either way I'm fucking you." His voice is silky. "I'm going to sink my cock so far in you and let my knot fill you past the point you think you can withstand."

My mouth goes dry, voice staying lodged in my throat as the image of him catching me on the forest floor plays out. "Deal." The word flows from me easier than it should.

His mouth spreads into a wicked smile, "Good girl. Tell me your limits."

My eyes blink slowly, a haze coming over me. "I don't like impact play, it's a hard limit. So is bondage, I *can't* be restrained." The words feel sluggish as if I'm in a trance. "I also don't love anal play, but it's not a hard limit."

He nods, "any others?"

I pause, genuinely thinking about it for a moment appreciating that he wants to know. "I can get uncomfortable with breath play, specifically choking, so if we do that, I need my partner to be mindful."

"Okay, and red, yellow, green, okay?" He asks, his hand

now tracing up and down my arm. I nod in confirmation. His hand lightly traces over my chest, his fingertips ghosting over me until they come to rest delicately on my pulse point. He raises an eyebrow as my heart accelerates, "run little reaper, run and let the big bad wolf hunt you down."

I count to three in my head before I bolt, ripping away from his touch, but not before I see his eyes start to glow in that inhuman way.

(Lay Low- Argy Remix- Tiësto)

Leaping over the lounge I push out onto the balcony allowing my legs to vault me over landing with a soft thud on the grass below. I don't risk a glance behind me, don't risk slowing down and losing this game.

"Times ticking." His voice carries out of the room after me, floating along the wind like a sensual caress before I hear the sound of a wolf howl.

"Fuck." I mutter. I had not considered he would shift; I assumed he would hunt me as a human. "Should have fucking told him no shifting." I won't last long against his wolf.

My legs pump hard, adrenaline coursing through me as something primal awakens and recognizes I'm being chased by a predator. My magic tries to move to the surface in response to the fear that is pumping through me, tattoos flaring to life easily giving away my location with their glowing aura.

Another howl has me urging my legs to move faster and forcing my magic to retreat so I stop glowing. *Five minutes. I just need to make it five minutes.* Sprinting into the woods I dart to and fro to throw off the trail. My lungs burn, and sweat drips down my back, as I look for a place to hide.

"*Pequeño segadora,* I'm going to catch you." His voice echoes through the space around us. His shift between wolf and man seamless.

Launching myself around a massive tree I stop to catch my breath. My body struggling to get the memo that we want to win this. No, all it wants is for him to sink his thick cock into me. To have me screaming and writhing under him as I come undone and beg him for his knot. The image plays out in front of me, my hands trailing over my body as I get lost in the fantasy.

"I can smell you," his voice and steps sound closer now pulling me from the visual roughly. "Smell your pussy, you like being chased. I bet you taste fucking divine." I shake my head confused by the strength of the daydream and move to push off the tree.

A low growl is the only warning I get before he's pulling me out from behind my hiding place. Out of pure instinct, I throw my hands out, my fist knocking his head back. I let out a gasp, reaching forward to apologize as his head tilts back down. The feral hunger blazing in his eyes as he licks the blood off his teeth stops my hand midair and my legs force me to back away.

"Fuck yes." He groans, his cock obviously hard as it juts out from his body. He swipes some blood from his mouth, rubbing it along his cock as he strokes his shaft. "I like your violence."

A soft whimper escapes me as I watch him stroke his length, but I don't give in, I flee instead.

Dios

(Sanctify Me- In this Moment)

Arcanna disappears back into the dense forest surrounding the lake. I smile, enjoying this game. I thought I had her, using my magic to send that fantasy. Thought she would have given in. The punch was unexpected but so fucking hot. My wolf shifts back out as I take off after the little reaper. Her scent so strong she has no hope of evading me. When I get close again, I move back to human form, whistling as I meander after her. To the left, I hear her heart skip a beat before it resumes its rapid assault on her chest. Her sandalwood scent permeates the air around us.

Allowing my magic to seep out the particles float, invisibly on the wind, until they settle against her skin, grabbing onto her soul once more. A low groan comes from behind a bush before she stumbles out. "What is this?" She groans.

"That my, *pequeño segadora*, is my magic." I walk to her, reaching out and grabbing her hips to drag her body flush against mine. "It's on your soul, allowing me to control your pleasure and feel everything you feel. Allowing me to send you little fantasies."

"That's cheating." She pants. "Same with using your wolf."

A smile splays across my face, "we never said no magic or shifting. Did we?" She shakes her head. "So, my *segradora*, time has run out and it looks like I caught you. I win."

She lets out another moan as my magic pulls at her arousal before she bites down hard on her lip and launches herself forward at me, attempting to turn and run. I throw myself at her, the two of us crashing to the ground. My body twists so she falls on me instead of the dirt. I barely manage to dodge her attempt to head-butt me. I wrap my arms and legs around her body without thought as she continues to thrash to get free.

"Wait! Red! Red!" She pants. My arms and legs release her immediately pushing her up to sit. I crawl around her so I can face her without touching, making sure she has space to breathe.

"I'm sorry, I shouldn't have restrained you," I say.

She glances up at me, "It's okay, I didn't tell you. I only said bondage. I should have been clearer."

I shake my head, "I should have asked more questions. What do you need now?"

Her cheeks flush, "I want to keep going." All around us the forest is quiet, the only sounds coming from our breathing and the slight shift of the wind to bring cool air through the thick trees. Pressing forward she moves her face so she's only a few inches from me. "I want you to fuck me. I want to cum on your cock while it's shoved so far in me, I'll be dripping your release for days."

"And Jax?"

"He can taste what we are like together."

A low groan comes from me at the idea of Jackson eating my cum from her. She launches forward, pressing me into the ground, mouth latching onto mine. We devour each other in that kiss. All our emotions pour into that one connection. Between the two of us we manage to rip her clothing free, allowing her naked body to touch the night air.

I hook my legs around her, turning us so I can settle with my face at her core. "Need to taste you," I growl, diving into her wet cunt. She lets out a long moan as I feast on her. She drips down my chin as I fuck her with my tongue. When I feel her at the edge of release, I crawl back up her body, notching my cock at her entrance.

Pushing into her feels like a homecoming.

My wolf surges forward, wrapping around her and dragging her to me.

"Right there! Right there!" She screams under me, her nails raking down my back. "Don't stop!" My magic moves through her body, focusing on bringing her to climax. My wolf howls, knot swelling.

"Your cunt is milking me so good. I'm going to fill you up my reaper. Fill you up so you never forget who you belong to." My knot expands, catching on the edge of her cunt. I slow my thrusts, pushing in with measured control that shocks me. "Fuck you're tight," I groan. She lets out a low mewl and I lean down, peppering her with soft kisses. "Almost there, you're doing so good." Finally, my knot is fully pushed inside her, the wet, hot, feel of her pussy sending shivers through me.

"Oh gods, you feel so good." She cries, tears now streaming down her face. "So. Gods. Damn. Good." I chuckle starting to move as she keeps milking me until I'm dragged over the edge and my release barrels through me. I let out a long moan as my hips buck forward, fucking her as best I can despite the tightness.

My wolf howls and I can feel my teeth elongating.
Mine.
Claim.
"Fuckkk," I groan as I fight the urge. "My wolf needs you, wants you. You are ours." My control seems to be spiraling as this female, my female, soaks up every ounce of pleasure I can give her. She palms her breasts, fingers playing with those barbells as I feel her cum again.

"Claim me." She pants. Head thrown back, next exposed. "Fucking do it, bite me. Make me yours."

"*Segradora. . .*" I hesitate, my body shaking as I fight the pull from my wolf, as I fight my magic now rising up to help my wolf.

"Fucking do it, Dios! Show me what it means to be yours, put that mark on me. I want it. I need it." Her nails dig into me. "I want Jackson to look at that mark, I want him to see it as he eats your cum from my cunt."

My wolf surges forward releasing any control I was pretending to have. Her words sending a feral need pulsing through me that overshadows any logic. My teeth elongate fully, and I know, without a doubt, my eyes are glowing as I lean down and sink into her neck. She screams out as our magic swirls together, our souls bonding. My back burns as her mark sears into me, the mark of a mate. *Guardián da alma.* Everything clicks into place as I finish filling her with my release, as her cunt continues to grip me hard. Her tattoos flare brighter, my eyes barely able to stay open as I drag my teeth from her and sit up.

Her pussy flutters, and her eyes are hazy as that magic dims. Our bodies both covered in sweat and forest floor. My chest heaves as I feel her coursing through me, feel her thoughts and emotions weaving into the very fabric of who I am. I feel my knot start to release us, but I can't bring myself to leave her, instead, I wrap her up in my arms under the canopy of trees and allow the bond to settle in.

Consequence be damned.

Arcanna

I should feel petrified, furious or any other number of emotions outside of content right now. Laying in Dios's arms I enjoy the feel of our bond, relish in the warmth spreading in my chest and the peace my soul seems to find with it. The canopy above us filters out the night sky, the moonlight managing to sneak through in small segments.

"Well?" Dios finally asks, breaking the silence.

I push up on my elbow and look at him, those mismatched eyes of his devouring me. "Well, what?"

He smirks, "I won our little game. Time to talk." I groan, my head dropping to his chest and eyes snagging on his cock laying against his thigh. My mouth waters and for a moment I think about taking him and sucking him down. A tight fist wraps into my hair. "No distractions. You can suck my cock later if you are a good girl."

He releases my hair and drags me back into his body, his hands stroking down my spine in a comforting wave. I stay quiet for a long time, focusing on the feeling of our bond, the feeling of his hands, and the scent of us combined. "The biggest issue is the magic in my veins. The Forest holds me, and fucking hell I shouldn't even have bonded with you just now." I glance to him and can't help wince at the pain that flashes over his face. "It's not that I don't want this, or didn't want it. But as Lady of Souls my first responsibility is to The Forest and no matter what I will always return there."

Dios nods, "That is a simple issue. Give me the real one."

I want to scoff at him because it doesn't feel simple. But instead, I let out a long breath, "I don't know if I'm ready to let go of the anger yet. I know that sounds. . . odd I suppose but letting go sounds scary." Dios remains quiet, that steady stroke still moving up and down my back. "It feels like cutting my safety line and free falling."

"You wouldn't lose a safety line, you'd gain wings." Dios whispers against my temple.

I snort, "I already have wings of my own."

"You know what I mean," he counters. I let out a long sigh struggling with how to explain the feelings I have, the complicated overwhelming feelings about bonding to Jackson after everything.

"I love him. I always have." I glance towards him. "When he came to me after I took the position as Lady of Souls he didn't fight, not really. It was so fucking easy for him to give up on us."

"One could argue that you gave up as well." He counters, not unkindly. And I can't argue with him because deep down I know it's true. I let him leave, I let his mother and Oisin win that day without so much as a fight. Dios pushes us upward until he can hold my face between his hands, eyes pinning me to the spot. "You both have healing to do, my reaper, so much healing and rebuilding. Why not try doing that together?"

"What about you?" I counter. He drops his hands free of my face before dragging us both to a stand. "Dios, what about you and Jax?" He scrubs his face with the hand that isn't clutching my own.

"He wants the bond as much as I do."

I nod, "so what is the issue?"

He pauses for a moment, the words building in his chest before he finally lets them free. "Magic like ours, together, is not something this world will want. We would have many enemies, the worst of all my own damn family. They will want to rip it from us. And if we had children? They would be just as in danger as we are."

His admission almost startles me because he is indeed terrified. His face showing the emotions clear as day as he talks. "Well lucky for you, you both have me. So, you wouldn't be facing this all alone."

Dios shakes his head, "I can't put you in danger as well."

I let out a dark huff of a laugh. "Dios. Look. I know you have guilt that your father would want to kill us. I get it. But I grew up with Jax. I know what it's like to be around snakes of all variety. We will be fine. All of us. Now let's go find Jackson."

Dios lets out a long sigh but nods his head. I reach up and plant a kiss on his lips, the cool steel of his piercings brushing against the heat I feel when we touch. I don't say anything as I pull away but I do lace my hand in his and squeeze it, just like with Jackson, before pulling us towards the house.

TWENTY-NINE

Harrowlena

The moment the ground shook I knew exactly what had happened, what was happening. I didn't need to see Jackson or Dios to have them tell me a gate was now open. And yet a part of me struggles to still believe he did it; he followed through with unleashing those creatures on an innocent city. My stomach rolls at the thought of all the lives that will, or have been, lost because of our end goal.

I don't think the blood on my hands will ever wash away. Not now.

Redemption and salvation are two things that will not find me or my soul.

Something has snapped in me.

A broken piece of my, once stitched back together, heart now seems determined to bleed me out. It had already started before Dios pulled me from that blood drenched hallway. But now? Now their words have filled the gaps pushing the stiches further apart. Leaving me with a gaping hole where my heart should be.

I want to be angry with them for putting the idea that The Order and Oisin, the only person who claimed to have cared for me, lied. That everything was a lie in the end. But I can't bring myself to point my ire at them fully. Because some of it does indeed lay with the person who gave me this scar on my palm.

Now, as I stand with fingers poised on it, I take a deep, steadying breath and press inward. With my eyes closed I feel the magic unfurling around me as I send my intention and location through that bond.

"You are taking a huge risk here, my angel." My eyes flutter open against the dark voice, and I stifle back a sob of both relief and shame to see my mate standing before me. My body moves without thought as I throw my arms around his neck, forgetting my anger and confusion for a moment. I relish in the warmth his body gives me and drink in his scent until I feel practically drunk from it. "But fuck am I glad you did. I missed you; did you miss me?"

"I. . ." Words fail me as I try to grapple with the rage and confusion, I had moments ago but instead, as my mate stands in front of me, all I can seem to focus on is how much I've missed him.

"Poor little Lena, at a loss for words already?" He smirks. My cheeks flame red, burning so hot I worry I'll catch flame. He laughs softly. "Gods I missed the way your cheeks turn red."

"I did miss you." I finally manage.

He smiles at me, the same smile that he used to give me when we would sit opposite one another in my old home before it falters and turns to a frown. "I was worried they poisoned your mind, worried they've been telling you lies about me." My stomach drops out and I feel myself suddenly filled with shame. "Ah, so they have been telling you sweet, little lies. It's okay my Lena. I can only imagine how hard this is. Being amongst them, having to see them every day and pretend to hate me."

More shame tries to drown me as I realize I had allowed their words to paint a different picture of my life; calling him here as proof of that. I never would have pressed that scar had I not doubted something. Doubted him.

As if he understands he presses a kiss to my lips, exploring almost lazily until I'm practically panting and my hands find their way back onto his body. He lets out a low moan, dragging me into him once more.

"You can make it up to me," he pants. "Fuck I missed the taste of your lips." He resumes kissing me, devouring all I have to give him until he's moving me backwards and pressing me down onto the bed. When he pulls away once more I watch through hooded eyes as he pulls his cock free of his pants, stroking it up and down. "I need that pretty little cunt of yours."

My body moves as if under a spell, slowly dragging my clothing away so I can expose myself to him. His gaze lands on my core, hot and hungry for me. "Oisin. . ." I groan as notches his head to my core and begins to push inward.

"So fucking tight." He moans. I wince a bit as his length fills me past the point of comfort. My body tensing as it tries to accommodate him with no preparation. For a moment I just watch him, observing his face as he focuses on fucking me. When he finally notices my gaze he pauses his own pleasure, sitting backwards so he can find my clit with his thumb. When he presses down on the bundle of nerves, I let out a long moan. "That's it, that's what I want to feel. I need you nice and wet for me. Need to feel you squeeze my cock." His words undo me and I allow him to take all the pleasure he wants from my body as he edges me towards my own.

"Oisin, please!" I beg.

He smirks. "Please what?" I shake my head back and forth, unsure of even what I'm begging for. "Please let you cum? Please fill you with my own?" His hips snap forward harder, thumb leaving my clit so he can grip my thighs and leverage himself easier. I feel it the moment he falls over his edge, filling me with his release. My own nowhere in sight.

Oisin stills above me before slowly pulling free, eyes still glued to my cunt. I feel his fingers as he dips deep within, fucking any of his cum that dared escape back inside me. "I want you to be full of me while you talk with them." He drags his fingers back out, painting my clit with his release and stroking gently. My back arches upward at the feel, the orgasm I lost now building back up rapidly. "I want you to remember it's me who brings you this pleasure, me who loves you and cares for you."

"Yes! Yes!" I pant. Agreeing blindly. My hips fuck his hand as my body desperately reaches for that feeling I'm craving.

"Always mine." He whispers, leaning in close. "Always yours."

"Always yours." I say back as I start to crest. "OISIN!" He slams his hand over my mouth as my pussy convulses and wave after wave of my own release falls over me.

"Fuck your beautiful when you fall apart for me." He groans. "Makes me want to stick my cock back in you and keep fucking you all night."

I think I beg him for that, my mind obsessed with the idea of more pleasure. But instead, he pulls his fingers free leaving me empty and quivering before pushing them in my mouth and forcing me to lick our release clean. I almost gag when he presses too far back and he lets out a huff of a chuckle at the movement. My cheeks burn with embarrassment as he drags the fingers free of my mouth and goes about tucking himself back into his pants.

"I'm sorry I called you here." I mutter softly. "I know it was a risk."

He frowns at me, "Why did you call me here?"

The words I wanted to say no longer exist, instead I utter the ones that I know he wants to hear. "We are going to The Well."

Jackson

"Ugh, where is Dios?" Kallen groans. "I'm bored. I'm ready to go do something."

Demon shakes his head even as Reaver snorts at her lack of patience.

"I'm sure he'll be along soon." I respond, dreading the idea of him showing up with Arcanna. I need a moment to prep her, to tell her who is here and why.

As if summoned by my thoughts, the door behind Kallen pushes open, drawing my attention, and Arcanna's body falls inward with Dios pulled in behind. Her face is flushed, cheeks a slight crimson and hair a mess. Dirt is streaked across the two and the happiness radiating off of them is electric. At least for the moment before Arcanna's eyes land on Rhea. The smile slips, her eyes grow hard, and she presses into Dios. My worst fears flare up again.

Dios cuts me a look that promises swift retribution, arms crossed protectively over her body as he looks between me and the group gathered in the room. "I suggest you explain rapidly, *mi cielo.*"

I hear Kallen let out a low whistle. "Looks like someone got fucked and mated."

Arcanna whips her head towards the female with a glare before turning back to me. My eyes snag on the fresh bite mark on Arcanna's neck and I stumble backwards. A cornucopia of emotions flooding my body as I war between being oddly happy they are mated and hurt that I wasn't good enough for either to complete the bond with.

My mouth goes to open, the statement about to roll off my tongue when Rhea cuts in. "Arcanna," she stands, her back straight and face sympathetic. When she moves towards her however, Reaver grabs her wrist as Dios pushes himself between the two. "I do not mean you, or Jackson, harm. I am only here to seek help in ridding our world of Oisin and The Order."

Arcanna says nothing, but her eyes? Her eyes remain cold and calculating as she assesses the female.

Rhea jerks her arm from Reaver, glaring at him. "I may be your fiancé but I can take care of myself, don't presume otherwise." Reaver lets out a low growl, his eyes flashing briefly.

"Fiancé?" Arcanna finally says, her voice quiet.

Rhea looks back to her, nodding. "Yes." Sadness seems to pass over her and my heart breaks for her. Rhea never wanted marriage. Never wanted to be tied to a man. And now she's with Reaver, who very clearly has feelings for her.

Arcanna seems to relax, giving Rhea a nod before looking back around the room, skipping over me entirely and landing on Kallen. "Never thought I'd see you again." She says with a warm smile.

Kallen offers up her own version of a smile, "glad we are Reaper. I have a feeling I'm going to have fun causing chaos next to you."

Dios looks over at me, no doubt seeing every single fucking doubt and anxiety wash over my face. Like he always seems to. "*Mi cielo. . .*" He starts.

I hold up my hand, "I'm happy for you two." I say it, and mean it, despite a slight pit in my stomach that he couldn't bond with me. That for some reason choosing me wasn't an option. I am happy they have one another. And I'm disappointed. Because I wanted that, with both of them.

I feel the anxiety attack the moment it starts to happen. My skin feels tight and my breathing restrictive. Arcanna's stormy eyes meet mine quickly, no doubt sensing the looming panic attack down the start of our bond. *The bond that she hasn't completed.* Anxiety doesn't give two shits if what it's telling me is rational or not, all it cares about is dragging me under and suffocating me. Force feeding me the reality it feels like painting, creating its own truth. And right now, its truth is that neither want me.

Dios unwinds himself form her and moves over towards me, gathering my tense body into his arms. "*Mi cielo*," he whispers in my ear. "Breathe." I follow his direction, dragging an unsteady breath inward again and again until I feel moderately in control. Dios pulls back from me, turning towards Demon and Kallen. "Pres, fancy seeing you here."

Demon pushes upward, placing Kallen on the seat he vacated, before clearing the space between us and pulling Dios in for a hug, slapping his back roughly. "I fucking missed you," he growls. When Demon pulls back, he has a wide smile on his face, dragging Dios's forehead to his own.

Kallen watches them with an intensity that makes me flush as visions of solstice flash over me. "Fuck," she groans biting her lip. "Now I just want a repeat of the holiday again."

The mention of our foursome has my cock hardening and lust blooming deep within my body. Visions of the night flash through my mind and I can still feel Dios as he knotted me in the middle of all the carnage that Kallen had left.

I cringe for a moment as my eyes dart over towards Arcanna but she looks more intrigued than anything, her eyes dilated slightly. "I think I need that full story," she says glancing between us all.

Kallen lets out a throaty laugh, "these boys know how to show a girl a good time. But I've got to be honest. . . Jax and Dios are something else to watch." She muses. "If you ever want to share them with me, I'm so fucking down." She lets her eyes roam over Arcanna's body. "Or if you want to play." Arcanna flushes a deep crimson and nibbles on her bottom lip.

"Ugh," Rhea groans. "You guys remind me of my brothers, no fucking boundaries."

Kallen's eyes light up and the thought of her meeting the twins has me interjecting finally. "Enough." I snap.

"Ugh fine," Kallen groans. "Ruin all my fun."

I glance to Arcanna, "Harrow agreed to take us to The Well. I never got to tell you that before all this bullshit happened."

Arcanna's shoulders seem to relax briefly but her face becomes serious once more, "While I am happy to hear that, I don't know if I trust her not to tell someone where we are going and what we are doing but I suppose given the moon is fast approaching we do not have a choice."

"Why does the full moon matter?" Kallen asks.

"Jackson is running low on magic; he needs to replenish. The Well will enable him to do that with the help of Harrow." Arcanna's words are explosive in the room.

Kallen glances between us, "why can't you feed him?"

"The Forest." She replies. "It might allow me to mate, but no one can feed from my magic."

"And you?" Kallen directs the question at Dios with a heated glare. He says nothing, she snorts and shakes her head. "I see you're still being fucking dumb."

"Kallen. . ." Demon growls low at her, a warning, which

only inspires her to snap her teeth at him before rolling her eyes.

"We go to The Well. Replenish Jax. And then we head to the city to hunt Oisin." Arcanna says, the plan sounding so easy coming from her.

"That's not all. . ." I feel Dios tense, knowing that my next statement is going to drop a bomb into the water. We all know what the original families did to Kallen and her mate. Out of the corner of my eye I see Reaver angle himself in front of Rhea ever so slightly, sensing the change in the room. "He brought back the original families."

The words are barely out of my mouth before Kallen explodes.

Arcanna
(Points of Authority/99 Problems/One Step- JAY-Z & LINKIN PARK)

Magic explodes outward as Kallen detonates in rage. My own magic moves up in a shield out of instinct, from my peripheral I can see Jackson's wings blown outward covering himself and Dios. Reaver has pulled Rhea down to the ground, using his body to protect her as six fully grown beasts pad into the space with lips rolled back, their essence coming from the shadows themselves. The space vibrates with their presence as they move to their master.

"Who?" She growls towards me, her voice sending shivers skating down my spine. Out of instinct my bone wings shift from my back. Her eyes glow with unholy fire as she looks at me. The feminine-feral rage she's held for lifetimes coming alive. "Who did they bring back?"

Swallowing to stay calm and steady my breathing I remind myself I am not the one she is angry at. "All the heads of the families, with the exception of the Carmine family."

She lets out a loud snarl. The sound reverberated through the space. Her magic dancing across us as it seeks out retribution. "Arthur?" She asks.

"Arcanna..." Dios's voice comes out in warning. "Come here."

I don't move though; I stand against the tempest that Kallen is throwing. I step towards her instead of away, earning a shout from Jax. But I hold my hand up silencing him. "Yes, Arthur. And Andrew Cosark, and Marianna Hoar."

Another volley of magic is unleashed as she lets go of a scream so agonizing that my own blood heats with both rage and grief for how she feels. Those covens created the creature in front of me, molded her through pain they deliberately caused her.

Her mate appears next to her finally. "Kallen," He growls. Bracketing her face with his hands so he can pull her forehead to his.

"I will kill them all." She pants.

He nods, "*we* will kill them all."

"I will paint the ground with their blood. I will rip apart their bodies and when nothing is left but their souls I will condemn them to the deepest pits of Hell. They will never know peace."

"I can give you the ability to do that." I say.

She turns towards me; I can understand in this moment why she is still feared. Despite no longer holding The Harbinger magic I see why people tremble in front of her. "Say more." She bites out.

I drop my shield, crossing my arms over my chest and pulling my wings back in. "I know a death dragon who can consume souls. And he's *very* fucking hungry."

Jackson

My wings pull in tight to my body but still ready to block any more magic Kallen may throw out. Dios's arms strained to hold me back from jumping between Arcanna and her. She may not be the Harbinger anymore, but she is just as deadly. And I have no doubt in my mind Demon would do very little to stop her from killing. "Drago?" Kallen asks, the mention of my sister's mate pulls me back into the conversation fully. "I knew that sneaky little dragon could do more than he let on."

I feel raw as I listen to the words. Everything starting to pile on me. My sister being gone, my lack of magic, Dios and Arcanna. My mouth feels dry and my heart sinks into my stomach as it all builds and builds.

"Why didn't you tell me?" My voice sounds broken as it leaves my mouth. The realization of who has been helping her watch over The Forest finally settling into me. Dios's arms continue to hold me, as if worried I'll launch myself at her.

She takes a step forward before pausing, her face sheepish. "You know it's complicated. The Forest has rules Jax, and I'm already breaking them by being here—"

"FUCK THE RULES!" I bellow. The pile of issues and emotions I've been holding exploding outward. She flinches, stepping backward. "Is this why you haven't completed the bond?"

"*Mi cielo*," Dios cautions.

Rationally I know it's not her fault, I know the gods damn rules. I'm the King, it's my job to know them and enforce them. But the older brother that misses his younger sister isn't rational, he's grieving the loss. A loss that I still haven't been able to mourn and honor properly.

"I'm sorry Jax, I really am." She says, tears threatening to roll down her face.

I jerk myself away from Dios, my magic darkening the

room before I regain control. "Ava deserves rest, peace, not hunting the creatures that put her there in the first place!" Nothing can seem to stop me from spitting the venom out. I shake my head, fists balling at my sides. "How could you allow this to happen?"

Her nostrils flare, tears now finally breaking out of her eyes. "She's my friend too you know?" She says through a small hiccup of a sob. "Do you think I want her doing what she's doing? Hunting things?"

I scoff. "Of course you do, now you don't have to do your fucking job. You can stay here and fuck Dios all you want." The moment the words leave my mouth I know I've gone too far.

A broken sob falls from her mouth as she turns and flees the room.

"Well, that was a dick move." Kallen says, breaking the silence that's invaded around us.

Dios grabs me by the back of the neck, dragging my gaze towards him and away from where Arcanna ran. "You go apologize." He growls, unforgiving. "And after that we'll talk about the bullshit you were just saying."

I don't argue, simply nod instead and let the walk of shame see me out.

Reaver

It's painful, watching my best friend finally implode. The shit he's kept shoved down for so long finally refusing to stay buried.

Dios mutters a curse before dropping into the low backed couch and draping his arms over the soft cushions. Demon clears his throat, "maybe you two should fill Dios in on what has happened, bring him up to speed."

Rhea lets out a tired sigh. I know she's exhausted and starving. She hasn't fed since we've been together and it's been weeks if not a month since she dropped into my lap, literally. The river of tears flowing down her face, and large eyes locking with mine before burrowing herself in my neck and breaking. Her sobs wracked her whole body, all the while I held her through it.

I was a dick to take advantage of her at that moment, to force her into the marriage. I would have helped her regardless, but my family? They would have been harder to convince. Her brothers dug the hole that she fell into, made it next to impossible for her to gain the trust of my family, but, I couldn't pass up the chance to snag the female who I've wanted since the moment I scented her. Even if she hates me for it, she's mine now.

"I'm not sure how long The Order has been spreading their poison in my city. However, it's clear it was long enough that they gained the support of many of our citizens who had started to push against my family for the support we gave the royals. Oisin came to our home as an advocate for peace, he claimed. According to him he was attempting to bring the truth to light about The Order. My parents and the council members all listened to him and bought his lies about Jackson and his family." She lets out a tired sigh with a shake of her head. "I tried to argue against him, I even reached out to my brothers, but in the end, I couldn't bring anyone to my side and had to flee my own home after he killed my parents." She says sadly.

"What was his gain?" Kallen asks.

"We may not be as big as the capital but we are powerful, should we have come to the aid of Jackson and his family I don't think The Order would have stood a chance." Rhea replies. "Once The Order realized they had turned the council members it was easy to turn the city against us. Most the upper and middle class have fallen in line with them, spouting the bullshit The Order feeds its people like gods damn scripture." Her body tenses, no doubt the memories invading her. "I barely managed to escape."

Anger ripples through me, "my armies are now in Divinity, taking control back and working on fishing out the little roaches." I say, my voice a deep growl.

"My brothers are working on it; I didn't need your help doing that." Rhea counters with venom in her voice.

I shake my head with frustration while suppressing an eye roll. I know she wants her brothers to still be who they were growing up, but truth be told they will never be those people again. Not after their loss. "Your brothers are part of the issue." I lean in closer, my mouth inches from her ear. "And it was my lap you dropped into, my home you thought of when you needed to be safe, not theirs."

She glares at me, pulling away from my breath and opening her mouth to continue the argument we haven't stopped engaging in since that moment.

"They are trying to split us up, divide our own meager forces so we can't stop him." Kallen highlights.

Demon nods in agreement. "It's smart. He's causing chaos in Gothic Grove, Divinity and still in the royal city. He's making it so we cannot all be in one place at the same time."

"Yeah, because he knows he'd fucking lose, little weasel cock." Kallen grumbles.

Dios drags his hand down his face as he leans forward. "No matter what we have to split up, he's already started this plan in motion. Reaver if you can keep control of Divinity that'll be huge. He may not have guessed your army would show up and instead assumed one of us would. That leaves you and Rhea on the playing field."

"And my brothers." Rhea says stubbornly. "I can get them; they can help more."

Dios nods even as I let out another hostile growl.

Kallen snickers. "I suppose we can go to the Primal Knights and get them ready."

Dios pushes to a stand, "Agreed. You can go back and forth the easiest. Once we get back from The Well we can join you in Gothic Grove."

Kallen mutters something of an agreement as she is starts dragging Demon out the door with a coy look at Dios who shakes his head and follows behind them leaving me alone with my stubborn ass fiancé.

Rhea pushes to stand only to wobble forcing me to lunge forward so she doesn't fall backwards.

I move in front of her, holding her shoulder with my hand to keep her steady. "You need to feed." I huff out. She goes to open her mouth, "don't even try lying to me Rhea. I know you haven't." I cut her off. She tries to shoot me a glare, but her movements are off and sluggish. "Gods damn it, Rhea! Fucking feed." I thrust my wrist towards her mouth.

"No." she says stubbornly, words slurring slightly now.

I growl, raising my flesh to my teeth and ripping into myself. Her pupils dilate and fangs drop down as she takes in the dripping mess of flesh. "You need to be alive to hate me, now feed."

Rhea is the most stubborn female I've ever met, even now I watch as she fights against her innate need to feed. Thankfully she lunges forward dragging my wrist to her mouth.

Her teeth sink into the flesh, and she pulls deep from the vein already opened. The sounds she makes as she sucks down my blood shoot straight to my cock. Her mouth is greedy as she takes pull after pull. Her own arousal perfumes the air around us. I grind my teeth down to avoid slipping my hand into her pants to feel how wet she has become.

"This means nothing," she pants, tongue licking the wound. "I'm turned on because I'm feeding and I'm only feeding because I have to."

I laugh, "you trying to convince me or yourself, princess?"

She snarls, biting in harder. The pain lights a fuse within me, and I drag her into my body, twisting so her back presses against my chest. She lets out a moan as my hand trails down her stomach to the waistband of her pants. She parts her legs and it's the only permission I need as I let my fingers dip into her bottoms.

"This all for me?" I swipe my finger in the mess she's created, dragging it up to her clit and pressing in hard circles. She bucks forward.

"Oh shit." She moans. Her head tilts back against my chest showing the blood painting her mouth and dripping down her chin. "Oh, fuck yes."

I push my fingers inside her. Her walls squeezing me tightly. "You're awfully tight princess." I keep pumping them in and out, "I want to split you open with my cock." A gush of arousal slicks down my fingers as she lets out another cry.

"Fucking do it then, stop talking and fuck me already with that big cock you like to talk about so much." She snarls.

"Fucking brat." I grumble. The arm she had been feasting on sneaks upward and grips her by the hair, forcing her towards the table. Between the two of us we rip her pants off right before she lays her chest on to the table, splaying her legs out wide. Her core dripping. "Fuck you're so wet, so ready to be filled." I keep staring as I unzip my pants, my cock bobbing free and glistening.

"Don't think this is about you." She growls. "I'm picturing Demon and Kallen."

SMACK.

The sound echoes across the room as my palm connects with her bare ass cheeks. She yips and goes to jump from the table, but I press my palm onto her neck, holding her to the hard surface.

"Talk about someone else while my cock is near your pussy ever again and you'll get more than a slap across your ass." I growl.

Leaning down I press my full weight into her. "Do you know what it means to fuck someone like me?" I drag the tip through her mess, the tip barely pushing in. She cries out, more begging and pleading. I slowly push inside her until I'm met with a slight resistance. I pause. "Rhea are you. . ."

"Shut the fuck up and keep going." She snaps. A dark primal need rises within me, a feral need to confirm exactly what I'm thinking. I plunge in with no ceremony, letting my cock impale her. She cries out, her body stiff and hands fisted against the table so hard I worry she'll break skin.

A sick satisfaction washes over me. She whimpers as I go to move my hips. "Shhh, breathe through it for me." I release her neck from my grip and sweep my hand under her and rub her clit in slow circles until I feel her body relax. When I start to thrust slowly her cries turn to a fever pitch, the wails filling the room so only the sounds of our pleasure exist.

"Oh my god what is that?" She cries as she feels the ridges of my cock start to expand. "Oh, fuck oh fuck." Her hips thrust back to meet me.

"That, princess, is what makes my cock more special. And why you'll never want another one again." I keep thrusting, allowing the four bumps to rub up against that extra sensitive spot deep within. My magic hums in my veins as they do, and I know the moment they start to vibrate.

"I'm going to cum, oh fuck oh fuck." She cries out under me. "Right there!"

"Thats it, Rhea, cover my cock in your cum. Show me what it feels like to have your pussy squeeze the life out of me." She cries out as I say the words and I feel her spasm, feel the warmth gush over me. It tips me over the edge and I'm cuming with her.

A few final thrusts and I collapse down, careful not to crush her with my weight, the two of us panting. I plant a soft kiss on her shoulder dragging my teeth over her skin as I do. "Fuck Rhea, you are magnificent."

"Get off me." She growls, shoving her elbow back towards me.

I frown sitting up and wincing as I drag my cock free from her, the ridges still exposed and wanting to be buried in her still. Her small hand manages to shove me backwards as she collects the remnants of her ruined pants. As I move to push my cock into my own clothing, I see the smear of our combined release and just under it, blood.

"Rhea?" I call out.

"What?" She snaps without turning to look at me.

"Were you a virgin?"

She lets out a choked laugh before turning and offering me a condescending smile. "Sure was. So thanks for taking that. Now I can fuck whoever I want without that pesky thing in the way."

"Oh Rhea, you just awoke the beast." I say with a deep growl. I launch myself at her, pinning her body to the door she had been making her way towards. Her eyes flare with fear but her scent blooms with arousal. "You belong to me.

Mind, body and soul." My fingers shove up inside her roughly. "And this cunt will never experience someone else. It's mine to fuck, fill and breed." Her pupils dilate until none of the color remains. "You like that idea, don't you? I'm going to do it all Rhea, fight me all you want but I'm done playing nice. I've got your virgin blood smeared over my dick." Her breathing heavies and she drags her full bottom lip into her teeth. "I'm going to ruin you princess. Rip you apart and forge you into my queen."

I pull my fingers from her core, bringing them to my mouth and licking them clean before pushing away from her with a cocky smile.

"Fuck you Reaver. Fuck you from here to the bottom of the underworld." She snarls. She rips open the door I had her pinned to and storms out, throwing her middle finger up as she goes.

I offer a dark chuckle. "Let the games begin princess. Let the games begin."

THIRTY

Jackson
  (Exile- Taylor Swift)
Anger is like a bon fire made of only brush, it's easy to ignite and quick to get large but its flame only lasts so long before it dwindles back to nothing and all your left with is ash and smoke. I had been filled with anger when I lashed out, my body burning with it like a raging inferno and now, as I follow Arcanna's scent, I'm left with nothing but extinguished embers.

I pause at Arcanna's door, shame rooting me to the ground. I know the anger was my own hurt over my mates not bonding with me. I allowed that emotional anguish to lash out at her and try to drag her down in the inferno. As soon as the words had left my mouth I knew I didn't truly believe them.

I should be better than that. I should know how to control my emotions.

"I can hear you out there, stop lurking." Arcanna's voice sounds muffled through the door. Letting out a sigh and shake of my head I let myself into the space she's claimed as her own. It takes a moment for my eyes to adjust to the dark room. When they finally do they land on Arcanna sitting in the middle of the bed with a massive blanket wrapped around her shoulders. Her eyes are red rimmed and puffy but the tears seemed to have long dried.

Approaching slowly, I sit down next to her, "I'm sorry I lashed out, I never should have said what I did."

Arcanna shakes her head, the long raven black hair shifting ever so slightly as she does. "I kind of deserved it after everything." She mutters. I go to counter her but she holds up her hand. "I ran, I listened to your mother and Oisin when I shouldn't have. I drove you away when you came to me. I kept it to myself your sister was with me. And. . . And I mated Dios when I shouldn't have if for no other reason than because I knew you should be the first."

Without thought I pull her body into mine, "there is no who should have mated first. I'm glad you and Dios found your connection. Even if we haven't found ours yet." I say with conviction. She lets out a small cry, the noise breaking my heart. "I let the grief take hold and my own gods damn insecurities. You aren't to blame. I am." I finally manage to say.

She pulls back to look at me, those tears silently tracking down her face. "I didn't complete out bond because I was scared about not only something breaking us apart but of The Forest. I have a responsibility to it, and the magic will not allow me to forget that. It was selfish of me to even let Dios bond with me."

She pauses taking a long, deep breath, slowly allowing it out breath by breath before continuing. "This will only end in heartbreak." She continues. "Ava isn't taking my place there, she's just helping. This will end no matter what when I'm called home."

I growl. My body vibrating with uncontrolled rage at

the idea of her leaving. "You are ours. Mine and Dios. And nothing is going to take you away from us."

(Snow on the Beach- Taylor Swift feat. Lana Del Rey)

She pulls back and looks at me, eyes watery and full of emotion. "It doesn't work like that and you know it, without someone to tend to it, I won't be allowed to leave while I'm alive."

"We'll figure it all out Arcanna. One day at a time we'll figure it out." I press my lips to hers, desperate for the connection before pulling back to look her in the eyes again.

"I was so angry Jackson. And I'm scared to let it go." Her admission sends more tears down her face and I drag her back into my body. Holding her tightly against my chest.

"I get it, fuck do I get it. It's easier to live in that space than face the unknown. Trust me. My anxiety does an excellent job of convincing me to stay in the places I've been." Pulling back I let my lips hover above hers. "But I'm willing to risk it, are you?"

It takes a full heartbeat before she parts her lips and presses them into mine. She tastes like salt water and anguish. Each kiss I give her is an attempt to heal the wounds that not only I ripped open, but the ones left behind by everyone else. I kiss each eyelid, trace my tongue over her cheeks to chase the tears, before returning to her mouth.

"Jax," She sobs. My name breaking across her lips.

"I know, wicked girl. I know." I lay her down on the bed, slowly stripping her off her clothing before I discard my own onto the floor. It's a slow exploration of her body with my mouth, my cock painfully hard and leaking precum. I lose myself in her taste as I feast on her. When my mouth finally lands on that tight bundle of nerves, she lets out a cry, back arching off the bed. I press one finger inside her as I let her grind into my face.

"I need you inside me." She begs. "Please!"

"Fuck you sound good when you beg." Crawling up her body I line myself up to her opening. Slowly I push in, making sure we each feel every inch as I disappear inside her. When I'm fully seated, I pause, watching her face. My magic swirls around us, the start of the bond pulsing under my skin as the tattoo burns.

She bites her lip hard, only a moment of hesitation before she nods. I feel it, her magic meeting mine and I have no doubt her own tattoo is burning now as well.

"You are my fucking home, Arcanna." My thumb finds her clit, the pressure causing her to cry out as I angle my cock to hit just the right spot. Magic flares around us, bright and sudden.

Her eyes grow wide, "Jax?"

The slight smile grows wicked, "see that? Thats our bond in real time. Thats our magic together. Because we belong to each other." Her hair is a cascade of black framing her face, the golden glow of the magic sending an unearthly aura around her. Her cheeks are flushed and eyes half lidded, she looks drunk with arousal and need as she whimpers. Her hips thrust to meet mine as we allow the magic to cocoon around us.

The moment the bond connects she cries out, back arching, and orgasm cresting over. My own cock spills deep inside her as we feel our souls link and the small kernel, we'll each share moves between us. Her emotions flood my side of the bond as it opens up in a spectacular array of lust, love, and magic. She cries out again as I feel her pussy clench once more, wetness pooling under us from our combined release.

"Jax!" She cries out.

I lean down, claiming her lips for a moment before pulling back, "that's right, scream your mates name while you cum." I nip at her neck and then ear lobe. "Scream so loud Dios can't help but join us." In a quick move I flip us so she's seated on top of me, her naked body glistening with sweat.

"Oh fuck, oh fuck." She pants as she starts to ride me, head thrown back in ecstasy. "Just like that Jax, that feels so fucking good."

I press my thumb into her clit, "that's right wicked girl, use my cock for your pleasure." She fucks me hard, her breath coming in quick pants as she gets closer to her release.

"Oh gods I'm going to cum Jax!" She cries out only seconds before I feel her clench and release. My own cock filling her one last time as the bond fully clicks into place and the magic ties us together. Her head drops to my forehead, our breathing coming in heavy pants as I remain deep inside her.

"I love you." I remind her again. I can feel my eyes tearing up allowing her to see how she affects me.

She lifts up, planting a soft kiss to my mouth. "I love you too."

My arms squeeze around Arcanna's naked body as she shifts in her sleep. My own eyes still closed as I enjoy the feel of our bond. My cock presses against her low back, still hard and aching to be inside her. We had both fallen asleep shortly after she slipped off my cock and now that I'm awake I want more. I want to stay in this bubble we've created for a little longer before reality comes calling. My hand slips forward, fingers exploring until they reach the apex of her thighs and I find her sticky with our release. When I dip deeper, I find more wetness pooled at the entrance of her cunt.

My eyes slowly blink open and are met with Dios's glowing ones as he leans against the far wall. "Don't stop, I want to watch." He commands softly.

I nod, allowing my fingers to dip inside Arcanna. She lets out a soft moan, her sleep now lighter as she rolls to her back and exposes her full breasts. Dios moves over and lets his tongue trace one of the barbells before sucking it into his mouth. Arcanna's eyes flutter and her hand comes up, pressing Dios's mouth into her breast harder.

"Are you awake wicked girl?" I coo, stroking her.

She groans, "fuck yes I am now." Her pussy squeezes my fingers and I chuckle. "A girl could get used to this."

Dios huffs out a laugh as he pulls off of her tit. She pouts but stops as she watches him drag his t-shirt up and over his head exposing his glorious body. When he starts to unbutton his pants my mouth waters and when his length springs free, I let out my own groan. He drags his hand up and down his shaft in a lazy fashion, collecting his precum as he does so he can drag it back down his cock.

"Did you eat her out?" He asks, still holding eye contact with her.

"Yes sir." I respond immediately.

He turns towards me, smirking. "Did you taste me inside her?" He leans down and claims my mouth with his own, kissing and biting, before pulling back and moving to Arcanna. Leaning in she accepts his cock into her mouth, eagerly licking and sucking it as he slowly pumps in and out. Her pussy squeezes on my finger and I slip another in, stretching her a bit more. Dios pulls free of her mouth after a moment.

"Hey! I wasn't finished!" She complains.

He shakes his head as he steps backward and lays on the bed next to her, "I want you on my cock and I want Jackson in your ass." She scrambles upward, my fingers pulling free, and positions herself over his cock. "Is that okay?"

She nods enthusiastically before looking towards me. "Just go slow, be gentle."

"Always." I promise. She smiles before going back to focusing on Dios. "She's hungry for us" I muse as I see her arousal dripping down her thighs.

"She's a slut for our cocks." Dios groans as she lowers down onto him. She takes him slowly, almost painfully slow. His length finally disappearing deep within her. Opening the bedside table I grab the lube before pressing her down onto his chest. Drizzling it onto her tight hole I let myself open her up slowly while she continues to let Dios rock into her.

"How are you feeling my wicked girl?" I ask, pushing my fingers in and out in the same rhythm she's rolling her hips on Dios.

"Fuckkkk," She hisses. "I need it all. I need it now."

"You set the pace." I reminder her. Pulling my fingers free I notch my cock to her entrance and slowly start to push in. "Oh Jesus, I can fucking feel you sir. I can feel you inside her." My cock can barely fit into her ass with Dios already lodged in her pussy and the feeling has me almost cuming. After an eternity I'm fully in her, the three of us panting as we get used to the feeling.

"Someone needs to move," she grinds out. "Now."

Dios huffs a laugh and we both begin to push in an out, slow at first, allowing Arcanna to get used to us. To stretch to accommodate us.

"Fucking hell. So full. So good." She groans. Her body loose and accepting as she finds her rhythm with us. The tightness of her ass and the feel of Dios against me is more than I can a handle and when her magic brushes against me I can't hold back.

"OH FUCK!" I shout as I pump into her. She squeezes around me as it happens, almost painfully.

"That's it, *mi cielo*, fill our girl up. I want to know both her holes are dripping." Dios commands. His magic snakes out and I feel it grip my soul, extending the orgasm as Arcanna falls over the edge with me. Our cries fill the room, a symphony of pleasure. "Fuck you two are beautiful when you come apart."

Arcanna collapses forward again, her body having pressed against mine at some point, and my cock slips free as the last of my cum is spent. I lay back and watch in fascination as my release drips from her while Dios fucks deep within her used body. When he stiffens, I know he is filling her, finding his own release deep within our mate.

THIRTY-ONE

Harrowlena

I had not expected to awake alone in my room yet I could not allow myself to be shocked by the action. It was a risk to bring Oisin here and he was kind enough to allow me to find pleasure in his body. The memory sends a wave of need through me that I force myself to shove away.

Dragging myself into the shower I almost want to keep the mess he made between my thighs as a reminder of his devotion to me. I had felt renewed in my purpose after our conversation, if not a bit embarrassed for allowing myself to be manipulated so easily by them, and yet. . . something still nagged in the back of my mind. A whisp of a feeling. Something that has barely taken root, yet it keeps trying to claw its way out of me.

The warm water flows over my body as my muscles attempt to relax. I let out a long sigh, dragging my nails over my bare arms in a rhythmic motion as I think back to the information I had gained, trying desperately to figure out why I still feel wrong.

"But what of the people?"

Oisin gathers me into a hug. "I will remove the creatures

as soon as we meet our goal. This is a means to an end." He assures me. "And before they put it in your head that I'm torturing some innocent victim and stealing her magic, just know that she's the one who has known what the royals were doing this whole time. She is no more innocent than Jackson is. And yet despite all that I promise to release her when I'm done."

Yes, there was someone being used for magic. But only short term, the magic was needed to finish the plan. Yes, the gates were opened but as a distraction only, everything would be fixed upon completion of the plan. It all made sense and felt so honest it almost made me feel bad for questioning anything.

I was lucky. As he responded with no anger only a soft smile and continued reassurance that all was well in hand and they were attempting to minimize the deaths of those who were not involved.

And yet still. . . something felt wrong.

In my bones and in my soul something felt wrong.

I slip down the wall, landing on the cool ground, closing my eyes, I tilt my face up to the cooling mist the shower is producing. My nipples seem to peak at the sensation and my stomach clenches. I frown, confused for a moment before another wave moves through me. This one stronger.

(Tennessee Whiskey- Austin Giorgio)

"I see you ignored my advice, little priestess." The rich scent of Dios invades the small room, the usual bergamot but with hints of warm vanilla and citrus laying on top of it. But it's not his cocky smirk I find, no, it's his brother.

Luz has his arms crossed over his chest and his eyes travel over my body in a lazy path that seems to devour every piece of me until my own body feels like it's smoldering and liquid heat pools between my thighs.

"What are you doing here?" I manage to squeak out as I try to cover my naked form.

"I'm disappointed though not entirely shocked." He says in that lazy way. My eyes dart around the bathroom. He tsks, stepping forward slightly, "no one knows I'm here. It's just us." He steps forward another pace until he's just outside the line of the water.

"You need to leave." I say, my voice shaking slightly, and back pressed against the cold shower wall.

He offers a crooked smile, "making sure you're okay." He glances around the room before dropping his eyes back to me, I squirm against the cool tile.

"Why? You don't know me." I ask as a strange heat starts to crawl up my spine, my body suddenly flushed while a longing starts to pool deep within. I should feel afraid right now, should be screaming for help as I sit naked in the shower with a strange man looking at me. But something about his sunset eyes makes me feel unafraid. Nervous? Yes. Afraid? No.

He shrugs as he pulls his shirt up and over his body exposing those hard abs and tattoos that cover him. "I have my reasons." He bends down until he is eye level with me "I wish you had listened to me. But you didn't. You called the one tied to you."

As if someone switched on the cold water my body turns to ice and my mind screeches to a stop. *Oh my god. I was lusting after this man after my mate just left.* I scramble upward as shame bubbles within me, licking up my spine and settling deep within my chest.

"I see you need time to panic, I'll wait." Luz says, leaning against the opposite wall.

His tone fuels a fire within my belly forcing the shameful feelings aside. "Excuse me? Get out." I snap. He only smirks. Adding to my annoyance. "Fine. I'll leave."

Newly embodied I go to move past him, looking far more confident than I feel as I let him take in my naked form. Luz lets his eyes trace over me, his gaze landing on my breasts and lingering before dropping down to the spot between my thighs. My body heats and I struggle to remain in control as I push past him. I wrap myself in a towel before fleeing into the main room.

"You know, you seem a bit flushed." He comments, strolling behind me lazily.

"Because you are looking at me." I snap back.

Luz chuckles. "I'm glad to see you have a bit of fire in you. No longer a little mouse, are you?"

I pause. The realization sinking in. I've been arguing with him and speaking freely. No pause, no hesitation, just free flowing words as they appear in my mind. I spin and face him, attempting to ascertain what magic he is using to pull this from me, to make me behave this way.

"Stop it." I growl. "This isn't me."

He raises an eyebrow, that lazy grin never leaving his face. One that I've seen Dios wear as well. "Have you ever thought it's not me who is doing this to you, but instead it's *him* who has caged you."

The words do something to me. Unlocking a door that should have remained locked and closed until the full moon. My body heats and wetness pools within me as rational thought ebbs away from my mind.

I push my hands through my hair confused and shake my head, "I need. . ." I start but can't seem to get the rest out, can't seem to figure out what I need right now. I shake my head in a desperate attempt to get the feelings out and regain my control.

"Something tells me I shouldn't indulge in you, that you may hate me later for it. But I can't seem to walk away." He says breaching the space between us suddenly. He sweeps me into his hold, his scent overwhelming me as I gasp at the sudden contact. His mouth hovers within inches of mine, our breath shared in the small space. "You're going to hate me eventually, *ángel caido*. Just remember, when that happens, it was me who was here for you. *Not them. Not him. Me.*"

He crushes his mouth into mine and the moment I taste him my body goes up. The flames of lust curling around me as he pillages my mouth with his own. A long moan manages to make it past my lips as I feel his tongue sweep in.

He's the second person I've kissed. The second person who I've touched. And if I was in my rational mind, I would note the difference between him and Oisin. I would notice the care he seems to have even as he grips my arms and pushes me back towards the bed.

But I'm not in my rational mind and all I want is more.

He pushes me backwards, my body landing on the mattress. I let my eyes travel over his body noting his tattoos and golden skin. They two silver barbells through his nipples twinkle in the low light. I bite my lip, a whimper just on the tip of my tongue. "You have no idea how hard it is to hold back right now." He growls out, his voice dropping low, and the sound makes my cunt feel so empty.

I whimper. "I don't want you to hold back," I say. "I want everything you have to give."

He chuckles, "I'm not holding back to spare you, I'm not the hero in this tale. You aren't the princess I'm rescuing. I'm the gods damn villain."

Luz

(Frozen- Madonna & Sickkick)

The little priestess looks up at me with her big, violet, eyes. The haze of her heat clouding them as she whimpers under my gaze. The full moon is still far enough away she should not be experiencing this and yet I knew, a part deep down knew, that she would start early. Whether by her own body deciding it had had enough, or the fucker who is tied to her using magic to mess with it all. It'll be a slow descent into it, maddening slow for her no doubt but still, eventually, she will fully be in the throes of her heat long before the full moon crests into the sky.

I drop to my knees in front of her still naked body, spreading her legs wide so I have her on display. When I glance up and catch her gaze once more, I watch as her pink tongue darts out before she drags her bottom lip into her mouth. She looks hungry.

She's chasing her demons away with my body, and I can't find it in me to stop her.

My hand creates a vice grip on the base of my dick to hold back from cuming too early as I let a finger trail over the wetness already pooling from her. When I bring it to my mouth I let out a groan at the sweetness of it. "You taste just like I thought you would." I murmur.

She groans, pupils blowing wide as I finally drop my mouth to her core. Her back practically levitates off the bed as I let my tongue ring press against her bundle of nerves before dipping within her heat. Her slick flows from her, soaking the bed beneath us.

"Yesss." She hisses out. Her hands finding my hair in a hard grip, forcing my mouth to stay on her core. As if I would dare stop before I have her drowning me. It's laughable really. I could eat this pussy as my last meal.

Her scent perfumes the room, and I groan as more of that delectable slick pours from her. With little preamble I push two digits into her tight pussy. The sound it makes filling the room around us. Her muscles clenching at my fingers as she arches up off the bed once more with a loud moan.

I rip my mouth free even as I continue to fuck her with my fingers. "Shhh, we don't want anyone knowing I'm here, do we?" I say. She whimpers at the loss of contact from my mouth. "Quiet now or I won't let you finish." I keep my eyes locked on hers as I go back to devouring her. Her legs wrap around me as her hands now find purchase on her breasts and squeeze.

"Oh, Oh, that feels so good." She cries in a whisper that is still too audible for my liking, yet I can't seem to care to stop. To remind her to be quiet. I continue to devour her until I feel her at the edge of release. "Right there. Please, Luz. Please I'm there." I smirk against her core as I bring her over the edge, her pussy fluttering around my fingers. She opens her mouth in a silent scream as her orgasm crashes into her.

"You're so tight, I can only imagine how it would feel to push myself deep inside you. Stretching you to the limit." Pulling myself free of the twist of legs Harrow has me in I pump my cock with my hand a few times, her legs spreading wider as if she wants me inside her. I can imagine how it would feel, to claim her like that, to remain locked in her heat. To fill her over and over again. "Fuckkkk." My cum splashes across her bare cunt and lower stomach pulling more sounds of pleasure from her. I stroke myself until my balls are empty and cock soft. I keep my eyes locked on her as I tuck myself back into my pants, still annoyingly wet from the shower.

"No," she cries as she reaches for me. Her eyes feverish and forehead beading with sweat.

I frown, "lets back that off a bit. We don't want things going too far before I have you in my domain." She looks at me with confusion painted on that perfect face. I let my healing magic drift out towards her blood pulling her heat back just a bit so she can feel calm and get some sleep. I give a small kick to the leash deep within her, smirking with satisfaction as I do. "Enjoy her while you can asshole, we are coming for you." I murmur.

Planting a kiss on her forehead I breathe in her scent once more before backing away slowly and allowing the shadows to gather me into their embrace.

Oisin

My chest cracks open, the pain launching me out of the bed as I gasp for breath. The tether in my soul searing as I rub at my sternum. My skin feels tight as I blink away the haze of sleep and push to stand. Walking over to the balcony I fling it open, the night air of Gothic Grove surrounding me as I step out into the darkness. The balcony overlooks the city and from below I can hear the screams of people caught by my creatures, but even that can't distract me from the strange sensation that dragged me from my slumber.

I growl low as I touch the leash again and feel it soaked in lust. No. Not just lust. Sated lust. And not from our time together earlier.

Fury radiates through me. My fists ball against the railing, magic crackling outward as my emotions take the helm.

"FUCK!" I scream as I let out the magic in a brilliant blast of light. I watch with sick satisfaction as it hits the building adjacent to mine and it crumbles in a fascinating display.

Walking back into the penthouse I grab my phone from the table, dialing quickly.

"What?" Feather's voice is filled with annoyance, not sleep, despite the hour.

"The timeline is moving up." I snap out.

She snorts, "call me in the morning."

The line disconnects without warning leaving me alone and stewing in my thoughts once more. If anyone else did that I would skin them alive, but Feather has proven useful, beyond the rest, and is the only one who isn't afraid of me.

Throwing my phone onto the couch I drop my body onto the opposite end and touch that leash once more. The lust is electric as it sears me, the level of it shocking, almost driving me to leave the penthouse and return to her. My body feels electrified by it and on edge, as though one wrong move and I might combust.

Snatching my phone again I send out a quick text message, dropping the device back down once I've received the answer. I shove my hand down my sweats and first my cock as it hardens. Dropping my head backwards I close my eyes and stroke myself from root to tip. I stroke myself slowly until I hear the doorbell ring.

"Enter." I yell. Not bothering to stop. The female enters, her tits out and cunt only covered by a thin g-string. The stripper meanders over, eyes on my cock already. I arch an eyebrow as my gaze drops to the ground in between my knees.

She folds herself between my legs, closing her mouth around my cock. She sucks and licks slowly at first. The pace annoying and doing nothing to deal with my frustration. Gripping her head on both sides I take matters into my hands thrusting hard up into her mouth until I'm hitting the back of her throat.

I picture my Lena between my legs. Her mouth the one chocking on my dick and not this stripper. The female at my feet gags, pulling me from the vision. Frustrated I rip free of her before dragging her body upward and switching spots. She leans over the back of the couch spreading her pussy wide for me.

"Come on baby," She moans. Her fingers sinking into her pussy. "Fuck me."

"Shut the fuck up." I growl as I shove inside her. "Don't fucking talk." It's easy, really, to imagine it's Lena's pretty pink pussy welcoming me as I slide home. It's easy to imagine the small pants coming from her mouth and those tits bouncing as I fuck her. I can smell her arousal around us, can feel the slickness of her dripping and easing the path for my length. I would tease her, edge her, until she was lost to the madness of it all and begging me to fill her, to allow her to cum.

I grunt as my balls draw upward and I unload deep inside the girl. I groan as I draw out my pleasure until my cock softens having nothing left to give and slips free of her.

"I didn't finish yet baby." She says in an annoyingly whiny voice.

Pushing against my tether with Lena I let her feel it all and hope it hurts. "I don't give a fuck if you did or not." I finally respond.

The girl whips around ready to snap at me but stops short. The look on my face clearly communicating the end of her life should she continue to talk. Instead, she scurries from the penthouse, leaving me alone once more.

"Soon," I muse, looking back out the window. "Soon I'll have everything I'm owed and more."

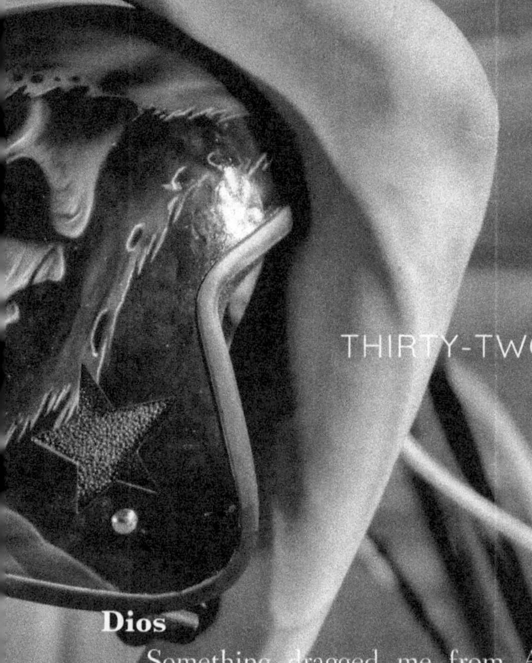

THIRTY-TWO

Dios

Something dragged me from Arcanna and Jackson. Something that had me on edge and needing to seek out whatever was making my magic, and my wolf, restless. Neither had moved as I slipped free of the bed to investigate.

There is a scent in the air that is far too familiar and should not be here, not in this home. Following the scent leads me to another bedroom door. The priestess's bedroom door. I don't bother to knock as I press it open with silent movements.

The room smells of sex and sweat.

Slowly I walk over to her sleeping form, her naked body on display with sheets twisted about and pillows knocked to the ground. Dragging in a deep breath I can smell my brother on her. The unmistakable scent of his citrus and warm vanilla with my own bergamot clinging to her.

I drag my hand down my face and frown noting the sweat beaded on her forehead. Even her hair looks slick with sweat in spots. My eyes glance out towards the lawn, annoyed to find my brother still here. I take one last glance at Harrowlena and make my way towards him.

"You had to fuck her?" I growl when I'm finally in ear shot.

He smiles. "She needed me."

I scoff. "That's a funny way to put it."

Luz shrugs as he makes himself comfortable on lawn chairs he managed to find. From behind he snags himself a beer before offering me one. I hesitate, the bottle out stretched between us. "Come on brother. Just because you have one beer with me doesn't me you have to announce our rekindled relationship."

I snatch the cold bottle from him. "We do not have a rekindled relationship, Luz."

"Sure sure." He says with a confident smile.

My body drops into the chair next to him, shaking my head as I do. A sudden weariness pressing in around me. "If you're using her to piss me off it won't work; I have no claim to that one."

"Of course you don't." He snorts. "You have two hungry mates in bed, you do not need a priestess too. And contrary to your believe dear brother I don't do things just to piss you off."

I cut him a hard look. Luz has spent many years pissing me off, even before we found ourselves in the space we are now. Even when we had the best relationship, we often found ourselves at odds with one another. A constant push pull.

"I will admit, lately my actions do seem to say I want to make you mad." He goes onto say. "But this was not one of those."

"So, explain." The soft waves of the lake brush against the shore, a few birds sending their song to sky as we sit in these beat up lawn chairs. It feels laughable to be sitting with him in such a peaceful environment. "Do you remember when we were kids and we wanted to move out to the mountains and live in a cabin?" I interject.

Luz pauses, beer half way to his mouth. His face is painted with something akin to shock before he offers up a smile and a light laugh spills from him. "Si. I also remember us going camping and deciding very quickly the outdoors wasn't for us."

"You decided that." I laugh out. "I was perfectly fine with it."

"So was I! Until those fucking bugs started eating me alive." He grumbles, a shiver moving over his body. I smile at the memory even as I feel a twinge of sadness that we lost that. Lost those people we once were. Luz clears his throat after a moment. "I didn't fuck her, make her scream yes. But not with my dick."

Rolling my eyes I shake my head, "same thing."

Luz pushes to a stand, his empty beer discarded back into a cooler that he managed to find. He looks me over with a sadness in his eyes and that pulls at the corners of his mouth. "I do not hate you brother; I don't want to harm you either. We may have our differences, but we also used to be close. Is it so wrong I would want that again?"

For a moment I want to believe him. I want to drag him in for a hug and tell him none of the past matters, because I miss him. I believe him. But I can't seem to do it, I can't force my limbs to move or my heart to fully give into it. Luz seems to understand, shaking his head and letting out a disappointed sigh. I feel our collective magic pull forward and the door to our home open. "It would be wise to use caution with her, brother. I would not trust the little priestess."

Narrowing my eyes I glance back to the still dark room where she lay sleeping before looking back to my brother who is already backing away towards the doorway. "Thank you." I manage to say just as he puts a foot through. He nods with a lingering look at me before he fully vanishes and the doorway closes.

Harrow

As my eyes blink to consciousness, I try to cling to the dream I had. The dream of Luz between my thighs. It had felt so real, and I wanted to indulge in the fantasy of that type of pleasure for a little longer. Stretching my arms upward I frown as I feel stickiness between my thighs. My fingers dipping downward. When I'm met with more of it seeping from me and the feeling of something dried across my pubic bone the world seems to tilt on its axis.

"Oh gods it wasn't a dream." I pant out. Shoving from the bed the sheets perfume our combined scents and my heart cracks apart. I rush to the shower, not caring that the water is freezing as I jump in and start to scrub the betrayal from my skin. The reality of the night punching me in the gut over and over as fragments of the night dance across my vision.

My body shakes as I turn the shower off and snatch a dry towel. I don't look at myself in the mirror, refusing to see if there are any remnants, any physical proof of what I did. *Oisin will never forgive me. I do not deserve him as a mate.*

The words taste sour as they spread over my mind. A piece of them falling on a dark part of my soul that enjoyed what Luz and I did. The dark part that continues to question the mate we are so desperate to return to. I force air into my lungs over and over, my heart beating out of my chest as the two halves deep within go to war with one another.

"How? How could I do this?" I cry, fresh tears falling down my cheeks.

You could do it because you know, deep down you know, Oisin is wrong for you.

I want to growl at that voice, to refuse to believe it. But the words keep hitting their mark. Making it harder and harder to avoid. Especially after spending time here, after seeing how Jackson and Dios and Arcanna are with one another. After feeling Luz's tender touch.

"Stop confusing me." I beg the room. Not caring that I'm only met with outward silence and inside that dark voice just laughs. My mind travels to Luz without permission, my body encouraged by the idea of that man giving us more pleasure.

I let out a long whimper as my body warms. Not as bad as it was last night, but still mildly uncomfortable. My muscles cramp and vision swims for a moment and I'm hit with the realization that my heat is in fact starting early and had Luz not helped me I would have given myself away. I would have begged for Oisin to return. Relief rolls through me, even if it's the kind of relief that is made of glass it's still relief.

Closing my eyes, I focus my breathing until the feelings pass and I'm able to feel in control again. If my heat is starting early, I need to get us to The Well as soon as possible. With a renewed sense of direction, I dress quickly before going in search of the three who I need to convince that it's time to go.

I move with poise and confidence that Lady Ornate always seemed to have despite being a liar. Head held high and eyes clear. When my bare feet are halfway down the long hallway to the dining room, I hear a clear feminine voice come from behind.

"I was wondering when I'd see you again." Kallen walks

into view, her long white hair flowing free around her shoulders. Her green eyes stand out vibrantly against it and almost appear to glow. Crossing her arms she stops in front of me. "Where have you been hiding?"

I swallow uncomfortably, unsure of this female. While she freed me from the mask that doesn't mean she is my ally. "I was in my room; I had a headache. When did you arrive?" I ask.

She smiles, eyes narrowing, like a cat who is toying with its prey. "Yesterday. But I suppose it's been a rather busy 24 hours so it feels like I only just did. You know. . . With the gates opening and all the killing."

My chest feels hollow as her words settle around me, throat suddenly dry and tight.

"You know, I've never understood the point of subtle threats or beating around the bush." Kallen continues, now circling me. My face pales, the color leaching from it as bile rises up in my throat. This is not a female I want to go against, banshee or not. She stops in front of me once more, that same feline gaze painted across her seems to turn feral at the color I've turned. "So, this is me not beating around the bush. I know a pet when I see one and you my dear are someone's pet. If I had to hazard a guess, I would say Oisin's."

"What?" I try to hiss out as if I'm shocked but the word seems to fall flat. Only confirming her suspicion.

A growl comes from the shadows and I watch in horror as two Hellbeasts step forward, the massive creatures dripping their poisonous saliva as they roll their lips up in a menacing growl. I step backwards, body ready to flee but Kallen grabs my arm, finger nails digging into the skin.

Dragging me towards her she leans down mouth grazing my ear. "Know this, priestess, if any harm comes to Dios or Jackson or even Arcanna, I will make sure you spend the rest of your life begging for mercy as I break you apart piece by piece and only when I get bored will I finally slit your throat and bathe in your blood." When she pulls back from me, I can see the promise of it in her eyes, see the events painted for me.

"I don't want to hurt anyone." I say, swallowing down my overwhelming fear.

She shrugs, no empathy or sympathy to be found. "You may not want to but you will. And you see Harrow I do like to hurt people, I love it in fact. So know that if you go through with this plan of yours, I will relish in hunting you down."

"Harrow?" Jackson's voice stops the conversation, "Kallen? Everything okay?"

Kallen winks at me before holding her finger to her mouth in a shushing motion. She whirls around to face Jackson. "Things are fine. I was just saying hello to the little priestess. I haven't seen her since I ripped that mask free for her."

Jackson, seemingly oblivious to my frozen body filled with fear, lets out a sigh as his shoulders relax. Kallen skips towards him, those beasts of hers following close behind. "Are you leaving?" He asks her.

She nods. "Soon. Demon and I have one last piece of business to tie up before we go back on the hunt."

He lets out a groan. "We aren't having an orgy."

Kallen cackles, even as my cheeks seem to finally get color back and flush crimson. "I know, I know. Dios told me to stop asking." She turns to me once more, removing the color stain on my cheeks by her sudden attention. "If you ever want a friend, Harrow, just send my little beast to me. He'll check in on you from time to time." The Hellbeast in question lets out a chuff next to my ear, startling me at its sudden closeness. "Toodles!"

Jackson shakes his head with a faint smile painted across his lips as he watches her meander back down the hallway. Once she's out of sight my body almost gives out, the tension falling from me in one swift movement.

"Harrow?" Jackson tilts his head as he now faces me. "You good?"

I muster up a smile and pray it's convincing as I nod. "Yes. I am. I was just looking for you."

"That's convenient because I was looking for you." He says with a smile. "Come on, the others want to talk."

I nod in agreement, barely registering the rest of the conversation as we make our way to the dining room. With Kallen aware of my plan, or that I have some type of plan, I cannot come out and tell them my heat is starting early. I can't demand we go to The Well, at least not until I know I can get away with what I need to do.

"Harrow?" I can see Jackson standing in front of me with arms crossed. Somehow we've managed to already arrive at the dining room. My mind having been too preoccupied to notice. "Are you okay?"

I blink several times before I nod, "Yes. Sorry. Just distracted. Were you saying something?"

He shakes his head no and instead pushes open the door. I'm greeted with 6 pairs of eyes all focusing on us as we enter. Multiple newcomers makes me wonder what exactly I've missed. Jackson goes about introducing everyone and making sure I have a comfortable spot before heading to be next to his mates.

"We were just discussing the plan." Dios says as Jackson plants a soft kiss on Arcanna's forehead.

The large man introduced as Reaver clears his throat as he continues talking, "As I was saying, The Order has spread lies nonstop about the royal family. My people have confirmed that with the loss of Ava, and you not being as present as usual, more people are keen to believe them." Jackson's jaw tenses at the news even as Arcanna mutters something about that being bullshit. "I didn't say I agree with them, just that those are the rumors."

"It's how they got us. They turned the people against my family." The other female, Rhea, taps her chin with her finger thoughtfully. "I think it would be helpful for you to resume business as usual. I think you need to go to the parties like you used to. Go to the street races. Do all the things that made you reachable and made you human in the eyes of the city."

"We don't have time for that." Dios growls. "We need to get to our destination."

I frown at the vagueness, are we not going to The Well? I want to ask.

I don't, instead choosing to continue to listen, to observe, and hope I get something out of this I can pass along to Oisin. Reaver nods, "no, Rhea is right. That could work."

"We have another issue." Demon says gruffly. "Apparently Rucker is unhappy with leadership and is trying to form some type of coo. He wants my patch. He's been talking to someone outside the club, bringing people in who aren't pack."

"Fucking asshole, we should have killed him long ago." Dios growls.

Kallen shakes her head, "If he takes the pack that might be an issue. At least short term, long term we would just slaughter him. But short term it would be an inconvenience to have to deal with that on top of the rest." She says it with the same unhinged, feral delight she had while confronting me in the hallway.

"So, you two can head and stop Rucker." Dios says, clearly confused as to why they weren't already doing so.

"We can't." Kallen growls. Dios looks between the two before landing on Demon, eyes full of questions.

Demon lets out a long sigh, "Kallen and I can't, we need you to go. We have. . . other business to attend to." Kallen offers another smile and I just want to scream at her to stop.

"So do both." Rhea says. "Invite this Rucker person here. Invite the pack here. Let them be at a race or a party and confront Rucker. Use him as an example. So not only are you connecting with the people but you're also showing him, and them, not to fuck with you."

"And The Well?" I ask. Despite wanting to keep myself from asking I do it anyway. Dios frowns, his mismatched eyes narrowing on me for a moment, his gaze dropping to my hand that had fisted itself around my own throat. I drop it quickly back to my lap.

"It's not a terrible idea," Jackson announces before looking over at me. "Should we still need The Well, we'll have time to access it before the full moon. This way is better because we won't be in Gothic Grove right away."

"But we don't have the magic, won't it take time to figure it out?" The line I walk for this conversation feels like it's wobbling and I'm about to slip off and plummet to my death with each question.

Arcanna shakes her head. "No, we got this." She says it simply with a smile that doesn't reach her eyes. "Besides, this all might be for nothing if this stubborn asshole decides to finally bond with Jackson." She jerks her thumb towards Dios who looks at her with an annoyed expression.

"But the magic. . ." I start to argue, panicked at the idea of what might happen if we do not get to The Well. "I'll still need help with it, still need healing."

"Which is why we have Luz on hand," Jackson cuts in. "He can help take the edge off and hopefully keep you alive." My mouth snaps shut and stomach clenches uncomfortably at the mention of Luz. My eyes drop the ground to avoid the gaze of the King.

"And Reaver and Rhea stay here?" He asks the room now that I'm not asking anymore questions.

"Until you flush Oisin and his creatures out, we will be here helping the city. Once you are planning to get him, we will come to you." Reaver announces. "What about you two?" He gestures to Demon and Kallen, the two strangely quiet.

"We'll be hunting down some individuals for retribution owed." Demon finally responds as he looks to his mate. The room chills at his tone, his eyes never leaving hers. "Kallen can bring us back and forth if we are needed elsewhere."

"We might need you both, not just for clearing out Gothic Grove but the final show down." Arcanna muses. "We have no idea the magic he has gathered, not with Bast and the covens at his disposal."

The shadows in the room swirl and I let out a gasp as another four huge Hellbeasts step in. Kallen beckons them forward, the largest stopping next to her and her mate. "Good boy," she coos. "You can go with this lot. Help them and bring me messages from them."

The beasts seem to understand, their heads bowing as they disappear back into the shadows. Minus the one standing with Kallen, it nuzzles her face softly, the same one that she told to watch me. The green venom and large teeth offer no deterrence to how close she gets to it. After a long moment it too dissolves back into the shadows.

"Dios, if Rucker is indeed an issue. Kill him." Demon growls. Dios offers up a wicked smile, one that promises violence and blood. "You and the King have my permission to make it as bloody as you need."

Kallen throws her head back dramatically, "see you go and do that, and I just want all of us to fight and fuck."

"You only get that at solstice." Dios says softly with a laugh. "And you'd have to talk with my mates." Arcanna smiles but Jackson has a look I can't identify. Still, all the talk of sharing makes me wonder how they are able to, how can they be mates but fuck other people?

You did. You fucked Luz right after you fucked Oisin. You fit in so well with this group.

I dig my finger nails into my palm and grit my teeth, desperate for that voice to stop but even more desperate to avoid the feelings of guilt and shame that I had forgotten about until now. Watching the interactions I know for a fact Oisin would never behave like they do, he would never forgive me if he found out about my transgression, heat or no. He has no interest in sharing me.

Kallen pouts as she and Demon stand up, bidding goodbye to the rest of the room. Reaver and Rhea are the next to leave. The dark-haired man hugging Jax hard before following the female out the door who looks to put as much distance between her and him as she can.

"Good luck!" Jackson yells after him. Only a muffled fuck off is heard in response before it's quiet and all the new bodies have seemingly left the lake house.

"That went as well as can be expected." Jax says, standing and grabbing a drink from the bar.

Arcanna lets out a long sigh. "I suppose you are correct in that matter. We have the best plan in a list of shit shows." She looks over at me, her gaze cautious and assessing. "And what do you think of this plan?"

My mind stalls out as I try to piece together thoughts I can share. "I think it's a huge risk for me, this plan." I say finally. "I think trying to help me weather the heat away from The Well is asking me to suffer needlessly when we could go and begin working on figuring out the ceremony." The words fall from my mouth with the same emotions I poured from my mouth in that final argument with my Nana, when she denied me what was rightfully mine.

She cocks her head to the side still watching me. "But if Dios and Jackson were already mated, this would be the action regardless." Her words, while true, do little to fix the rising tide of anger and guilt and frustration that is bubbling up.

"I *deserve* to know the ceremony. I'm the High Priestess. It's my job to know and understand that magic. And not just so I can fuck someone for a week so I don't die." My words feel powerful, my banshee magic adding a little push to them.

Dios leans forward, eyes narrowed as they listen to me rant. I half expect him to cut in, to confront me but it's Jackson who interrupts my anger. "None of us are owed magic. Even you, Harrowlena. We do not want you to suffer in any capacity but if we don't have to risk going to The Well while Oisin is still alive then we won't." I bite down on my lip hard to keep my retort in my mouth, knowing if I push more I'll end up incriminating myself. "The plan for Luz to help you is a good one. It buys us the time we need. And keeps you alive."

"And you just trust your brother?" I counter towards Dios.

He doesn't say thing, instead just casually observing me. My stomach rolls and body feels hot as I swallow back the magic pushing upward in my throat. Red hot anger fills my veins as I realize Jackson is not going to listen to me, not going to give me what I want or need. Right now, he feels like just another person keeping me from what is rightfully mine. I want to scream at him, not just as a banshee, but as a female. I want him to know that he is making choices at my expense. I want to rage.

The three seem oblivious to my fury though. Jackson now giving his attention to the other two. Arcanna lets out a small groan of pleasure as I watch Dios's tattooed hands trail down her exposed chest as he delicately tilts her head to the side and plants kisses upward before licking over the bite mark she now proudly shows.

My breathing picks up, the anger and rage now sharing my body with the first prickle of arousal. My nipples feel tight and a desperate hunger works its way up my body until it feels like I'm choking on it and it has all but replaced the powerful emotions I was having only moments ago.

Something is wrong.

I push to a stand quickly, startling the three, as if they had forgotten I was still in attendance. I think I manage to say I will All I know is whatever Luz did to help me last night is no longer helping.

Against all odds my body really has started going into heat early.

Arcanna

(Something in the Way- MXMS)

Jackon's silver eyes focus on the door that Harrow disappeared through for a brief moment before they turn back to me and watch as Dios licks and nips up and down my neck. His lips lingering on the bite mark he left on my shoulder the other night. I shudder at the feel, arousal washing over me swiftly.

"She seemed pretty mad we weren't going to The Well." I pant out.

Dios huffs against my neck. "She did indeed."

"We just need time to think. And keeping her from The Well as long as possible gives us that." Jackson continues to watch us, eyes following every movement Dios makes with his lips. "We could make it real you know? We could bond, truly take her out of the equation." Dios pauses against my neck for a moment, his hot breath stuttering over the skin. He doesn't say anything but I can feel the tension radiating off him. Just as I'm about to tell him to stop being such a cock about it all and complete the mating bond Jackson lets out a long sigh.

He presses a hard kiss to the mate mark on my neck, sucking it deeply. A long moan flows from my mouth at the feel and I swear to all the gods I could cum just from the sensation.

"You smell divine, *segadora.*" His nose drags upward to the shell of my ear before he nibbles my lobe. My eyes flutter shut, his hands exploring my shoulders in feather touches until he's rolling the knots out of my muscles. The action drags a moan from my lips, the sound filling the room. I feel his hands dip closer and closer to my full breasts in a tantalizingly slow motion. When his fingers finally graze the barbells in my nipples, I can't help but arch into his touch, demanding more.

"So greedy." He chuckles.

My eyes open finally, locking with Jax who looks feral. His cock hard against his pants as his eyes follow wherever Dios's fingers go.

"He likes watching us," Dios whispers. "Do you want him to watch me fuck this tight little cunt with my fingers? Do you want him to watch you come apart all over my hand?"

He applies his teeth to my neck again, "yes." I pant out desperately. "Fucking yes."

Dios moves around me, pulling his hand free of my shirt

as he does. Picking me up he deposits me onto his lap so I'm facing towards Jax, spreading my legs wide as he pulls my long skirt to the side exposing my drenched core to him. The idea of him watching me fall apart on Dios's lap ratches up the arousal, my pussy leaking uncontrollably. Dios sensual movements of his fingers on my thigh drive me to insanity. Every time he skips touching my core and goes down the other leg I whimper.

"Take your cock out, *mi cielo*. Show her how turned on you are by this." He commands. Jax doesn't skip a beat, allowing his cock to spring free of the tight pants. The end already leaking. He grips himself hard, holding the base as if he could lose himself any moment. Dios takes that moment to press the pad of his finger to my clit.

"Oh fuck!" I scream, back arching. "Yes, please please. Your fingers feel so fucking good." I cry out as he continues to circle the tight bundle of nerves over and over. Edging me to the point of insanity. The world swirls around me as he finally pushes two thick digits deep into my pussy. The sounds it makes are nothing short of obscene.

"She's dripping all over my lap, so fucking wet." Dios groans. "She feels so good, so hot and tight. Squeezing my fingers." He picks up his pace before pulling out and circling my clit with my own wetness. "I want you to cum on her bare cunt, cover her and I'll fuck you into her."

Jax doesn't hesitate, moving across the room and in front of us in a flash. He jerks his cock at a punishing pace as Dios lazily caresses my pussy. When I feel the first splash of Jax's cum I let out a long whine, overcome with desire. Dios doesn't pause, even while Jax is still cuming on me he's pushing the release deep inside.

"Oh yes," I cry out. "You feel so good. So fucking good to have your cum inside me and on me. Mark me up. Oh, fuck I need to cum." I fuck into his fingers, even as I grab some of the cum off my lower stomach and push it into my mouth. The taste explodes over my tongue finally pushing me over. "I'm going to cum! I'm going to cum!"

Dios doesn't stop, he lets me ride out the waves of pleasure on his lap, even as I squirt and leave a mess all over his once clean jeans. When the waves finally end, I slump backwards onto his chest, his fingers still deep inside me. Everything relaxes within me, sleep trying to pull me under.

"Good girl, *segedora*. You did so good. So pretty when you fall apart." Dios murmurs.

"She looks good with your fingers in her." Jax whispers.

The last thing I hear is Dios, "She looks good with us both."

Dios

Carefully, I lay Arcanna on the couch, her scent still plastered to me making my cock painful. I cover her with a blanket before turning back to Jackson who has tucked his length back in his pants now. The movements are swift and determined and I know I cannot avoid the conversation once more.

"I want this," he says as he crosses the space towards me. "I'm yours and you are mine. Fuck everyone else." His lips find mine and I allow myself to melt into him. Let him take the lead in an uncharacteristic move. My resolve slipping as I feel him.

I try to find the words, to explain why I'm holding back on this, but they keep missing the mark. I shake my head as I try to clear them out and search for a better way to explain, for some way to show him that I while I want this more than anything, I won't put him in the crosshairs of my father. I open my mouth to at least try but he shakes his head. Placing his warm palm over my mouth, he pushes me back to the chair I had been on with Arcanna. My ass lands hard on the cushion as he straddles me.

Those silver eyes bore into me, flames licking behind them. "Dios, you. Are. Mine. For better or worse. Which means we can figure it out." He keeps his palm firmly over my mouth as he keeps going. "We are both well aware of the dangers of our magic being joined. We both know there will be a target painted on our backs. But that would assume those people could touch us. No one is getting to us."

"You don't even know my father, my family," I growl. "You don't know what you're agreeing to." When he tries to push in for another kiss I grip his throat, holding him back. His silver eyes flash black, anger coursing through his body. I squeeze harder, holding his furious gaze. "We cannot bond, *mi cielo*. As much as I want this, we cannot complete that."

"You bonded Arcanna." He growls low, unable to hide the hurt in his voice.

"My wolf claimed her, and you know full well that bond is different. She doesn't feed off my magic, doesn't *share* magic. You would." I counter. "It would make you a target for every one of my enemies." He strains against my grip on his throat. Stubborn determination shines in those silver eyes, refusing to drop my gaze first. I shake my head, almost proud of him for this given his submissive nature with me normally. "The one time you choose to be a brat and we aren't even fucking." I mutter releasing him.

Jackson pushes off my lap, shaking his head and backing away from me. Alongside that determination is a flash of hurt that seems to be seeping into the silver. "When we go with Luz I'll show you how well I can handle your family, Dios. I'm not backing down on this."

"Fuck." I groan after he leaves. "Why the fuck did I have to have such a stubborn mate."

THIRTY-THREE

Jackson

Leaning against the car, the next morning I do my best to wait patiently for the rest of the group to meander out. The light of dawn hasn't even attempted to push through the clouds yet and despite that, the humidity already feels oppressive. Even the slight breeze through the open garage door does nothing to cool me down. Exhaustion tugs at me as I raise the coffee to my lips. I hadn't slept, instead I had paced the room waiting for Dios to make an appearance.

Again.

A move that I seem to be getting very good at. *Always the one waiting for them, always waiting.*

When the door had finally creaked open and Arcanna peaked her head in the smile on her face was one of apology as she climbed into my bed alone. We both knew who I was waiting for. What I was waiting for. And no doubt she had even tried to get him to follow her.

The white 4-Runner rumbles behind me, the air conditioning already on full blast to keep the interior cool for the long journey. Soft music plays from the speakers as I feel the change in my bond deep within, as the one who has part of my soul nears.

As if summoned by my thoughts Arcanna comes into view. Not even bothering to change out of her pjs, she stumbles from the house with coffee in hand. Her dark hair thrown into a messy, uncontrolled bun atop her head. When I offer her a smirk, she flips me off, "You know how I feel about mornings." She says by way of greeting.

"Nice sweatshirt." I say, noticing immediately that it's one of Dios's. The Primal Knights logo spanning across her chest. I open the door when she gets close enough and allow myself to enjoy the sight of her full ass in the small flannel shorts, she has on.

"Take a picture, it'll last longer." She taunts

Grabbing her around her center I pull her back into me, burying my face into her neck and breathing in her sandalwood scent. "I would love to take a photo of you, naked, on your knees with my cock in your mouth."

A low groan is pulled from her, and I don't need to see her face to know the eye roll is happening, "it's too fucking early Jax. I need my coffee before we have sex talk. And let's be honest, it wouldn't be me on my knees."

A laugh is ripped from my throat as I release her and let her climb into the car. Even as my dick comes to attention at the idea of praying at her feet and drinking from her cunt.

Dios clears his throat behind us pulling my attention as he stretches upward so his shirt allows his abs to peak from under the thin material. The morning light looks good on him, even with my anger and hurt still boiling my blood I can't help but watch him. My mouth dries at the sight and I want nothing more than to spend the morning worshiping his body.

"Where is Harrow?" Arcanna asks, yawning as she peeks her head out.

Dios jerks his head behind him just as she peaks through the door. She keeps her gaze locked on her feet as she walks towards us. "Good morning." She murmurs softly finally glancing up. The dark circles under her eyes stand out in stark contrast to her skin. Even her hair seems to be dull and lifeless. It would seem I'm not the only one who didn't get sleep.

I offer her a similar greeting before she's climbing up into the car, her form disappearing into the back as I climb up into that driver's seat.

Dios slides into the front with me, "Good morning *mi cielo*." The low tenor of his voice sends shivers through me. "Don't think I didn't see you eye fucking me just now." I suppress the eye roll.

"So, what's the plan?" Arcanna grumbles. "It's too fucking early to be going to street races."

I can't help but laugh at her. "That's very true, but with the Primal Knights coming into Hell we have a lot of work to do to set up a club house for them."

"They are bikers how picky are they?" She groans.

Dios snorts out a laugh, glancing behind to her. "You'd be surprised."

While the two continue to go back and forth I focus on heading towards the city and forming a plan on how to get the man next to me to finally bond. The first part? Showing him his club can fit here, his life can fit here.

Harrow

My knee bounces with nerves.

Two full days out in the city of Hell and it feels like a lifetime since we left the lake house.

Glancing up at the flashing motel sign I watch as Dios

and Jax disappear into the lobby. The rain pelting the window clouding the view. They had decided to spend the night here, apparently the owner had known Arcanna back in the day. The justification that they would spread the word that Jackson was out and looking to race. It feels like a pageant and it's making my skin crawl.

I can feel my throat tightening as a fresh wave of symptoms tries to push into me. So far, I had been lucky, avoiding being in close proximity with any of them when a wave hit. Escaping into the car or whatever bed I was staying in until it passed. And for some reason I've held my tongue, refused to tell them, refused to beg to be taken to The Well.

I feel my pants start to dampen as a wave of arousal tries to crest over me, "you should go check on them," I say to Arcanna over the steady rhythm of the rain against the car roof.

She offers me a small smile, her own dark, storm cloud eyes moving from me to her mates and back to me. Of the three she has started to pull away, unlike when we first met and she offered to show me yoga, now she keeps our interactions at a minimum. I didn't think it would hurt, to lose the option of her friendship, but I find myself wishing it could be different.

For a moment I worry she won't get out of the car, my inhale of breath holding in my lungs until she finally nods and scoots out. Quickly I dive into my bag and grab a small washcloth, shoving it down my linen pants to soak up the slick I can't avoid. My stomach cramps and I bite down hard on my lip to avoid crying out. I send a silent curse to whoever thought this was a good way to deal with magic, and to my Nana for not giving me the ceremony in the first place.

Shower. I need a shower. Something to wash away any evidence that my heat is here, that it's slowly taking control of me. Part of me still wants to deny that's what this is, but the closer we get to the full moon the less I'm able to avoid the reality.

It never should have started this early.

The mystery as to what triggered it and why is one that plays over and over in my mind. Part of me is convinced it's punishment for everything I've done. All the failures and all the betrayals. And that perhaps The Elders were indeed correct about staying pure. And lest we forget allowing Luz to bring me pleasure, allowing myself to get lost in his body. Maybe that was the biggest push, the biggest failure in a test the universe was giving me.

Arcanna opens the door to the SUV, the fresh scent of rain washing through me dragging me away from the spiral I was descending into. "We got rooms, come on!" She throws a hoodie at me, and I scramble to pull it on. "I told them I should be the one to go ask for the room, old man Henry is picky as fuck." She gripes. I manage to scramble free of the car, finally, rushing towards the rooms through the deluge of rain.

Once in the covered breezeway I pull the hood off my head and follow close behind her. Jackson and Dios each stand next to the doors located at the farthest back corner of the motel.

"This would have been way faster if you listened to me." Arcanna spouts off.

Jackson drags his hand down his face. "Yes. I'm aware." He groans. "Henry made that very clear after you walked away."

Arcanna laughs, loud and clear, the sound so free. So very unlike how I'm feeling right now.

Dios eyes me, his lips pressed in a grim line before Jackson hands me a key. "You'll be in here," he pushes the door open, and I'm greeted with a plain room with white walls. The bed has an old checker print comforter, and the AC unit hums in the corner. "If you need anything we are right next door."

Exhaustion pulls at me and despite the state of the room all I want to do is curl up in the bed. Dios lingers, even as Arcanna and Jax say their goodnights, eyes tracing over me. "Like Jax said, we are right on the other side of that wall." He says his voice a low growl. "And the walls are very thin."

I shiver at his words and for the first time I wonder if he knows.

I wake the next morning, drenched in sweat and no more rested than the previous evening. Haunted by dreams filled with eyes that are the color of the sunset and dark hands gripping my thighs. Luz's face had been the one to swim through my fantasies as I slept, his voice the one that coaxed my release free. But the dream had quickly morphed into a nightmare, with my beloved appearing. The look of disgust on his face plain as day and the words he spat chased me out of my slumber.

"You betrayed me, my Lena. After all this you allow him to fuck you? To defile you? You truly are the whore The Elders claimed you to be."

The tears are still fresh on my face as I stumble out of the bed. Making my way into the bathroom, energy waning from the lack of sleep, I forgo a shower and quickly run a washcloth over my sensitive areas before pulling on fresh clothing.

My mouth feels like sandpaper as I exit the room and trail behind Dios to the SUV. Arcanna and Jackson getting in ahead of us, their energy practically vibrating out of them as they chatter about the races coming up. I'm hit with envy, watching the exchange and realizing Oisin and I have never had moments like that and maybe we never will.

I push myself ahead of Dios to get in the car quicker hoping to maybe get some sleep before the night's events. Or at the very least sleep through the physical and emotional whiplash I'm feeling. Just as I'm about to reach for the door Dios's warm hand closes around my wrist, dragging me back an inch.

I hear him draw in a deep breath against my neck before releasing me. "I would think long and hard about the secrets you keep." His voice is rough against my ear as he whispers to me. "If you hurt either of them, if you bring anything upon them, I will forget about my promise to protect you."

He releases my wrist and heads to the passenger side once more. I let myself take a long, deep breath for a moment to force my heartbeat to slow as I slowly start to reach for the car. My fingers shake as I grip the handle and open it. I'm greeted by the sounds of Jackson and Arcanna still talking, unaware of what just occurred. When I slam the door shut Dios catches my gaze for a split second before looking at Jax again.

There is no doubt in my mind Dios will kill me if he finds out my secrets.

THIRTY-FOUR

Jackson

Arcanna and I are buzzing with excitement for the evening, the feeling reminiscent of how it was when we were younger. She continues to argue which car is better, which engine is actually faster (doesn't matter the horse-power, according to her) and how she plans to kick my ass.

"You haven't raced in forever, Jax. You can't possibly think you'll win against me." She says with arms folded over her chest. "Even if I'm not racing with my car. I'll still beat you."

I haven't bothered to tell her she'll be racing her actual car, the one she raced with me long ago. Her Dodge Demon has sat in my garage since she left and tonight, she'll finally know.

I snort out a laugh as I make a turn and head towards the renovated club house we managed to throw together for the MC. "You keep talking like you've been racing this whole time. You've spent just as long as I have outside the scene."

"You don't know, I could have made a whole fucking race circuit in the City of the Dead." She counters.

"Did you, *segradora?*" Dios purrs, finally joining the conversation. I want to laugh as Arcanna pouts the movement so unlike her. "It seems like, perhaps, you and Jax are on the same level then."

Harrow too has remained utterly silent, chewing on her fingers the whole time until Arcanna finally batted her hand away and glared at her. My eyes drift to Dios but he says nothing and remains locked on the gates to the compound looming ahead. I had seen him say something to the priestess, saw her body go ridged and terror melt through her. It was on my list of things to confront him on whenever we had a moment alone.

I slow the car to a stop as a Primal Knight walks out towards the entrance. Kallen had managed to portal them all over late in the night. The SUV has barely parked before Dios jumps out to greet him. The two clap each other on the back, the prospect flushes under Dios's scrutiny. I cock my head to the side in curiosity as I watch the two.

"He doesn't look like someone who should be in a motorcycle club." Arcanna reflects, her breath suddenly hot on my ear as she leans into my space. While I don't disagree, I keep my mouth shut having recognized him as the one Kallen pulled from the trafficking ring. He is simply trying to find his way in this world, figure out what his freedom means.

Dios turns towards our vehicle and motions us forward, the prospect eyes widening as he realizes Dios has people with him. I huff out a laugh and shake my head, this kid is definitely not cut out for this life.

Harrow finally breaks her silence, her throat clearing with a cough. My eyes snag on a small amount of sweat gleaming on her brow. My brain works to try and calculate exactly how long we have until the full moon when Arcanna lets out a hiss. My eyes drag upward as I spot

Rucker walking out, body tense, and hands shoved in his pocked. His eyes hold the promise of violence.

(Start a War- Klergy & Valerie Broussard)

"Fuck." Ripping open the SUV door I leap out, gravel crunching under my boots.

"You think you can just bribe your way back into this club?" Rucker spats. "You and Demon have failed this club. Bringing us here only proves that."

"I would think long and hard about this." Dios warns Rucker as I move up to him. Rucker looks more furious and unhinged up close, his skin flushed with anger and his eyes wild, his wolf just below the surface. His body vibrates, close to giving into his shift. I give a subtle shake of my head, my wings unfolding behind me. Those dark eyes flash between us, calculating his odds of survival.

"Zero percent," I say in a hard voice. Overhead lightning crackles, answering the call to my magic. People often forget what my magic is, and just how powerful and destructive it can be. Even weakened like it is.

His gaze lands on me, "what?"

Pushing my hands into my pockets I repeat myself, "you have a zero percent chance of surviving an altercation between us."

Dios smirks, pressing into me. Rucker looks between us, disgust on his face. "You need him to fight for you now huh? My my how the mighty have fallen." His eyes focus on my wings still spread behind me. "And you, King of Hell, how is that magic of yours?" *Fucking hell someone has been talking to him.* I move to step forward, to show him that I'm not the weak King he seems to think, when Dios places a hand against my chest, stopping me.

"Threaten any of the people with me, Rucker, and you'll learn how I earned the title *El Dador De La Muerte*." The promise of violence sends shivers through me.

"It's not a threat, Dios. It's a question." He sneers, his lip pulling back. "Watch yourselves, you aren't as untouchable as you think." He spits onto the ground in front of us, turning back towards the clubhouse and walking away. Dios and I don't move until he's back inside, a collective exhale seemingly leaving us.

"He's going to be an issue," I say. "Someone is obviously working with him from Hell."

Dios shrugs. *"Algún día conocerá a su segador."* The words send a chill down my spine and not for the first time I wonder if the Primal Knights truly know what Dios is.

Dios

Ari looks over at me as I walk next to him, Jackson on the opposite side and Arcanna following behind in the car. "He's been very short tempered lately." His voice is soft, too soft for this life. And it makes me want to shake some sense into the damn dragon that has marked him.

"He's always been a fucking prick. Ever since Dahlia left." I respond.

Ari's eyes dart around before he stops short. "He keeps talking about how you and Demon shouldn't be in charge. That he's the one who has stepped up and taken care of shit."

"And the pack believes him?" Jax asks.

Ari shrugs. "Some do and some don't. I think having us all come here, creating this whole place for us, has shaken things up. Even those loyal to Demon and Dios are wondering what's happening now."

I scrub my face and curse. This was an outcome I did not foresee when we created this plan. The pack has every right to feel as they do, with the two of us gone we've offered very little support or guidance. It makes sense that Rucker would "step up" and take over things. And if it was any other wolf that would be fine. "Anything else we should know?"

The wolf shifts back and forth on his feet, "Well. . . um. . ." He stutters.

"It's okay Ari, your safe." I reassure him.

"He's had people visiting. People from here."

Even if this is confirmation to what we already suspected I still clench my fists hard.

"We'll take care of it." Jackson's warm hand circles mine as he slowly uncurls my fist. His touch calming the rage that had been building. Ari nods and mutters thank you before scampering off towards the club house.

"What's taking so long?" Arcanna yells from the car.

Jackson snorts and shakes his head. "Let's get inside and make a plan." I only nod, allowing Jackson to pull me towards the space we've managed to create into the club house. A place that once would have felt like a homecoming but now? Now it feels like a goodbye.

<hr>

"You going to tell me what's going on?" Jackson steps through my bedroom door, his body leaning on the door frame with arms crossed. He looks good, like he belongs here in this life. Belongs with me. My magic can't help but attempt to reach for him before I tamp it down.

"What do you mean?" I ask as I drag my hand down my face. "I'm fine." He scoffs and shuts the door, closing me in with his delicious scent.

"You just got some pretty serious confirmation that Rucker is betraying us, betraying the pack. You want to pretend like that's not bothering you?" He snaps at me.

I shrug. "I'm not pretending anything, but we came here to deal with this, it's not as if I should be shocked."

Jackson lets out a long sigh, dropping down onto the one chair we have. "Doesn't mean it doesn't hurt for that to be confirmed. These are your pack members." He leans forward. "If you don't want to talk about that, want to talk about the fact that you threatened Harrow as we left the motel?"

I curse under my breath. "You are far too observant for your own good."

He lets out a laugh. "Come with the territory of being King."

I drop down onto my bed and brace my arms on my knees. "I heard her call out for Oisin last night right before the unmistakable sounds of her getting off."

"Fuck," Jax growls. He grabs two beers from my mini fridge, opening both and passing one to me before he starts to pace around the room, the chair discarded.

"Its not like we didn't know she was still involved with him in some way, but everything feels like its on a hair trigger right now. Her cuming with his name on her lips just felt like the match getting struck over gasoline." I say before taking a long sip of my beer. I watch as he picks at the label of his own, the condensation losing it.

"We should call Luz, he can bring us to your family now. Get Harrow out of here and away from The Order." He says.

"No." The word falls heavy between us before I continue. "I don't trust Luz and I don't want him near us until we absolutely have to."

He glares; silver eyes alight with flame. "He's your brother, you really think he'd do something to us?"

"I think that not every sibling set has a relationship like you and your sister did." I say it cautiously not wanting to cause him pain but also needing him to understand that my family is not like his. "Luz is my father's puppet. Whatever the King commands my brother does. So, if it was my fathers will to harm you, harm us? Then yes, I do think my brother would do it."

Pity flashes through those silver eyes as they trail over me before they seem to fill with determination. "So, we complete the bond. Nothing can touch us then." He says it with such conviction he almost has me believing it. "Dios we are fated, this is what we are supposed to do. Who better for the King of Hell to sit next to than a Death God?" He prowls towards me, landing between my legs so my head rests just at the button of his jeans, forcing me to look upward at him.

"Careful, *mi cielo*." I warn. "You are not the one in charge here."

He offers a cocky smile, his dick hardening in the jeans before me making my mouth water. "I think I'm more in charge than you want me to believe." He counters. I move to grab him; to throw him on the bed and fuck him into submission but he steps backwards and out of reach. "The next time we fuck will be when we are mating and not a second before that, *Sir*."

A deep growl reverberates up and out of my mouth as I watch him move away from me. My darkness stirring within, furious at not touching him. My hands ball into fists against the old comforter on the bed as I fight with myself to avoid launching after him. He says nothing as his silver eyes hold me, backing away until he's out the door leaving me alone with my magic and lust.

Jackson

(Like a Stone- Audioslave)

The crisp night air is filled with the scent of salt water,

leather, and motor oil. A hint of smoke shifts towards me as the wind kicks up again. Leaving Dios in the room had been a testament to my own damn stubborn nature. And I'm damn proud of myself for doing it. Fuck, the man oozed sex appeal and I wanted him, wanted his claim, his bond.

Standing partially obscured by the dark, I watch as the club members interact with one another. The air feels charged tonight, as if one spark and it will explode into flames. The clear divide between pack members who follow Demon and those who have been swayed to Rucker is evident. Bringing them here was never meant to add to the issues. The clubhouse creation itself had been Arcanna's idea, "a way to make them feel at home," she had said.

Arcanna's laughter draws my gaze, and I watch her talk animatedly with a few of the pack members as she points towards their bikes. She's blended in seamlessly here, though it's not surprising. She's always known her way around mechanics better than most. Even now I would bet money on her over anyone else being able to take apart one of these bikes and put it back together with no issues. The sound of engines drags my attention to the gates and a wide grin spread across my face.

* * *

Arcanna

I watch as cars pour into the area, the smell of exhaust filling the space around me and pulling a wide smile over my lips as shivers erupt over my body. Jackson steps out of the shadows, rolling the sleeves of his flannel up on his forearms as he greets the first person. They embrace with a long hug. One after another friends and acquaintances from the past seem to show their support for him. He falls back into it easily, the smile on his face genuine as he greets each person. The pack shifts nervously, the ones loyal to Rucker, no doubt, questioning their previous ideas of how easy it would be to take out the King of Hell.

A twinge of sadness washes over me as I think about the race. It's the first time I won't be using my car. I've never asked Jax what happened to it, and he's never offered up the information. It leads me to believe she did not make it once I left the palace. The memories imprinted in her leather seats are ones I'll cherish forever, and it kills me that she's gone.

People wave at me and beckon for me to join them. Standing up I swallow down the grief and head towards them when a family rumble sounds in the distance. The deep, low growl followed by the high scream as the engine revs. I allow the sound to roll over me even as my skin erupts in goosebumps. I'm pulled forward, as though the sound is a lure and I am its prey. Jax turns when I'm only a breath away from him, silver eyes full of delight as I see my baby pull into the lot. The red paint shining and sparkling, rims gleaming and the black tint gobbling up the light around it.

Tears fill my eyes as I behold my very own Demon. "How?" I manage to whisper out.

Jacksons warm air brushes the shell of my ear. "I had it moved to the lake house a while ago. I wanted it safe, just in case."

I spin to face him. *Just in case.* In case I returned. He had held out hope all this time that someday we would find one another again. I throw my arms around his neck and devour his mouth in a kiss that sends flames licking up and down my spine. He laughs into me even as he grips me hard.

I allow myself to get lost in him until we hear a familiar squeal. Ripping free of my mate I turn to see Ophelia climb out. She flings herself towards us, her soft body enveloping me in a hug as she sobs and laughs. "I missed you all so much!"

I can't help but let out my own choked cry as I hug her back before pulling away. "How? I mean what are you doing here?"

She laughs, that warm sounds so familiar and so comforting as she scrubs the tears free of her freckled face. Her long curly hair is half broken free of the band holding it back, but she doesn't seem to notice, or more likely she doesn't care. "We got the message that the oh so mighty King of Hell was calling for races." She rolls her eyes even as she shoots Jackson a warm smile. "And when I got the personal message asking me to bring your car we couldn't say no!!"

"We?" Jackson finally speaks up.

Ophelia seems to look nervous for the first time, tucking her hair behind her ear. "Oh um, yeah. . ."

"Deva."

Jackson freezes next to me and down the bond I can feel the turmoil of emotions he's going through. Anxiety peaking next to regret as Nyx shuts the passenger door of my car. I frown, confused as to what I missed.

"I'm sorry Jackson, you know him. He wasn't going to let me come alone." She says quietly.

"I know. It's okay." He manages to get out. His eyes stay on the man who now lands in front of me, next to his mate.

"What's going on?" I ask as my eyes dancing between them.

Nyx shifts his lazy gaze to my own, "Nothing. I just wanted to bring you your car. Can't have you racing some piece of shit can we now?" He says it like he used to, with ease and confidence but his eyes hold darkness and a pain that is new.

"Nyx." Jackson starts but stops short from the look his friend shoots him.

Ophelia elbows Nyx with a hard glare before it softens as she casts her gaze back to us. "I'm happy to have gotten to see you both. I've missed you."

"You aren't staying?" Even as I ask, Nyx is already walking away.

"No, sorry. Nyx has had a hard time with. . . everything." She looks at me apologetically, as if she understands that I clearly don't know what's going on.

"I'm sorry, Ophelia." Jackson manages. "For all of it. I should never have allowed what happened. You were my family, both of you, and. . ." I grab Jacksons hand, squeezing three times, as he stumbles over the words. "And I let you down."

She offers a sympathetic smile, dragging us both in for a hug. "I know Jax, and he does too. Give it time." When she pulls away, I feel a sense of loss as she disappears back into the crowd.

When I turn to Jax he lets out a long sigh. "I know. . . I know. . . I'll explain later. But first can we just enjoy the fact that your car is here and safe?"

The words are enough to distract me, my body pulling from his and rushing to what was once my only safe haven.

THIRTY-FIVE

Jackson

Exhaustion pulls at the corners of my psyche. Seeing Nyx and Ophelia had made me realize, once more, how many mistakes I've made. Having to push that aside to race, to focus on keeping not only myself safe but Arcannas well was taxing to say the least. The thoughts had continued to try and force my anxious hyper-fixation to stay on them, even as I let the race try to take me away.

Now as I'm standing here watching everyone, my body is struggling to keep up with the post-race parties. It makes me snort; I used to have no issue doing this. No issue allowing the adrenaline of the races to own me before using booze and drugs to chase away the withdrawal of it when it was all over. Now, however, all I want is to fall asleep with my cock in one of my mates.

Taking a sip of my beer, I let my eyes drift over to our priestess who is politely sitting just outside the circle of wolves at the fire pit. The flames illuminate her pale face and sweat starts to bead over her brow. She didn't come to the race, her absence noticeable. Between that and talking with Dios about her I've made it my mission to keep an eye on her. After all, I brought her into our group, so if she truly is a danger to us, it's on me to deal with it.

I bring the beer to my lips again as she excuses herself, keeping to the edge of the group, and heads inside the building. Following her I note how out of place she looks in her jeans and sweatshirt having swapped her normal linen attire. Her long silver hair is bound up in a braid going around the crown of her head leaving her neck bare.

When she enters the dark hallway, that leads to the rooms, we are staying in, I pick up my pace allowing my feet to sound on the floor. Alerting her to my presence at last.

She whirls on me, her violet eyes almost luminous in the dark space around us. Her hand flies to her chest, "you scared me." Her voice is soft.

"Sorry," I reply, allowing my body to lean against the wall opposite her. "Wanna let me in?" I nod my head towards the door.

She hesitates, chewing her lip again. Narrowing my eyes I push up and crowd in on her. "You've been acting odd." She shakes her head to try and argue but I hold up my hand stopping her. "You can either let me in and we can talk, or I can let myself in and we can talk. Either way we will be talking."

The fight seems to leave her as she opens the door, the two of us stumbling inside the small room she's claimed as her own. Flipping on the light I watch as she sits down on the twin bed pushed against the wall. I take up residence against the door, arms crossed, and eyebrow raised. It's purposeful, blocking her exit path.

Her hand fiddles with the buffalo plaid blanket laid across the bed. The material pilling up in spots that she picks at. I don't push her, instead I let the silence build around us. A skill I learned; one my father never did manage to master. Silence makes people uncomfortable in the best of circumstances, and in the worst? They break so beautifully.

She lets out a defeated sigh finally. "I think my heat is starting early." She starts, keeping her eyes pinned to the floor.

"What?" My stomach drops out as I push up straight, "how long have you known?" Every worst-case scenario piles up in my head. While I had hoped she was simply a backup plan Dios has still stuck to his choice of us not mating. And without him she's my only choice in gaining my magic back. "We could have gone straight to The Well. Completed the fucking ceremony while we had time." I say through clenched jaw.

She shrinks back from me, the movement pulling at me enough to force my body to sit, to make myself seem less threatening. "The day we chose to leave, I had felt off." She lets her eyes trail around the room, still not meeting my hard gaze. "I didn't realize it was my heat; I thought maybe I was sick." The lies flow from her lips like poison honey and it takes everything in me not to laugh at her. To call her out on her bullshit.

"Fucking Hell." I growl in frustration. Did you even think about the fact that this doesn't just impact you?!" My voice echoes in the room and she shrink back even further from me. Shaking my head I close my eyes, forcing my body to release the anger building in me. When I open them again, I watch as she trembles.

"I'm sorry." She manages to whisper out, eyes shimmering with tears as she sits on her knees looking at me. The whole thing makes me sick and a wave of disgust rolls over me knowing she still holds the assholes who abused her in such high regard that she would threaten her own life like this.

"Harrow, you know this could kill you right? Our plan

had been created when we thought we had more time." I swallow the anger trying to burst free, refusing to let it show right now.

"Jax. . . I'm sorry." Her voice breaking. "But I mean, really. . . how much earlier is it? You knew you would need to figure this out sooner rather than later! I'm sorry, I didn't say anything. Truely I am but I just. . . ."

I don't bother looking at her, don't bother placating her or acknowledging the sorry's she keeps spilling out over her bleeding lip It's easy to forget she's never lived a life outside of The Order, truly. Even being with me she kept herself sequestered before The Order snatched her back. "Why did you leave with Dios?" I finally ask. "Why did you leave and come to us?"

The question seems to take her by surprise. "You know why... the mask." She tries to say but her voice shakes and her eyes? They betray it all.

I cut her off, "Don't lie to me anymore Harrow. I'm fucking done with it." She shrinks backwards and its all the confirmation I need that something else is at play here. That she is not the innocent, damsel in distress that we've all assumed, no I assumed, she was. Arcanna and Dios have had their suspicions this whole time and I've continued to allow it to be the truth.

I bracket her body into the wall with my arms, my wings unfolding behind me. "You will stay here, in this room, and when I return with Dios and Arcanna you are going to answer all our questions, or I'll slit your fucking throat. Consequences be damned."

THIRTY-SIX

Arcanna

My body feels at peace, the race still flowing through my veins and the scent of leather still clinging to my body. Fuck it had felt good. So good. To be that free again. It's why I practically gasped for air when, for a brief moment, I felt murderous rage flood my bond with Jackson before it was cut off and contained. I frown. Touching our bond carefully, asking for him to reopen it but it remains shut.

"What is going on?" I ask Dios. He turns and looks towards the spot where Jackson vanished. His eyes glowing with hunger. "Fucking Christ, go complete the bond with him."

He cuts me a glare, "stay out of it."

I raise my eyebrow at him, "Want to try again death pup?"

Dios remains silent. His body tense and eyes glued to the club house where Jackson resides "Dios, we both know it's inevitable. The bond. Do it now and put us all out of our misery."

He downs the last sip of his beer and chucks the bottle.

"I'll be back later." He doesn't wait for a response before leaving me alone in front of the crackling fire.

"Go get some!" I cat call after him, others joining in. He flips me off and keeps walking.

Shaking my head, I take another long drink of the vodka cranberry. All around the party continues to rage. The excitement overflowing from most the pack. I could get use to this type of life. Used to working on bikes and cars, racing every night again, and the feel of family within the pack.

The smaller wolf who greeted us sits down across from me at the fire pit, his innocent face covered in a smattering of freckles that dance around in an uncontained pattern. His eyes remind me of the moss on the floor of my Forest as they peer out from behind his glasses. His lanky body still holds the awkwardness of a youth who hasn't figured out how to carry himself, and his blonde hair is an unruly mess of curls on the top of his head. When he catches me looking at him his cheeks burn red. It's endearing.

"I'm Arcanna." I offer up. "I don't think we ever got introduced."

He looks around, as if he's shocked, I would speak to him. "Oh, uh I'm Ari."

I offer a warm smile, "it's nice to, officially, meet you Ari. Now tell me, how did a wolf like you end up here?" Even without looking at his hands I can tell he doesn't work on bikes or cars.

"Kallen, she's Demon's mate. She rescued me." he says as he stumbles over his words. I watch as he fiddles with his vest for a moment, his body shrinking inward as if just talking about any of it is pushing his mind elsewhere. "I know I don't fit here. . . I'm not really the prospect type but I had nowhere else to go and Dios said he'd help me figure it all out."

I lean forward, careful not to startle him. "Hey," his eyes

pull to mine. "I may not know this MC well, but I do know Dios well. If he thinks you fit here, you do. The Primal Knights seem like good people, for the most part." My gaze goes over his head to Rucker.

"He's not very nice." Ari whispers, knowing exactly who I'm looking at.

I frown, "What makes you say that?" The little wolf avoids my eye contact and looks at his feet that he shuffles against the ground. "Has he hurt you?"

"I don't want to cause any issues. . ." He looks nervous, cheeks red.

I try to keep the bite from my voice as rage settles deep within. "Ari, you are not causing trouble by telling the truth. It's Rucker who is the issue here." The rise and fall of his chest seem to be more rapid. And his body seems to close in on itself more. "Has there been other people?"

Ari nods, "He brings me out, with a few other pack members, to different places. He says he has meetings to attend to. The men are. . . not good."

I let my anger flow down my bond towards Dios and Jackson as I stand up. "Stay here." My voice hard and unwavering.

Ari goes wide eyed, a panicked look going over his face. "He'll hurt you. Please it's not worth it! I'm not worth it!"

The words only stroke the fire. "He can try to hurt me. But I promise you he will fail." Pushing my hair to the side I expose the bite mark on my neck, "I'm bonded to Dios. So, in my eyes I'm part of this pack, and I protect my pack. Which includes you. You are worth it Ari."

Rucker doesn't see me coming as I slam into him, taking his body to the ground. People around us step back wide eyed. He thrashes against me but my magic pulls from the earth helping me hold him. My body glows and I let my wings ripple from my back. The skeletal appearance casts fear over him as he takes me in. "Listen to me you pathetic piece of shit, keep in mind that when you die here your soul comes to me. And I whole heartedly believe in karmatic justice."

"Fuck you, I don't know what you're talking about." He growls, even as his face pales slightly. His wolf tries to push to the surface in answer to that fear. Down the bonds I can feel Jax and Dios move up behind me. They don't intervene, but the message is clear. Fuck with me and you fuck with him them.

"Don't play dumb now." I growl. "I know what you've been doing here."

"You're nothing but a fucking whore." He spats with courage that doesn't reach his eyes. "Oisin was right about you three, disgusting." I hold back every emotion at the name as it flows out of his mouth. Refusing to give him the reaction he so desperately wants.

"You're working with that piece of shit?" Dios growls out.

The smile that pulls over the wolf's face only confirms Rucker just wanted a reaction, and Dios gave it to him. "He promised me, and the pack, power. No more dealing with bullshit politics. Just pussy, drugs and violence."

Jackson snorts with disgust. "And what does he get? What did he ask of you?"

Rucker smiles madly, a long laugh dragging from him. It chills the air around us as he goes on and on.

I grip his face, pulling his gaze to me again, finally cutting off the laughter. "I can make the rest of your miserable existence here a nightmare but compared to what will await your soul it'll feel like paradise." I lean in closer to him. "I can get very creative with punishment and torture. So, I suggest you start convincing me why I shouldn't kill you."

"I think my gift will be you, I want you and before Oisin kills your mates I'm going to let them watch me fuck you over and over again." Rucker spats out.

"*Segradora*." Dios's voice melts over me. The nickname a command to move. Pushing to a stand, my back presses into Jackson as Dios edges in front of us to block Rucker from trying anything. The rest of the pack is quiet, watching the drama unfold. Rucker sneers before he too attempts to pushes to a stand only for Dios to let his magic loose.

I see the moment it touches Rucker's soul, his body suddenly freezing. Dios casually looks out towards the gathered crowd watching us before back to Rucker. "You forgot who I was didn't you? Forgot what I was capable of." Rucker has the decency to look horrified, his eyes the only thing allowed to move as Dios grips his soul. This time Dios looks to the crowd, his voice.

booming over the collective gathered. "I wouldn't want this to be confusing for anyone. If you intend to side with Oisin or anyone from The Order you will not be met with forgiveness or kindness. If Jackson does not kill you, I will. I will hunt you down and rip your soul apart piece by piece. This man is the King of Hell and the rightful one. I suggest none of you forget that."

The crowd is silent as his words sink in. I glance out and watch the reaction. A few shift nervously but overall, they all appear to be nodding along with Dios.

"I'll get answers from him; you and Jackson go back to the clubhouse." Dios glances towards Ari, who looks utterly terrified. "He won't bother you again."

Ari's eyes fill with tears, and he offers a grateful smile, "Thank you." He says before he flees back into the clubhouse.

Dios grumbles, "all we need is Kai getting wind of this and we'll have a toasted clubhouse at the very least." He looks to us. "You two go enjoy yourselves, I need some time with this one."

I frown, "We can help."

"This needs to be done by me." He says. "And Demon."

"Whatever you need, we are here." Jackson says, cutting off anymore argument I may have. He nips at my neck, "I need to taste you."

My eyes flutter shut as I lean into his body, "you want to be my good boy?" I purr.

"Yes," he groans. "Please. Let me be good for you."

Jackson

(Seven Nation Army- White Stripes)

Everything else seems to flee my brain as I drag Arcanna into the clubhouse. Including that I thought I saw a flash of silver hair outside with us. She shoves me into an open room, slamming the door behind us as she hungrily attacks my mouth. Her kiss is fierce and claiming. She's pulling at my clothing at the same time I grab at hers, both of us scrambling to get naked.

Her hands explore my body in a ravenous, unhinged way. My own hands find her thick thighs and I lift her up so she can wrap herself around me. I slam her back into the wall as I grind into her, only pulling my mouth from hers so I can bite down her neck.

"Yes Jax." She moans, the heat from her pussy already burning. "Fuck I need you."

I take a risk and allow my magic out, the tendrils pushing out and holding onto her full breasts, the cool metal barbells she has pushed through her nipples are an easy target as I play with them. She writhes against me, crying out as my magic pulls back and I spin us.

Dropping her onto the small bed I kneel between her legs. I pant as my eyes travel over her. "What do you need?"

She pushes up on her forearms. Her legs spread wider, exposing her core fully to my heated gaze. "Feed yourself." She commands with a sultry smile.

Without hesitation I dive into her wet pussy, sucking the arousal from her that is already dripping down onto the bed. I lose myself in the taste and sensation, my tongue pushing inside her before licking upward and sucking her clit into my mouth. She doesn't attempt to hold back her moans, the sounds filling the room around us as she cries out for me.

Her hand fists my hair as she starts to climb towards her climax. She fucks my face hard before she pulls me off, "I need you in me." She pants.

Bracing over her I notch the head of my dick to her entrance before pushing in with a swift movement. My head drops to hers as I adjust to her tightness. But it's only for a moment before I'm snapping my hips back and slamming into her.

"Give it to me, give me everything Jax. Fuck me so hard I won't be able to walk. Leave bruises on my body so I can be reminded of tonight." She demands. I let myself go, wings flexing out behind me despite our small space. The magic in our bond weaving between us.

"Fuck you take me so good." I cry, watching myself slide in and out of her. "I want you to cum for me, squeeze my cock until I have to fill you." My eyes roll back in my head as she wraps those thick thighs around me, meeting me stroke for stroke.

"Make me cum. Make me tip over that edge. I want to be dripping." She demands. Our sweat slicked bodies glide against each other, the room heating with our combined magic. I allow some of my own to fuse with the barbells in her nipples, sending small jolts of electricity through them. Just enough to edge her with pain. "OH FUCK!" She screams, her pussy convulsing against my hard length. Her orgasm rips through her body in an uncontrolled wave.

My own release washes over me until my cock is emptying inside of her, "fuck you milk me so good. Taking all my cum like such a wicked girl." I moan as I fill her up. She writhes under me as she takes everything I have to give.

My hips finally slow, my thrusts becoming shallower as I lean back and allow my cock to slip free of her. She frowns at the loss, and I chuckle as I press a kiss to her forehead.

"I love you." She whispers to me.

"You have my soul in your hands, my wicked girl." I respond.

She looks up at me, her eyes seemingly glowing in the post orgasm bliss. "What happened earlier? I felt you. You were pissed."

I shove my free hand through my hair, "you felt that huh?"

She doesn't say anything, only raises an eyebrow at me as if to say duh. Shaking my head I allow myself to take this moment of calm, to cherish it with all my heart and soul because I know once I leave this room with her, once we interrogate the priestess and Dios finishes with Rucker, we won't have a moment of calm for a long while.

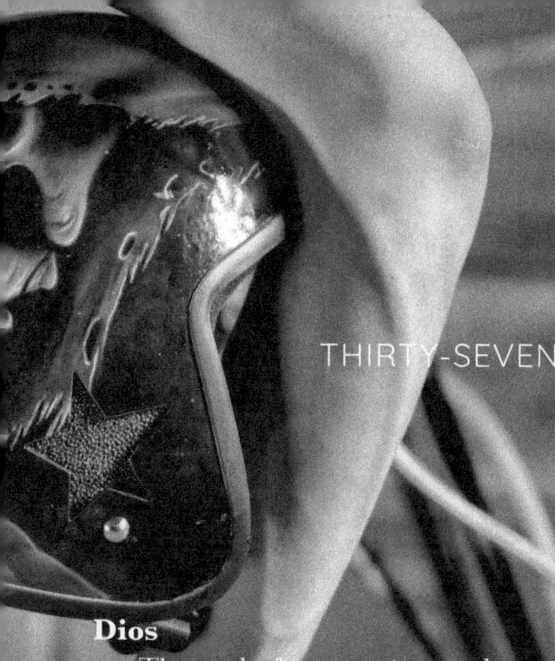

THIRTY-SEVEN

Dios

The smoke from my cigarette burns down my throat as I stare down at Ruckers body. The slash across his throat bleeds out onto the dark asphalt under his head and his eyes stair lifelessly up at the sky. I take one last drag before dropping the cigarette onto his body and pressing my shoe into it. The golden embers sizzling against his clothing before extinguishing.

No part of me felt bad for killing him. Not after everything I've heard from the other members of the pack. Not after his confessions of working with The Order. He was the reason Oisin gained Bast, apparently, having found Dahlia and her. He was the reason Oisin had discovered Ava as well. I shake my head; no wonder Dahlia ran from him and the pack.

"This won't look good to the dragons." Demon mutters as he joins me. His anxiety around drawing unwanted attention from the massive shifters so clear in his tone.

I let out a long sigh. "It isn't on you." I can understand his feelings; with the secret he's harbored around the death of Shadows mother. If the dragons figure it all out there is no doubt in my mind they would try to come for Demon.

"It is though, this is my club, my pack. It's my job to know what the members are up to and keep them in line. The fact that Rucker has been helping that piece of shit this whole time? Fuck Dios that's years and years he's been a spy." Demon shoves his hands though his hair in frustration.

I had called him the moment I had secured Rucker. And the moment he heard Rucker had been a spy for The Order he had appeared through a portal, Kallen waiving at me with a large smile over her blood splattered face. A look she seems to have frequently. We had spent hours interrogating Rucker until every secret had been drawn and we finally finished him.

"I'm going to need someone to take his place that I trust. . ." He says as he looks over at me.

I roll my eyes, "I'm not taking the job Demon."

A pause before, "Why? You are perfect for the job, and I trust you with my mate."

It's high praise, him trusting me with Kallen. Though truth be told Kallen does what she wants no matter what. Him trusting me has more to do with trusting Kallen not to murder me. Still. . . . With Luz's deal being called into play at any moment I can't accept the position when I doubt, I'll return to Hell much less Gothic Grove.

"Dios?"

"Look, you should find someone for my spot too most likely." Silence stretches between us. Uncomfortable silence filled with tension.

"What the fuck are you talking about?" He growls.

I go to open my mouth, to say goodbye to him when a delicious scent moves across the air, sweeping away the metallic tang of blood as the wind shifts. My body is moving without permission, following the lure of that sweet smell.

Rounding the corner, I'm hit with a burst of pheromones that almost brings me to my knees while I simultaneously curse the gods.

Harrow

My fingers dig into the brick wall that is supporting me as I breath through my nose with clenched teeth. The early morning light barely breaking over the horizon over the now quiet clubhouse. The last of the members heading to their rooms hours ago. I had waited hours for Jackson to return, something in me accepting that this is how it was to end. In my new reality I had now created, they would interrogate me, and I would break. I would tell them everything and in doing so I could finally be free. They would pass me off to Luz and allow him to heal me through the heat so I wouldn't die. It wouldn't be a betrayal to Oisin because I would have no choice. Not really.

I had accepted it.

Accepted this was the consequences of all my actions.

And it had felt, nice, as though I could finally breath again knowing all the lying was soon to be over. Nicer than I thought the acceptance would feel, honestly. I could live my life without fear of secrets being discovered, without fear of being hurt. Yes I would be away from Oisin but I couldn't feel bad for that, not when it was never my choice to go with Luz.

When he had not shown I went looking for him. Resigned to my fate and almost eager to get it all over and done with. But when I heard Dios talking about what he would do to those who betrayed Jax? I knew there would be no mercy for me here, no blissful escape. Only more pain and suffering. So, I turned back around and got ready to flee once everyone was asleep.

Now as I try to enact that very plan I realize how idiotic

it was.. My body is on fire and sweat trickles down my spine beneath the layers of clothing despite the cool air washing over me.

That had been a mistake.

The words flow over me nonstop as I bite back a groan of pain as a fresh wave of excruciating cramps moves through my body. My thighs suddenly wet with the arousal I'm producing.

This was such a mistake.

This is the consequence of my actions, a punishment sent from the goddess herself. My heat starting early. If I had just trusted Oisin, trusted the process and never allowed the doubt or Luz to weasel into my body and mind it wouldn't currently feel like part of my soul is being dragged free of me with each breath I exhale.

Forcing another shuttering breath through my nose and releasing it through my mouth, I will my body to move.

I can do this. I can find him. We can figure this out together. He won't be mad at me. We can go to The Well and figure it out, together. It'll be fine.

Another wave of cramps hits and I bite down on my hand to keep from crying out.

"You won't feel any pain during it, we'll complete the ritual together, Harrow. You'll see. Everything will be okay. We'll get through this together." The words Oisin spoke filter through my brain even as Luz's face swims in front of my eyes sending shame and guilt cascading over me like a waterfall.

A tidal wave of pain drops me to my knees, a cry ripping from my lips before I can stifle it. My vision swims as I topple over clutching myself. I hear feet scrape against the ground and my world darkens from a shadow looming over me.

Strong hands grip me, dragging my body upward and my nose is filled with Dios's dark scent.

Dios

Harrowlena is curled in a fetal position, her scent cascading off her in waves. She cries out, hand reaching out blindingly as though she is searching for someone or something to save her.

"Fuck me." I growl and race to her. Bending down I scoop her up, a soft cry coming from her. Her body is hot, sweat dripping from her, and the sweet scent of arousal perfuming around us.

Instead of moving towards the clubhouse I head back to the 4-runner, placing her delicately on the leather seats. She cries out, reaching for me as soon as our skin is no longer touching. "It hurts so bad." She sobs.

From behind I can hear Demon talking to someone on the phone but Harrowlena's pained scream ratches upward as she attempts to throw herself out of the seat I've placed her on.

"I need to get to him! Please! You can't keep me from him!" She screams, her nails biting into my skin as she scratches and hits at my arms.

"Calm down," The words are for her and me as even as dread coils itself into me with the understanding that if she's gone into her heat early, we have little hope for Jax gaining his magic through her. Leaving our bond the only option. And the reality that we will indeed need my brother once more. I wrap my body around hers, dragging her to me. "It's okay Harrowlena. Breathe for me. It's okay." I can no longer hear Demon and I can only hope he is getting Jackson and Arcanna.

She pauses for a moment, soft cries and whimpers

falling from her lips. "It wasn't supposed to be like this, this isn't what is supposed to happen."

I frown at her words. "What was supposed to happen?"

Her body stills and for a brief second, I think she's returned to a rational place as her eyes snag mine. Until she lets out a feral growl, right before her head connects with my nose and blood pours from it. Her screams bouncing across the parking lot. "YOU'RE KEEPING ME FROM HIM!" She screeches, her magic starting to build behind each sentence she throws together.

I wince at the feel of it giving Harrow enough of a distraction to slip my grip. I tackle her to the ground, my body landing hard on top of her. "Gods damn it!" I grind my teeth down as I keep her pinned to the concrete.

"LET ME GO!" She screams, this time infusing her banshee magic in it fully. My grip loosens once more as I brace against the cry. Glass rains down from above as the SUV windows shatter.

Everything is ringing as I snarl in her ear, "I don't want to hurt you."

"You already are, you aren't letting me go to him!" She lets loose another scream, this one much stronger. My grip loosens fully this time and that's all it takes, like a wild animal she senses the weakness and flings her head back. Catching me in the already broken nose. My body falls from hers and through hazy eyes I see her take off running.

Rolling from my back to stomach once more, I push to my hands and knees, I swipe the back of my hand across my nose in a desperate attempt to clear the blood as I try to stand.

Arcanna and Jackson meet my gaze wide eyed as they come out of the clubhouse. Concern and confusion mirrored in their eyes.

"Grab her!" I shout pointing towards the fleeing priestess.

As Arcanna moves to intercept Jackson grabs her bicep, pulling her into his body and whispering into her ear. She shakes her head, flexing against his hold as she tries to pull away towards Harrowlena.

My eyes travel to the priestess who slams into the chain link fence that borders the property. She screams in frustration, clawing at the metal like a rabid beast. She backs up, drawing in a breath as she prepares to unleash more magic when just behind her a familiar figure walks up.

"Now now little banshee, we wouldn't want you hurting yourself, would we?" Kallen grabs Harrow, wrapping her arm around her neck. "I warned you what would happen if you made this choice." Demon steps up and shoves a syringe into Harrow's arm. The tiny priestess freezes before her body goes limp and she is pulled under by whatever drug they gave her.

I breathe out a sigh of relief. A gurgling sound draws our attention as her body begins to seizure in Kallen's arms, the female swearing as she drops down to hold the priestesses steady. It goes on for a few moments before her body stills and then she retches up water and bile.

Kallen shakes her head before looking up at the rest of us, "We need to get her to a healer. Now."

As if summoned I close my eyes against the voice that is determined to drag me back to the pits of the underworld. "Someone call for a healer?"

THIRTY-EIGHT

Harrowlena

My body only knows pain.

The fire licking through my vein seeks retribution against me for being so far from the one I need. The one who promised to help me. There is a void that has wrapped around me, trapped me, imprisoned me. It keeps me from the one who would save me. The one I was promised.

"It hurts." I think I say to the void. "You promised me!" I attempt to yell. But my voice feels broken, my throat raw, and the sound is barely a whisper.

"You deserve to be punished; this is retribution for all the failures."

"I've done everything you asked, please!" I think I yell, my tears hot against my skin.

My pussy clenches as arousal rips through me again and again. With each wave of unmet need comes another of scorching fire. I sob as my body is wracked with spasms and an inferno rages through my blood. The feeling of burning from the inside out a constant companion.

"Lena. . ." the voice I need, the one I've been begging

for is soft against the maelstrom of pain I feel. Fingers penetrate me, giving me brief relief. *"Lena we are going to do amazing things together my sweet mate."* This. This is what I need. My mate's fingers in me.

"You came." I breathe out. "You came. You came. You came." I repeat the words over and over as I move my hips.

"I will always come for you my sweet Lena. You are mine."

I want to nod in agreement, but I feel my body clench and my release moves through my body in a crescendo. I sob from the relief I feel, and my hands reach out to hold my savior, to draw them in so they can finish what they started. But I'm met with cold, empty space, and the fingers I once felt deep within are gone.

I'm ripped from my relief and thrown back into a reality I don't recognize. Hand's that don't belong to him, to my mate, seem to have taken up residence on my body. My power building and building. Rough hands push me down, hold me to the hard surface under my back. Angry voices above me as I try to force my eyes open. Memories of being bound by that mask surface and fear moves through me. Is that what this is? They want to rebind me?

I scream out for my mate, scream for him to save me. "Why?! I did everything you have asked, why are you punishing me?!" He promised that he would help and take the pain away.

"But did you? You have failed me so often my Lena. Even now you fail me."

"I'm sorry!" I sob. "It's not my fault this time." Though my body shouts at the lie I tell. Because it is my fault. All this is my fault. The goddess is punishing me by throwing me into my heat early. So yes, this is all my fault and maybe I do deserve to die for that.

Jackson

Dios doesn't say anything as his brother appears with hands in pockets, a smug smile painting his lips.

"I see you are up and moving my lovely reaper." Luz says.

Arcanna growls low, "I'm not your lovely anything."

He chuckles softly, unperturbed by her hostility.

"Who the fuck are you?" Demon asks, stepping in front of Kallen who still holds Harrow. The movement would make me laugh if the situation weren't so dire given Kallen would undoubtedly be the one to go against a god.

Luz follows his movements and for a moment his eyes seem to flash with genuine concern over Harrow before landing on Kallen. He lets out a low hiss, eyes flaring wide. "You."

She narrows her eyes at him in that Kallen way that promises either death or fucking depending on the next words the person uses. "Have we met?" She asks sweetly.

Luz shakes his, and expression of awe painting his face. "It's not very often I meet someone *divine tocado*." His gaze travels around the group of us. "Honestly Dios, I'm offended no one knows about me. I'm your baby brother after all, does family mean nothing?"

Dios stays silent.

Luz rolls his eyes, "The drama." Arcanna steps forward and drops herself next to Dios, her head tilting just enough to show the new mate mark. A reminder that Dios isn't alone.

"I am here to personally escort you to our home. I can even heal your broken priestess there as a gesture of good-will." He pushes his hands back into his pockets as he steps closer to see Harrow. Demon snarls, his wolf surfacing. Luz looks more annoyed than anything as he looks him over. "Move aside wolf, I would never harm your mate."

"Like you could," Kallen laughs. "Trust me when I tell you, *no one* is going to harm me or my mate again." Her tone sends chills down my spine. Luz has the decency to give her a head nod, his eyes filling with an odd amount of respect.

"Harrowlena with die if you do not bring her to my home. She is in the throes of heat right now; she's literally burning alive from the inside out."

My stomach drops at his words.

"What about her replenishing Jax?" Arcanna asks. No doubt sensing the fear and anxiety moving its way over me. Dios hisses a warning, cutting her a sharp, angry look. A look I know well. One that is based not in actual anger, but fear. He does not want his family knowing I'm weakened.

Lux frowns, the expression cutting across his face as he looks between me and Dios. "I see you are still just as naïve as ever," he grumbles. When he looks to Arcanna he adds, "She will not be able to give up any magic, the moon isn't full so the ceremony cannot be done. Either she dies here, or you follow me. Which will it be?"

Dios

I can't seem to bring myself to look at my friends even as Arcanna and Jackson push by me, following Luz carrying Harrow limp in his arms through the door he created to our home.

Arcanna pauses before she steps over the threshold, holding her hand out to me. I take a deep breath turning to Demon and Kallen finally. The two regarding me with varying emotions.

I shrug, "I'm sorry." The words sound lame, even to my ears, and they don't do the situation justice.

He snorts and shakes his head, dragging me in for a quick hug that I can't get myself to return. "When you come back you owe me a drink and an explanation." He says into my ear.

I squeeze my eyes shut and can't bring myself to tell him I won't be coming back. That once I step through this portal and into my home the likelihood of me being allowed to return is slim to none. I barely managed to escape the first time, there will be no seconds.

My body feels wired, the tension refusing to leave me as I step out of his embrace. Kallen doesn't move to hug me however those green eyes cut into me hard as she grips Demons hand. "I have no issue going after you Dios." She says with a tone full of violence. "I went against covens; I'll go against your family. No matter who they are. Just remember that."

Turning from them I glance at the still open portal, Luz's form rounding a corner and disappearing. I let out a long sigh, grabbing Arcanna's hand, and not giving credence to her statement. Because there is no reality that she could hold her own against my family.

Against my home.

Home.

The space I've avoided for so long and now I'm right back here with my mates. The two people who shouldn't be in spitting distance of my father. When I step over the threshold it feels like I'm marching to my death and when the portal closes behind me and the sounds of Hell are cut off it feels like the lid to my coffin is now shut.

"Luz said we can stay in there," Arcanna's voice pulls my eyes open, apparently having shut them against the sight of my home. She gestures towards my old room and the one it connects to. Her voice is quiet, but it still puts me on edge, worried it will summon *them*, my parents.

I half expected them to be waiting in ambush. But now I suspect they are biding their time while their dog enjoys his toy in the room across the hall. Because that's all my brother is to them, their dog. The one they send out to fetch whomever, and whatever, they want and need.

And he obeys his master's without question, every single time.

I shove at the unwanted memories of my departure as they try to struggle to the surface now that I'm back here. The idea of stepping into the room, my old room, rooting me to the spot. My feet feel like lead, too heavy to dream of picking up and using to transport myself forward.

Jax and Arcanna seem less apprehensive and make themselves at home, pushing into the room before me as I still linger in the hallway.

"You coming?" Arcanna calls out to me. Either oblivious to my distress or giving me space, the latter the more likely scenario. Knowing if she starts talking to me I might break apart.

Rubbing my neck, I take another large breath before allowing it to slip free as I move towards the other door. Stepping over the threshold of my childhood bedroom I'm hit with a sense of nostalgia. Everything is the same, yet everything feels different. It's like I'm standing in a museum of my life.

Even the blanket my abuela made me is still stretched across my bed, as if I just woke up that morning and ran out to get coffee. My fingers trail over the material, the rough yarn snagging on the callouses I've built up over the years working on my bike. When I reach the end of it, I move to take my leather cut off my back, laying it on my bed with reverence. I snort out a sad sort of laugh as I realize the vest won't be part of my attire anymore, or my identity.

I continue to catalogue my previous life as my eyes roam the room. When they snag on the dark crown placed under my desk lamp my body goes cold. It's a message from my parents, one that confirms my fears.

I'm never getting out of here again.

I back away from the offensive metal like it might strike out at me, spinning on the ball of my foot and heading to the adjoining door. Needing to find space and reprieve from everything that is happening.

Pushing it open I'm hit with my mates overwhelming scents, my cock growing stiff and my mouth watering. The two are sitting against the couch, Jackson massaging Arcanna's feet, her legs draped over his lap. . It brings a small smile to may face, the action so normal and domestic. "So, this is your home?" Jax finally asks.

"This is where I grew up, yes." I make a point to avoid confirming this is my home, because it isn't. Not anymore. Not since I joined the Primal MC Knights. Even if I'm trapped here forever this will never be my home. *My mates are my home.*

Arcanna snorts. "This place feels like an old medieval castle or some shit."

I don't say anything despite wanting to tell her that some of the prison cells are indeed that old and are still stained with the blood of past victims. They might even currently have people locked in them given my father's lust for torture.

"So, are we just going to trust your brother to take care of Harrow?" Arcanna asks. "I would bet money he had his claws in this."

"I can assure you I had nothing to do with her heat starting early, that is purely biology." Luz breezes in, reeking of sex, his hair messy and eyes feverish as he pours himself a drink. His pants hang low on his hips while his chest is exposed and two barbells glitter in his nipples. The silver matching the ring he wears in his nose. "I'm just cleaning up the mess you three were too stupid to realize had been created."

"Excuse me?" I growl.

Luz rolls his eyes. "You ignored my warning not to trust her, and here we are."

"I already didn't fucking trust her fully!" I spat. "How were any of us supposed to know she was going into heat?"

"It's a good thing you'll never be King, Dios. You truly do not have the observational skills for it."

I lunge for him only to feel Jackson's arms wrap around my mid-section. "It's not worth it." He whispers. Arcanna glares at Luz as she drags her legs up and under her now that Jackson is holding onto me.

Luz smirks, "yes listen to your mate big brother."

Jackson growls, the feeling vibrating my body. "Either talk to us or leave."

My brother sighs. "I could use a drink, I'm exhausted."

"Get. To. The. Point." I grind out.

He eyes narrow, "play nice brother or not only will I refuse to save the priestess, but I'll reverse the healing I did on your little female." This time it's me holding Jackson back as he attempts to launch himself at my brother. "Everyone is so touchy." He chuckles darkly.

Arcanna's fist connects with Luz's chin before she plants her hand around his throat. His eyes alight with feral delight even as her glaive appears in her hand. "I will slice you up and feed you to a dragon that I know who is dying to get another soul in his belly."

Luz spits blood off to the side and only nods as she removes her hand from his throat and backs away until she presses into Jax, his arm circling her as he nuzzles her neck.

I brace myself as Luz grins in a sadistic way, a grin that promises I'm going to hate whatever he has to say next. "I'll continue to heal her but you three are required at a dinner event tomorrow evening, mother and father are *dying* to meet your little playthings."

"We don't have time for this," Jackson growls out.

Luz shrugs, "One night of dancing and enjoying dinner. You'll be here anyway little King given the priestess. Enjoy the festivities and you and your mate can leave the following morning." He glances to me as he says it, his eyes shining. The message is clear, Jax may be leaving with Arcanna but I will be staying.

Harrow

I am lost to a sea of pain and endless need. A constant gnawing hunger that is never satiated. Each time I think it's ending another wave pulls me under, and I'm drowning all over again. Living like this is agony, and I beg for death. Plea for it. Offer up everything I have left to give if my misery will just end.

"You will not be dying right now priestess." A warm voice answers, the sound beautiful within my head. It wraps around me, pushing the broken pieces of my mind and body back together. Warm tears cascade down my face, and I want more than anything to express my thanks as my body finally relaxes. The spasms and endless need finally ceasing and giving me a moments peace as warmth spreads through me like golden light. *"I know who you are Harrow, I know* what *you are, I see in your soul."*

A chill runs down my spine at her words, as she shares a prophecy that I had no decision in being a part of. The golden light dimming for just a moment as desperation claws my stomach apart as I try to resist hearing her.

"The more you resist, the more you ignore the truth right in front of you, the worst this will be. You cannot defy fate

like this." More warm, golden light flows over me soothing my aching body. "I *will grant you the peace I can, for now. And in return I ask that upon your waking you stop being ignorant to the world around you.*" The voice seems to float away, leaving me with the haunting words alone in my mind.

THIRTY-ONE

Luz

Watching the priestess sleep I can't help but feel a small amount of gratitude towards her captor. Without him I never would have found her. The past 24 hours with her have been a beautiful nightmare, helping her through her heat while healing the infection that piece of shit put on her soul. Her scent is burned into my skin now, a permanent part of me that will never go away, even when this body has long rotted away.

Taking a sip of my drink, I tap the glass with my ring as I watch her twist this way and that in the sheets, her naked body slipping free to show her peaked breast and the sheen of sweat still coating her. My cock hardens as I'm hit with a fresh scent of her arousal and when her legs spread slightly, I can't help but find myself kneeling between them, whisky discarded as my tongue goes in search of something better.

I take my time, savoring her flavor on my tongue as I swirl through her slick folds before sucking her clit into my mouth. The swollen bundle of nerves has her body quivering around me and when I press a finger inside her she releases her orgasm almost instantly, a soft moan dragging from her lips while she still slumbers.

"I should have known you would spoil my fun," I huff as I pull my finger free and lick it clean. A feminine chuckle is the only answer. Pushing to a stand I turn towards the spot I had previously sat to find my whiskey glass empty. "How did I earn a visit from the illustrious L."

She rolls her white eyes, the color standing out starkly against her thick black hair. Her long Victorian dress clings to her frame and her red lips make her look like she should be haunting Dracula's castle. "Really Luz, one would think you aren't happy to see me."

I keep my face passive as I move and pour myself another drink, "you ruined my snack."

Her soft chuckle fills the air, "on the contrary, she got off, didn't she? So, you got your snack. You just didn't get the full meal."

"Semantics." I say waving the full glass at her. "Now are you going to tell me why you took the risk of coming here? I know it wasn't to drink cheap whiskey or watch me eat her pussy."

Her eyes grow feral with hunger, "I would gladly watch you eat her pussy all day." She purrs. "At one time we were quite the team." She pushes upward and invades my space, her long, pointed fingernail dragging down my cheek until she hits my bare chest and smooths her whole hand out across my pecs. I let her explore, her hands moving up and down my body as her eyes devour me. When she reaches my cock, now hard between us, I fist her throat with my hand and drag her mouth to mine.

She moans as she swirls her tongue over my lips and piercings, eagerly licking up whatever cum is left from Harrow before she pulls from me. She lets my hand hold her throat still as she bites down hard on her lip before step-ping back. I let her push me down onto the bed directly next to Harrow as she mounts me, her cunt tight and wet as I slide home. She groans, those sharp nails digging into my chest hard enough that I can feel the trickle of blood. When she leans down and licks my chest clean, I let out a groan at the feel. "You taste just like you used to." She muses.

"And what's that?" I ask, the end turning to a moan as she starts to ride me.

Her pussy trembles as she positions herself just right, so my cock hits the magic place deep within. My fingers dip under the skirts she never removed and press her clit, the piercing in it adding to her pleasure. Her mouth goes slack and her orgasm rushes through her before my own cock finds its release. We both ride our pleasure out, the room filled with the sounds of our bodies and panting breath until she stills atop me.

Leaning down she bites my ear lobe before her tongue sweeps out to soothe it, "You taste like every bad decision I could make."

***

Harrow

For the first time in a while when I awake I feel clear headed, the heat still simmering below the surface but not a raging wildfire trying to kill me. My eyes blink open slowly, the light streaming in through large windows so bright it's almost painful. Everything feels raw, my eyes, my body, my heart. I grimace when I shift, and I can feel the stickiness between my thighs and flashes of my time with Luz meander through my memory. My cheeks heat as my pussy starts to drip arousal again even as the guilt, I feel for betraying everything I've known, tries to nibble away at my mind.

"You're awake." Luz meanders into my view. His chest on display and coffee skin glowing in the morning light. His nipples each have the same silver piercings that are in his nose and tongue. He's not as tattooed as Dios is but there is a spattering of ink across his body. I have the urge to trace them with my tongue. He clears his throat, and I snap my focus back to his face, a knowing smile spreading over his mouth.

"Where are we?" I ask quietly, my throat painful, the words dragging across my tongue. Luz frowns and quickly grabs me a glass of water from the bedside table, handing it to me and allowing me to take a long sip of the cool liquid.

"We are at my home." He explains blandly. "What do you remember?"

I frown; my memory hazy at best. "The last thing I remember. . . ." I trail off.

He leans forward, arms going on either side of me on the bed. "You were being very naughty. You've gotten yourself into quite the predicament, haven't you?" His voice sends shivers over my body, my nipples hardening between us. "Do they know?" My eyes widen a fraction before I can think better of it. He presses his nose into my neck, breathing deeply before his tongue peeks out and tastes my skin. "I can taste it you know; the poison he has left in you. Smell it too. It covers that normally delicious scent of yours."

My breathing feels erratic, "I don't know what you're talking about." My body wars with itself, there is still a desperation in my blood. His hand reaches up and cups my heavy breast, softly playing with it, forcing me to arch into his touch. His scent envelopes me as his hands explore and before I realize it, I'm lying on my back once more with his heavy body on top of me.

His mouth hovers above my own. "He wants to keep you for his own personal battery. Never allowing you to realize your true power." He says. "But I would unleash you." His mouth claims mine, our kissing growing hungry as his hand dips between my thighs. He growls low when he feels how wet I am.

"That's my good girl, so ready for me." The praise shoots through my body like a bolt of lightning. It takes away any argument that was building in me, any refusal of what Oisin was or is doing to me.

I feel him push down his pants and the head of his cock notches at my entrance as he plays with my clit between his fingers. He keeps teasing me, pushing me to the edge before dragging backwards, the head of his cock never fully pushing into me.

"Please," I stutter out. "Please, Luz."

(Endgame- Klergy)

"Fuckkkk," He cries. "My name on your lips might be the only prayer I ever need." He sits back up his eyes glowing with lust and magic. He keeps his hand firmly fisted around his length, pumping it slowly before he starts to feed himself into my tight channel. My pussy burns with the stretch and I arch upward as the pain seems to light up my pleasure receptors.

"Fuck me," I demand. "Please." I beg.

"Oh I'll fuck you my *ángel caido* but after we will be having a little chat." He pins my arms above my head before my body freezes entirely. The need that was trying to devour me suddenly replaced with panic.

"What is this?" I hiss out. The control my body had previously vanishing.

"Just my magic, enjoying flowing through your blood."

He does not release my hands, nor let up on the pressure he is leaning into me. "The one you claim as your mate has deceived you little one, he has been poisoning you with a false fucking bond."

Even if he hadn't been holding me with magic, I would have frozen. "No." I breath out. "No that's not true."

"You say that as you are fucking another man." As if to prove a point he thrusts into me harder dragging a cry of pleasure that is all me, my heat held at bay and no longer burning me. "You can lie to yourself but never to me, I can taste it in your blood."

"No!" I cry out. "I'm not lying."

He laughs, cold and unforgiving, as he keeps manipulating my pleasure. "You are not sheep to be led around and controlled, and yet here I find you with a pretty leash and a master." Luz growls. "You are meant to bring kingdoms to their knees."

The truth of his words wash over me. Even as a child my Nana and mother led me through our way of life, no choice given to me in how I was to behave or interact with the world around us. The Order was no better, and *him?*

A strange acceptance flows through me. As though a veil was removed and suddenly things feel clear once more. Luz controls my body like an expert master, pushing and pulling at my arousal as I allow myself to settle into this newfound realization. This newfound clarity.

"And you?" I whimper out as he hits the perfect spot. "Will you fall to your knees for me?"

Leaning in close, his breath caresses my ear. "Oh my sweet *ángel*, I will do better. I will bring you sacrifices daily. Slay any who wish to interrupt your reign." He slips a hand down between our bodies and strokes my clit. My body arches into his as I feel my orgasm cresting towards me. "All I ask is you return to me when I call."

"So, I'm trading a cage for what?" I manage to pant out.

He lets out a soft chuckle, "A crown."

Luz

I can see the wheels turning in Harrow's eyes, those violet windows to her soul wide despite being filled with lust. Her body arches into mine as I release my magic bit by bit and give her control back, give her heat back. I needed her to have clear mind for this moment, despite the danger of holding back that heat.

She flushes a deep red, her pale skin practically glowing. I wasn't lying when I said I would give her a crown. I want this woman to unleash herself upon the world. I want to watch as she topples kingdoms and slays the nightmares that haunt her. My fingers find her clit and I let myself massage the tiny bundle of nerves, watching her face the whole time as she starts to come apart at the seams.

I feel her pussy convulsing around me as she lets out a silent scream. "That's it," I coax her. "Let it all go. Let me feel you soak my cock." She writhes beneath me, a seemingly never-ending orgasm claiming her body and soaking the sheets beneath us.

Pulling my cock free I move up to her face, "taste us." I growl, pushing the head past her lips. She eagerly follows my instructions, licking her arousal from my still hard cock. "Good girl. I want our taste to live on your tongue." I grunt as my balls draw up and I'm cuming down the back of her throat in waves. She drinks it down, never missing a drop and her violet eyes remain locked on mine. A clarity in them that marks the end of her heat coming.

Pulling free of her mouth I scoot down giving her room to catch her breath as I grab a drink. "You shouldn't have done that." She says voice horse. "*I* shouldn't have done that."

The glass practically cracks in my hand as I attempt to reign in my rage at her statement. "My cum isn't even in your stomach yet and you are going to tell me we shouldn't have done that?" I turn back towards her, my gaze pinning her to the bed. "Your cunt is still dripping from your own orgasm and you are going to tell me that was wrong? Tell me, does he ever satisfy you? Does he leave you breathless? Does he make you squirt and scream?"

She balls her fists in the sheets. "Stop it." She growls. "None of this is real."

"You know that's not true, you knew it while I was balls deep in you because I used my magic. I held your heat back." I spat the words out. "I doubt he even knows where your clit is."

"Stop talking." She commands again.

"I think he would rather use you as his own personal cum dumpster." I say, refusing to allow her to backtrack.

"I SAID STOP!" Her voice flows from her in waves of magic as her banshee side takes over. Everything around me shattering and splintering. I watch with fascination as she screams into the void before pulling it all back with wide eyes. Her chest heaves with the exertion.

I raise my glass to my lips, the liquor burning down my throat. "That was impressive."

"How. . ."

I snort, disgusted at how little she understands. "I'm a God. I can withstand anything I want. But it also helps I was testing you and knew to shield before that happened."

Harrow drags the sheet over her naked body, covering her tits and holding it against herself like armor . She smells of our joining. The scent intoxicating to me as we occupy the space together. It hasn't been a hardship for me to fuck her, to use her, if anything she's become a new addiction in my life. Something that I crave to return to.

Truthfully, I'm not sure how I feel about that. She was never meant to be something I *need* to keep. "You can keep denying the truth but it's in you now. I've made sure of that. So, when you're ready to talk I'll be here."

I don't let her respond, fleeing from the room before I do something I'll regret.

FOURTY

Jackson

The summoning to see Dios's parents comes the next morning. Luz appearing with a dark look in his eyes demanding our presence in the royal hall. Dios had rushed out after him, their voices hushed and angry as I tried to listen at the door. When he returned to the room he looked defeated. Locking himself in the adjoining room and staying there until we all exited into the hallway dressed in clothing presented to us by servants.

Luz, Dios and I were all dressed in similar attire, dark button up shirts and slacks. Arcanna, however, wore a long emerald green dress that hugged her body tightly. Two slits on either side landed just at her hip and the top cut down low in the back and front. Her chest seemed about ready to spill out. Her dark hair had been spun up into a braid show-casing her stormy eyes and full lips, along with the claiming mark from Dios's wolf. She holds her glaive in her right hand, the blade shining.

"You look beautiful." I whisper into her ear, pressing a kiss just below. She flushes from face to chest and offers a soft smile. Dios whispers something else, the words lost to me, causing an even deeper crimson flush to move over her and arousal to wash through our bond.

The door from across the hall opens, Harrow stepping free from it. Nerves seem to pepper her as she twists and pulls at her fingers, regarding each of us with those violet eyes. "I owe you all an apology." She says softly.

Arcanna scoffs and shakes her head, arms crossed. "We don't want an apology; we want the truth Harrow. You put yourself and us at risk by not telling us you went into heat early." Harrow flinched, the words landing their mark.

Luz slips his arm around her waist, his thumb landing just below her naval. Harrows pupils dilated and she leans into the touch. "Let's not be late, you know how mother and father feel about that."

———

Harrow
(Ave Maria- Tommee Proffit & Stanja)

Luz escorts us towards his parents. His hand never leaving my body, whether on my back or holding my own he keeps me grounded. And I couldn't be more thankful for it right now. Arcanna's words had hurt, I hadn't realized how much her budding friendship had meant to me until now, until it was clear that bridge was already on fire. No, not just the bridge, my whole life feels on fire right now. Everything unsteady and confusing.

Luz's words from early follow me through the hallway, I can't seem to shake them now that their claws are in. They keep chipping away at the bond deep within, chipping away at the memories that I once thought fondly of. My head feels full, too full, and everything is heavy. As though the air itself is attempting to crush me and my internal monologue is attempting to drown me in screams.

"After you brother." Luz says as we land outside a large door. He presses a kiss to the back of my hand, his eyes bright as he releases me and steps backward. Dios, Jackson and Arcanna all file in before me and I'm left trailing behind them, acutely aware of how alone I feel now.

The great hall surrounding us is painted gold, with deep plush red carpets lining the white marble floors. The grand pillars holding up the ceiling are carved with skulls and skeletons that are twisted into grotesque shapes. Flames move across them throwing their shadows onto the walls giving them the appearance of dancing. All around us eyes track our movements forward, the only sound is our shoes when they hit a patch of marble instead of carpet.

Directly ahead of us sit Dios's parents, with Luz having managed to appear standing just behind them. His father's black throne is a twisted heap of charred bones that have been dipped in iron and steel. He has a stern look on his face, and a golden crown sits atop a full head of thick black hair that is cut short to his scalp. He wears his shirt open exposing his well-toned golden chest and his green eyes burn bright as they skate over the group before landing on me. His eyes lingering on me long enough my stomach twists and turns uncomfortably.

His mother, sitting upon her own golden throne, watches us with curiosity as we approach, a small smile tugging on her painted lips as she spots Dios. Dressed in a tight red dress that leaves little to the imagination she has her stark white hair pulled high up in a ponytail. While she wears no crown she has a small diadem across her forehead with a glittering white jewel in the middle.

After what feels like an eternity we land in front of the king and queen. The God and Goddess of Death.

"Mamá. Padre." Dios nods towards his parents. If they are offended by a lack of title they don't show it. "Estos son mis compañeros. These are my... companions. Harrowlena, Jackson and Arcanna." He points to each of us. Both his parents look us over, judgment painting the King's face whereas curiosity shines in his mothers.

"Trajiste un segador aquí. You brought a Reaper here." His father glares at Arcanna who is clutching her glaive in her right hand, her face cold and unforgiving as she looks at the King before he lips pull into a cocky smile.

"Y el Rey del Infierno. And the King of Hell." His mother adds her voice oddly whimsical. "And this must be Luz's new. . .friend he found." The look she gives me makes me want to shrink into the ground but it's nothing compared to the Kings.

"Every prince needs his whore." His father says cruelly. The lust in his eyes as they rake over me says he does not find me distasteful.

The Queen sneers at him, "you would know." She says it quietly, but I catch it none the less.

Dios steps forward slightly so his body is moderately blocking us from his parents.

"Luz offered to help us. We won't take up your time." Dios says, the formality in his voice shocking.

"We know why you are here, and had your brother consulted us we would have denied the request." He glances backwards at Luz who keeps an annoyed look on his face as he shrugs.

"I was bored." He replies simply.

The King keeps that sneer plastered to his face and returns his gaze to us before schooling his features to something more neutral. Gesturing to myself, Arcanna and Jackson, "you three may leave now." He commands. "You've gotten what you came for."

I glance between everyone before looking to Luz, confused.

"What is he talking about?" Arcanna asks.

Dios's father yawns, "Dios will be staying here. He knew if he returned this is what would happen. But he's bargained for you, the would be king and his whores, to leave this place unharmed as long as he remains behind."

"What?" Jackson hisses stepping towards Dios.

Dios says nothing, his jaw clenching as he glares at his father.

"You cannot keep him," Arcanna counters. "He is our mate."

Dios flinches as his father lets out a truly evil laugh. "You may be bonded to his wolf, but you are not his true mate, and we all know he will never mate with the piss poor excuse of a king standing next to you." Anger I've never known pulses through me, my power rising in my throat as they insult the people, who in a different life, could have been my true friends. "He knows what the consequences would be."

"Separating mates is cruel." I say, my voice barely above a whisper. "It could kill them." His mother looks at me with sadness in her eyes before she blinks and it's gone, painted in indifference once more.

Luz clears his throat as he shoots me a quick look before addressing his family, "father, they have agreed to attend the ball. It is a good opportunity to show how merciful you are choosing to be. Letting Dios have one last night with his mates." Calling it mercy feels like salt in the wound and entirely untrue but I hold my tongue still. This new fire in my belly, the fire to defend these people, too new to me to understand how to harness it through words.

He cuts him a hard glare, eyes narrowing for a moment before he lets his mouth spread into a wicked smile that provides no warmth. "It seems your brother has more compassion in him than I. Fine, you will all attend this evening and show the members of our court that their prince has returned for good."

Dios balls his fists at his side before giving a curt nod.

"No! This is bullshit!' Arcanna yells, magic flaring brightly on her tattoos. "We aren't leaving without him." She turns to Dios, panic in her eyes. "We aren't leaving without you."

"*Segradora,*" he murmurs softly arm reaching for her.

She jerks back from him, "No! Is this what you were doing? While we thought you were locked in your room you were really talking with them?!" She uses her glaive to point at the royals earning a hiss from the King.

"Get control of your beast." His father growls, inspiring laughter throughout the room.

I go to step forward, to defend Arcanna, but Jackson beats me to it, his wings unfolding elegantly behind him and seemingly gobbling up the air around us with the darkness. His hands are planted in his pockets and his silver eyes are cold as they look to the King and Queen on their thrones. "If Dios does not come with us, I will return for him." He turns and looks out at the gathered crowd. "I will slowly take apart each of you. . . Piece by piece and when your people are all dead I will burn this place to the ground."

"We are gods what can you do against us." His father laughs loudly.

Jackson cuts him a look that is made of vengeance and holds a promise of blood, his silver eyes so cold I'm shocked the royals are not frozen to their seats. "You are not untouchable because of your title."

Uncomfortable silence spreads through the room as the threat lays over the crowd like thick fog. The King's face is red, the Queen's pale. Luz looks amused at the whole thing, a smile pulling at the corner of his mouth. Jackson says nothing as he pulls Dios from the room, Arcanna following closely. I hesitate that fire in me growing and demanding I speak up for them. It's burning up my throat and into my mouth.

"Come along, friend. Let us retire." Luz's sudden touch acts like water over the flames, extinguishing the feeling. I swallow. Frowning as I allow him to lead me out of the room. The King's face is the last one I see before I'm swept away and the look in his eyes sends chills down my spine that have me gripping Luz harder.

"Do not allow him to see that fear." Luz hisses, digging his fingers into my skin to ground me. "You do not fear the weak and mundane."

I swallow back my response as we finally exit the throne room. I don't know how to tell Luz I'm not who he thinks I am. I'm not the fighter he wants me to be, even as I try to deny that fire that was just burning through my body.

Dios

(Bound- Indiana)

Jackson shoves into the room, slamming the door into the wall hard enough I know it'll leave a mark. I can't blame him for his rage. I should have known my father wouldn't keep it a secret I had talked with them. I don't know why I believed he would offer me that courtesy.

"*Mi cielo. . .*" I try to start.

"Just don't." He spits out.

Arcanna casts me a worried look as she reaches for our bond. My magic pulls my wolf back, docking the inferno of emotions that is blazing under my skin. The crestfallen look on her face is enough to break a man.

Enough to break me.

"Why would you agree to stay here?" Arcanna asks, tears shimmering in her eyes.

"There is a curse on me." I begin, voice shaking. The two look at me with confused expressions as Jax pulls Arcanna into his lap on the chair across from me.

Scrubbing my face with my hands, I take a deep breath before exhaling slow.

"The darkness didn't appear right away, according to my family. But when it did, I was. . . not myself. I often didn't remember what had happened when I came out of it but the carnage around me? Let's say what I left when retrieving Harrowlena is nothing compared to what it was then." I begin.

"So what?" Jackson grumbles. "I don't give a shit about that."

I smile at him, loving him for wanting so desperately to accept me. "Everyone feared me, and rightfully so. I was a child with no way of controlling the dark magic that lived within my veins. My brother was the only one who did not. We became best friends; he seemed to help balance me out. Two sides of the same coin. My father, however, had different plans,to see me learn control. He wanted to unleash me, to use me as a weapon. Unbeknownst to me he began to drive a wedge between my brother and I."

Jackson leans forward, Arcanna crawling from his lap and wrapping her arms around her own legs. "So, your father has always been a prick." Jax scoffs.

I huff out a broken laugh. "Yeah, he has." Letting out another long sigh I try to prepare for the rest of the story. "When we turned 18 was when it all changed. Luz had been pulling away from me for a while, leaving me feeling unsteady and alone. My father stepped in to fill the gap. He had been training me, shaping me into a weapon he could use against his enemies. He saw me as a way to conquer the world."

Jackson stands up, his body pacing back and forth as he listens. "I'm still not understanding the point of this story and its relevance."

"I know, *mi cielo*." My voice fills the air with a somber vibe as I near the end of the story and prepare to say goodbye to this. To them. "My abuela saw what was happening. She watched as her own son turned her grandson into a mindless creature of darkness. So, she helped me, she got me out. And it cost her everything. My father is not merciful, even to his own mother."

"How did he find out?" Arcanna asks, sorrow filling her body.

But it's Jackson who answers. "Luz." He says quietly but the fierceness behind the name cuts me to the core. This man, the King before me, loves me with every fiber of his soul and I have no doubt in my mind he would rip my brother to shreds if he could.

I nod. "I told Luz what was going on, I wanted to say goodbye to him. And, in the end, he betrayed me." Standing up I begin to pace the room as if it will chase the memories away. "My father will come for anyone who keeps me away. He has made it very clear he will kill you Jax if we mate."

"He doesn't know we would join powers, does he?" He asks without missing a beat.

For the first time in my life, I feel true fear at the words that spill from his mouth. True, gut wrenching, body paralyzing fear as I realize there is something worse than Jax dying. It's him being used by my father. It's us being held here. Visions of my father torturing Arcanna to force us to comply fill my head, the intrusive thoughts battering me into submission.

As if sensing my spiral Jackson pushes towards me, grabbing my face between his hands. "Your father is a fucking fool if he thinks he can control us or use us. And he will rue the day he ever made you understand the type of fear I just saw flash through those beautiful eyes of yours." He crushes his mouth to mine, lips frantic as he releases his emotions into the searing kiss. Heat flares through me as I give myself over to it, let myself get swept away in the feel of his body against mine.

Arcanna moves up to us, lust and need pouring through the bond. Pulling myself free of Jackson I watch Arcanna loop her arms around his stomach, her fingers playing with his abs. His silver eyes lock onto me and heat flares in them as he watches me pull my shirt up and over my head. I make a show of slowly slipping my jeans down allowing my semi-erect cock to spring free.

"See something you want, *mi ceilo?*" I ask, my voice low and husky.

He bites his lip as Arcanna peers over his shoulders, her eyes electrified as she lets them graze over my body. When they land on my cock, I can't help wrapping my fist around it and jerking it.

"I'll tell you what I want," I say. "I want you both. I want to fuck you in the ass, Jax, filling you with so much cum that when we go to dinner tonight it's still dripping out of you." I travel around the two of them. "And I want to watch you fuck Arcanna's tight pussy at the same time."

Jax groans. "Oh, he's getting so hard." Arcanna says in a breathless moan. "So hard."

I let my finger trail down her exposed back until I hit the zipper of the dress, "do you want to taste? Touch? What do you want?" Slowly I drag that zipper downward until I'm able to start peeling the dress off her.

The scent of her arousal blooms in the air just under Jackson's scent. "I want him to taste me while I taste you." She groans when her dress finally pools at her feet and I'm able to grab a handful of her ass. This. This is what I need right now, what we need right now. To forget, just for a moment.

I chuckle, "you heard her *mi cielo.*" Jackson scrambles to drag his shirt up and over his head before pushing his pants down. His cock stands out against his body, the tip angry and dripping precum. He lays down onto the floor at our feet, eyes hungry as he watches me peel the underwear from our mate. Arcanna drops down, her thighs bracketing his head and bare pussy hovering just above his mouth. I step closer, standing over Jax so my cock bobs directly in front of Arcanna's mouth.

"*Te ves hermosa de rodillas, segadora.* You look beautiful on your knees, reaper." I say as I stroke myself. She licks her lips, eyes hooded with desire.

"Don't get used to it." She says a playful smile on her lips.

I chuckle, "I wouldn't dream of it." I slowly push the head past her waiting lips. Enjoying the feel of her warm lips wrapped around me. Her tongue flicks up my slit, collecting the precum that's already started to bead out. "Fuckkkk." I groan.

It's at this same time that Jax clearly takes his opportunity to taste her because she jerks forward, a moan vibrating through her chest as she takes me fully into her mouth. She gags as I hit the back of it. When I go to back off, she grabs my thighs and drags me back, allowing the tip to slip down her waiting throat. Her hips grind into Jax's mouth, his own answering sounds filling the air.

"Gods, that's so hot. Watching you eat her pussy like such a good boy. Keep going, don't stop until she's squirting all over you. I want to taste her release on your mouth." Arcanna lets out a long moan in answer to the command I'm giving Jax. She works harder and harder on my cock as I watch her hips grind into her mate below. "Can I cum across your face?" I grunt out.

Arcanna's eyes blink open, hazed with arousal and need. She gives a small nod of confirmation before her eyes close again and she's lost to the pleasure. Closing my own eyes, I fuck her with abandon until I feel my balls pull up and I'm yanking free to cover her in my release. She lets out a long scream as her own release barrels into her. My cock never softens as I look at her with my cum dripping down her chin to her chest.

"Oh fuck, oh fuck Jax. Just like that! Oh fuck oh fuck." She screams out, the orgasm rolling through her body over and over. When it releases her from its clutches, her body sags forward, my hands catching her under her arms as I hoist her upward. Jax smiles, his mouth and face glistening from her cum. His cock painfully hard.

I cock my finger, beckoning him forward to stand. When he does, I drag his mouth to mine, not kissing but cleaning with my tongue until nothing is left of the orgasm Arcanna left on him.

"Fuck reaper, you taste so fucking good on his mouth." She groans as I dip my fingers down to her core. "You ready to feel Jax inside you?" I ask.

She nods; her eyes hazed with arousal to the point that I worry she's already slipped away from us. But when she blinks, they clear, left with only sharp need and hunger. "Jax will ride me, and you'll ride him." I command. Neither of them argues. "On the bed reaper, hands and knees."

Arcanna doesn't argue as she spreads herself open on the bed. Jax groans at the sight, her pussy wet and ready. He moves up to her, his cock notched at her entrance, his eyes casting back to me waiting for permission.

"Such a good boy waiting," I praise. "You may fill her." He pushes in swiftly, pausing once fully seated. I let my hand dip down to feel where they are joined, pushing my fingers in and out with his cock. Once wet enough I focus my attention on his tight hole, pressing him forward as I start to work my fingers in and out of him.

"Oh fuck," He cries as I spread him. "That feels so fucking good."

I chuckle, "I had intended to prep you more but I need to be in you, need to feel you."

"Someone fuck me already I'm dying over here." Arcanna grumbles.

I press the head of my cock against his heat and slowly move in. "Fuck your hole is tight."

I feel his hips shift forward as he slowly starts to fuck Arcanna. The reaper throwing her head back with a moan. The sounds send me over the edge. Spiraling as I lose all control and turn to primal instinct. Our scent swims in the air, merging and blending as we find pleasure within our joining.

Jackson's ass is tight, the muscles strangling my cock. I let my magic take hold of him. Keeping him from finding his release as I start to fuck him slowly. With each thrust, I edge him closer and closer to what he needs most, before pulling him back again. Arcanna groans as the torture I'm inflicting on Jackson goes into her, his body straining to keep fucking her while I'm edging him. Her moans and curses are sent into the atmosphere joining Jacksons.

The reason behind avoiding mating him getting further and further away from me with each thrust into him and moan I pull from his beautiful mouth. My magic keeps demanding we mate, my teeth descended, the canines pointed and sharp. Madness has invaded my mind, madness fueled by the primal lust I feel for this man and the need to have the three of us fully bonded. Rational, logical thought has been chased away.

"Oh shit. Oh fuck. Don't stop. Don't stop." Jackson pants. "You feel so fucking good."

My hand grips him so tight I have no doubt he'll be bruised. "I don't intend to stop until you are taking my knot in that tight ass and I've claimed you as mine," I growl, my voice no longer mine but the part of me I keep chained away. "Now beg me." In the distance I think I hear Arcanna groan out her own release.

Jackson whimpers, "fill me up. Please. Fill me with your knot. I want you in me. I want you to paint me with your release. I want to feel you when I walk. Show me what it means to be yours. Fucking claim me."

Any restraint I was holding onto vanishes, and I feel my dick pulse as I press my knot into him. His body tenses under me, no doubt feeling an overwhelming pressure given my size.

I pull my magic back, releasing my hold on his cock. "Shhh *mi cielo* you can take it. You are such a good boy. You can take my knot." I lean over him, glancing down at Arcanna whose eyes are practically rolled back in her head. She falls over the edge, orgasm slamming into her. And dragging Jax with her, his dick filling her up. "That's it, baby, let me hear you cum while I fill you up. Squeeze me with that tight ass."

My mouth hovers over his neck. A silent question. One last chance to opt out of this.

"If you don't bite me right now and take me for your own, I swear to all the gods I'll kill you." He growls. "And Arcanna will find your soul in the afterlife to continue to punish you."

"He speaks the truth," Arcanna groans out under us.

(Bedroom Hymns- Florence + the Machine)

I bite down hard as my knot fully penetrates him. He cries out, another release flowing over him and squeezing me harder. The taste of his blood fills my mouth as I hold him down by the bite. My magic swimming between us to meet his. His blood sings against my own. The feeling pulls my orgasm from me, my dick filling him just beyond my knot.

We stay like that for an unknown amount of time, but

it's long enough that Arcanna is able to slip free of our hold and my own cock softens just enough that my knot finally releases us.

Pulling off the bite mark I pull him onto my lap so I can face him. I tilt my head to the side, offering up the expanse of my neck for him. He lunges without question, his teeth digging into my skin until my blood flows into him. . Our bond settles into place, warm and content against the one I have with Arcanna. The three of us now connected forever.

When he releases my neck, his silver eyes are almost fully black with a tinge of hunger.

"Feed. Now." I command.

There is no hesitation on his part as he latches onto my mouth dragging my magic deep into him. The feeling is pure ecstasy. My cock hardening once more at the feel, an intoxication flowing through me that I know will be my new addiction. Our magic intertwines, neither of us knowing where one begins and the other ends.

Something within my chest unlocks like the bond was the key to opening up a vast well that had been shut off to me for so long. The power we create is nothing short of otherworldly, the air around us shimmering with it. The ground below our body quaking from the release. Everything within me settles, my soul comes alive with the power.

Jax keeps pulling more magic from me. My cock filling the space between us with cum as I get off over and over again. Even my wolf feels more powerful as we continue to strengthen the bond. When he finally pulls free from me Arcanna is there, pressing her lips to mine before doing the same to Jackson.

Nothing and no one will stand between me and my mates now.

I would dismantle all the heavens and underworld to protect them.

I would wage war in their names and think nothing of it.

When this is over, they will sit atop a throne built from the bones of those who went against us.

My wolf lets out a long howl in agreement.

Jackson

Drinking from Dios's well of power lit my soul on fire, the bond between the three of us coming alive. The feel of their naked bodies against mine makes me want, no need, to fuck them again. The shimmering white mate tattoo stands out against Arcanna's hip and now a matching one paints Dios's chest. Over his heart. I flex my hand and enjoy the tingle of the new mark on my own body.

Arcanna drops against the couch next to us. Her leg going over the back of the couch so her pussy is bared and open to us. I can see my release dripping from her.

"You lay like that and you might find someone feasting on that pretty little cunt of yours." I growl.

She laughs, eyes closed. "Promises, promises."

Dios bends down, his body laying over my lap as he laps at her center. His tongue scooping out our joining. He takes his time, slowly exploring her as she starts to knead her breasts and play with the barbells through each peaked nipple. My cock feels painfully hard against Dios and I shift to gain friction. He lets out a low moan.

My hands find his ass cheeks and I grip him, an idea forming. Bending down I allow my tongue to find his hole. I feel his body jerk in surprise before another long groan is pulled from him. He tastes divine, my cock dripping from the tip as I devour him.

"I clearly missed the invite," Luz's voice pulls me from my meal and has Dios growling low and feral over Arcanna who lets out a loud moan as her orgasm hits her just as he pulls his face away. Luz eye's turn feral. "You sound beautiful cuming like that."

"Get. Out." Dios growls.

His brother only smiles. "Just coming to tell you mama is sending someone with clothes for y'all." He turns around with a chuckle, slamming the door behind him.

I groan slumping back and looking down at my cock which is painfully hard. "At least you got off, wicked girl."

She lets out a laugh, "Very very true."

Dios

(Gangsta- Kehlani)

Sitting on the mockery of a throne that my parents set up I survey the crowd. We had barely gotten covered up before my mother's attendants came in to provide us clothing for the evening's festivity. We also hadn't had time to talk about the plan. Bonding may have been pure instinct and while I don't regret it, I also don't know what to do about my father. While I rationally know I'm not the kid he manipulated years ago I still have a fear of him taking everyone I love from me. He took my brother, and my abuela, I can't let him take Jackson and Arcanna.

The bond between the three of us swirls around, hungry for the release we were denied earlier. Well, me and Jax were denied, fuck his tongue felt good. It almost made me want to feel what his dick would be like. Almost.

I glance at Arcanna, the only one of us who got off. She's lounging on red pillows behind me. Her body adorned with another black skin tight crop top, golden chains hanging in swoops across her arms. Her black hair is pulled back in a tight, high ponytail and her smokey eye makeup has my dick hardening. She smirks at me, no doubt my arousal trickling down to her through the bond. If this were any other party, I would fuck her right here. Let everyone see how I claim my mates.

My eyes cast around the room, searching for Jax, who had declined to come with us to the party. He had simply said he would meet us here before disappearing back into the bathroom once more. Harrowlena had also refused the knock on the door, her room silent as I stood outside it. I don't find either of them in the crowds. Instead, I spot my brother, Luz, who holds up a glass of champagne towards me and offers up a smile as he meanders over.

"Hello brother, you look festive," he looks towards Arcanna eyes traveling over her exposed body. "And you look good enough to eat."

I can hear Arcanna snort behind me, "in your dreams." She mutters.

"Oh, I will be, now that I know what you sound like when you cum." Luz laughs as I growl low, my wolf threatening to burst through me. "You are so easy to rile up big brother, honestly you would think you would have grown out of that."

"Is there a reason you're haunting us right now?" Arcanna snaps, standing to her full height.

"Just making the rounds. Curious to find the missing King and our little priestess." He raises his glass to his lips taking a long sip.

"Touch him and I'll kill you." The bond still fresh as my powers attempt to surge outward, my wolf pulling against the restraint I'm desperate to hold.

Luz tsks, "I have no interest in your mate." Looking back towards Arcanna he offers his hand to her, "let's dance Reaper."

"Like Hell am I dancing with you," she growls.

Dropping his hand to his chest in mock pain he smiles wide, "I like you, Reaper." He drains the champagne before pushing his hands in his pockets and moving into the crowd again.

"Your brother is certainly something." Arcanna mutters, crossing her arms over her chest as we watch him meander through the crowd. "Though I do wonder, if Harrow isn't with him and he's asking after her. . . . Where is she?"

"I have no idea." While we may not need her to fulfill the role of High Priestess for Jackson, I still don't want to allow her to sneak off. I go to tell Arcanna I'll look for her when the main door to the hall opens and my mouth drops open.

Everything goes silent in my mind, the world disappearing as my eyes zero in on Jax as he enters the room. His bronze chest is on display in a tight-fitting v-neck shirt. The black making his silver eyes pop. His dark linen pants cling to his muscular thighs as he walks, and the hint of his cock is outlined. Atop his perfectly tossed hair sits the crown that had sat upon my desk. The one I refused to wear tonight. His eyes cast around the room with an air of authority.

My grip tightens on my drink as I pray my father doesn't see this as the challenge that I know Jax is throwing down. I watch as he meanders around the room, eyes tracking over various men. I take a sip of my drink to keep myself from vaulting off the chair and slaughtering everyone who's looking at him.

"Careful Dios," Arcanna whistles. "He didn't come to play."

I growl low at her. Whatever she sees in my eyes causes her to back off, a look of surrender on her face. "I'll just go get another drink." She murmurs. Slinking towards the edge of the room.

(Vegas-Doja Cat)

When my attention is pulled back to the floor I search for my mate. His body having been swallowed up by the large crowd my parents gathered. When I fail to spot him right away fear starts to edge its way in. Until the crowd parts and my eyes land on Jax making his way to where I sit on the throne. "What are you doing?" I growl, eyes moving up the crown. "This isn't the time or place to decide to be a brat." My fingers dig into his strong biceps as I spin him and pull him back against my chest, driving my hard cock into his ass.

"You don't like it?" Jackson says with a playful tone. I dig my nails harder into him earning a hiss from his beautiful mouth. "I figured one of us should wear it, your father needs to know he isn't the only King in the room."

I growl next to his ear. "You're drawing attention to yourself."

Jackson turns in my arms, dragging me closer into him so he's only inches from my mouth. "You think I draw attention?"

My eyebrow raises even as my magic swirls through us. "Be good, mi *ceilo*."

"You aren't giving me a choice, I didn't magically forget about you staying here." He gives me a pointed look even as he grinds himself into me. Jackson leans in closer, his tongue swirling around my neck. "You think we are going to leave you here? That's not happening. It's best your father figures that out now." Jax applies his teeth to my neck, biting just hard enough that I know I'll bruise.

I grab his wrist hard sending a jolt of magic into his soul. His pupils blow wide, the darkness almost fully eating up the silver. "You are playing a dangerous game right now," I growl, my wolf peeking out. Jackson growls right back, his eyes hard with no give.

I don't stop to think and instead drag him out of the crowded hall, away from prying eyes.

Jackson

The moment we are outside the party Dios shoves me against the brick wall, my breath being pulled from my lungs by the sheer force. I barely recover before his mouth is claiming my own. I let out a low moan as his magic pulses through me. My eyes roll back in my head. This right here is all that matters. Not the kingdom. Not Hell. Not Gothic Grove. Just the feeling of this man's hands on me.

"Fuck yes." I moan out at the feel of him on my body. He lets one hand trail up into my hair yanking my head back so he can look me in the eyes. I whimper as his other hand grips my cock hard. The need for him to dominate me overwhelms everything, my skin crawling and my body antsy. *We* need this. I need to remind him of what we have when we are alone.

He smiles wickedly before pulling back, much to my displeasure, and leading us down the hallway. He roughly shoves me through the large door. The dim light of candles barely illuminates the dark bedroom, the fire casting a hypnotizing glow across Dios's face.

When he turns his full gaze on me he looks like a true god. "Kneel." He commands. I drop to my knees, eager to worship at his altar. My cock juts out painfully but I keep my hands pressed to the tops of my thighs, ignoring the appendage. "I think I like the crown on you, *mi cielo*. But I think I'll like it better after I fuck you so hard it tumbles off your head."

I moan out a yes please. He walks around me, looking me over as if it's our first time. He pushes me forward with his boot, so I land on all fours, the crown barely staying atop my head.

"You forgot who you belong to." The pants are ripped from my body. When his hand slaps across my bare ass I let out a needy moan. He does another and another until my ass is tingling and the only thing keeping me from making a mess on the floor is sheer willpower.

"*Sir*," I cry. "Please."

He doesn't answer, a chill moving through the room as his body shifts away from me. I'm met with the sound of a click, his warm presence behind me once more, and cool liquid drips down my ass. The first press of the plug sends a hiss from my mouth as he slowly works it in. When my muscles finally relax and accept it the sounds I'm making are animalistic. Shimmying my hips I desperately try to work it into just the right spot. To gain relief from the overwhelming arousal coursing in my body.

"No no." Dios growls low. "You won't be cuming anytime soon." When he walks back into my line of sight I'm met with his naked, bronze body. The tattoos blend into the dark room like demons waiting to be released. His thick cock juts out from his body. He pumps it lazily as he looks at me, pulling those piercings into his mouth as he bites his lip. He moves backward until he sits on the edge of a chair, motioning for me to crawl to him.

Driven by pure, feral, need I move towards him as quickly as I can. My only purpose to get his dick into my mouth and his taste on my tongue. When I'm safely tucked between his knees, I slide the thick head past my lips enjoying the taste of him.

"Your mouth is fucking perfect." He groans as he allows me to explore him. Up and down, I take him in, my tongue slipping over the thick veins before circling his head again. Pulling free for a moment I dip down, taking his balls into my mouth while my hand lazily works his cock over. Dios lets out a string of curses all in Spanish. His body is on a hair trigger.

Without warning he drags me up by the hair and thrusts me down onto his hard cock causing me to gag before he lets up and presses me down again. Over and over he fucks into my mouth, using me for his pleasure. My eyes fill with tears and saliva pools out of my mouth.

"Fuck..." He growls before pulling from my mouth. "Open." My mouth opens, tongue out, as I wait to accept his holy communion. He pumps his dick a few times before he releases it across my face and mouth. My tongue is desperate to catch as much as I can. When he's finally finished, he doesn't allow me a moment to rest, he uses his fingers to wipe the cum that missed my mouth. His fingers gag me as he breaches my lips and forces me to take every bit of his release. "Good boy." He says offering me a rare smile.

I preen under the attention. He pushes me back as he stands, his eyes snagging on my angry cock that is dripping pre-cum on the floor. A long string of it pooling. "That looks painful."

"It's okay Sir." I reply. "I want to please you."

He narrows his eyes slightly before pushing me back gently so I'm flat on my back, the crown finally rolling off my head. His warm mouth envelopes the head of my dick and I let out a long moan as I'm reminded of the plug in my ass in this new position. He swirls his tongue around the head of my cock as he takes me all the way and I hit the back of his throat. My hips move with a mind of their own, my release almost achieved until I feel him take control, his magic holding the orgasm back.

A desperate cry is pulled from my lips. I look down where he is sucking me off and his eyes dance in wicked delight.

"Fuckkkk, Dios. Please please." But he ignores my begging as he pulls his mouth free of my cock. He flips me over in a rapid movement, hoisting my hips up so my ass is up in the air presenting for him.

"Gonna fuck this tight ass. I'm going to fill you up. Going to ruin you. No one will question who you belong to after this." He pulls the plug free, my body bucking forward before I feel him plunge his thick cock into me.

No matter how many times Dios has fucked me I always go breathless with that first thrust. His sheer size pushes the limits of what my body can handle. Even with the edge of pain, I hear myself begging for him to fuck me.

"I'm not going to last long." He moans out. "Fuck I want to knot you again so badly."

"Do it!" I beg. "Please do it!"

His hips buck forward but he doesn't give me what I want, the delicious pain that goes with the knot is kept at bay as he cums while gripping the base of his cock. I cry out even as my own orgasm rips through my body and my cum splashes the ground beneath me. "Next time." He soothes. "Next time, when we are home, I'll fill you with my knot again."

The promise is enough for me.

He's coming home with us.

Arcanna

I sip my wine as I watch Jackson get dragged from the room by Dios. I snort. Jackson had told me of the plan. And I couldn't disagree with him, Dios may have bonded Jax but he was still planning on remaining here. Leaving us alone in Hell while he was forced to deal with his horrid parents. And I had seen the way he looked at that crown, the way his face paled and hands shook. Staying here would kill him, and neither of us would stand by for that.

"I see you've been left alone." As if summoned by my thoughts, the voice of the King comes from my left. I take another long sip of my wine before looking towards the man.

"It would seem my *mates* had some business to attend to." I reply in a lazy fashion. His father's face goes blank for a moment before his eyes narrow with rage. I smile, "I think the crown looked spectacular on the King of Hell, didn't you? My two mates, how did I get so lucky?"

"Dios will not mate the King, he knows the risk." He spats. "And you are nothing but something to pass the time, to fill his animalistic side. A warm spot for his knot."

A genuine laugh pulls from my lips as I push to a stand. "You don't know your son very well. And I think you greatly underestimate the bond the three of us have, the *very mated bond we have*. I would be careful on who you threaten." I offer another smile as I set my wine down, the King processing my words. "Now if you'll excuse me." I push past him with no bow or other acknowledgment to his status.

"Bitch," he seethes. "You will show me respect."

I brace for the inevitable my magic forming a shield around me, but no hand pulls me back, no magic hits into me, instead it's silent. Everyone has wide eyes as they look just beyond me. Turning slowly, I find Luz between myself and the King, the latter with murderous intent plastered on his face.

"I was just coming to offer to escort our guest to her room for the evening." Luz says with a pleasant voice. "Thank you for finding her father." He turns towards me, looping his arm through mine without permission and dragging me forward.

"What are you doing?" I hiss, trying to pull free.

His hand grips my forearm, "I'm saving your life. Just shut the fuck up and follow my lead." Against my stubborn nature I do as he says, recognizing that I may be powerful but these are gods and it would be foolish to turn away help.

The walk through the door into the hallway feels like the longest walk of my life and when we finally reach the end I rip myself free of his grasp and put distance between us, glaring. He smiles, a bit sarcastically at me, as he shoves his hands into his pockets.

"Why?" I growl. "Why help me?"

He shrugs, "I was bored." Turning his back to me he heads down the hallway before stopping and throwing one last look at me. "See you for breakfast, Reaper."

Oblivious to everything else, Jax and Dios slept through the night. Tucked in one another's arms. It was precious. And yet sleep had evaded me. A restlessness taking up residence in my bones screaming something was wrong. Not just with the King but Harrow. . . The missing priestess.

The morning is crisp, the humidity yet to turn suffocating. I know in a few hours I'll be thankful for not bothering to do my hair and just pushing it into a bun. Despite the cooler air my thighs are sweating as they sit bare against the wood bench at the large table, I've found myself sitting at for breakfast after the failed search for Harrow.

Glancing up at the table that Dios's parents sit at I desperately attempt to ignore the looks his father keeps shooting towards me, it's a little to smug and pleased for my liking. His mother, on the other hand, seems to be pretending my existence is inconsequential sips on her coffee.

"Is something wrong, Reaper?" Luz asks, dropping down next to me.

Taking a sip of coffee, I glare at him, "Are you trying to ruin my breakfast?"

He laughs, "Just making conversation with you, you seemed lonely. Where are you're lovely mates? And the priestess?" The mention of Harrow has my stomach dropping low, my assumption, or maybe my desperate hope, had been he was still helping her. That she was with him.

"Jax and Dios are sleeping. . ." I respond carefully, my mind running through the various scenarios that would leave Harrow missing.

Luz tsks. "They left you alone? You could have joined me if you had wanted, I would have loved to have those thick thighs wrapped around my head." The grin on his face is dangerous.

Swallowing my disgust down I narrow my eyes, "Careful Luz." I growl out the warning. "I don't tolerate assholes very well. Where is Harrow?"

He brings a piece of red fruit to his mouth, chewing thoughtfully. His eyes glance up towards his father before they return to me. The deep sunset within them seems to harden for a brief moment before they glitter with the promise of mischief. His casual nature seems to only add to my frustration building.

"What do you know?" I finally ask, breaking the quiet between us. Another grin pulls at his full lips as he pops a raspberry into his mouth. "Speak." I hiss.

"I don't know anything, I'm honestly just enjoying your reaction." He leans closer. "Working you up is the most fun I've had in awhile." Right before I go to slap him across the face Luz scoots away from me.

Just as Dios and Jackson meander into the room hand in hand.

"Coward." I huff towards Luz.

"Smart." He responds, the glimmer of mischief returns to his eyes.

Jackson and Dios take a seat next to us. He opens his mouth when he looks to me but his father clearing his throat has us all turning towards the King. The serpentine grin spread across the man's face makes my stomach clench.

"I believe I have someone who you are all dying to see."

From behind him Harrow walks out, a long white chiffon dress adorning her body, the sheer panels layered over her arms and chest while leaving a slip of her stomach open. Upon her head rests a golden crown of sunbeams that mark her as a High Priestess. I glance at Jackson who is frowning, but it's who meanders up beside her and presses a light kiss to her cheek that has me gasping.

"Oisin." Jax growls.

Jackson

(Smells Like Teen Spirit- Tommee Profitt & Fleurie

The world narrows as I see Oisin press that kiss to Harrow's cheek. "Hello lover." He purrs, nuzzling her neck. Her cheeks turn crimson and she keeps her eyes glued to the floor.

"You piece of shit." I stand from the table, fingers digging into the thick wood. Oisin lets out a harsh laugh with a look of smug satisfaction painted on his scarred face. "What the fuck are you doing here?"

Oisin gestures towards Dios's father, "my friend informed me he had something that was mine. Something I needed returned to me." He glances down to Harrow.

"She isn't your property." Arcanna bites out. "She's a fucking human."

"She's my mate. Of course she is my property." The words fall from his mouth, and while I knew that deep down, she still had a connection to the man I'm stunned with how deep it runs. Harrow, for her part, looks ashamed and fiddles with the panels of the long skirt. Still refusing to look up at all of us.

Words seem to get caught in my throat as I try to work out this betrayal, the betrayal towards my mates. It was me who trusted her, me who begged Dios to retrieve her, and even me who asked her to watch over Ava. And all the while she was playing us as fools.

Darkness overtakes me as I look at each face of the people who betrayed us, finally landing on the Kings. the smug look on his face faltering as he takes me in. Takes in my rage and when I drag forward Dios's magic it pales.

He gasps "you completed the mate bond."

Next to us I think I hear Arcanna huff something about 'I told you so.'

"Yes." I growl. My voice no longer my own but some feral beast dragged from the deepest pits of Hell. "You tried to keep my mate from me, from coming home. And now you allow this filth to enter this kingdom? You will pay."

Dios's mother backs away from the King, Oisin and Harrow slowly. Her eyes never leaving them as if they are dangerous beasts waiting to strike. Arcanna, Dios and Luz all stand next to me as the four of us look towards them. Oisin whispers something into Harrows ear, a small smile pulling at her lips and her eyes softening as they glance up at him. She loves him. The truth of it in front of us plain as day. She loves this man and had no intention of leaving him.

A ripple of magic moves through the air, cutting off my thoughts of her betrayal.

"Someone opened a portal." Luz says, alarm finding its way into his voice.

"Impossible," Dios counters. "No one can do that here but us."

Oisin chuckles. "You'll find I can do plenty of things when I have a goddess fueling my magic." He steps forward, body slightly in front of Harrow now. "Including opening a portal. Your palace and streets are surrounded, my creatures and my people own them now."

"What do you want?" Dios asks, his voice steady and unwavering.

Oisin's eyes glance to Arcanna and my world tilts. "Everything. But for now, I'll take your little Reaper."

FOURTY-FOUR

Harrowlena
**   A few Hours Prior**
**   (Broken Crown- Mumford and Sons)**

Luz's words haunt me as I walk through the halls of the palace, my feet carrying me with no destination in mind aside from away. Away from Luz. Away from Arcanna and Jackson and Dios. Yet the words, his damn words, will not let me escape. They follow me around like a ghost taunting me and sending poisonous thoughts through me. The doubt he's sowed refusing to leave. The scar on my hand pulses and I look down at the pale line, tears shimmering in my eyes.

"I had my doubts about you," The King's voice is harsh as he appears beside me in the dark hallway. "But Oisin assured me you were loyal to him, and him alone. Even if you had my son's cock stuffed in that cunt of yours."

My cheeks flame with embarrassment and guilt. When the King arrived at my room and told me who he was working with I knew that Oisin would find out about my transgressions. He would know just what happened when I went into heat. Who I found relief in.

We round the corner, the King herding me towards his chambers.

I feel like I'm walking to my execution.

When we arrive at the thick wooden doors of his room the King pauses once more, looking me over with a sickening leer. "I told him I would be more than happy to take you off his hands, should he not want someone so used." I blanch, vomit rising in my throat. "He said no, but remember. . . . I will be around for a long time, and I will make it known the option is always available."

I have no chance to recover from his words before he's pushing me into the brightly light room.

"My Lena." The voice wraps around me. "Returned to me finally."

My eyes adjust to the blinding light compared to the dim one in the hallway. Oisin looks beautiful and kingly as he stands in front of me. His clothing pristine and hair swept under a crown he stands tall as he looks down at me. His hand lifts as if to cup my face but I step back from it. He frowns, eyes darkening as I hold his gaze.

"I. . ."I try to start.

He pushes back into my space, lips finding me for a moment, the kiss igniting all the feelings Luz had chased away and yet. . .

Something in me feels sick from his touch. The part of me that wanted to scream at Dios's father. The part of me that believed in what Luz had told me. That fire in me does not like his touch any longer.

I press my hand to his chest, desperate for distance. "I need to talk to you." I stumble over the words as my tongue tries to hold it all back. "Alone." I add.

The King behind us snorts and Oisin frowns once more. "We can speak later. We have things to do on a very short time table."

"I already went through my heat." I cry. Not the words I wanted to say but none the less they pour out. "It's done. I'm sorry."

He rolls his eyes, fully stepping free of me and his body turns cold. "I know you did, trust me. You think I wouldn't feel it? Notice it?" I flinch with each word he throws at me. "I know you whored yourself out. But thankfully for you I have a solution and we haven't lost anything yet." Tears fall from my face as I listen to him, as I physically feel his words smashing into my body as though it were his fist. He watches me break apart for an unknown amount of time, his face blank, no emotions. My mate, watching me break apart piece by piece with no ounce of empathy or love or anything.

"Are you really my mate?" I practically vomit out through the tears as my knees crash to the floor.

For a long moment I wonder if Luz was indeed correct, if Oisin has lied this whole time. Created a false bond between us so he could gain The Well. For a moment I believe all the things, once more, that he told me and I can see the truth in it when looking at how Arcanna, Jax and Dios all take care of one another.

His dark shoes invade my line of sight, knees next, and then his hands are on either side of my face as he gazes into my eyes. "Why would you ask that? What have they said?" I shake my head through a broken sob. "Oh Lena, I thought you trusted me. Believed in us. It saddens me that you would listen to their nonsense."

"Is it true?" I whimper out, tears now flowing down my cheeks.

He rolls his eyes, dropping his hands from my face. "Of course it's not, stupid girl. But I can see you do not take the bond as seriously as I do." He leans in, take a deep whiff of me. "You still smell like him, smell like his cum. Yet here I am, still touching you. Still willing to do what I need to do."

Everything in me shatters as I feel the tug of the bond between us and a deep well of shame and regret bubble up smothering the fire that was putting doubt in me. "I'm sorry," I sob out. "I'm so sorry Oisin I never meant to hurt you."

He tuts, dragging me upward and lifting my chin with his hand. "You are so naïve; I should have been more careful with you. I knew you'd be easily corrupted. I take owner-ship for this as well. I'm just sad this is what has become of the one I chose as a mate."

I beg more. "Please let me make it up to you. Show you I love you."

He has an almost patronizing smile painted on his. "I have just the idea."

"How?" I ask between sniffles.

He wipes the tears from my face gingerly. "I need the Reaper. She has the magic we need. You'll have to help me get her." I reel back, shocked and confused by what he is asking. "Lena. You must do this. Otherwise, I cannot guar-antee forgiveness."

I hate myself in this moment for agreeing to what he says but the voices in my brain are too loud and I can't filter them to know which I should listen to.

"Good girl." He praises before looking over my head at the King. "Now let's go greet our guests."

Now, standing in front of them all I can't bring myself to look in their eyes. I can hear Oisin speaking, hear Jackson arguing with them but I can't look at them.

"Harrow?" Luz's voice wavers, the sound trying to send

456

me into another breakdown. It's his tone that finally draws my eyes to the group, against my wishes I look at each of them. Jackson's hard gaze is pulled into a frown, his silver eyes holding a promise of bodily harm as he pulls Arcanna into his chest.

"Harrow you don't have to do this." Luz says in a soft dangerous way.

"Ah the man who made my mate a whore." Oisin says with a cruel, cold voice.

I flinch at the words and avoid looking at Luz. My eyes tracking to Dios who looks at me with nothing short of disgust.

"He killed Ava, killed your whole fucking family. How do you not see this? How do you still believe his lies?" Arcanna screams, pulling at Jax to release her. His arms don't move though, the strong cord of muscle keeping her furious body contained.

Her voice feels like a physical slap causing me to wince.

Oisin scoffs, "she's been tied to me since the very beginning, and without me she wouldn't survive. She knows that."

"You really are going to go with someone like this?" Jackson says, voice filled with judgement. "You are better than that." I shake my head, words choking me. If I could speak, I would tell him I'm really not better than this.

"He's not your mate, *ángel* You know that. Don't do this." Luz says, his voice still so quiet yet the loudest of them all.

"Did you forget he put that mask on you?" Jackson adds, the betrayal in his voice cutting deep into my soul. "He's the reason for those scars on your face. The reason for your nightmares. He's the reason my sister is dead and your own family, it's all him. All that means nothing?" It's almost worse that his voice stays level, that he doesn't scream. The neutrality of it burns like living fire.

My violet eyes close for a moment, a break from watching the confusion morph to pure hatred. "You don't understand." It sounds weak even in my ears. "You could never understand, he's my mate."

"No mate would do the things he has." Arcanna counters with sympathy in her voice.

"That's enough." Oisin's voice cuts through it all as he moves up behind me, his hand linking with my own. "My *mate* has given you more courtesy than I would have."

Luz steps forward. His eyes hard as they seem to almost darken, the sunset red taking on a deep, horrifying crimson. "You cannot hope to win." He says to Oisin. "You have no real magic. And *they* will not let you take The Well."

Oisin lets out a long, loud laugh. "I have more magic than I know what to do with. As I said it makes all the difference having a goddess tied to me."

Luz shakes his head. "The one you have is not unlimited. You will drain her to the point of death and then what? You'll be out of magic with no hope to stand against us."

"I don't need to drain her. I will have everything I need before long." Oisin snaps.

"What do you get from this father?" Dios grounds out. Dios's father looks on with a smug, satisfied look as his personal guard joins the fray and surrounds the group. Ignoring his son's question. "You won't win this."

An ear-piercing scream from the Queen draws my attention from him to the beasts that have been allowed in, Oisin's creatures destroying everything in their path as the banquet hall erupts into chaos.

It's enough of a distraction for Oisin.

He disappears from my side, reappearing behind Arcanna. His arm coming up across her neck before he jabs a needle into her arm. She's barely unconscious before he's back at my side with her.

"ARCANNA!!!" Jackson's voice bellows across the room, his eyes wild with emotion. One of the guards raises a sword, the blade poised to slice into the King's neck. Jackson doesn't even turn to look at him, his magic radiating outward and dropping the guards body to the floor. The room darkens, lightening beginning to crackle over head. Jackson's wrath locked on us, pinning us as the next target for the magic he is building.

"What did you do?" I pant. Reality snapping into me as Jackson screams her name in a broken, furious plea. "They'll kill us."

"I secured our future." Oisin growls. A portal opening behind us. One of his creations, another testament to the power he is using.

He dumps Arcanna's body through the portal, her head cracking on the hard floor. The sound echoes through the room. The scream that is wrenched from Jackson will haunt me even into my death as Oisin steps through and over her body. He holds out his hand to me, eyebrow raised.

"You go with him like this, *ángel caido* that's it. No going back." Luz says. I bite down hard on my lip to keep the sob from being wrenched from my chest.

"Hurry up, mate." Oisin growls. "We have things to do, sins to atone for." It's enough of a reminder that my feet carry me over the threshold.

"Harrow!" Luz yells. "Remember what I said!" His voice the last thing I hear before the portal shuts and seals us into my new reality.

Harrowlena

The silence is louder than any of the screams once the portal shuts. When I turn, I'm no longer met with the banquet hall of Dios's family, instead it is a large bay window overlooking a skyline. The city lights sparkle in the deep black of night, the buildings popping out against the velvet backdrop.

"We aren't in Hell." I breathe out.

Oisin snorts, "No. We most certainly are not. We are in Gothic Grove."

Turning towards him I watch as Arcanna is dragged off by a few witches, her body limp over the shoulder of the largest one. My eyes linger on the blood smeared across the spot she was laying.

"Will she be okay?" I sound too loud for the space and cringe at my own voice.

Oisin meanders further into the home, throwing his jacket against the couch and exposing his white button-up shirt before tossing the crown to the cushion next to him. Grabbing a bottle of wine from the expansive kitchen countertop he pours each of us a glass. I take mine hesitantly looking down at the swirling red color. "Drink up, you've been through a lot." He says as he turns, dropping down on a chair that faces the door, his back to the expansive windows.

I hesitate for a moment, not wanting to feel the effects of the liquor but also not wanting to disappointment him. "Maybe later?" I say hesitantly.

Oisin rolls his eyes, "Arcanna will be fine, for now." I watch as he drinks his glass in two gulps jerking his head towards my glass. "Drink up so I can rip that pretty little dress from your body." His gaze turns hot as it runs over my body.

My body heats as I brush my free hand down the material, suddenly very aware of my naked form under it. Even if I hadn't picked it out, hadn't wanted to put it on, I still thank him and the desperate side of me that wants him, wants his attention and affection preens. Though that fire in me squirms uncomfortably, disliking the fact that we still need his approval, are still desperate for it.

I throw the wine back, gulping it down and practically choking on it as it floods my taste buds and flows down my throat. The spicy, sweet flavor cloying as it swirls around my body. When it's finally gone, my glass empty save for a tiny drop, he crooks two fingers, beckoning me forward. He smiles, not the wicked sort, but one that is tinged with sadness. It reminds me of the boy I fell in love with long ago. The one who held me so lovingly on a cabin floor, who braided my hair after a bath and who promised me happiness. Maybe it's that reminder that has my feet moving over the cool tiles of the penthouse floor. Or maybe it's the fuzzy, warm feeling blooming in my blood that has me moving. Either way I feel drawn to him, drawn to my salvation or my doom but none the less drawn.

Once I'm in front of him, he pulls me down onto his lap

so I'm straddling him, cupping my face with his hands. "I never should have allowed them to do any of the things they did to you. Never should have followed through with this plan. If I had been smarter, you would not have fucked someone else. You would still be my Lena."

"Am I not yours anymore?" I ask, a slur to my words. I shake my head, trying to clear it, trying to gain the clarity I had before the wine. But it won't clear. It stays fuzzy and somehow seems to rekindle the long quiet bond that lay between us.

He goes to kiss me, but I turn my head at the last minute. Unable to allow him to touch me when the question still lingers on if I am still his or if I have lost everything.

"I need this Harrow. We need this if we are to erase what you've done. His tone is sweet and caring but the words are far from it. They highlight every fear and negative thought that has crept into my head, solidifying the rightness of it. A broken sob is wrenched from me and for a moment he drags me into his chest and holds me as I splinter further. "This will show me you are still mine, will *make* you mine again."

"I'm sorry," I cry into his chest. "I'm so sorry I failed you." His scent burns my nostrils, providing little to no comfort as he shelters me in his embrace.

He lets out a dramatic sigh, the sound brushing past my ear. "Shhh, it's over now. Show me how much you trust me. Show me you believe in us." He says softly. "Can't you feel how much our bond needs this?" I nod enthusiastically because I do feel it, that place so cold and sad.

(Cold- Aqualung and Lucy Schwartz)
Moving my shaking palms up into his silky black hair and dragging them down his face, I trace his long scar, before landing on his neck and finally down to his chest.

Slowly, my fingers start to unbutton his shirt exposing his chiseled chest followed by two pierced nipples.

Oisin stays still, but his breath picks up as I lean down and let my tongue taste his skin. His heart pounds under my hand that's landed flat against him. His cock hardens under me, but still, he does not move. He continues to allow me to explore, to taste. I move down his body, my mouth tracing every inch of his skin until my knees hit the floor and I'm wedged between his legs. And still, he says nothing despite his breathing now a loud pant, as if he can barely contain himself from dragging me back up his body and plunging himself deep within my waiting channel.

Shaking fingers undo his pants, and with his help, I'm now staring at his thick cock jutting up in front of my face. My eyes trace back up to his face, pure hunger in his red eye as he looks at me on my knees for him. I don't let my gaze waiver from him as I suck the tip of his cock into my mouth, my tongue lapping up the small drop of precum he's already produced. He says nothing, his teeth digging into his lip, as if he's afraid I'll stop should he open his mouth.

As I take him fully into my mouth and down my throat, however, he lets out a long groan of pleasure. The sound shooting straight through me, my pussy suddenly weeping. I lose myself in sucking him, the taste and feel of his cock in my mouth giving me an odd amount of pleasure. The guilt is still there, but guilt and I are long time lovers, and I've become an expert at pushing it aside.

Oisin finally snaps, pulling me up and off his cock and pushing me back onto the ground. His hands pull at my long skirt, dragging it down before he rips the lace panties off me exposing my cunt to the air. "Fuck you look good." It's the first and last thing he says before he dives into me, his tongue hungrily pushing into my center. I arch up at the feeling a low moan being pulled from me.

He fucks me with his tongue for a few moments before he pulls out and moves to my clit, pressing his thick fingers into my heat as he does so. The feeling is maddening, my hips fucking upwards. My body lost to the pleasure he is providing.

(Die for You (feat. Akylla)- Excision)

"Oisin." I moan out his name, my inner walls beginning to quiver, my lower abdomen tightening. "Don't you stop," I command him, my hand finding his head and pushing even harder into my clit.

He lets out an approving moan and his fingers start to pump into me harder and harder. I begin to crest over the edge, my orgasm impending before he pulls back, dragging and angry growl from me. He only smirks as he lines his thick cock up and pushes inside of me.

He continues to pull pleasure from me, the curve of him hitting that perfect spot deep inside. He unleashes himself and fucks me into the hard floor. "You are mine, forever. I will fuck you and fill you and take from you. We are the endgame for one another." He cries out as he finds his own release, still denying me mine. The bond between us shimmers, the bond that according to Luz did not truly exist the one he claims he healed within me, and I let out a pained cry as it opens again and floods into me.

He roars out, the feel of me pulling another round of release from him. When it's finally over he drops down, his head resting at the crook of my neck, his cock still inside me. "You are mine." He pants. "Never forget that."

As his cock slips from me, I feel his cum drip down, I feel his pleasure at the idea of his essence being in me pulse down the bond that lingers in my chest. And I hate myself for the hunger that pools deep in my belly. Hate myself as I roll over on top of him and grind my wet pussy down onto him until he's hard enough that I can slip him back inside of me, as I chase my own release.

(DARK ARIA <LV2> (Feat. XAI)-SawanoHiroyuki[nZk])

When I wake the next morning, I'm tucked into a large bed with soft, black sheets. Pushing up I find myself alone, the opposite side of the bed cold and empty. I groan as I clutch my head, the wine having left me with a headache that feels like someone is hammering on the inside of my skull. In the darkness of the room suddenly everything that seemed so clear and so right last night now feels muddy and wrong.

My thighs still hold the dry evidence of our night together and everything feels tender. Even my breasts seem to hurt. And the bond? The bond feels wrong, like oil sitting on top of water. Bile rises in my throat and I throw my bare legs off the bed as I race towards what I can only hope is the bathroom.

My stomach heaves as bile and water and the last bit of the wine come back up, the sound echoing against the marble walls and tile floor. My body breaks out in sweat as a heat flash moves over me.

After what feels like an eternity the heaving stops and I rest my head against the edge of the bathtub next to me. The cool stone of it calming the inferno currently ravaging my body. I breath in steadily, forcing my heart rate to calm and my stomach to settle. Everything hurts. I want nothing more than to sit for a while longer but with the upheaval of my stomach also came the upheaval of last night. Now no longer feeling comfortable with how Oisin treated me.

I will not drink that wine again.

The internal proclamation is the first thing that feels right since leaving Luz. Everything else has felt muddled and confusing and wrong. At least until the wine.

Pushing myself up off the floor I snag the silk robe off the door, pulling it over my naked body. Not bothering to shower, or caring to, I pad out into the living space my eyes drawing to the large balcony off to the side. Oisin's naked, muscular back faces me as he braces himself against the rail. With nothing but a pair of sweats on I take a moment to observe him, catalogue the marks and tattoos he has on his body. While I would normally feel a sense of want, now all I feel is something akin to disgust.

Is this really my mate?

"I feel you back there Lena." He mutters.

I frown, "where is Arcanna?" I step up next to him, taking a seat on one of the chairs and pouring myself coffee from the French press.

He looks down at me, his dark hair falling in front of his scarred eye. "That's the first thing you say to me? Your mate."

I wince at his tone. I may be second guessing everything but he's not. "Sorry. I have a headache, the wine. . ." He only looks at me, the wind shifting his hair in the morning breeze. "I don't think I want to drink it anymore."

His lips pull into a frown. "Why? Because you're hungover? We always drink that wine" he says, crossing his arms over his chest.

Setting my coffee cup down I take a deep breath, "I know. But it makes me feel weird and I just don't think we need it. We can be together without it, right?"

He rolls his eyes at me, "Stop pretending like it's the wines fault you spread your legs for me last night." My cheeks flame with embarrassment and shame as I think back to the previous evening. My mind feels hazy, the events not fully appearing except in brief blips and clips of our naked bodies writhing on the ground. "Look if you are going to start regretting every whorish activity you do, you should probably start looking at the cock you fell on that wasn't mine?" His tone is vicious, angry, and spiteful.

"That's not fair." I say weakly. "My heat. . ."

Suddenly he's in my face, pressing me back into the chair with a hand braced around my throat. "And why did you go into your heat early? You fucked us Harrow. You should have known better and maybe your heat wouldn't have started. But because you couldn't keep your legs shut, with me or anyone else, it started early." Oisin squeezes, cutting my air off, before he releases me again. He looks at me with disgust as I gasp for air and massage my throat. "The Elders were right about you. This is your fault, all of it. You are the reason we are failing. So, when I need you to spread your legs you'll fucking do it because you owe me that much now."

Silent tears stream down my face but no sound comes from me until he slams the door leading back into the house. Then, and only then, do I allow the wind to gobble up the sob that bursts from me.

Oisin

I have always assumed the magic I tied us together with would withstand anything but Luz, fucking Luz, has crept into my little priestess and started to pick at that bond. I felt it, as we fucked, felt the part that had started to breakdown, his healing magic so potent. Felt his fucking influence nestled deep within her. I had thought giving her more of the wine would help, more of that magic, but it seems like it wasn't enough. Now I'll have to rely on her piss pour self-esteem and violence to keep her with me.

"So much more work." I groan under my breath.

"Oisin, my lord!" Arthur Mori's booming voice interrupts my thoughts. The annoying coven leader walks into my home like he belongs, trailed by the other coven leaders whom I've had no interest in to learn their names. They are a means to an end, a distraction for The Harbinger and my half-brother. "Feather tells me you were successful in bringing the woman with you. Shall we head to The Well?"

My hand shoots out, gripping him hard around the throat and dropping him to his knees in front of me. "Do not begin to think you give me orders, understand?"

He pales slightly nodding, though I don't miss the way his eyes flash with annoyance. This is a man who is used to controlling others, not being controlled himself. And it's becoming more of an issue every day.

"I'm sorry sir." He chokes out as I release the grip on his flesh.

For a moment I picture shoving my fist through his chest and ripping his beating heart out. The hallucination so vivid I can practically feel the warm blood on my hands. He would lay there and flounder until his brain finally caught up and the life would seep from him. The other coven leaders would know, would understand I'm not someone to fuck with. They would give me the respect I deserve.

The elevator dings forcing me to leave the reality I crave. "The city is in chaos; I have cameras on each section." Feather walks forward, not looking up, with an iPad in her hands that takes her focus. Her long acrylic nails fly over the screen. "The people are flooding towards The Playground and Club Eufori seeking refuge, just as we hoped."

When Cordelia had discussed finding her, I hadn't been

supportive but her use of healing magic along with her ability to hack all of Gothic Grove has proven beyond valuable. And unlike Lady Ornate, Feather has no interest in my cock.

"And my brother?" I ask tentatively.

"They are occasionally leaving The Playground to kill things but, overall, they remain sequestered within its walls. Only allowing a select few to find sanctuary within their domain. Kai, on the other hand, has opened up Club Eufori to anyone and everyone." She snorts. "It's a free for all and he can barely keep up."

A deep well of satisfaction opens up as I think of my brother and his mate falling from grace. I needed his reputation, and hers, tarnished. Needed Gothic Grove to turn against them in the wake of the dragons and Ava leaving. That way, when I kill them, the people will view me as their savior. Will worship me.

I glance to the coven leaders, "open up the gates to your grounds. Spread the word that safety can be found within your sacred lands." They look uncomfortable at the thought but for this to work I need some people to survive. "Tell them The Order is here to help."

Feather huffs out a laugh as the leaders grumble but otherwise agree, turning to leave the penthouse to do my biding. "Oh how the mighty have fallen." She mumbles with a wicked grin.

"Have you woken Arcanna yet?" I ask as I meander towards the kitchen and pour myself a drink, ignoring her hostility towards the men. She follows behind, her heels clicking on the marble floors.

"No sir, not yet. I want to be fully prepared before I allow her to regain consciousness."

I raise an eyebrow, "are you not equipped to handle this?"

She finally raises her eyes from the screen and cuts me a hard glare. "I'm not stupid. Arcanna is a Reaper and Lady of Souls. She has magic I do not and will not have. I would be a fool to wake her without proper precautions."

Another thing I enjoy about Feather. She's practical. Knows her limits. "Make sure we open another gate closer to the clubs. Unleash whatever beasts we do not need for protection at The Well." I say, nodding with approval. She doesn't respond, instead refocusing on her iPad, sending out commands or whatever the fuck she does on the thing. "Feather, continue to make me happy you'll be rewarded at the end of this."

Overall, her looks are unremarkable. But the fire and drive that burns in her brown eyes as she looks back at me? That makes her radiant. "I don't want a reward. I want revenge." She says with a cold voice.

When she doesn't offer an explanation, I nod in acceptance. She takes the dismissal, and I watch her swiftly walk back towards Arthur who is sheepishly standing by the front door, waiting on her no doubt. My gaze travels over to Harrow who is still standing on the balcony, her hair blowing wildly in the breeze as she looks out at the city below.

"Sir," Feather calls out as she waits for the elevator, Arthur now dragging himself with her. "Be careful. We need her for our plans. After all the work I put in to figuring out how to restart her heat and how to do the ceremony I would be very annoyed if I had to find a body to experiment on for this."

I roll my eyes and grind my teeth down. "Understood." Feather had made it abundantly clear that while she was confident with what she had learned thus far, she would not have the same confidence if it wasn't Harrow's body, we were using to channel The Well. Which would mean more testing, more experiments, and more time I do not have.

"Whatever you just did to her, apologize. The more she doubts you the harder it will be to hold onto her. Whatever magic is in her, it will take hold of her more as that doubt grows."

"Feather. . ." I warn. I hear the elevator ding and the doors slide open. She says nothing more on the topic and exits the penthouse. Leaving me alone to figure out how to play nice with Harrow when I simply do not care to be nice anymore.

Jackson

(Recover- Ruelle)

I can't seem to get myself to move. Can't seem to lift my body from the rubble that I collapsed onto when I watched Arcanna disappear. It was like watching Ava die all over again. The world narrowed and I couldn't breathe. Her life-less body flung over the witches. Seeing Harrow follow Oisin was another dagger to the heart. Even now as I listen to Dios and Luz fight it feels as though the sounds are muffled, that my vision is so tunneled I can't comprehend what's going on.

"What did you do?!" Dios screams. I don't need to touch our bond; I can hear the rage and grief in his voice.

"I didn't do shit!" Luz yells back. "I healed the priestess, saved her from dying. It's not my fault you three are too fucking dense to realize she was tied to *him* still."

I hear a thud and a crunch, the sounds making me turn my gaze from the last place I saw my mate to the two broth-ers. Luz stumbles back and wipes the blood from his lip as he shakes his head. Dios stands with fists still balled and body coiled with tension. My mate radiates danger.

My only mate left.

Fuck. I've lost her. What if I lose him too?

My breathing seems to be coming in short bursts now, as if I can't drag enough oxygen in as those irrational thoughts worm into me. I know that Dios and I are power-ful, I know that if we had time, we could be more powerful than The Harbinger most likely. But even with all that power we still lost Arcanna.

"Breath for me, *mi cielo*." Dios kneels down in front of me, gripping my face so I have to look at him. "Don't let yourself get dragged away. I need you. Arcanna needs you." I nod, following his instructions. Reminding myself she isn't dead. Oisin needs her.

"You knew something, and it allowed our mate to be taken." I growl, turning towards Luz. "You should have told us, been up front that she was tied to Oisin."

Luz shakes his head, spitting blood to the ground. But it's a soft feminine voice that speaks up, not him. "My son did what he had to do, what he was instructed to do." The Queen walks into the space, her crown still high atop her head despite the dark hair that has escaped the twist she had it in. "And it was not the priestesses who called him here. It was the King."

Dios sucks in a breath. "Where is he?" The three of us look around, realizing the King has vanished.

The Queen moves to Luz, gently checking over his wounds on his face and muttering something in Spanish. His eyes soften towards her and she offers a sympathetic smile before turning back to us. "He fled no doubt, with Oisin." She snorts and shakes her head. "Too long I allowed him to rule over this place and now look at it. My boys have no relationship, and far too many innocents have died."

"You owe us an explanation." Dios growls. His mother flinches at the tone even as she nods.

"It is a longer story of gods and betrayals," she pauses looking at Luz who gives a curt nod and then brushes her eyes over us. Whatever she sees in me has sadness filling them. "But maybe we shall start with the short version so you can find your mate."

I nod, my control slipping, my grip on reality slipping. I drag in a deep breath, allowing Dios's warm scent to bath me in grounding magic before I move away from the warmth his body provides. "You have ten minutes. Ten minutes and then I'll be destroying every person between me and my mate."

"As you wish," she says with a low bow.

Dios

My mother finds a chair and slumps into it, her long dress swishing around her. She snags the tipped over bottle of wine and manages to drag a few drops from the bottle before dropping it back on the table. One of her attending ladies appears out of thin air, producing another bottle quickly as though we aren't standing in the middle of a ruined throne room.

"Ten minutes." I grind out. My mother takes a deep breath before nodding.

"I know, I'm sorry. I'm trying to figure out where to start."

She looks to Luz who simply shrugs, "I don't know why you're looking at me, I told you long ago when this blew up in your face, I wouldn't be the one to clean up your mess." He pushes his hands into his pockets and heads towards the doorway.

"So, you are just going to leave?" Her voice takes on a slight panic as if being alone with Jackson and I worries her.

My brother snorts, "yes. Because whatever retribution they are going to take on you is not one I'm going to shoulder. I told you how I thought we should do this and you chose not to listen." He pauses as he hits the large doorway that is now blown apart, half the door hanging on its hinges still while the other has a Jackson size hole through it. He turns to look at me and Jax, his eyes shining with emotion. "If you need help finding Arcanna let me know, I'll be cleaning up the mess Oisin left behind in our city." It's all he says before he's gone.

Mother lets out a long, defeated sigh. "You cannot be mad at him any longer, mi hijo,"

"I think he gets to feel however the fuck he wants." Jax spits coming to my defense quickly. I turn towards him slightly shocked, and thankful, realizing that someone besides Demon has my back. My chest fills with warmth and my heart swells. My mate looks over at me, his silver eyes swimming as he feels my emotions through the bond before he turns his gaze back onto my mother. The silver going glacier.

My mother looks between us, "I am glad you have found one another. And I am truly sorry your other mate was taken. This. . . This spiraled out of control."

"Oh, come along Lisbeth, you always knew this was a risk." The voice comes before the sound of heels clicking on the hard floor. The owner, while still shielded by the dark hallway she approaches through, is familiar.

"You." I hiss.

The female enters, her white eyes still just as shocking against her dark hair. Again, her attire matches that of some old Victorian era western mix. The crimson skirts gathered and layered over a black corset. My mother watches her approach with apprehension. "What are you doing here?" She asks.

The female smiles, her white teeth unnaturally bright behind her crimson lips. "I just couldn't resist seeing your darling son again." My mother goes pale at her words and the female smiles even larger. "I do so love the men in your family."

Jax steps in front of me, "Who are you?" He growls magic pulling inward.

"You didn't tell your lover about me?" She purrs.

I roll my eyes, "this is the female who told me of Bast."

She scoffs, "Female? That sounds so bland." Holding out her hand towards Jax she trails her eyes over his body. "Hello little King. It's a pleasure to meet you finally." He doesn't take her hand, only looks at it like one would look at a viper. She finally drops it after a long moment.

"Who. Are. You." He bites out. His magic barely contained.

"You can call me Lilith."

It had taken longer than ten minutes to explain what the fuck was going on. A few hours longer to be exact and by the end Jackson was deep into a spiral and myself? I was barely holding on to my reality having now gained the full history of my family and what The Order was planning to use Arcanna for, according to Lilith. I can't help but feel anger towards my mother, even if I understand the why behind her actions, she still allowed me to suffer. And because of her poor choices we lost Arcanna in the process.

Lilith had left before us, a promise to hunt down my father and figure out where the 'weasel fucking coward' was hiding. She promised to send the pieces home to us if we wanted them, my mother had gone pale at the words which pulled a long laugh from Lilith before she winked from existence. Nothing but her scent of roses and lily's left behind.

"Dios you have to promise to forgive your brother,

promise me that and I will do everything in my power to help you find your mate." She begs with fresh tears in her eyes, gripping my hands tightly. "You don't have to forgive me, but your brother. . . Please."

I carefully extract my hands from hers, stepping back and into Jackson's warmth. "You will help us regardless of my future relationship with my brother." She stifles a sob, eyes blinking rapidly. "You will help us because that's the right thing to do after you fucked this up."

"And, if you don't, I will burn this place to the ground." Jackson says coldly.

She widens her eyes before managing some composure and straightening, taking a long deep breath and suddenly returning to the Queen once more, her role as my mother tucked back away. "Your brother has been looking into things for us, he found that Oisin has seemingly opened the coven grounds up in Gothic Grove for its citizens. They've created some sort of refugee camp for anyone who can make it."

Jackson shakes his head, "they are doing exactly what they did to Rhea's kingdom."

"For what gain? Gothic Grove doesn't have anything, no ruler." I remark.

My mother raises her eyebrow, "They have The Harbinger."

Fuck.

Jackson

There have been times in my life I have questioned if I would make a good King. So many times I think I've lost count at this point. But as I stand in front of my friends, my people, and swallow down the skin crawling agony of the bond between Arcanna and I being so quiet I realize whether I make a good one or not I'm all Hell has at this point. And it makes the decisions I'm about to make hard as fuck.

"They aren't at The Well yet." Rhea comments, Reaver nodding along with her. "My brothers have also confirmed they aren't in our home any longer either."

Dios crosses his arms, shoulder brushing my own as he stands next to me. He and I had finally agreed that returning to the lake house was the smartest choice until we figured out where Oisin and Harrow had taken Arcanna.

"We've been watching the coven grounds, and while they've brought a ton of people there, we haven't seen Harrow, Arcanna or Oisin." Kallen says. Her green eyes burn bright, feverish even, as she speaks and I don't miss the hand Demon has on her. His knuckles white with how hard he is gripping her hand. As if he's worried, she'll flee any moment.

"That doesn't mean they aren't there." Reaver counters. Dios grunts in agreement.

Dragging my hand down my face I breathe deeply for a moment, willing myself to be calm, to exclude calm down my bond with Dios. "We know the end game here. It's The Well." Every part of my body screams in protest as the plan locks into place in my mind. "We go there. We wait for them."

Dios hisses out a breath as he realizes what that means for us and for our mate, yet he doesn't argue with me only grips my hand as tightly as Demon grips Kallen.

"And what of the city? Of Gothic Grove?" Rhea asks. "Those people are suffering and will continue to suffer as my people have."

"That's our home. We will take care of it." Kallen says with fierce determination.

"We will need your help," Dios says as his eyes drag from her to Demon. "The pack's help."

Demon snorts. "I already told you; the pack is ours. Me, you and Kallen. They will do what we need because that's what family does."

"The last time I went against men like this I was alone." Kallen says softly, her eyes far away as if she is seeing a different time and place. When they finally refocus, I flinch backwards, the smile spreading over face full of blood, violence, rage, and madness. "I *ruined* them. Dismantled them piece by piece until all that was left is the crumbs they are so desperate to pick up now." Shadows swirl around her and her pack comes out, all of them, the Hellbeasts each flanking one another as they take in the room.

Kallen releases herself from Demon, walking to the largest of the beasts and nuzzling it gently. "They all begged in the end, every single one of them. Begged and pleaded and pissed their pants when I killed them." The room is silent, crackling with tension. Even Demon looks unsure as he watches his mate stroke the coarse fur of her creature.

"Kallen?" He asks hesitantly.

She turns to him, eyes blinking a few times. "Imagine how much worse it will be for them now. They will beg and plead and I will never again grant them the mercy of death. No. Even when their physical bodies are gone I will keep their souls. I will play with them and torment them and only after I grow so bored I couldn't possibly think of any other way to harm them will I grant them true death."

"Fuck me," Dios groans. "I don't know if I'm terrified or turned on."

"I think I'm both." Demon says.

I, however, watch Kallen with apprehension. For the longest time she has told us Astrea has been the danger to have in Hell, that it is her who we should fear going to the dark side. It's been easy to forget Kallen's own dark history with everything going on. But now? Watching her in this moment. It's a stark reminder that she is still the female who destroyed the original witch families, the one who spent so long with Alexi just so she could torture those witches descendants.

I glance towards Reaver and Rhea, both with eyes on Kallen as though they to see what I see.

A ticking time bomb.

One that I'm knowingly sending out into the world and hoping it goes off.

Arcanna

It's the steady dripping noise that has me pulled into consciousness followed by the smell that fully jolts me awake.

"I was wondering when you would wake." A weak voice says through the dim lights. My eyes blink rapidly as they attempt to clear the drug induced sleep and make sense of my new surroundings. My stomach swims as I try to sit up. "Careful, you'll puke if you get up too quick."

"Thanks for the warning." I groan as I lay backdown. Turning my head to where the voice resonated from, I can just make out someone chained to the opposite wall. Her wrists bound upward with metal cuffs that attached to a ring even further up. "Bast, I presume?"

She manages a slight smile. "The one and only." She muses before descending into a fit of coughing. It takes a moment for her to catch her breath again, the coughing finally subsiding.

"How long have you been here?" This time I push upward again. Forcing my eyes closed as I let the nausea wash over me.

"I have no idea." She says weakly. "I can tell you that you've been here two days though."

My eyes open wide. Two days? Two full fucking days since Harrow betrayed us. "That fucking dumb little girl." I growl. My body tries to move, tries to push off the bed but my foot snags on my own tether I failed to see.

"They wanted you to remain on the bed, so they kept your binding longer." The chains jingle a bit as Bast readjusts. "They are scared of you, it's why they kept you asleep. One of the witches refused to wake you unless she could guarantee she had everything ready."

I drop back down on the bed. While it feels mildly satisfying, they fear me, and not my mates, I can't help the chill that runs through me. "Have what ready?"

"Oh Bast you can't give away all the fun without us." Oisin appears from the main door, Bast shrinking further into the dark wall and away from him. He smiles at the reaction, a sickening smile that makes the nausea come back into my stomach.

"Hello Ossy, I heard your helpers were scared of me." I coo, feigning the confidence I most certainly do not have right now.

His old nickname pulls a scowl from him before he raises an eyebrow at me, "you can't pretend with me, Arcanna, I know you too well."

"Fuck off." I snap back.

He lets out a laugh as Harrow peers in behind him, hesitantly looking at me before remaining just behind his body. Oisin grips her hand and drags her further into the room, her body looks stiff and uncomfortable with his touch. When Oisin moves further inward lights flick on, illuminating the priestess. She looks bad, her lip swollen with dried blood cracked to it and dark circles under her violet eyes.

"Grass doesn't seem greener does it?" I mutter under my breath. Harrow's eyes shine at me, hurt flashing through them before she looks back down at the ground.

Oisin leads Harrow to a chair close to the bed I'm chained to, the back forcing her to sit up straighter then could possibly be comfortable. "Harrow understands that anything that happens is penance for what she did while away from me. She knows that in order to remain the High Priestess she needs to atone for her sins." I want to vomit at his words, but more than that it makes me feel bad for Harrow. A new understanding of her predicament coming to light.

"Looks like the consequences of your actions have finally caught up to you, daughter." My mother sweeps into the room, head held high as though she is the most important person in the world. The sneer painted on her face seemingly reserved for everyone but Oisin who she looks up at with a disgusting amount of lust.

"Hello bitch." I sneer. "Sad to see you're still alive."

I don't even have time to brace before she's in my space and the sting of her hand is against my cheek. Blood pools in my mouth from my lip. "You won't be so cocky once you see what's in store for you." She grinds out through clenched teeth. I cut her a hard glare before spitting the blood onto her white clothing.

"Fuck. You."

She only offers a smile as she steps backwards and I'm able to see Oisin and Harrow once more. Like a little doll, Harrow allows him to place her body in various positions before putting an IV into her arm. Her eyes remain locked on the floor and no sounds come from her mouth. Confusion runs through me as I realize that just beyond Harrow's chair lies what looks to be more medical equipment.

"What's the plan here?" I ask finally. Oisin says nothing, my mother rolling her eyes and shaking her head like me asking is the dumbest thing in the world. Harrow, however, her eyes drag up slowly to me and I can see the conflict in them, as though she wants to tell me, wants to talk to me, but can't find her voice anymore.

"Harrow knows her place; do not think you will get information from her." Oisin says with a smug look at his face before he starts to walk towards me. I back away from him as far as I can get on the bed as I try to drag my magic upward. But nothing answers, my tattoos remaining dull.

"What the fuck." I whisper suddenly more scared than I was before.

"It's the chain, you won't be able to get to your magic with that on you." My mother says with pride. As if she invented the damn things.

Oisin leans in, gripping my arm hard and driving another IV into me. I let out a growl, struggling against his firm grip and the pain of the roughly placed IV. "Because our little Harrow couldn't stop whoring around, she waisted the magic meant for me. The magic I am owed. So, we are going to use your magic to restart her battery, so to speak." He lets out a chuckle at my horrified expression. "I can't believe I hadn't realized it sooner; we had the perfect solution all along to this. You. Your magic. Your connection to The Forest."

"You can't do that," horror bleeds through my tone. "That will kill The Forest."

He shrugs, "What do I care? Gods can't die anyway; I have no need for your grove of trees." From behind a witch enters, the blank look on her face impressive given the scene she is walking into. When she nears, I see her holding a grimoire and everything else fades away as I realize how well and truly fucked I am. When she starts to mutter an incantation the needle in my vein starts to pull, my tattoos suddenly shinning bright as my magic is yanked from my body and shoved into Harrow.

I let out a scream, a broken sound that echoes through the room and no doubt the space we are staying. It rings in my own gods damn ears until it's the last thing I'm aware of and the room fades to black.

Jackson

I let out a long sigh, a heaviness pressing in around me. I try to reach out and touch my bond with Arcanna but once again I'm met with a void of silence, for a moment I had thought I felt something. As everyone had left for the night I had reached out and for a brief flash I felt fear and pain before it was gone once more.

My fingers tap on my thigh, as my anxiety kicks up, the voices convincing me I've lost her again, but this time it will be forever. No redos, no way to try again. That bond forever broken. Warm hands move over the hard planes of my stomach, dropping down to grab my hand. Dios holds it firmly. Forcing me back from the spiral I was descending into.

"It's okay *mi cielo*. We will get her back." He plants a soft kiss on my neck, the feeling loosening my shoulder muscles.

I let out a long sigh at the feel. "I know we are making the right choice. Going to The Well. But I hate leaving her longer."

"I know, I do too. But we also couldn't know where she is right now. This is the best plan we've got, regardless of how shitty it feels." He continues to kiss and lick my skin, a slow exploration that has me closing my eyes and dropping my head to give him more access. He slowly spins me, pushing me up against the large window gently. "What do you need?"

The question startles me, I'm not sure what I need right now. My anxiety tells me I need to be in control while another part of me feels desperate to let go. The two pushing and pulling against one another so hard my head wants to split in two. Dios seems to understand because he drops to his knees in front of me, dragging the zipper of my jeans down before slowly peeling them away from my legs. My cock, only half erect, spills out. Dios looks up at me as he takes me into his warm mouth. He sucks slowly, no rush in his movements. Allowing me to slowly harden in his mouth.

He moans as he takes me to the back of his throat, his hands now moving up my naked thighs to grip my ass cheeks on one side and cup my balls with the other. The gentle movements are at odds with how we normally are. My hips begin to thrust forward, testing him, testing the boundaries. He doesn't stop me from doing it again and again.

When he starts to probe my tight hole with the tip of his finger my cock jerks in response. He huffs out a chuckle before breaching me, his finger driving me closer to my edge. Nothing is rushed or hurried, his tongue slowly caressing my cock. I run my hands over his shaved head, admiring how he looks on his knees before me.

He works another finger into me as I observe him, the intrusion delicious. His dark skin against my lighter-colored cock looks beautiful and for a moment I lose myself in watching that, the tattoos moving as he grips my shaft. My heart cracks with the love I have for this man, this beautiful man who never gets on his knees for anyone but me. This beautiful man who knows exactly what I need without me needing to ask for it. For a moment guilt slams into me, guilt over enjoying this while Arcanna is. . .

"I need to feel you, need you to take me." I say, the words a jumbled mess pouring from my mouth as I push the guilt down and try to stay in the moment. "Please." It's not lost on me this might be our last time together; nothing is guaranteed in battle and the one we are heading into? I want to be okay with being selfish right now. . . So badly I want to be okay with it. To enjoy his body on mine.

Dios doesn't stop right away; he keeps bringing me closer and closer to the edge before dragging me back again.

"Oh gods I'm going to cum!" I scream as the orgasm washes over me. Dios drinks me down greedily, taking everything, I have to give and more until I hiss with sensitivity. Pulling off my cock he stands quickly, pulling his own clothing off as I drop down onto all fours, presenting myself to him.

"Such a good, needy boy aren't you." Dios coos. I hear him slick up his dick with lube before I feel the cool press to my ass. I groan as he pushes in, no waiting, just filling me up with his cock from root to tip. He fucks me slowly, allowing me to build my arousal back up until my cock is hard and dripping once more.

"Need you," I pant. "Need your knot."

He groans as his hips snap forward and he's fucking with reckless abandon. "Use your hand *mi cielo*, get yourself off." I don't hesitate as I grip my shaft and start to jack myself off. I feel the moment his knot starts to inflate. The tissue catching on my rim as he pulls in and out until he finally pushes it all the way in and he fills me. "Fuckkk you feel good. Your ass is clenching and milking me so perfectly." He rocks back and forth as my own cock spurts cum over and over again.

The feeling is nothing short of bliss. The two of us

locked together in pleasure as we writhe on the floor. "You take me so well." He praises once more. "So perfect." I feel my eyes flutter shut as he holds me, every so often cuming deep within me again. My body starts to drift as sleep starts to drag me under. "I love you," He whispers into my ear as exhaustion finally claims me.

Harrow

Rubbing the spot on my arm that Oisin keeps shoving the IV in I cringe at the tender feel as I watch him and Dios's father talk. The two making plans for our trip to The Well.

"They are in Hell already." His father says. "My sources said they returned to the lake house to regroup."

Oisin snorts. "No doubt thinking they'll catch us by surprise at The Well."

"My son was never smart," the king laughs. It makes me realize how little he truly understood and knew Dios. Even in my short time with him I could see how smart and calculating he was. Part of me wants to open my mouth and tell them that but the small movement of my mouth reminds me of the sore jaw courtesy of Oisin's hand this morning. It keeps me from saying anything.

"Our armies are already in place; they won't have much hope in stopping us at this point." Oisin continues.

"And the dragons are taken care of as well!" Another witch, this one from one of the covens Oisin resurrected moves in. His stride confident seemingly screaming that he is more important than he truly is.

Oisin claps his hands, "Excellent! No need for my ex-bride to show up with her reptiles."

"Ava?" My voice finally manages to escape. He cuts me a glare, one that promises violence later.

"Yes, we will be at the edge of The Forest of Souls." My stomach bottoms out, the world narrowing inward as I take in his words. He snorts at my reaction. "You didn't think you could avoid your homeland forever, did you? Where the fuck do you think The Well is?"

Home.

Oisin is taking me home.

My arm is pulled upward from the chair as my brain tries to catch up with the words. Someone's fingers digging into my tender skin. I don't need to look at where we are heading, I know it's time for another infusion. Another hour or more of sitting with Arcanna as her hate builds towards me. And another hour of my own self-hatred building only to come a crescendo when I know I'll beg for him to fuck me once more after the infusion is done. When my blood feels like it's boiling as the magic mimics my heat. I'll beg and plead and get lost in his body. And when it's done, I'll go back to hating myself once more.

"You need to start behaving better," Oisin hisses as we near the door. "We'll be leaving soon, and I need everyone to know we are united."

"We were," I try to say. "Or are. But. . ." I hesitate.

He halts our journey, his grip loosening on my arm as he spins me to look at him. For a moment I get lost in his eyes, in his scent, and just for that moment I can see a flicker of the man I loved. "I'm sorry," he says. Shocking me. "I know I've been. . . unkind to you. We are just so close to finishing this. So close to getting what we've always wanted."

My palm reaches for his cheek, resting on it for a moment. "I don't want anything but you, Oisin. The revenge, the power, all of it means nothing if in the end I don't have you." They are desperate words. A last-ditch effort to drag the man I loved, the man I wish was still with me, to the forefront.

His eyes search my own, face devoid of emotion as he absorbs it all and for a moment, I think he'll agree. I think he'll step away from it all until I see that familiar darkness pass over his face as he shakes his head, stepping free of my grip. "We need the power Harrow. And you'll get it for us."

My heart breaks, the last little piece of it I was clinging to falling away as I let him drag me through the door.

Arcanna

My brain feels fuzzy as I regain consciousness, my body barely able to keep the astral projection up as my magic is siphoned from me and pumped into that traitor's body, the longer this goes on the less forgiving towards her I feel and the more murderous thoughts invade my mind. Ways to make her suffer for doing this, right after I gut Oisin.

I can hear voices around me, someone calling my name as my eyes finally flutter open. It takes a moment for the world to stop spinning and my home to come into view. The canopy of trees above me sways in the wind and the smell of rain-soaked leaves invades my nostrils.

"Arcanna?" Ava's voice accompanies the shadow of her body as she leans over into my view.

"Hey," I manage to croak out. Slowly I sit my body upward, taking another moment for my vision to catch up before I look at Ava. Behind her Drago and Shadow stand, arms crossed and faces grave.

"What are you doing here?" Ava asks. "And what is wrong with you?"

I glance down at my hands as the projection flickers in and out, "Shit. I don't have much time."

"So, talk." Drago commands. "You are here for a reason."

"Drago." Ava hisses.

I try to wave my hand but the amount of effort it takes forces me to keep it in my lap. "Oisin has me. He's using me to power up Harrow."

Ava cocks her head in question, "The priestess?"

"Yes, she's, his mate." The words get heavy, and I take a moment to ground this form here as my physical body tries to pull me back. This is a calculated risk, using this much magic when I'm already so low. It could kill me. "I wanted you to know he is going for The Well, using my magic as a catalyst to drain the whole thing. He doesn't care that he's also killing The Forest in the process."

Another form moves forward into my view. Shadow. "Where are Ciaran and Astrea?"

I shake my head. "I don't know. But I know Jackson and Dios are coming for me. I figured maybe you all want in on all of this." I pant.

If I weren't on deaths door I would cower before the look that passes over Drago. Pure dark, feral rage moves swiftly over him. The whole forest trembling around us as he pulls his power back in. Ava reaches up and grips his hand, squeezing once.

"We don't have to do this," she says. "We are happy here."

He shoots her a look of disbelief before catching his other mate's eye, "are we?" He asks

Ava pauses for a moment before shaking her head sadly, "I suppose not."

Shadow huffs a laugh. "Besides, we should probably show them the pathetic magic they placed around The Forest isn't actually going to hold us." He says.

"What?" I freeze.

Drago rolls his eyes, "The fuckers put up some wards to keep us in. I assume they knew you'd try and ask us for help."

"Or that we would just show up." Shadow adds.

"But they won't hold us, we've already poked at them." Ava says with confidence. I let out a slow breath as I feel myself pulled back again. The ability to remain here waning with each passing moment.

"Thats good because I don't know how much help I'll be." A cough racks my body and my vision swims. The feel of the grass on my cheek suddenly present and Ava screaming my name echoing in my ears. As my form finally let's go and I'm yanked back to my body.

Harrow

Sitting in silence, aside from the occasional deep breath I take, I know the exact moment Arcanna projects from her body. Even if I didn't feel the interruption between us, I would have known. She may have refused to speak to me the first few hours of being in here but regardless we were here together. Now I'm just here with a shell of a body.

My brain drifts back, to the moment I realized Oisin had no intention of coming back for me.

"Where is he?" I croak out as Feather pokes at the needle in my arm.

She rolls her eyes, "You fell in love with the wrong man little priestess." I can't tell her that I'm well aware of that but my face must say it regardless because she snorts and shakes her head. "He's busy preparing for our arrival."

"How long?"

She glances towards the door for a moment before back to me, "Four days. You've been here four days. But the good news is you are almost done, almost free."

The sound of vomit hitting the tile floor pulls me from my thoughts. The word free lingering and taunting me. I will never be free.

"Well, that is disgusting." Oisin remarks. I turn to find my mate standing in the doorway with a look for revolution on his face as he watches Arcanna retch again. "What's wrong with her?" He asks me. Arcanna seems to pale further as her soul is now firmly back into her body. I can only guess where she went, but I hope she found some peace wherever she was.

"It's the magic removal. It makes her nauseous." The words tumble out of me without thought. The lie suddenly appearing within me and escaping just as rapidly.

Oisin narrows his eyes and for a heartbeat I worry he'll question me but instead he walks up and kisses me firmly on the lips, shocking me. "I miss you in my bed." He groans. "Miss you warming my cock with that tight pussy." Already I can feel my nerves responding and already that deep hunger is churning inside me, so much more ravenous now that her magic has been feeding me for so many days nonstop.

My cheeks flush as he kisses down my neck and his hands find my breasts. "Oisin. . ." I warn. But he doesn't stop his exploration. "Oisin, Arcanna is here. We can't."

He lets out a laugh against my throat before his lips travel further down to my chest. "She can watch." He moans as he lets his tongue dip into my shirt and find my nipple. "If memory serves, she liked to watch me and Jax, I'm sure she'll love this."

The words make me pull back as I'm reminded of all the time Oisin spent with Arcanna and Jackson. Of the life he was living while I was suffering under the hands of The Elders. It's another reminder of the vast difference between those I've seen with a mate bond and us.

"You both are disgusting," she says, her voice hoarse and stiff.

Oisin pulls up off my body as he manipulates me into a position that allows him to spread my legs. His hand dips down into my skirt, his fingers grazing over my sex. Already embarrassingly wet. He chuckles. "My little Lena wants it. She's dripping." I hate the moan that he manages to pull from my lips as he strokes my clit. "You, see? She needs this just as bad as I do."

He's right. I do need this. I need him. The sudden hunger hits me full force and the whimpers and cries he draws from my lips fill the small room. I don't even notice him notching his cock to my pussy until he is pressing deep inside and fucking me hard. My body quivers, on the edge of release as he uses my body.

"That's my little slut, you love me fucking your cunt in front of her, don't you? Love that while we drain her life force and magic you are getting filled with my cock and cum." He pants.

The words make me crash, my orgasm fleeing me at the reality. But Oisin continues until he finds his release and I feel it splash deep inside me. When he pulls out, he doesn't notice I never came, he only throws a towel at me after he is done wiping his cock clean. The piece of cloth hitting my bare thigh and leaving a wet spot.

"Clean up, we'll be heading out soon. I need you dressed and ready." He demands. My eyes catch Arcanna's and I, once again, realize just how different Oisin is towards me. His *mate*. Even now as the word bounces around in my head it feels wrong, no longer providing me comfort and instead sending a deep chill through my body.

Luz was right. He was right and I still betrayed them all.

His tone is patronizing as he heads out the door, leaving me with his cum still dripping from my sex. "Oh, and Lena, if you ever lie to me again, I'll make sure that mask goes back on you so you can never be tempted to betray me." I'm just as much a prisoner in this room as Arcanna is. We just have different cuffs holding us in place and different key's that are meant to free us.

"Why did you lie to him?" Arcanna finally asks. It's been less than an hour since Oisin left me with his seed drying on my legs and my body unsatisfied. Yet even in that small amount of time my mind has fixated on every single interaction I've had with my supposed mate. From the very start, until today.

"I don't know," I finally respond honestly. Arcanna scoffs. I turn to look at her, her usually shinning black hair dull and the tattoos faded to a light gray, her magic all but drained from her body. Her lips are cracked, blood dried to parts where they've split open. The vomit on the floor is still there, though thankfully the scent has faded.

"He's not treating you any better than he is me." She pushes. "If anything, it's worse. This isn't how mates treat one another." The words sting. I let a sigh out and turn away from her, my gaze locking on the door that separates us from whatever is happening in the penthouse. I can hear people coming and going, hear the preparations being made and I can even hear Oisin walk by. His voice muffled behind the wood but still evident.

"Harrow, you show him your angry and he'll put that mask back on you. . . He's already threatened you. Don't tempt fate." Arcanna warns.

"You should be happy given everything that's happened is my fault." I snap with tears in my eyes. "You should want me to suffer."

Arcanna sighs, "I may be pissed at you, but I also know you're a misguided, ignorant girl who lost her family and spent years with these fucking wack-adoos. I can't fully blame you for your actions when you've been manipulated your whole life."

Her words are harsh, despite the truth behind them, and I can feel my face flame and heat crawl up my spine. She's not wrong. I know what The Order has done, and is doing, is wrong. I know they lied about me needing to be pure and the things they did to me were abusive. But Oisin? I had held out so much hope that he wasn't the same as them, that he truly cared for me.

Ultimately, it was the hope that blinded me and landed me here.

"I didn't know," I whisper. She cocks her head in question. "I didn't know this was the plan; I didn't know that he was working with Dios's father."

She blinks, those large eyes swirling with emotion. "What did you think would happen though? Truly?"

I blanch at the question despite its validity. My voice is lost for a long while, as I think on her question. Because what did I expect to happen? I went into this whole endeavor wanting to find revenge for my family, but truthfully that left my body long ago. But the need for a family, the need for someone to love me, that stayed. And I think a part of me truly hoped that doing the things I did would show Oisin I was worthy of what I craved from him. I was the ignorant and naive girl that Arcanna said. Worse, I was willing to allow myself to be blinded by everything in the desperate attempt to cling to the lie I've been fed for my whole life.

"I think," I start. "I think I wanted to believe in the delusion I've been fed my whole life. I wanted to believe that I would be enough for that man. That showing him I was willing to do anything for him would turn him from this quest and we could live happily ever after." I stare at the door holding us in this room for a long while until I finally look at Arcanna who holds so much pity in her eyes it burns my soul. "I think I was a stupid, naive, selfish girl who wanted the fairy tale at any cost. And I think I deserve every consequence coming my way."

Arcanna

I'm at a loss for words as I listen to Harrow. Even long after she stops talking, I still watch the priestess as she comes to terms with her new world view. Part of me loathes that I feel any ounce of sympathy towards her plight, but another part can't help it. I can't help but soften towards this broken female in front of me who has so clearly wanted, no needed, companionship that she clung to someone like Oisin. I may have been furious with Jackson, but I've never known the type of loneliness Harrowlena has felt, no doubt.

"What happened to the other girl?"

I blink quickly, realizing Harrow has spoken again. Glancing over to the side I see the empty cuffs that held Bast. I had passed out, not long after the first 'treatment' and when I awoke the goddess was no longer with us. Her chains still as death and the room cold without her presence. "I'm not sure." I respond finally. "Harrow, Oisin doesn't intend for me to live through this. And I don't think he cares if you do either."

Her eyes look lifeless, the emotions that had raged earlier no longer there. "I know," Her voice is equally as listless. "We are going to my home after this, I guess it's nice I'll see it again before I die."

"You need to fight." I hiss. "Fucking fight for once in your gods damn life don't be a fucking passenger in this. Take the wheel and fucking drive."

She says nothing, those lifeless eyes watching me until the door to our room opens and a group of witches' meander in. Feather leads them, quickly directing each of them to one of us. "Hurry up," she says. "We need them prepped and ready to move." She doesn't look at me, not once, but I see her frown at the state Harrow is in. I see the look on her face when she realizes the substance drying on her is cum. The last thing I see before the witch who has me knocks me unconscious is Feather leading Harrow to a bathroom.

Harrow

(Angel in Hell- Klergy)

Feather washes me off with no words. Moving my body with care but refusing to meet my eyes. Arcanna's words sparked something in me once more. The fire that had died, the ember that had seemingly been extinguished suddenly re kindled now. I want to be angry at her for doing it, I was ready to die, ready to be put out of my misery but she had to remind me I didn't want to fade away. And more importantly, my fate was tied to her. She needed to survive. I owed it to her and to Jackson and Dios. I can't let my actions cost her, or them, any more than it already has.

I shove the small pieces of me that are broken apart, the pieces that love Oisin, into a box. And the box I push into a closet before throwing chains around the door in my mind. Someday I'll come back for those parts, or I'll die, and it won't matter. Either way those pieces will not serve me with what I need to do now.

Feather pushes my priestess clothing into my hands as she exits the room. I don them as someone who would put armor on. I braid my hair back as the plan forms in my head, and I place the sunbeam crown atop my head as I let the acceptance of my fate wash over me. As I allow the girl free who I've held back for so long. With back straight I walk back into the room, Oisin holding his hand out to me next to the portal that opens to the place I thought he rescued me from all those years ago.

"Are you ready?" He asks.

"I am." I say with confidence. The first real, honest answer I've given in my life. And when I take his hand in my own, I cling to that confidence refusing to let it drop away as my bare feet land on the soft grass.

The girl in me, the scared one who followed Oisin without question, doesn't want to look around at my biggest source of guilt and regret but the new me? The one now burning in my veins? She looks. She takes it all in and marks every scorch mark, every torn apart home, and every broken memory that resurfaces and adds them to the armor. Adds them to the reasons why this plan has to work.

"Take her to Arcanna, I want the last of that bitches magic in her before night fall." Oisin commands. He releases my hand, dropping it without a goodbye as he stalks off to speak with Arthur Mori. I offer none myself, watching his retreating form with a detached level of interest.

Fingernails dig into my arm dragging my focus to the person he is leaving me with. Lady Ornate sneers at me. "What are you wearing?"

I blink for a moment and then smile. A true smile. "My clothes."

"You are in High Priestess attire." She hisses as she tries to start dragging me away from the group, but I keep my feet dug into the ground.

"Yes, because I am now the High Priestess. Am I not?" I respond with a cool, calm, tone. "After all, you have no magic of this nature. I do. You were merely a place holder. You are no longer needed."

She reels back, dropping her hand from my arm with a

shocked look on her face that morphs to fury. "You little cunt." She growls.

Stepping into her space I grab her wrist. Squeezing it as I force her to hold my eye contact. "Careful. We both remember what happened when you were at the receiving end of my scream the last time. Imagine how powerful I am now." I drop her wrist and step back. Satisfied with the pale, horrified look on her face. "I can find my own way to Arcanna."

With my back to her I allow another smile to spread over my lips as I go find the female who I owe so much to.

Jackson
(No Rest for the Wicked- Klergy)
Looking out over the army that Oisin has collected feels surreal. Smoke pours into the air, shouts and screams echo outward into the now desolate space that is between us and The Well. Even from here I can feel the faint pulse of power emitting from it. Those old ruins that look little better than a crumbled stone house. The Forest, Arcanna's old place of residence and now my sisters, is barely hanging on. The patches of dead trees stand out like scars while other parts burn as Oisin allows his ilk to do as they please.

I shove down the fear of what it could mean for Arcanna.

"I don't see the coven leaders." I comment.

Dios grunts, "maybe they stayed in the city?"

"It seems unlikely, Oisin raised them from the dead for a reason." I respond. "And he's not one to waste that type of magic."

Kallen walks up beside me, "They are here. I can fucking smell them." She growls. Demon drags her backward into his chest, protectively wrapping his arms around her middle.

"Is everyone in position?" I ask, a calm washing over me as I open up the part of brain that stays calm, that plans. The one trained by the previous King of Hell. This is the side of me that was forged through my own blood and sweat at the hands of the man who I called father. This is the part of me that's covered in old battle scars, that could enter a race and zero in on how to win; shutting the rest of the world out. It's the part of me that was in no way shocked that Oisin was already here, that he believed he could beat us.

Dark winds ruffle my hair, my gaze pulling to the right as Nyx meanders up, taking a long drag of the cigarette in his mouth. His mate, Ophelia, stands next to him. Her bright eyes looking horrified as she takes in the devastation around us.

"You came." I say to one of my oldest friends. To one of my friends who was shoved aside the moment I became King. I owe him so many apologies. I wasn't even positive he would show when I sent the request, not after what he had been like at the races.

He offers me a nod, his eyes hungry for blood before softening as they glance down at his mate. Ah. He came for her. Not for me. "Deva," he says softly.

She holds up her hand, "don't you dare say another word. I'm helping. For Ava." She holds my gaze when she says my sister's name and the look on her face threatens to break apart the wall I've put up to avoid my emotional side. I offer a nod of thanks, not trusting my voice.

Nyx sighs out, long and exasperated but does not argue with her.

"Alright, let's do this." Kallen says with a little too much glee. "No one fucking die, I don't want to have to go grab your soul from its new keeper." She growls as her and Demon stalk off into the night against the howls of her pack she is about to unleash.

No goodbye, just a command to stay alive.

And a promise that we will not stay dead if she has anything to do with it.

Dios, drags me into his chest, laying a claiming kiss across my mouth as he allows me to pull from his magic. When I'm done my eyes blaze with his magic. "You come back to me," he commands. I say nothing. Learning long ago it doesn't do anyone any good to acknowledge the inevitable may happen. Instead, I kiss him hard, before stepping back and allowing my own wings to unfold, leaping into the air to find our mate.

Arcanna

(Will You Fight- Klergy & Beginners)

I never considered myself someone who would break. But now? Now I question that. My bones, my body, my very soul feel flayed apart. Oisin had come to me, and I knew what would happen, knew it in my bones. He never wanted me to survive this, and this torture session seemed to be edging me closer to the end. Harrow had walked in as he landed a particularly brutal hit against my body. To her credit she had cried and begged for him to leave me be but he had a mission, in the torture he administered, one he succeeded in spectacularly.

And when he was finished with me, he went for Harrow. Her torture felt worse to witness. The brutality of it made worse as he continued to tell her he deserved a better mate then she was. When he had finished with her, he left her lying half naked on the ground, laughing and joking that he might let the guards have a taste of her after all this was over.

It made me want to throw up.

Now, the priestess and I sit in uncomfortable quiet as we each process the day's events. My eyes track over where she sits, and they widen briefly as I see the blade she drags from under her clothing. Harrow holds the knife between us, and for a moment I worry she's about to stab me. However, she brandishes it against the metal between us, slicing through the chain in a manner that begs the question exactly what type of blade she holds, before tucking it back against her body.

"You need to leave. Now." She says with urgency.

I blink, confused for a moment, as the dehydration and lack of food truly has started to take its toll. "Why?" I stutter out.

She shakes her head at me, biting down hard on her lip and struggles to help me to stand. "Because I think I've made enough mistakes to last a lifetime. I don't need to continue to repeat the cycles. Do you have enough magic to get yourself out?"

I nod. Whether it's true or not I don't care. I need out. I refuse to let that man touch me again. "Take care of yourself Harrow."

My magic wanes, the little I have left, as I land in the middle of Oisin's makeshift camp. My vision swims and my knees threaten to buckle but I grip my glaive hard, the tool still coming to me, thank gods, using it as a support staff more than a weapon. My nose is clogged with smoke and eyes water as I glance around at the creatures who are helping him. Renewed rage replaces the broken feelings as it fills my blood as I take in the full destruction Oisin has reaped upon my Forest.

For a moment no one moves, his army surprised by my sudden appearance, a coven of witches looking to each other unsure of who I am, but when I send my magic out in a burst of fire, they realize I'm not here as a friend. I lose myself in taking apart the creatures around me, my glaive taking down one as my magic takes another. My body going numb, and my only focus on each of the creatures. I have precious little time left before I'm drained completely and even less time before Oisin sends his executioner after me.

The chain on my wrist still rattles as it clinks against the staff end of my glaive when I wield it. Part of me is still shocked she helped me; another part worried for her survival when Oisin figures it out. Because he will, he'll know exactly who freed me.

The distraction costs me and the blade of one of the vampires catches me across the cheek. "Fuck!" I scream as I teeter on my feet. The vampire smiles sadistically as he starts to step towards me before his body suddenly drops to the ground, lifeless.

A shuddering burst through my mate bond before a deep growl fills the air as Jackson slams into the earth. His magic, combined with Dios, ripping the souls free of the creatures around us. A small whimper is dragged from me as relief fills my body. His hands catch me right as I start to slump towards the ground.

"Fuck wicked girl, don't you ever do that again." He slams his mouth into mine. I sob into the touch, desperate to erase the horrors of the days with Oisin. But Jackson pulls away too soon and I hate it. "We need to get you out of here." He pants with his forehead against mine.

The tingle of magic on my skin sends warning bells off and I only just manage to throw a shield around us before one of the witches hits us with a wave of magic. My knees buckle as I brace against it. The last of my magic coming up from the depth of my reservoir.

"Motherfuckers." Jax curses. He glances at me, frowning at the sweat rolling down my temples.

(Dark Outside- Klergy & Maire Gallo)

"They drained my magic," I pant out. "I can't hold this." Rage rolls over him in thick, suffocating waves as his eyes go black. "Jax don't!" But it's too late. I'm cut off as he steps back from me and takes off up and over my shield. I watch as he breaks through their defense in a matter of moments, the witches falling to the ground dead. His combined power with Dios is astronomical, the feel of it sends shivers down my spine.

I slump down to my knees, my magic finally dropping to nothing and my body giving out. Even if I wanted to, I couldn't force my body to stand, to move. My magic completely gone from me now.

"*Segradora.*" Dios's smooth voice appears behind me and his warm hands pull my broken body into his. His scent smothers me and all I can do is hold on to his arms with a desperation I hate. Tears roll down in silent rivers as I watch Jackson cut down more demons and vampires. Unable to hold back the emotions that keep tumbling through me.

"This feels too easy." Dios mutters as he lifts me upward in his arms. "Something isn't right." His eyes continue to look over the area, assessing and searching for whatever ripple in the air he seems to sense. Jackson turns towards us eyes wide as if he too feels it.

"He has the original coven." I manage to get out. My throat feeling raw. "He has the grimoires." Just as I say it the air above us explodes with magic as a portal opens and out steps the original witch families, with Arthur Mori leading the group. His family grimoire held tightly in his hands.

Dios

I watch in horror as Arthur Mori sends out his destructive magic from that fucking book. Jax barely making it to the ground before it passes over us all in waves. From behind him wave after wave of Hellish creatures pour out, hidden from sight previously. I drag Arcanna to stand, her body wavering as true fear pulses over me. Jackson is now hidden from my sight as he is overwhelmed by the creatures.

"Go," Arcanna pants. "Go help him." She's barley standing, her face pale, tattoos a dull gray and her eyes? Her eyes seem to hold nothing but haunted memories that I know will make me want to destroy Oisin in the most painful way possible.

"I'm not leaving you." I snap back.

She manages to shove out of my embrace, clinging to her glaive as her body tries to give out once more. "Help. Him." I hesitate. Unable to make the choice. Leaving her feels like I'm choosing Jackson's life over hers, but staying. . .
.

A flash of white to my right pulls my attention as it races towards Jackson.

Demon.

He shifts for a moment to human, gripping his battle ax hard and offering me a nod before shifting again and racing after his mate who has used a portal to drop to the spot I last saw Jackson. Relief pulses through me along with a deep well of gratitude.

Kallen's rage is a living beast, her magic a whirl of retribution. Her golden whip taking creatures out as she focuses her furious gaze on the coven leaders. When she lets out a scream Arthur has the decency to falter for a moment and when his eyes connect with hers, he looks scared. Whether because he knows it's Kallen or because seeing his dead daughter is a shock is unclear. Either way he has the mark of a dead man walking now.

The visual has me far too distracted to stop what happens next. In slow motion I turn as I hear Arcanna grunt and hit the ground with a thud, her body somehow too far from me as though she had been inching away from the safety of my arms the whole time. On top of her is an Elker, the beast having speared her through the chest. Her face goes even more pale, if possible, as her name slips free from me in a guttural scream that echoes across the battlefield.

A large black mass slams into the creature as my foot steps forward. A Hellbeast. The largest of Kallen's pack rips into the Elker, the creature screeching as the venom from the beast sinks into it. My body finally seems to move, the world fast forwarding now as I sprint to my mate. Her breathing is heavy as I scoop her up.

"I can't seem to avoid getting hurt, you're bad luck." She jokes, blood dripping down her lips.

"You're going to be fine *segradora*. Stop talking." I command. I reach down the bond with Jackson. "Please hear me." I beg. A shudder of magic is the only response before silence descends around me. Bodies drop with sickening thuds as I look from Arcanna and see Jackson walking across the battlefield to us once more, eyes wholly black, and focused on the body in my arms. I can vaguely hear Kallen laugh out madly before cursing Jackson for not leaving more for her.

I can feel the drain of magic, on both of us, and know he won't have much longer using this magnitude of magic all at once. And I won't be able to help him replenish, not this quickly. But none of that seems to matter right now, as Arcanna coughs and blood hits my cheek. Because if Arcanna dies, it won't matter how much magic we drain from our bodies. No, none of it will matter because we will drain it all if it means destroying the person who hurt her.

So, I do the only thing I can think of, passing Arcanna to Jackson who has finally made it to us, I let loose the side of me that I've held back.

I let loose the Death God.

Harrowlena

**(My Love Will Never Die feat. Claire Wynd-
ham- AG)**

My hair stands on end as Oisin looks out at the path to
The Well with a hungry expression. All around us are the
screams of the battle. The magic being cast off by those
fighting feels suffocating, even as my own body is burning
up with the borrowed magic from Arcanna. I keep forcing
myself to breathe through it, to stay rational and calm and
keep to the plan I've created in my head.

A scream pulls my attention from his sickening expression. My violet eyes search the groups fighting until the
source of the scream is found. I watch in transfixed horror as
one of Kallen's Hellbeasts pulls an Elker from Arcanna, one
of its long talons being left behind in her chest. She drops to
her knees, her eyes blinking in confusion as she looks down
at the thing sticking out of her.

"No!" I cry out. Oisin grips my wrist hard as if he could
sense my body being pulled to her. My stomach rolls at his
touch, at the memory of what he did to me early.

"Your place is with me. Not them." He growls before

turning back to Arthur Mori, speaking to him of the ritual he'll use to drain The Well.

By the time I look back, the fight has swallowed up my view of Arcanna's dark hair. A flash of white however draws my gaze to the right, Kallen. Her golden whip arcing through the air as she takes out enemy after enemy. A wild smile is plastered across her blood-splattered face. Next to her is a massive wolf that I can only assume is her mate. His muzzle is covered in gore as he shreds into a witch.

Time moves in slow motion as I finally land on Jackson whose dark wings are flared wide, Arcanna's limp body now in his arms. He manages to send out wave after wave of his dark, electric magic but even I know he'll tire eventually against this type of onslaught. Arcanna doesn't move, blood pouring from her in a way that I can't imagine she would survive.

Reaper or not.

Dios's magic courses through the ground as he pulls the dead into the fight. Controlling each one like a divine puppet master. His body practically vibrating from the amount of magic he is using.

"This fight will be finished in no time at all." Arthur says smugly.

Oisin chuckles, "they made a poor choice going against us all. Would have been better to just roll over and let it happen."

"And once done here we shall reclaim Gothic Grove." Arthur comments. "Those who do not follow our rule will be dealt with swiftly."

Lady Ornate smiles at him, her affections having seemingly switched to him over Oisin. "Already those who you rescued are working towards bringing others into the fold. You will have full control in no time."

"You couldn't get Oisin's cock so you have to go for

Arthur?" I snap before I can think better of it. She gasps and I roll my eyes at the mock outrage before turning towards Arthur, my rational side seemingly no longer in control and instead only that part that holds my fire. "Your daughters may have something to say about your supposed rule."

Oisin cracks me across the face hard, the back of his hand splitting open my lip. "Shut up you ungrateful slut." I glare up at him through my curtain of hair as I wipe the blood from my lip.

"What do you mean daughters?" Arthur snaps at me, drawing my gaze. A smile spreads over my mouth, no doubt unhinged with blood decorating my teeth. Sweet satisfaction bubbles up and a laugh pours from me. A laugh I can't seem to contain as I brace myself on the ground. In the background I can still hear Arthur demanding answers, demanding what I meant.

"Get up." Oisin hisses, dragging me upward by the arm. His grip punishing and no doubt leaving bruises. But still, the laughter continues to crack free of my chest.

"She's lost it." Lady Ornate says. "Finally showing her true colors."

The only thing that stops me from continuing the descent into madness is the sudden shuddering of the earth. As if the ground itself has taken a breath and let it out rapidly.

The movement causes a pause. The witches momentarily stop their casting. The beasts stop and sniff the air. Another shudder, this one more violent. And then a roar so loud I cover my ears, shutting my eyes against the sound before black flames scorch the earth in front of us.

(…Ready For It?- Taylor Swift)

"You said the dragons would be contained!" Oisin screams in fury.

Astrea's father looks nervous, "I thought they would. That spell was flawless. No one could have broken it."

I watch in awe and relief as a massive skeletal dragon drops to the ground, unleashing not only his black flames but his death magic. The ground around him, and anything close vanishing into dust. Not just dead, but gone, bone and blood nothing but dust to the wind. The beasts and witches immediately retreat from the death dragon as they suddenly understand exactly what has landed in their presence.

"How is he using his magic in dragon form?!" Oisin screeches, his careful control of his emotions fraying at the edges.

"I. . . I do not know." Arthur stumbles over his words.

Oisin digs his nails into my flesh, "What do you know?" He hisses. Spit flying into my face. He shakes me back and forth as if he'll drop the answers from me with the movement. But I have nothing for him. Nothing left to give.

"Hello father, it's been oh so long." The Harbinger herself drops down from another dragons back, this one made of golden and black scales. Atop his back he also carries Ciaran who drops behind his mate followed swiftly by Ava who moves seamlessly around everyone in her ghost form. Astrea looks at her father, Oisin, and me with pure hatred.

Arthur pales, "how? How are you alive?"

She offers him a wicked smile. "I'm hard to kill."

Her magic twists and turns around her body in a black smoke that seems to have a life of its own. Arthur's beady eyes narrow in on it, cheeks now flaming red. "That magic is not yours." He hisses.

Astrea shakes her head, "It's not yours either," She grips two blades in her hands and the movement pulls her father's attention, his eyes widening at the look of them as though he is seeing a ghost. "Shall we explore how you came about this power? How the covens created it?" The man slams his mouth shut but the look on his face offers nothing but pure retribution for his daughter.

Oisin edges himself in front of me drawing The Harbinger's attention. Her cold gaze grabbing my eyes. I feel myself recoil. This. . . this is what everyone was terrified of. This is who, alongside her mate, keeps the creatures of Hell in check in Gothic Grove. Even having a death dragon nearby nothing compares to taking on The Harbinger head-on.

Astrea moves rapidly, flipping one of those blades in the air as she catches it once more by the handle, her dark magic unfurling further as she lets go of the two snakes normally tattooed on her. I keep my eyes locked on her, keep them focused as the green in them disappears to be replaced by black. And it's in that change that something in my brain clicks. A door opening that has long been kept shut. A realization that has been kept at bay by the man currently digging his claws into my arm.

Are you ready? The soft voice whispers through my head. *Are you ready to reclaim what was yours? What should have always been yours?*

For a moment I'm too stunned to say anything, too stunned to recognize the voice as it continues to whisper through my mind. My eyes shift to Oisin, tugging him slightly towards the space I need him to go. It's a small shove, a small suggestion, but he grabs it rapidly.

"Keep her occupied." Oisin growls at Arthur, who looks to still be in shock, as his grip drops to my hand, and he starts to pull me towards The Well. The movement violent forcing me to trip and stumble, landing hard on the ground. Oisin yanks me up harshly. "Come on, I need you if we are going to finish this!" He yells. Another reminder of what I am to him. And what I'm not. Another confirmation that I'm doing the right thing.

(MIDDLE OF THE NIGHT- Elley Duhé)

I hear the roar of another dragon right before the heat hits me. My head whirls and I see a river of lava heading towards us as the gold and black dragon spews it from his mouth. I send a prayer upward that I'll survive this and force my body to run, force my legs to pump harder than ever before as I flee from the death that dragon promises.

The Well lies directly ahead of us, the vision of it settling me in a way that I haven't felt in a long time. The relief I feel has me letting out a broken sob. The relief that this will all be over soon, provided we make it to The Well alive.

"OISIN!" Ciaran screams out, shattering my moment of relief. Shadow overtakes us, his dragon dropping the vampire in our path before he continues onward. Ciaran points his sword at us. "Harrow, this is between me and my brother. Leave so I don't have to kill you too."

Keep going. You must keep going. You must follow the plan, stick to the plan. The voice comes again into my brain, the soothing sound a balm to the chaos around me.

I shake my head, drawing a deep breath. Reminding myself this is the last time. "I'm sorry Ciaran, I can't do that." I push Oisin aside, my magic rallying deep within me. "Be ready to run," I whisper to the deceiver next to me as I unleash my banshee side. The scream rips from me, Ciaran throwing up a shield of magic that blocks it just enough that the blast doesn't kill him. I don't wait, I grab Oisin's hand again and bolt towards The Well. I don't stop to see if Astrea is now coming for me because I went after her mate.

We hit the sacred building, my body barreling into the old door. "I am a Priestess of this realm!" I scream, my throat burning from my use of power. "I demand to be let in!" The cry is broken and hoarse. My palm flat against the runes carved into the wood, my blood from the fall smearing across the dark oak. "Please," I beg my voice barely a whisper now. "Please, I seek sanctuary. Please let me in. Please help me." I send my desire into the words, the need to put a stop to this, to keep my friends safe.

"What are you saying?!" Oisin growls.

You will always be welcomed here.

I feel the ward drop, the door hiss open and I drag Oisin through. My nose is invaded with the smell of damp earth as the heavy door shuts behind us, the darkness brief before glowing blue erupts around us. My veins thrum with power as my body reacts to the magic within this space. Everything in me is keyed to The Well, every part of me knows my purpose.

"You did it," Oisin says, pushing past me to look at the glowing orb of power that floats in the center of the room. Magic seeps out of it into the ground like the roots of a tree. The power that is both given and taken from Hell. He turns and faces me, lust in his eyes. Not for me though, no, lust for the power I can give him. Unlimited power. "Now hurry up, let's do the ritual."

His words open that chained up door, the little broken pieces of me peering out. My heart hurts, and my body feels as though I'm being cleaved in two. He has no interest in me, never has. His goal has always been this power and I am a means to an end. I shut my eyes against him, focusing on my goal. My intent. Because with any magic intent is everything, and this is no different.

Something in me pulses, the feeling pulling me forward and past Oisin. Like a puppet being controlled by a master I allow the magic to take me where I need to go. Put my trust in it that it understands my intent.

Oisin continues to speak, to tell me how it'll be once he

has the powers. All empty promises and lies that at one point may have swayed me, long ago. But having met Jackson, Arcanna, and Dios? Even Luz. Emptiness isn't good enough.

Stopping directly before the ball of light I tilt my head, slowly blinking and looking at it.

Hello child. The voice is louder here, in my head, and yet motherly. The feel warm in my body.

"Hello." I respond out loud.

"Who are you talking to?" Oisin asks, a slight tenor in his voice revealing that he is nervous.

You've come a long way. Suffered greatly.

I bow my head in a small nod.

(Heavy in your arms- Florence and the Machine)

Warmth wraps around my body as if someone is drawing me into an embrace.

You will not suffer any longer. You have done so well, protected this magic, protected those you love.

"I hurt the ones I love," I say, ignoring Oisin altogether now as he continues to demand answers from me.

You did what you needed to do. You survived. They will survive because of what you did here today.

A sigh of relief cascades through me as the magic shows me Arcanna, injured but alive. Followed swiftly by Jackson and Dios, both still fighting but alive as well. The dragons, Kallen, Ciaran. . . everyone is alive. A sob is pulled from me as my face spreads into a smile.

"Thank you. Thank you so much." I cry.

Now finish this. The voice commands.

I don't stop to think and don't allow myself the chance to second-guess what I am about to do. Instead, I draw the magic into me at the same moment I pull the knife free that I've kept hidden on my body. Spinning rapidly, I stab Oisin in the stomach, pushing the blade in deep as his blood pools across my hands.

I twist as I scream, the pain of hurting him ripping at me, tearing at my soul. Whatever magic used to tie us together thrashing against my intent to kill him. My body desperately tries to stop, tries to fight as I drag the dagger upwards with every ounce of strength I have. The magic of The Well flowing into him at the same time his blood is flowing out. If the dagger doesn't kill him the power will burn him from the inside out.

"What?" His face is full of confusion, his eyes looking at the dagger I have pushed into him and back to my face. "What have you done?"

I sob, the sound echoing through the ruins. Because part of me did love him. Part of this wasn't just the magic binding. "I had to. This was the only way to end it." I cry out. My vision blurs, "I wanted you Oisin. Just you. But you lied to me all this time." The magic now pulsing through him at a dangerous level. "We could have been happy. But you had to lie, you had to pretend I was your mate! You used me!" It's the last thing I say before I rip the dagger free the blood spraying me in the face.

His body drops down in slow motion, his eyes still locked on my own in disbelief. The cry that is wrenched from me as his life finally fades out rattles the old building. My knees drop down, the knife clatters from my hands as I wrap myself into a small ball. I lose track of time, rocking back and forth as I look at Oisin's body in front of me.

Luz had promised it wouldn't hurt.

No that's not right.

He promised it wouldn't kill me if I freed myself from him.

Which feels worse now, to live with what I've done. To live with the memory of Oisin's face, the feel of his blood on my hands. The hypothetical of it all felt so much better than the reality that is crashing in around me.

Eventually, the sobbing stops, everything stops, my heart slows, and I become numb. Not the detached feeling I had earlier, no, this one is very different. It's the numbness that settles in when your body knows that you cannot handle feeling anymore.

I killed my very first love to save the people who I've come to care for. Those same people who want me dead because of everything that's happened. I look at the knife that's still lying by Oisin's body, his blood still shining on it. It beckons me like a beacon of hope, an answer to my prayers.

My fingers feel stiff as I reach for it, as I try to end it all.

And then, "No *mi ángel co. T.* That's not for you."

Luz's face swims in front of my own, his aura a comforting light, before my eyes close and I let the world fade away.

Drago

The pathetic creature at my feet wheezes, life still stubbornly clinging to him as his blood, no doubt, fills his lungs, slowly drowning him. It makes my cock hard thinking about it.

"Are we good, dragon?" Luz interrupts my erotic thoughts of the man dying at my feet. Glancing up I see the priestess limp in his arms still unconscious from absorbing the power of The Well. The knife she used to stab Oisin now lying at the feet of the man who holds her, the blood still shimmering and fresh across the blade.

"We're good." I say, my eyes glowing golden in the dim cavern.

Luz clears his throat, "It's not dead yet." He uses his foot to point at Oisin who is now grasping at his throat with blood coated hands.

"Good," I say with a smile. "I want him to suffer for much, much longer in this physical body before he begins his suffering in the afterlife."

Luz snorts out a laugh. "Here, I'll help you a bit." He shifts the female in his arms and slowly bends down with arm extended. Oisin seems to breathe a sigh of relief once Luz touches him. When he pulls back, Oisin's face has some color back in it and his breathing is no longer as labored as it was. "Now he can suffer longer."

Shoving my hands in my pockets I nod my head in thanks. Luz turns his back to me, meandering slowly from the cavern towards the portal he is opening. "Long may the gods reign, Drago." He calls over his shoulder. I don't bother answering him as my dragon starts to take over.

"No, please!" Oisin sputters as he beholds the horror, he has unleashed upon himself.

"The time for begging is over. It's time to pay homage to the god that stands in front of you." I lean down, allowing my full power to take hold. "You'll become very acquainted to praying at my feet by the end of this. Very. Fucking. Acquainted."

His screams are sweet and the only thing I hear as I unleash my vengeance.

FORTY-TWO

Luz

(Your losing me- Taylor Swift)

Harrow looks out blankly at the lake, her eyes tracking the gentle ebb and flow of the waves. Her silver hair is drawn up in a simple ponytail with wisps escaping in front of her face. There is a finality in her posture, an acceptance of one's place in life. Neither sad nor angry but a carefully placed neutrality.

"You can stop lurking." Her once soft voice, now forever raspy it seems, says over the breeze.

A smile spreads over my lips as I allow my feet to carry me forward. When I fold my legs down next to her, she finally turns and looks at me. Her once violet eyes are leached of their color and instead swim with the white crackling energy of The Well. I had been shocked when her eyes fluttered open for a moment, my mind flashing to the only other person I know who has those milky eyes.

"I wasn't lurking." I growl. It pulls a small smile to her face before that mask of neutrality goes back up. She draws her gaze back to the water, mesmerized by its movement.

"*Ángel caido.*" The term of endearment falls from my lips without thought.

The sounds of nature overtake us for a moment, the water, wind and birds a soothing symphony against our weary souls. For a long time, we say nothing, her looking at the lake and me watching her.

"When I met Oisin he was a different person," she finally says. "He was this bright light in my life, someone who saved me from the things that went bump in the night. Someone who gave me what I so desperately wanted."

"What was that?" I ask.

She chuckles. "Love."

My mouth feels dry as I listen to her, "do you regret it?"

She turns those, now white eyes, on me again, "I regret many things that transpired, but that does not change the fact that I *ache* knowing he's dead by my own hands." She glances down to the appendages as if the blood will still stain them. No words come to me as she lets the confession free, but I slip my hand into hers. Hoping it can convey everything words cannot.

Small tears pepper her face in silent tracks, but her body remains still, her breath even. "I think a part of me died with him. And I'm okay with that. She had to die, I think, in the end."

"Harrow…" I start but when she turns and looks at me head on the words of comfort die in my throat. Placating her with sympathy won't heal what broke when she felt Oisin's warm blood on her hands. So instead, I pull her in, placing a soft kiss on her forehead.

The movement breaks her, the quiet cries now turning into full body sobs. I allow her to fall apart against my chest, holding space for the grief I will never understand for a man I wish had died by my own hands. Because this is what you do for someone you love, you hold space even when you don't understand it.

For a long time, we stay like that, even after the sobs have quieted again. It's an extended goodbye, one neither of us are in a hurry to finish.

Daylight fades into twilight and as the first few stars begin to pepper the darkening sky she finally pulls back.

"They wanted to say goodbye. . ." I start to say but the lie dies on my tongue. None of them wanted to see her, my brother included, despite the fact that she saved so many. The scar across Arcanna's chest a vivid reminder of what they almost lost because of the actions of Harrow.

She pushes to a stand, dragging me with her. "You don't have to lie; I know what I lost. I made my choice."

Her eyes pull behind me and I know who stands there without turning. I know my brother is watching us from the windows, despite having no interest in saying goodbye to her, I know he's watching to make sure we leave. He's keeping his healing mates safe.

"I hope they find happiness," the sound of her voice overtakes nature. "They deserve it."

"So do you," I counter. She just shakes her head sadly.

Without thought I drag her into my body, my mouth laying a long claiming kiss. When she pulls back fresh tears glitter in her eyes before she's pulling from my embrace and walking away. I turn and follow with gaze as she makes her way towards my mother's outstretched hand.

"Come my dear," my mother says. "Your new home awaits you."

Arcanna

I watch Luz's mother lead Harrow through the portal as I rub at the new scar across my chest. Behind me Jackson lets out a puff of air, his sleeping form rolling over facing away from me. His toned back has new scars across it, bruises now sprouting up across his ribs. He drained himself so low, all to keep me from bleeding out until Luz could heal me. I'm racking up IOUs with the god at an astronomical point now.

Slipping on a pair of his sweats and my tank top I quietly push out the door into the hallway.

"Going somewhere?" Dios's deep voice startles me, the door shutting louder than I want as I spin towards him.

"Fuck," I pant. "You scared me."

He offers me a smirk, "clearly." I roll my eyes at him which earns me an eyebrow raise. "Careful, *segadora*. You are still healing but that doesn't mean I won't punish you later." His eyes smolder with the promise of long nights.

"You should be careful yourself." I bite back, enjoying the feeling of how normal the banter is. "I might give it back to you just as hard." He and Jackson have handled me with kid gloves and while I appreciate it, it's starting to get on my nerves. I have no interest in dealing with the trauma of my time with Oisin, not now, maybe not ever. I refuse to allow that man to take anything more from me. Maybe it's unhealthy, or not smart, but it's working for me at the moment.

He's in my space within a heartbeat, his mouth firmly over the mating claim he left on me all those nights ago. His teeth press into it making my knees go weak and pussy flood with arousal. My body lights up as his strong hands grip my hips, a low moan pulling from me as his tongue swirls the bite mark. When he pulls away it takes everything to hold back a whimper.

"What were you saying, *segadora*?" His breath is hot against me as his hands explore my body while I'm pushed against the door. When his hand dips into my sweatpants I can't help the sound he draws from my mouth. "Shhhh, you'll wake up Jax." He warns. It only makes me want it more. The idea of being caught suddenly making my body catch fire. He laughs, his fingers dipping into me.

"Oh fuck," I cry. The feeling of him surreal. He slowly pumps in and out, occasionally bringing my wetness to my clit. He works me until I can't breathe, my breasts heavy and nipples pushing against my tank top painfully.

"Do you want to cum?" He taunts as I feel his magic grab hold of my soul.

I throw my head back, hitting the door hard. "Oh fuck, oh god. Please please please." I pant. "I need you, please." My hands move of their own accord grappling at his pants as I pull his cock out. Wrapping my leg around his hip I sheath myself in one move.

"So wet and ready for me." He pants as he thrusts into me. I dig my nails into his shoulder hard as I drag his mouth to my own. I'm lost to the feeling, his pleasure pulsing down our bond. The intensity of it all pulls tears to my eyes and when he finally releases my soul and lets me cum, I feel the tears flowing down my face. He finishes just behind me, his cock filling me with his release.

We both stand panting, foreheads pressed together. When his cock slips free of me, I feel lost in the sensation of his release dripping down my legs.

"Now wherever you go you'll smell like me; they'll know who you belong to." He whispers as he pulls my pants back up.

Grabbing his hair, I kiss him again before pulling back. "Make Jax suck your cock, let him taste both of us." Without missing a beat, I let my magic pull me back to my Forest.

(Arsonist's Lullaby- Hozier)

I materialize at the edge of the woods atop a hill overlooking all that remains of my Forest. As soon as he had died the massive wave of magic pushed outward, scattering the creatures that remained alive. Their carcasses still dot the landscape that is speckled and scarred from the battle. The path to The Well forever a reminder of the battle, and the ruins just beyond? They are nothing but a smoldering pile of rock now.

The coven leaders escaped, despite Astrea and Kallen's best efforts. Arthur, the little rat he is, sacrificed witch after witch to escape his daughters with that damn book. He hasn't made it a secret, either, that he still lives. Setting up shop in Gothic Grove like he never left. Taking over the old coven grounds, and subsequently the gate to Hell that Oisin created. Even worse he has seemingly drawn people to him, twisted the story so he and my whore of a mother look like the saviors of the city. They've done an excellent job turning the citizens of Gothic Grove against Astrea and Ciaran.

"I was wondering when you would come back." A deep voice from behind, more animal than man, has me turning. Drago stands with hands in pockets, his white hair longer than usual and eyes weary. Behind him Shadow and Ava stand. The two pressing in close as if they are worried he'll disappear.

"Have you come to officially resign your position to us?" She asks. I blink, stunned for a moment. She lets out a bright laugh. "I mean, your mated to my brother and Dios, I just assumed our interview was taking care of the place the last month. Though truth be told if that was our interview we probably failed."

"No, none of this is on you. This is all Oisin." I respond firmly. "I'm sorry to ask this of you." I offer weakly. Even as gratitude swims in my chest as I look at her and her mates.

Shadow scoffs, earning a glare of Drago. "What?" He asks. "She acts like you aren't a dragon of death and she isn't a princess of Hell. We are meant to be here."

The truth of his statement settles into my bones. For the first time I look at Drago with different eyes, understanding suddenly dawning on me. He offers me a ruthless smile.

Taking a deep breath, I nod towards him, "thank you. Thank you all of you."

"Arcanna, you deserve happiness." Ava says in understanding.

"So do you." My eyes swim with tears.

She looks between her mates, "and I have that. All I wanted is right here. We'll take care of it from here. You take care of Dios and Jax."

I glance back towards The Forest, "The souls and The Forest need healing." I shake my head. "This place is too important to allow it to fall to ruin."

"We've got it." Drago says. "Go Reaper. Leave this place to those of us who are already owned by death."

Relief floods me as I let go of the chains this place has held on me. I send a silent goodbye and thank you to the place that kept me hidden for so long. To the place that allowed me to heal for a brief time.

"We'll be here when you need us." Ava says.

I ignore how ominous that sounds, praying that nothing catastrophic happens for a long time, however naive that hope maybe. "Take care." I reply. When I close my eyes, I feel The Forest push me one last time, sending me straight back to the people who I call home. And when my feet touch down on the soil, I feel the emptiness of the place that my Reaper magic once occupied and only a small dusting of the elemental magic I possessed prior. And instead of the grief I expect to come from the loss I feel a calming acceptance. Because in the end I have my mates, and Ava has hers.

Gothic Grove is no better than it used to be. The streets still smell like sewer water and the people that inhabit it are just as corrupt. The only difference? During the day the city streets are virtually empty, and at night they are alive and thriving. Otherwise even who rules the desolate city is the same. Fucking Mori witches.

Grabbing the tray of drinks, I offer a sweet smile to the bartender, pressing my tits out just enough that he can see straight down into my shirt. "Thanks doll." I say, blowing him a kiss. I sashay my hips just enough as I walk away to distract him from where I'm headed. The VIP rooms. Once where Drago sat and watched over club, Kai now holds court.

Careful to avoid the lights shining directly on my face I make my way up the stairs into the space above. Kai sits on a large leather couch, his right leg crossed over his left and white shirt unbuttoned just enough to expose the massive tattoo across his chest. His almond eyes are dark as they peer over the top of the crystal tumbler in his hand and a dark strand of his hair hangs down in his face coming loose from the tie, he has the rest in.

To his right stands a giant ginger man, his hair pulled back in a low bun. His leather vest gives him away as a motorcycle club member, but which one is unclear with how his arms are banded over his chest. His watches the room casually, as if he is bored and ready to go home already. He's a variable I did not account for and one I hope to avoid.

The last one I notice is the massive Viking, his form taking up residence against the dark wall, his eyes assessing the area. The blue in them seems electric in the low light, as if they could pierce the inky darkness of the shadows, I prefer to stay concealed in. I would know him from anywhere and I breathe a sigh of relief that he is alone, his mate nowhere in sight. That would have been a complication I did not want or need.

The music pulses a sultry beat as I put the drinks down on the main table directly in front of Kai. Pushing my hips out I let my ass pop out from under the small skirt. I know how to make men want me, even mated men can fall prey to someone who knows how to use their assets.

"I don't know you," he says. His voice sultry and smooth. "But you seem oddly familiar." His eyes feel like fire as they track the movement, my skin growing hot. Only years of keeping my reactions under lock and key allow me to stay steady and calm.

I offer a shy smile and let the pink wig fall in front of my face obscuring it more praying that he doesn't try and look closer, and that my make up holds to cover the mark on my face. "I just started." I say coyly.

He raises an eyebrow at me and for a moment I worry he doesn't believe me. After a heartbeat he jerks his head towards the cage in the corner, the demand easy to read. I offer a sweet smile, sashaying my hips as I make my way towards the platform, he wants me to perform on. I can feel

Kai's eyes as they track me and once more my skin heats and tingles and I send a prayer to the gods that don't give a shit that he won't figure out who I am. Won't *remember* who I am.

After all. He's not my target. At least not anymore.

(Digital Sea-Thrice)

The music picks up and I let my hips drop and sway to the beat, hands traveling over my body despite none of the men paying me any mind. I lose myself in the beat while trying to pay attention to anything the men say.

On my next spin I notice the redhead talking. "I don't have all night. Lord knows she'll come get me if I'm not back, and I don't think any of us want that."

Ciaran snorts, "you've got your hands full with that one, Demon." I file the name away for later. To figure out what club he belongs to.

Demon shakes his head with a smile, "you aren't any better."

The vampire just shrugs, not denying anything as he takes a long sip of his drink. I keep moving my body in time to the beat. Keep waiting to hear anything useful to my hunt.

"We are just waiting on— Ah, there you are! Was wondering if you got lost." Kai's voice swirls around my mind. With my eyes still closed and back to the room I can't be sure who entered.

Until that scent hits me.

When I complete my next spin, I open my eyes knowing who they will land on and knowing this is the end of the line for me. Peeling them open I'm met with the eyes of the two twins who still haunt my nightmares. Their eyes connecting with mine in furious recognition.

"Tell me Kai, why do you have Hansley Mori dancing for you in a cage?"

Well fuck.

THANK YOU FOR READING

Thank you for taking the time to read Ruined Kingdom. If you would be so kind as to leave a review it would mean the world to me!

Before you leave, subscribe to my newsletter newsletter to get all the up to date information on the upcoming releases, events and more. You also get early access to books, merch and sales.

ACKNOWLEDGMENTS

Thank you so much for reading Ruined Kingdom! I hope you liked it and I hope you can forgive Harrowlena for some of her choices in the end. I would be remiss if I did not take this moment to thank certain people for making this book happen.

Bre, my lovely amazing editor dragged me kicking and screaming through all this. The amount of voice memo's back and forth was astounding and I'm sure I sounded unhinged more than once. But she kept at it, kept pushing me and challenging me and making sure the characters got what they needed. So thank you, my lovely lovely human.

Thank you to my husby for giving me the space and time to lose my mind over this book. For the random weekend days where you took the kiddos out of the house, sacrificing yourself for the greater good of the smut world. You mean the world to me. And these books would not exist without you.

To the Gothic Grove fans, the HOA, and the desperate house witches this world wouldn't keep going without your constant support. Every review you leave, every message you send and every post you create or share truly keeps me going and gives me the fuel I need to keep writing.

Love you all endlessly! Stay spooky and spicy.

PEOPLE, PLACES, AND THINGS

Because Gothic Grove has grown so much I wanted to give you a little extra help in keeping track of all the people, places, and things we are introduced to. **Because this is a comprehensive list it may include spoilers. So please beware.**

Places

Gothic Grove: City that our lovely story takes place in. Home to witches, shifters and other supernatural creatures alike. It's Gotham City meets Seattle.

- The Playground: Kink club/bar previously owned by Ava. Currently under control of Ciaran and Astrea.
- Club Eufori: Previously owned by Drago, this place is currently being ran by his right hand man, Kai.

Hell: Welcome to Hell! Not just anyone can come here, only the elite. And those who know how to sneak in.

- Royal City of Hell: Think steampunk Las Vegas. This city houses the royal family. It also is thee place to go for street racing, gambling, drugs and sex.
- The Priestess Forest: The previous home of the royal priestesses.
- The Forest of Souls: Ran by the Lady of Souls this forest is dedicated to those who have passed on. The forest is a place of healing should you need it. It borders the priestess forest.
- The Land of the Damned: Think of this as Hell's jail. If you are naughty enough, or our Lady of Souls dislikes you enough, this is where you will spend eternity being punished.
- City of the Dead: This city houses those who have passed through The Forest of Souls and are ready to begin their afterlife.
- Kingdom of Divinity: The second largest royal city within Hell. They have a long standing relationship with the royal family of Hell, including an engagement, at one time, between their children.
- Southern Isles: A small group of tropical islands that generally keeps to themselves. They have had mutliple 'wars' with the Kingdom of Divinity and tension simmers between the two.

People

Known Mated Pairs:

- Astrea Mori and Ciaran Helvig: Witch and Vampire/Witch Hybrid. Astrea currently holds The Harbinger magic.

- Kallen and Jameson 'Demon' Knight: Kallen is the former holder of The Harbinger magic. Currently her soul is possessing the body of Reem Mori. She holds the following magic: Glamour, Realm Walker, Elemental, Mind Control and other unknown powers. Demon is the president of the Primal Knights MC. He is an alpha wolf shifter.
- Shadow, Drago and Ava: Shadow and Drago are stepbrothers. Both are dragon shifters. Shadow holds fire affinity and is a Realm Walker. Drago holds death affinity. Ava is the former princess of Hell with unknown magic.

Other People:

- Oisin: Leader of The Order of Infernal Sin. Ex-boyfriend to the current King of Hell and ex-fiancé to the former princess of Hell.
- Jackson: King of Hell and brother to Ava.
- Arcanna Ornate: Lady of Souls.
- Dios: Death God and wolf shifter who is currently part of the Primal Knights MC. He is best friends with Demon.
- Reaver: Prince of the Southern Isles and best friend to Jackson, King of Hell. Magic and powers are unknown.
- Rhea: Princess of Divinity.
- "The Twins" Aelius and Kalani: Brothers to Rhea and former princes of Divinity before they gave up their crown for their sister to rule.
- Original Witch Families: The covens that ruled over Gothic Grove until Kallen, with the help of Alexi Helvig, destroyed them.

- Alexi Helvig: Father to Ciaran. Killed by Astrea. Helped to torture and kill the witches of Gothic Grove while under the influence of Kallen who was attempting to locate the magic that the families stole from her.
- Kai: Drago's right hand man, currently running Club Eufori
- Ari: Wolf shifter rescued by Kallen who is currently living with the Primal Knights.
- Nxy and Ophelia: Friends of Jackson and Arcanna

Things

- Poppy: Astreas fox familiar.
- Samhain: Ava's crow familiar.
- Hellbeasts: Vicious creatures that historically answer to no one. However, Kallen commands a pack of them as her familiars.
- Vampires: Creatures that feed off blood AND magic to survive.
- Shifters: Individuals that can shift into different creatures at will. Thus far this includes dragons and wolves.
- Demons: Beings of Hell.

Venomous Love: A Gothic Grove Prequel Novella

Gothic Grove

Heavy Is The Crown

The Demons They Forged: A Gothic Grove Novella

Ruined Kingdom

Preorder untilted book (releasing summer 2025)

ABOUT THE AUTHOR

JA is a spooky, spicy human who is living her best witchy life in the PNW. She has two dogs, a cat, two gremlins aka children, and a loving mate who always makes sure she has coffee.
She has been writing since before she can remember and found a love for reading way back in the day when her dad would read her The Hobbit as a bedtime story. Now she indulges in dark romance whenever she can.

www.ingramcontent.com/pod-product-compliance
Lightning Source LLC
Chambersburg PA
CBHW070259310726
48976CB00005B/1490